A qualified parachutist, Harvey Black served with British Army Intelligence for over ten years. His experience ranges from covert surveillance in Northern Ireland to operating in Communist East Berlin during the Cold War where he feared for his life after being dragged from his car by KGB soldiers. Since then he has lived a more sedate life in the private sector as a director for an international company and now enjoys the pleasures of writing. Harvey is married with four children. For more from Harvey, visit his website at www.harveyblackauthor.org.

Also by Harvey Black:

DEVILS WITH WINGS

Devils with Wings
Silk Drop
Frozen Sun

THE COLD WAR

The Red Effect
The Black Effect
The Blue Effect

FORCE MAJEURE

Purgatory

G000038457

PRAISE FOR HARVEY BLACK

Book 1 of Force Majeure *Purgatory* was selected as Editor's Choice by *The Bookseller,* May 2015.

"Black makes a world waiting for heroes, and there are some in this story, but even the heroes have to adjust. He explores the human condition very well stripping away everything to show what we are – mammals, primates, shaved apes, risen hominids, nothing more – yet he leaves that spark, hope." – Paul Comerford

"Chillingly realistic take on life in Britain post nuclear war…" – Philip

"Thrilling read. Had to keep putting it down and couldn't…" – Roy S

"Thoroughly enjoyable read. The sort of thing to give nightmares considering recent events in Eastern Europe." – Cat Whisperer

PARALYSIS | HARVEY BLACK

FORCE MAJEURE 2

Published in 2015 by SilverWood Books

SilverWood Books Ltd
14 Small Street, Bristol, BS1 1DE
www.silverwoodbooks.co.uk

Copyright © Harvey Black 2015

The right of Harvey Black to be identified as the author of this work
has been asserted by him in accordance with the Copyright,
Designs and Patents Act 1988.

All rights reserved. No part of this publication may be reproduced,
stored in a retrieval system, or transmitted in any form or by any means,
electronic, mechanical, photocopying, recording or otherwise,
without prior permission of the copyright holder.

This novel is a work of fiction. Names and characters are the product
of the author's imagination and any resemblance to actual persons,
living or dead, is entirely coincidental.

ISBN 978-1-78132-379-3 (paperback)
ISBN 978-1-78132-380-9 (ebook)

British Library Cataloguing in Publication Data
A CIP catalogue record for this book is available
from the British Library

Set in Bembo by SilverWood Books
Printed in the UK on responsibly sourced paper.

To my wife Melanie, for her continued patience

CHAPTER 1

PARALYSIS | GROUND-ZERO +28 DAYS
BRAVO TROOP, EAST OF CHILMARK

The Land Rover slid sideways as Rolly wrestled with the steering wheel, coaxing the vehicle around the mound of drifting snow, the shape of an abandoned car beneath its surface. The back wheel dipped, a hidden ditch enticing the tyre into its depths, Rolly tapping the accelerator just enough to give power to the other wheels linked to the four-wheel drive system to force the vehicle forward and out of the trap. The Land Rover suddenly jerked forward, jarring its passengers, the tyres gripping the less slippery surface of the tarmac beneath. The trailer wobbled as its right wheel dropped into the same hole, but Rolly was back in control and applying more power, pulling it free and continuing to steer the vehicle through the white carpet ahead. The wipers flicked left and right and repeated the cycle as they desperately tried to clear the steady fall of white flakes attaching themselves to the windscreen. The incessant fall of snow was UK wide, carpeting the country in a steadily thickening blanket. A layer of white was forming on the bonnet, the mound of white crystals on the spare wheel threatening to block the driver's vision completely.

"This fucking weather's shite," growled Greg, thrown sideways in the passenger seat. "Where the fuck's it all coming from?"

"Precipitation falling from the clouds, forming flakes of crystalline water ice on its way down," came a voice from the back of the vehicle.

"Do you know what, Plato? You're too smart for your own good," Greg responded to his fellow soldier, and friend, sitting in the back.

"It's called a university education."

"Bloody waste of time, if you ask me."

"It's here for the duration by the looks of it," added Rolly as he stared through the ever-thickening snowfall, seeking out the best route.

"How we doing, Rolly?" asked Glen, stirring in the back.

"Making about forty K. Any faster and the tyres start to plough."

The falling flakes were forming a sheet of white ahead, blending in with the ever-thickening drifts on their route, and the vehicle's front wheels were often having to plough through them. The vehicle slid, Rolly twisting the wheel, turning into the slide, until they were back on track, the front wheels breaking through a frozen crust of ice beneath them. The freezing temperatures, down to minus eight two nights ago, had formed a film of ice beneath the six-inch layer of snow that had descended the previous day. In the early hours of the morning, the snow had restarted, the troop now having to make their way through over half a metre of snowfall, drifting to well over a metre in places.

Glen looked at his watch, then at the surrounding area, the snow falling from the grey skies restricting his view. "It's eleven ten. We can push on for a few more hours at least. Later, we need to keep our eyes peeled for somewhere we can hold up for the night. You OK, Rolly?"

"Yeah, no problem, boss," Rolly responded confidently, but without taking his eyes off the road. As a consequence of the lack of traffic movement around the UK since the nuclear strikes, apart from the few military and civilian vehicles still drivable of which there weren't many, there had been no vehicles around to flatten the snow, so the troop's Land Rover had to create its own path through the ever-thickening layer.

"This is going to fuck up our timings."

"You in a hurry then, Greg?" asked Plato, a grin across his face.

"Less time I spend cooped up in here with you lot the better."

Once they had agreed on their next mission, consenting to work in conjunction with the Regional Government Centre back in Chilmark, they had set off south, cutting around the southern edge of Salisbury, skirting the northern tip of the New Forest north-east of Christchurch. Then, heading north-east, steady progress had been made between Winchester and Basingstoke. Soon they would be leaving the A31.

"Hang on tight, lads, we're coming off here, might get a bit rougher."

"With your driving, that's a given," groaned Greg.

Rolly swung right, leaving the A31, and headed for Binsted. The A31 had been relatively clear of vehicles, just a single line of abandoned cars facing both ways, and the centre of the road had been kept clear for use by military vehicles. Occasionally, a vehicle whose driver had chosen to break the rules had blocked their route, but they managed to manoeuvre around it and continue their journey east. It would have been a better road to continue along, but they wanted to avoid the larger towns and villages, such as Farnham, and the military towns of Aldershot and Guildford, keeping away from any potential refugees. The troop had seen some evidence of life on their journey: plumes of smoke from houses that appeared to have survived the worst of the nuclear storm. Most of the housing stock in the UK that had survived appeared to be those in the outlying areas. That's not to say that the countryside had got off scot-free, or that all of the population in those areas had survived. The initial wave of radiated fallout had deposited a thin veneer of toxic particles across the entire country – England, Scotland and Wales – nowhere had been omitted from exposure to its life-taking poison. Even the Emerald Isle, along with Northern Ireland, had received their own share of nuclear bombs and missiles. Once the Russian President had made the decision to strike at NATO, Russia had unleashed every available nuclear weapon in its arsenal, from over 400 land-based strategic rocket forces, with over 1,500 warheads, up to twelve SSBN nuclear submarines, with over 500 warheads, and eighty bombers capable of carrying over 800 cruise missiles. With the US, British, French and German retaliatory strike, consisting of nearly 2,000 warheads, mutual destruction was assured.

On the road east, just before Binsted, the area opened up, exposed to the elements, the locality less protected by trees. As a consequence, a strong current of air buffeted the Land Rover trying to push it off the road, Rolly having to steer into the wind in order to keep the vehicle on a relatively straight track. They passed through Binsted, but with the steady curtain of snow restricting their visibility, no signs of a fire, smoke or life could be seen. Rolly and Greg, in the passenger seat, were on the alert for any threats as they drove through, but the passage was uneventful.

Once past the village, the road, in a shallow dip, was slightly better, and the trees either side helped to reduce the effect of the wind. This also meant that fewer snowdrifts had built up, allowing Rolly to up their speed, pushing forty-plus kilometres an hour, but not wanting to risk going any faster. If he spun the Land Rover or they came off the road into one of the deep ditches either side, the consequences at worst could be fatal, at best seriously damage the vehicle or delay their journey. Rolly needed to concentrate every second if he was to keep the vehicle on the road. It wasn't quite a white-out, but he would be relieved when Greg took over in an hour's time, giving him a breather. It had been agreed that no one would drive for more than two hours, such was the concentration required to avoid abandoned cars, always on the alert for an ambush, and keep their transport on the road. He drove along the Binsted road for a further three kilometres until they reached Alice Holt Forest where he turned right, heading south along Dockenfield Street, eventually turning east through Dockenfield itself. Here, they did see signs of life, thick black smoke from a chimney, a fire that was obviously burning green or damp wood gathered from the surrounding area. As agreed, they chose not to stop.

Frensham followed; then Tilford. At Tilford, if they wanted to stay on a decent tarmac road, they needed to turn left for Farnham, considered a risk, or right for Rushmoor, taking them on a long detour. Greg and Rolly consulted the map and agreed to take a track, at right angles to their current position, going north-east. The hard-packed track was a bumpy ride, but after a kilometre and a half it saw them at a T-junction, taking them back onto a more solid route. Rolly took them left at Elstead, then right, the road winding and even more treacherous in places than the track they had just left, before pulling up next to a small wood, Halesmore Wood, before Puttenham Common. They all agreed that, before they swapped drivers, a brew and a leg stretch were called for. Rolly, at six-two, was particularly pleased to give his long legs a break from the confines of their military vehicle. Rather than just a brew after the leg stretch, it was decided something more substantial was required. Two tins of soup were heated up, and they sipped at beef broth while remaining in the warmth of the Rover.

"Best not stay here too long," warned Glen, steam rising from his mug as he cupped it in his hands. "We'll be blocked in."

"Definitely snowman-building weather," added Greg. "So much for bloody global warming."

"At least we've found a solution for it," suggested Plato.

"A solution? Blowing ourselves to bits? We should have stuck with rising seas and hotter summers, Plato mate."

A smile passed between Glen and Plato, both knowing how easy it was to wind Greg up.

"Why did you join the regiment, Plato? You should have taken up a job as a philosopher or something."

"Couldn't have a unit full of just gorillas, you know. We need some brains in the outfit to lead the way."

"Wanker."

Glen pulled himself forward so his head was between the seats, peering in between Greg, now in the driver's seat, and Rolly on the passenger side. "Let's have a look at the map."

Rolly held it up and to the right so they could both see it.

"We need water. What can you see, Rolly?"

Rolly studied the map. "Here, just before Puttenham Common itself, we cross over some standing water a couple of klicks away, fed by the River Wey, I think. Looks a fair size. We can stop there."

"Won't it be contaminated?" asked Greg.

"No," responded Plato. "Any contaminants will have sunk to the bottom by now. So long as we don't disturb the waterbed, we should be OK. Value of a university education, mate."

"Wanker."

"Still sterilise it, though," added Rolly.

"Check for dead animals in the area," Glen reminded them. "There will be a fair few, I reckon."

"Not just animals either," advised Plato. "The human death rate is bound to be pretty high. There will be millions of rotting bodies out there, so we need to take note, especially around built-up areas and any water we access. I don't need to remind you guys that dysentery, typhus and cholera are going to be a real problem. Any tight-packed communities, living in insanitary conditions should be avoided like the plague, pardon the pun."

"Going through London's going to be a bit of a pig."

"That it is, Greg," agreed Glen. "Once we get a bit closer and have conducted a few recces, we can finalise the route we'll take to Pindar."

"Still giving Northwood a miss?"

"Yes, Greg. It will have received a number of direct hits. They wouldn't stand a chance, but Pindar, on the other hand, was much better protected."

"I suggest we do a recce of environmental conditions as well as access. We have no idea what state the city's in, but, if I had to hazard a guess, I'd say many of the roads will be impassable."

"We'll soon know, Plato. ETA, Rolly?" asked Glen.

"We need to cover some seventy-odd Ks. Head for Peasmarsh, Chilworth, then turn north before Wotton here." He pointed at the map. "That will take us to Effingham, then Cobham, crossing the M25 beforehand. East, then north about four klicks before Epsom. North, north-east until we hit Wimbledon Common. North-east from there will take us into the heart of London, through Battersea, Lambeth, then north to Whitehall. Complete the journey in two stages. Stop overnight in the Putney area, as we agreed, and tackle the inner city the next day." Rolly looked at his watch, showing twelve thirty. "Let's say six hours to Putney at the latest, dependent on this." He indicated the snow still falling on the bonnet, an ever-thickening layer forming on the cooling metal.

"Crossing the Thames will be the tricky bit," warned Plato. "The bridges are bound to be out."

"If that's the case," reminded Glen, "we know the two options open to us. Swim or the tube."

"We'd best get moving, boss, before we do get bogged down in this shite."

"Succinctly put, as ever, Greg. Right, gentlemen, let's make a move. Wake me in two hours, Greg."

"Will do, boss. I'll be ready for a kip by then."

Glen closed his eyes, taking the opportunity to catch as much sleep as possible, knowing that once they got into London, rest could well elude them.

Plato plugged the earphones of his iPod into his ears, listening to an operatic overture from *The Marriage of Figaro* composed by Mozart, glad that he had been able to top up the iPod's battery using an adaptor and the Land Rover's electrics. He also had an emergency charger that was powered by dry-cell batteries, should he need it. He stared out of the window, determined to ensure he always had a stock of spare batteries on hand so he could indulge his passion for operatic music. He looked up at the dark clouds, thinking the solar charger he had in his bag would be of little use.

Rolly studied the map, and Greg started the engine. Putting the Land Rover into gear, Greg applied gentle pressure to the accelerator, not wanting to spin the wheels and get them bogged down. It might be in four-wheel drive but the conditions were rapidly deteriorating. Once on the road, he steadily increased speed, and they continued east. The next stop would be for water.

CHAPTER 2

PARALYSIS | GROUND-ZERO +29 DAYS
BRAVO TROOP, LONDON

Glen, Rolly and Plato looked across the Thames, the shattered Wandsworth Bridge in front of them. Struck by conventional missiles, air-launched cruise missiles, fired by a Russian Tupolev, the centre of the suspended span of over 100 metres was nothing more than a gaping hole, and the remaining cantilever sections of steel had fallen into the river with just the anchor arms standing on the banks either side. Unless struck by a direct or very close nuclear bomb or missile, the bridges could have possibly survived, Russia having to resort to more conventional means to ensure their destruction, locking the UK's major city into gridlock. The wharves across the other side of the river were strewn with snow-covered wreckage. The luxury multi-million-pound waterfront apartments that had existed to the right, with their staggered balconies facing the water, were no more. In fact, London was no more. The majority had effectively been levelled, and the only depiction Plato could conceive as a comparison was with the photographs he had seen of the bombing of Hiroshima during World War Two. The best way to describe it, and how he imagined it would look from above, was that of a black and white photographic negative: the lighter images of what had once been major roads, and the darker patches that of rubble – what used to be houses, shops, stores, apartments, and office blocks. At present, the only three-dimensional structures were those that had once been tower blocks, now nothing but jagged forms jutting upwards like rotting teeth, torn apart by the ferocity of the blast and the firestorm that followed, leaving nothing but a shattered infrastructure on the skyline, defiant but unserviceable. The tallest structure they could see was probably the Shard, or what was left of it. Out of the over 300 megatons that had descended on the UK, London had received over ten per cent, thirty-plus megatons, ensuring the complete destruction of the capital city of the United Kingdom. The only area that appeared to have survived, if that was a term that could be used for the crushed remains, was the south-west, the London Borough of Croydon.

Their planned overnight stop at Wimbledon Common, expecting to camp out in the local forest, had been a ghostly experience. Many of the trees had been blown over, either bent at an angle or snapped at the trunk bases, the forest floor now criss-crossed with their shattered remains, the route through or into it impassable. The few trees that had survived the onslaught and remained upright had been burnt and stripped bare of their foliage, now looking like tarred toothpicks pointing skyward. The soldiers had backtracked and found a location north of Epsom, a more acceptable location to spend the night.

At first light, avoiding major roads as much as possible, the four men had driven the last ten or so kilometres to their current position, the southern riverbank at Wandsworth, passing around Ewell, north-west of Tolworth, through the area of New Malden, circuiting Wimbledon Common. Although they suspected the bridges were down, a sure target for the enemy bombers, they felt it worth having eyes on to confirm. Satisfied there was nothing more to see, the three men returned to the Land Rover to join Greg.

"Done," called Greg, tightening the last nut of the Land Rover's front nearside wheel before packing up the jack and wheel brace. Such was the poor condition of the roads that, in the final approach to the bridge, a jagged piece of steel reinforced concrete, hidden beneath a half-metre layer of snow, tore a gash in the tyre that was now beyond repair. Fortunately, they still had a second spare wheel in the trailer and the third one still on the bonnet, but they would have to take extra care during the remainder of their journey.

"Knew you could do it," responded Plato.

"Wanker."

"You sweating, Greg?" asked Rolly.

"Don't you bloody start," responded Greg, pulling his combat jacket and NBC suit jacket back on as he now started to feel the chill, the heavy work of changing the wheel having been finished.

Although the fall of snow was currently light, the newly barren landscape allowed the wind free passage, and it whipped around the legs and shoulders of the four soldiers.

"I wonder how long this weather's in for?" queried Rolly.

"We could have these low temperatures for a week, a month, maybe even a couple of years," answered Plato.

"You're full of the joys of spring."

"It's what we have to be prepared for, Greg mate," replied Plato.

Glen brushed the vehicle's mudguard free of snow and placed a plastic-coated map of London and the surrounding areas on the cleared space.

"Once we get Pindar out of the way, we need to reassess our future," concluded Glen. "If Plato is correct, and I have no reason to doubt him, the future doesn't look promising. We have to start thinking about the long term."

"Chilmark?"

"Possibly, Rolly, but let's not get into that now. We have Pindar to deal with first."

"Is it worth bothering?" asked Greg.

"I believe we have to close this one off, find out whether or not there's anyone in command. If you all want to open it up for debate again?"

"No, you're right, boss. We need to stick with it."

Rolly and Plato also nodded their consent.

Glen went back to the map, pointing to their current location. "Let's push along York Road. But take it easy, Plato. Just detour where you have to. We need to protect this," he said, tapping the bonnet.

"Yeah," agreed Greg. "We'll be stuffed without it."

"The bridges still need to be checked out. Even if we can't get the vehicle across, we may be able to get across on foot. We'll check the Vauxhall Bridge last." Glen tapped the map where the bridge crossed the Thames from Vauxhall to Pimlico. "Then south-east to the Oval and find somewhere as a forward operating base." Glen folded the map, stuffed it inside his NBC suit, shivering as the cold air was let in, and headed for the trailer. "Spin her around, Plato, and we'll hook the trailer back up.

Plato jumped in the Land Rover, his turn at the wheel, started her up, and manoeuvred into a position where Glen, Greg and Rolly could lift the trailer hitch while he reversed closer. With the trailer hooked up to the Land Rover, the three men jumped on board, and Plato started the slow journey to their penultimate destination, the Oval.

The six-kilometre drive was tortuous, for both the vehicle and the occupants inside. With the route ahead hidden by a layer of snow, it was only the higher mounds of snow-covered rubble that gave Plato any indication of where the road wasn't. Fortunately, the A3205 was relatively wide, and the centre itself was reasonably obstacle free. Although most of the cars and other vehicles in the area had been thrown violently into the air, crashing down at various points across the landscape, or up against the buildings nearby, some of the heavier ones had remained in place, or at least within the vicinity. They had been irreparably damaged though, burnt out, but their snow-covered shells acted like giant traffic cones guiding Plato along the road. It was far from perfect, often coming up against the remains of a building, or smashed vehicles blown off the road and taking the Land Rover in the wrong direction. When that occurred, the other three soldiers would jump out, using long staffs, cut from trees in the Epsom Forest, to probe the area until they could get back on track. They passed Battersea Park to their north, then the Battersea Dogs & Cats Home, the famous Battersea Power Station now nothing more than a pile of rubble. They passed what was once the New Covent Garden Market on their right, then the shattered buildings of the Vauxhall Underground and mainline stations.

Other than hazards of driving, the six kilometres had been fairly uneventful, apart from the constant stopping and starting, but they had seen signs of life. They often saw trickles of smoke spiralling skyward, apparently coming from the centre of concrete structures that, although demolished, had enough of their infrastructure intact to form an enclosure, open to the elements from above but offering a perimeter within which survivors could huddle, sharing the heat of an open fire. They had passed within fifty metres of one such group, clustered together in what was once Hamilton House. Five people, bundled in layers of thick clothing, had bounded towards them, waving their arms frantically, delirious yells on seeing evidence of what they considered to be bureaucracy, government control, hope, coming to their rescue. One of the individuals running towards them wildly tumbled over onto the snow-covered ground, tripped up by an unseen network of bricks, reinforced concrete, cars, girders and other debris, the new surface of most of the City of London. They were within ten metres of the soldiers as the military Land Rover crawled past them, looks of hopelessness and despair on their faces as it slowly dawned on them that the military didn't intend to stop. As the vehicle growled its way along the undulating road, getting further and further away, they stopped running, stopped waving, any flicker of hope they had dissipated. Maybe, just maybe, one of them thought, the soldiers were part of an advance guard, wanting to complete a reconnaissance of the city before making contact; a larger force behind them, bringing food, water, blankets and shelter. After another five minutes of watching the army unit slowly disappearing from view, swallowed up by a curtain of snow, they headed back to what was now their home, to sit around the fire that was keeping them alive, keeping them warm in between sessions of scavenging, scraping the snow aside, pulling anything out of the rubble that could either be eaten, worn or burnt as fuel for the fire.

Further back, just south of Battersea Park, the soldiers had come across a more hostile crowd, as many as twenty-plus. Some were armed and quickly moved to cut off the soldiers' route of advance while a second group came around behind them. Glen, Rolly and Plato quickly dismounted and walked alongside their transport, weapons clearly visible, their intentions towards the hostiles obvious. The crowd, recognising that a few shotguns and carving knives were no match for what were obviously healthy and very heavily armed soldiers slowed their advance. The group at the front backed off, and the soldiers were allowed to continue their journey towards the centre of London unmolested.

It took them four hours to make the six-kilometre journey, and all were pretty exhausted by the time they reached Vauxhall Bridge which, not coming as a surprise to them, had been destroyed. It was impassable both by vehicle and foot. Had the gap been a few metres wide, they would have attempted to grapple the other side and rope across but, at over 100 metres, it was a non-starter.

After looking at the Vauxhall Bridge, the destroyed remains of Vauxhall Cross to their right, the base for the British Secret Intelligence Service, MI6, now utterly destroyed, they moved on. Negotiating collapsed railway lines that crossed in front of them, Rolly drove them the last kilometre to the Oval. It took another hour to make that short trip. He drove around the southern section of the Oval, England's famous cricket ground, now just rubble, the viewing terraces collapsed and the once green, professionally tended cricket pitch covered in snow. However, beneath the snow lay a layer of black ash, rubble and dust scarring the pitch forever.

Glen, who was taking his turn in the driving seat, giving Rolly's aching arms a rest, covered the last few hundred metres, steering the Land Rover down the A3 Kennington Park Road. In spite of the fact that it was also covered in debris beneath its blanket of snow, it was proving to be relatively accessible.

It was now fifteen twenty-four, and the priority was to find somewhere to hold up for the night, somewhere secure, somewhere safe. Although not in huge numbers, clearly there were some survivors occupying the city, and they would no doubt be sick, hungry and desperate. He and his men may be armed to the teeth but, if bounced unexpectedly and by a big enough crowd, the tables could quickly turn against them. Glen was having doubts about their mission to reach the Pindar Bunker and considered raising the cancellation of it with the team again. But, deep down, he knew it was in their best interests to have come all this way: to gain a better understanding of the condition their capital city was in and to also confirm or deny there was a higher command, a government in control of the country. Once they knew that then he and his men could think about their longer-term future and consider the options open to them.

As the vehicle crawled past Kennington Park, the soldiers looked at what were once healthy, well-manicured trees, now nothing more than scorched trunks. Many had been felled, the cream-coloured stumps jutting out of the snow. No doubt the wood had been hauled away to be used for burning, to keep people warm.

"We're too far from the tube, boss. We should turn back," suggested Plato, scanning the area from the front passenger seat. He slid the side window open, brushing some of the snow away so he had a better view of the surrounding area.

Glen nodded in agreement and took a slow, wide turn, checking the trailer in the wing mirrors, making sure it wasn't tilted at too much of an angle or would catch on a large fragment jutting out of the snow he had just circumvented. He headed south again.

"There," called out Plato. "The church." Although not immediately recognisable as a church, its location tied in with the map. It stood opposite the entrance of the Oval – not the cricket venue but the tube station. "All the trees are gone, so the area should be left alone. If we can find a nook behind it, we can tuck our stuff away."

"Worth a try," Greg's voice echoed from the back.

"Pull over, boss. Greg and I'll go foxtrot."

Glen brought the Land Rover to a halt close to the snow-covered mound, three or four times the height of the vehicle, of what was once Saint Mark's Church. Greg and Plato quickly got out, Rolly following and then jumping back into the vacated passenger seat, an extra pair of eyes as he and Glen kept watch. Both Greg and Plato pulled on their personal load carrying equipment (PLCE), attached pouches with which to carry their ammo and other key items. They also pulled up the nuclear biological and chemical (NBC) hoods of their NBC suits and donned their helmets. Greg cursed as his foot caught on something, nearly causing him to completely lose his footing and hit the deck. He used the canvas-sided Land Rover for support.

Plato looked back, white clouds of frosted breath escaping from his scarf-covered mouth, crystals of frost already forming on its surface. "Steady now."

"Wanker."

Plato led the way on foot, placing his boots carefully, testing the ground before releasing the weight from his back foot. He headed for the black railings he could see poking through the snow, the broken tops of four sandstone posts indicating the entrance. He scanned 180 degrees in front, Greg doing the same but in the opposite direction, watching their backs. Four metres took them to the entrance, the slab-lain path providing a solid footing unless obstructed by one of the collapsed blocks of stone or parts of the collapsed ornamental clock tower beneath the snow. Either side of the path, Plato was sure he could feel the softer texture of grass or earth beneath his feet until that too was blocked by or covered in fragments of the once proud building. He pointed to the ground, indicating to Greg footprints off to the side, the tree stumps yellow-centred with a black ring, evidence that they had been cut down sometime during the last week. In some respects, that was good. If the grounds of the church had been cleared of everything useful, it was unlikely people in the area would return, preferring to focus on the remaining trees at the far end of Kennington Park, some 400 to 500 metres away.

Plato signalled with his hand that they move right and made his way across the front of the church. When he reached the far side, a gateway on his right, wide enough for vehicles, and a driveway to his left that ran down the side of the church, he signalled left. The drive was fairly clear beneath the snow, the building having collapsed away from it. As he moved alongside the remnants of what was once a substantial building, he noted that the trees had been felled and spirited away from here as well. His eyes lit up once he arrived at the back of the church. The rear section, although crushed by the force that destroyed the church in the first instance, possessed an inner space. The masonry and blocks of stone that had collapsed on top of it afterwards had been partially deflected by the decorative but large stone columns. A yawning hollow space, wide enough to hide their vehicle, was visible. All he had to do was to see how deep and secure it was. It was no good having shelter if there was the slightest chance it could come down on top of them.

Plato called Greg forward and indicated the cavern. "I need to check it out," he hissed.

Greg nodded. "Let's give it five."

"Agreed."

The two soldiers crouched down and listened, taking five minutes out to take in their surroundings, check if anyone or anything was taking an interest. Apart from the whistle and the force of the wind as it whipped down the drive, it was silent. The engine of the Land Rover had been turned off, not only to conserve fuel but also because the sound of a diesel engine ticking over could travel a considerable distance, particularly if windborne, advertising the presence of the four soldiers.

After five minutes, satisfied that no one was in the immediate vicinity and having received no warnings from Glen and Rolly, Plato tapped Greg on the shoulder and pointed towards the black cavern. Plato flicked on the torch attached to the side of his helmet and started to walk into the depths of the chamber. It appeared to go back a distance of between eight and ten metres, judging by the number of Plato's strides. Along the back, two of the ornate columns had collapsed inwards towards each other, wedged, forming a barrier that prevented the stone blocks along the back wall, or the sides, from caving in. He took out a second torch from his NBC suit trouser pocket and shone it around the dark space above him. He estimated the height to be just under a metre above his head. The roof of the chamber looked as though it was supported by a mass of haphazardly interlinked stone blocks, placed so that they were preventing a complete collapse. He wouldn't like to be here when it did go, but he felt confident it would hold for the immediate future. However, the steady increase in the weight of snow would slowly add to the downward pressure, and something was bound to give eventually. Perhaps that's why it had not been used as a place to shelter: the fear of the entire structure collapsing overpowering the desire for shelter. For all Plato knew, there might be better places hidden amongst the ruins of the city for the survivors, so this place was not needed. Narrowing towards the back, it would be a tight squeeze, but if they manhandled the trailer so it was positioned across the width of the rear of the cavern, all should just about fit.

Plato returned to the entrance and made contact with Greg.

"Well?"

"It'll do. Not the safest of places, but hopefully we won't be here long enough."

"Let's join the lads then. Bloody freezing my ass off here."

"Stop your grumbling."

Greg took point and swiftly led them both back to the Land Rover where they briefed Glen and Rolly. Agreeing that it was the right choice; they reversed the Land Rover and trailer down the drive, a tricky manoeuvre but expertly carried out by Rolly. What made it harder was keeping the revs down, the troop not wanting to give any survivors in the area notice of their arrival. For once, they were actually thankful for the thickening snow, visibility now down to less than 100 metres. And the snow would cover their footprints and the tracks left by the wheels of the Land Rover and trailer.

The four men manhandled the trailer to the back of the chamber, turning it so it lay across the back wall, allowing enough space for the Land Rover to reverse into the chamber, leaving a metre of space free so its nose didn't stick out, exposing its position. Before they settled down for the night, Glen and Rolly completed a recce of the tube station. Although the upper part of the complex structure had been flattened, they still managed to find a way in. Inside the collapsed structure, the floors had crumpled, the wreckage of the building falling into the lower levels. Despite the fact that it would be difficult, the deeper levels were accessible by roping down if the men were unable to find any undamaged steps. What they would find at the bottom was anyone's guess. The two men returned to the hidden Land Rover.

Satisfied they were secure for the night, they settled down to some hot food. Suspending two large pieces of hessian from the roof of the chamber, one either side of the Land Rover, blocking visibility from the outside, they were able to use a gas stove. After two tins of stew between them, plus a couple of dried crackers each and a mug of tea, powdered milk and sugar, they soon felt warmer and their hunger was sated. Despite the space being cramped, the men managed to fit four director's chairs, stored in the trailer, in the space available, and to sit down and plan the next day's actions.

Glen held a sheet of paper on his knees, and the other three positioned themselves as best they could so that they could also see it. A camping light helped.

"This is how I remember the tube system in this area. Jump

in if you think I've got it wrong. I know Greg has completed some counter-terrorism training beneath the streets of London, but I'm sure you and Plato haven't."

"Not me," agreed Rolly, and Plato concurred.

"The reason I've chosen the Oval and the Northern Line is that, where it passes under the Thames, two other lines also go under at that point." Glen tapped the three lines he'd drawn crossing the double line that represented the River Thames

"All three lines, the Jubilee, Northern and Bakerloo, pass beneath the river. So, if we have problems getting through one, we have two alternatives. The Northern Line and Bakerloo Line will take us to the Embankment, whereas the Jubilee Line doesn't connect with another station until Green Park, which will be our last resort. I want to see if we can get out at the Embankment, as a fall-back option, but prefer it if we avoid the city and make our final destination Charing Cross. Once at the Cross, and we're satisfied there are no immediate threats, we can go and find Pindar."

"Do you know why it was named Pindar?" asked Plato.

"No, but I'm sure you're going to tell us," jibed Greg.

"It's named after an ancient Greek poet."

"A poet?" questioned Rolly.

"Yeah, his city, Thebes, was razed to the ground in 335 BC, but his was the only house that survived."

"Lucky guy."

"He was that, Glen. Alexander the Great spared him."

"Now we've had our bedtime story, Greg, Rolly, do a 360 out there." Glen indicated outside the hide, slapping Plato's arm. "Me and the philosopher here will sort out a kit list for tomorrow."

CHAPTER 3

PARALYSIS | GROUND-ZERO +29 DAYS
TOWER TRIBE, CROYDON

Bill shuffled along the line of survivors who were crouched, shivering, outside a line of derelict, smoke-grimed buildings on Mitcham Road, firing them up with as much encouragement as possible, promising them they would find a new home soon. They had spent the night huddled in the ruins of a supermarket off Pitlake, Bill wanting to get them off the streets, hidden from prying eyes while he and the leaders of the group planned their next move.

"That's our home that's burning," sobbed Sally. Her green eyes, framed by curls of dark hair sticking out of the hood of her jacket, reflected in the light of Bill's partially shielded torch.

"We'll find another," comforted Bill, crouching down next to her, placing an arm around her shoulders. Kelly, a seventeen-year-old that had attached herself to Sally, who had reciprocated, having lost her own daughter to the nightmare that had befallen them, was huddled next to her.

"We just need to stay strong until we do." Bill looked up and back at the reddish glow that lit up the early morning sky, the glow of the still smouldering tower that they had escaped from the previous night and that had once been their temporary home. Furthermore, Bill felt angry that another's greed had forced him and his group out into the desolate streets of the city, forcing them from what was becoming a secure sanctuary, somewhere from which they could have started to build a new life. It was only after everyone was out that he was able to complete a count: only fifty-two had survived out of the eighty originals.

He suppressed his anger, squeezing Kelly's arm gently. "We move out in five minutes, so get ready." He stood back up. "We move out in five minutes," he hissed as he walked down the line of what were now refugees, effectively vagrants out on the streets, without a home.

Once at the head of the column, he met with Robbie. "Have you felt it?" asked his number two.

"What?"

Robbie held his gloveless hand out, and Bill could just pick out small flakes of snow melting once they touched the palm of the man's hand. Bill pulled his face mask, a thick yellow scarf, down from over his nose and mouth and looked up, white flakes passing in front of his eyes, cold crystals stinging his face. His tongue flicked out, catching some of the falling flakes, the bitter, acidic taste causing him to grimace and spit the melted substance out. "Shit, that tastes foul!"

"Must be all that crap that's still up there." Robbie indicated towards the clouds with his hand. "Better tell people not to drink it."

"They won't need telling," added Bill. "The taste will be enough."

The powerful form of Owen joined them. "We're about ready, Bill."

"Told everyone that they're not to leave anything behind?"

"Sure, Bill. They know we'll need everything we have. Still the same plan?"

"Yes. We have water, but, if our estimate of two days' supply is accurate, that has to be a priority. So, we'll head for South Wimbledon, going via the common to restock. We'll have to scavenge for other stuff, if we get the chance that is, on the way."

Simon also came alongside the huddle. At five seven and on the slim side, he looked almost petite standing next to the two strapping men and the tall Robbie, but Bill still had confidence in him. "I have two guys up ahead, out to about 100 metres, so ready when you are, Bill. Christ, this snow is starting to thicken," he added, looking up into a steady swirl of greyish flakes floating down.

"Let's move. Robbie, take the lead, Owen, tail end. I'll post Trevor somewhere in the middle. Simon, you do your own security thing. Just keep me posted of any threats."

"Sure."

Bill walked across to Aleck, who was next in the column, telling him and Alan behind to follow Robbie who had moved to the head of the column ready to lead the way. Owen headed to the rear of the group, positioned there by Bill to make sure that no one dropped behind, dumped any of their precious supplies or needed assistance. Bill stood at the side as the heavily wrapped figures started to push themselves up from the cold rubble, gathering their belongings and the supplies that had been allocated for them to carry. Robbie pushed ahead, and Aleck was the first to pass Bill, the man nodding positively as he walked by. Alan, then Martha and her three boys closely followed him. Patrick, the eldest at nine, was carrying almost as much as his mother. He now saw himself as the man of the family, helping to take care of his mother and two younger siblings.

"OK, Martha?"

"We're fine, Bill. Me and my boys won't let you down."

"I know you won't."

"None of us will," added Andrew, next in the line as he shuffled past.

The steady stream continued to stumble past: Ken, Ellie, now without her husband Howard who was killed during the attack on the tower, and Mathew, who Bill whispered to as they crossed paths, "We'll need to do some scavenging later." Then came Sally, closely followed by Kelly. Elisabeth, now on her own, her newly wedded husband Curtis killed during the attack, was not far behind Kelly.

Once they had evacuated the building, the tower ablaze above their heads, Bill had done a quick count of survivors. Curtis had been killed prior to Bill and his group arriving at the tower, and Jake had died alone in the back of the van, killed by one of the intruders. The guards on the tower entrance had also been killed, along with Howard and seven others that had put up a fight to defend their home. The rest of the group's casualties had perished in the fire, trapped in smoke-filled rooms higher up, running there to escape the gang that occupied their home. Kenny, along with his two sons, had run and hid, but paid the price, burnt alive somewhere in the upper limits of the tower block. The family was far from popular and would not be missed. Now, with only fifty-two left, Bill knew that time was not on their side. They had to find, he had to find, a new home if they were to survive beyond the next few days. If he didn't, they would either die of cold, hunger, or thirst or succumb to the gangs that still roamed this borough of London. He clung onto a suggestion he had made earlier: to use the tunnels of the London Underground, one of the tube stations. It was a long shot, but worth a try. There was a risk that the tunnels were already occupied and well defended, or that they had collapsed as a consequence of the violence of the nuclear blasts that struck the capital city of the UK. He knew from previous sorties that the further north they went the worse the damage. He would have to lead, the word 'tribe' sprang to mind, and he smiled to himself at the title of tribal leader to South Wimbledon, Colliers Wood, or maybe even Tooting Broadway. Morden was not an option, the line there along with the station being above ground.

Nearly thirty kilometres of the Northern Line consisted of a deep-level tube, which had hopefully survived the nuclear holocaust. Even if the tunnels were undamaged, and were unoccupied, there was still a risk that the destroyed or collapsed buildings, along with the tons of rubble strewn across the city, prevented access to the safety of the tunnels below. First, they would need to make for Mitcham Common, where they could acquire water. It wouldn't be fresh and could possibly be contaminated, but, if boiled, it would prolong their survival. If there was nothing there, he knew of a tributary off the River Thames, the River Wandle, which fed the Beddington Sewage Treatment Works. His first port of call after that would be South Wimbledon. Then the worrying would truly start if access to the depths below was not possible.

The last in the file, other than Owen who was watching the back of the line, were Maurice and Justin, two Territorial lads in their late twenties, and Terry and Vincent. The families of the two men were somewhere in the centre of the procession, the ex-soldiers remaining at the rear to cover their backs. The TA lads had proven useful and both Terry and Vincent had also shown that they had what was needed in a fight.

Bill walked alongside them, turning back to Owen. "All clear?"

"No sign of anyone following."

"Keep a good lookout. It's not difficult to miss this lot." He pointed to the long line that snaked ahead.

"Sure, Bill, I've got our arses covered."

Bill turned to Justin. "Once we get settled again, I want to search for that TA centre you told me about."

"We can both lead you there, Bill." Justin turned to Maurice, who nodded in agreement.

"I think it's worth a try."

"It's just moving the rubble though. If the building has collapsed," responded Justin, nearly tripping over as his foot caught on a piece of debris.

"We'll find a way, don't you worry." Bill left them to focus on where to place their feet, the rubble treacherous in places, and walked faster, making his way along the column, calling out encouragement, heading to the front of the column, ready to divert their route should he need to, or to identify any scavenging opportunities. It worried him a lot. In fact, it scared him. Scavenging, although necessary, was tough and would only keep them alive for as long as processed foods could be found. Beyond that, they would have nothing. A layer of snow slowly thickened around his shoulders, the flakes becoming larger and visibility worsening. He brushed a few clumps off his shoulders, the waterproof keeping the clothing beneath dry. But he knew that although many of the group had warm clothing, once that got sodden, or even just damp, they would encounter problems. They must find shelter, they must find food, they must find protection. He must find a solution.

Once the group had crossed over the second railway line that passed through the suburbs of Croydon, Bill led them north-west, along Mitcham Road. Although more exposed, it kept them away from the mass of now derelict houses that had been burnt out in the firestorm immediately after the nuclear strikes on London and the surrounding area. Wandle Park was about 300 metres off to their left, and to their right was the sprawl of what was once the thriving population of Thornton East. There were burnt out wrecks, and abandoned cars along the road. A high proportion of the UK's cars had been left stranded on the major roads leading out of the city. At the next junction, on their right, either side of Leighton Street, what was once an open-air car showroom, displaying second-hand cars for sale, now displayed over 100 burnt out hulks. Although walking down the centre of the wide section of road kept them away from the depressing destruction either side of them, it did leave them slightly exposed to a biting easterly wind that cut into them. The snow wasn't heavy, not yet anyway, but its steady downfall, occasionally whipped around by the wind, meant that that any exposed skin was stung by icy particles, the acidic element causing the unprotected flesh to first itch then burn.

After a two-kilometre hike, the group reached the Lombard Roundabout, Purley Way joining it from the south. A large Chrysler showroom, once a showcase for new cars, had now completely collapsed, the once huge windows shattered, leaving a layer of broken glass strewn across the road, the crunch magnified as they trekked across the steadily thickening layer of snow. Bill led them to the centre of the roundabout, heavy foliage providing some cover from the snowfall and the wind. Sentries were posted and the group took a ten-minute break.

The break was soon over, too quickly for some, and Bill and his leaders were soon coaxing everyone back on their feet. Loads were picked up, heavy baggage weighing down on the shoulders of most of them. The fitter, stronger members of the group helped out where they could, but they had their own burdens to carry. Most were carrying food and water, plus some form of bedding to keep them warm during overnight stops. The bulk of the clothing they possessed was actually being worn, with just a few spare items in a bag or rucksack. Bill had also insisted that they take camping gas stoves and as many gas bottles as they could find before the burning tower forced them out. He continued to lead them along Mitcham Street once on the other side of the roundabout. Now they had the Beddington trading estate off to their left, no more than 300 metres away, and Croydon University Hospital a kilometre away, in the centre of the residential area spread out on their right. Bill walked alongside the snaking column, roughly in the centre of the line of march. His group stretched out over 100 metres along the road. Some had their heads down and just placed one foot in front of the other; some chatted with a friend or family member as they walked; others took little detours to peer into the burnt out and rusting shells of cars, either out of curiosity or in the hope of finding something useful. Bill checked for gaps between each individual. None appeared to be lagging behind, not yet anyway.

Then something caught Bill's eye: Justin was waving his arm in a wide arc to catch his attention, the red of the bubble jacket standing out in what was becoming a near white-out as the snow started to thicken.

Bill shouted to Mathew, ten metres ahead. "Mathew, get everyone to close up. Snow's thickening."

"Right on it, Bill. It's sure coming down thick and fast now. Shall I get the lead to pick up speed?"

"Not yet. Let's get everyone closed up first."

"OK."

Mathew started to chivvy those as they passed him to increase their stride until they were in touching distance of the person in front. In the meantime, Bill made his way to the rear of the column, passing on the same instruction to everyone he passed.

"Keep close to the person in front. Move up, move up. Weather's closing in. We don't want to lose anyone. Keep moving. We don't want anyone left behind."

He eventually reached the last in the line: Justin, one of the ex-army lads, along with Owen.

"What's up, Justin?"

"Not sure, Bill. Something following us."

"You mean people?"

"No, too small. Unless they're on their hands and knees."

The three men walked backwards, keeping their eyes on what might be following them, but not wanting to get separated from the rest of the group. Bill peered into the cascade of snowflakes which seemed to be softening, forming slush beneath their feet. The swirling flakes made it difficult to see more than ten or twenty metres ahead of him. A dark shadow appeared for a fraction of a second before disappearing into a swirl of sleet.

"There," pointed Bill. "Nah, it's gone again."

"That's what I get. Just a fleeting glimpse of something dark. Then it's gone in a flash."

"You seen it, Owen?"

"Not sure. Stare long enough, and the bloody cars seem to move."

Bill looked over his shoulder: the last person in the line was no longer in view. "We need to catch up."

All turned around and picked up their pace, taking five minutes to reach the chain of people again. Turning back, Bill couldn't fail to miss at least three shadows amongst the swirling sleet, but disappearing out of view in less than a second.

"They're dogs, they're bloody dogs," uttered Justin.

Bill agreed. "But how many of them?"

"Shall I fire a shot in their direction?" asked Justin, holding up his shotgun.

"They're too far away. Anyway, we don't want to announce our presence to all and sundry."

"Do you think they're after us?"

"Oh yes. Just like us, they need food, and it looks like they have us at the top of their menu."

"What shall we do then?"

"I'll get Maurice to join you, but we'll have to pick up the pace and find a place where we can make a stand."

"There's too many of us for them to take us on, surely."

"That depends on how many of them are out there and how hungry they are. Let's go. Cover us while I get some help."

"OK, but don't be too long," Justin said, a slight tremor in his voice.

Bill started to move back up the line. "You need to pick up the pace, Terry. We've a pack of dogs on our tail."

Terry's eyes widened, and he immediately stepped out, shrugging the rucksack higher onto his shoulders and gripping the two bags he held more tightly.

Bill's boots splashed through the slush, the snow well and truly having turned to sleet, the waterproof jacket and hood keeping him dry, but his combat-like trousers were starting to absorb the wet as the sleet drove into his body. He wasn't panicking, but he was worried. Just snow, they could have coped with, but with this driving sleet and potentially a pack of dogs on their tail, the odds had just tipped out of their favour. He continued with his warning until arriving two-thirds of the way along where he asked Vincent to continue with the message and that the column needed to pick up speed.

Trevor joined Bill. "They're saying we're being hunted."

"I don't know about being hunted yet, but we have dogs trailing us, and we can't take any chances."

"Dogs'll be hungry."

"Bound to be. Most of the carcasses will be well and truly rotted by now. They'll need to prey on fresh dead or even fresher meat."

"Yeah, like us."

"I want you to join Justin, Maurice and Owen at the back. I'll be with you in a few minutes."

"Gotcha."

Trevor moved quickly to provide additional support to those covering the rear while Bill almost ran to the front of the line where he found Robbie and Simon in control.

"Hi, Bill. We got the message: pack of dogs."

"We don't know there's a pack out there as yet."

"Still, the last thing we need. Especially in this shitty weather."

Robbie looked absolutely drenched, and Bill imagined that he probably didn't look much different. Bill walked alongside him and Simon as the tribe continued to move along the road. "We need some cover, and soon."

Robbie wiped his face, clearing the sleet out of his eyes. "We'll be at Mitcham Common in about half an hour."

"We'd be out in the open there. No good."

"Isn't there a warehouse on the left, just before the common?"

Water ran down Bill's face, soaking his scarf and invading his lips and nose. He spat the sour-tasting water out of his mouth, cursing. "Bloody stuff! Yeah, there is, a builders store, I think."

"There then?"

"We've no idea what condition it's in. But I don't see as we have much of a choice. It's our best option. Go for it. Keep everyone moving."

Bang...bang...

"Shit. Get everyone moving now. Sounds like Owen and the two army lads are in trouble!"

Bill broke into a run, the *slap slap* of his feet on the slush-covered road interspersed with shouted orders to the group. "Run, we need to move quickly." *Slap...slap.* "Mathew, give Martha and the kids a hand." *Slap...slap.* "Ken, you need to help carry Elisabeth's stuff. We can't slow down." *Slap...slap.* "Vincent, Sudhish, with me. Get any weapons you have at the ready." *Slap...slap...slap...slap.*

Justin, Maurice, Owen and Trevor suddenly came into view, a semi-circle of emaciated dogs no more than three metres away, one clearly wounded, two metres beyond the nearest dogs.

"How many?"

"At least a dozen," responded Owen. "Maybe more."

"Watch your backs. Some of them are sneaking around the sides," warned Justin.

Bill scanned the area. As well as the dozen or so in front, two smaller groups were moving backwards and forwards as they edged closer, wary, but hunger driving them to take the risk. Three or four on each side were making their way around the fringe of Bill's group, trying to close the circle, trapping their prey.

"We need to keep moving," ordered Bill, looking back, seeing that the bulk of the main party had disappeared into the curtain of falling sleet. He wiped the water from his face and eyes, constant drips of water running off his hood, burning his lips. He blinked continuously, trying to retain vision through his now reddened and swollen eyes.

The group started to shuffle back, forming a wide semi-circle, maintaining their distance from the dogs in front and keeping pace with those trying to reduce the gap behind them.

"Pick up speed, lads. We're going for a warehouse. About ten minutes away. Keep it together, and don't take your eyes off those bastards."

No sooner had Bill finished speaking when three dogs darted forward. Maurice moving more slowly than the rest, suddenly found himself separated by a couple of metres from the main body of defenders. A Jack Russell terrier darted ahead of the other two, fangs sinking into tissue, savaging the man's ankle, the terrier twisting his neck from side to side aiding his strong jaws and teeth to strengthen their grip and tear into the victim's flesh. The taste of blood overloaded the dog's senses, a red mist descended, and the frenzied attack gave the opening for other animals in the pack to launch. An Alsatian leapt at Maurice's arm as he bent down, struggling with the load he was carrying, trying to club the terrier with the chair leg, his chosen weapon. A third darted in, a bullmastiff, sinking its teeth into Maurice's thigh, the powerful jaws locking down on his limb, pulling the man down, a scream reverberating from the stricken man as pain lanced up his leg.

Bill was the first to respond, dropping his baggage and running towards the attackers as he saw more dogs closing in for the kill. Fearful of using his shotgun and hitting Maurice, he swung a boot at the bullmastiff, hearing a satisfied yelp as he then clubbed it with the butt of his shotgun. Mathew, who had just joined them, stabbed the Alsatian in its side with his makeshift spear, a carving knife strapped to the end of a broom stale, the pitiful squeal evidence that it had been critically wounded and taken out of the fight. Bill now fired a single shotgun barrel out to the front, hitting a black labrador and dispersing the other dogs it was leading to the fray, and quickly turning 180 degrees to fire another blast behind them, scattering the dogs that had taken the opportunity to encircle the humans.

What happened next gave them the break they needed. The Alsatian, now dead, was suddenly set upon by a pack of six, ripping at its coat, tearing into its muscle tissue, then turning on each other in a mad fever of snarling, growling, snapping and biting. The wounded mastiff, not wanting to miss out on a meal, joined in, but the smell of blood dripping from the wound on its head inflicted by the shotgun butt just attracted other dogs, their hackles up, the hunger pangs driving away any sense of normality as they also tore into the bullmastiff that was now fighting for its life.

"Run! Run now!" Bill shouted.

The group didn't need any encouragement. Picking up their discarded loads, they broke into a sprint, leaving a pack of howling dogs, maddened by the scent of blood and the chance of a meal for the first time in over a week. Bill picked up his own baggage took one of the bags off Maurice and grabbed his arm, dragging him towards the others, Owen coming to his aid. With just the rucksack now and support from Bill and Owen, Maurice managed to hobble along the road, the sleet swallowing them up, the dogs disappearing from sight, and just the sounds of growling, snarling and howling behind them.

Ten minutes later found them at the warehouse. Robbie and four others were standing out in the sleet, weapons at the ready, prepared to fight off any threat. Bill and his rear group threw themselves through the doorway, crashing onto the floor and safety.

CHAPTER 4

PARALYSIS | GROUND-ZERO +29 DAYS
MOTORWAY TRIBE, NORTH-WEST OF CHELTENHAM

Judy ran as fast as she could from her camper van to the makeshift medical centre. The two scarves wrapped around her head and neck flapped in the bitterly cold snow squall that blew with force across the motorway, and the snow and ice bit into any exposed flesh, buffeting her face, blinding her. She stumbled as she approached the door of the bus, once a luxury coach but now with flat tyres, blistered and flaking paint, grabbing at the door to help keep her footing. She pressed against the foldable door, forcing it open, pushing her head through the blankets that acted as a draft excluder, protecting the occupants inside from the bitter draught that eked its way through the gaps in the partially buckled doorway. Once through, she pulled the scarves down off her face. The smell assailed her nostrils instantly, causing her to gag: a smell of bodies, urine, gangrenous wounds, rotting flesh, and vomit. The coach now served as their medical centre, a hospital. Every alternate seat had been torn out to provide floor space for the patients to lie down. The abandoned cars along their stretch of the motorway, over a thousand of them, had been stripped of anything that could be used to make the patients comfortable: cushions, car seats and camp beds to lie on and car blankets, coats and sleeping bags to provide them with some protection from the debilitating cold.

Philippa, the group's only medically qualified person, a nurse, a sister in fact, acknowledged Judy. "Hello, Judy, I take it there's no change in the weather?" She said it with a smile, seeing and feeling the blustering snow and wind pounding at the coach and its windows.

Judy slumped into one of the remaining coach seats with her back to the window, her feet on the seat, pulling her knees up and wrapping her arms around them to keep warm. "How are our patients doing?"

Philippa sat on the seat on the opposite side of the aisle, turning to the small camping stove on the foldaway table in front of it. "Tea?"

"Please."

"Might get enough out of this for two," she said, holding up a pale-looking teabag. "This will be its fourth scalding."

"Wet and warm, it'll do for me."

Philippa put a small pan of water on the stove and whispered, "They're all asleep except for George at the end. Daniel and Ollie are looking pretty good. The soldiers did a good job of fixing up their own handiwork."

"It wasn't their fault, Philippa."

"Yeah, but you got the hots for that Glen." She laughed.

Judy blushed, changing the subject. "What about George?"

Philippa shook her head. "Only a matter of time. The radiation must be eating him from inside. He's coughing up blood, and his faeces are streaked with blood, lots of blood."

"Nothing we can do?"

"Even if I had the expertise, I don't have the facilities." The water came to the boil and she worked her magic with the used teabag, handing a steaming mug of watery tea to Judy. "Saying that, I doubt even a fully equipped specialist hospital would be able to do much. He's not moving from here, Judy, that's for sure. The move still on?"

Judy cupped her hands around the mug, using its heat to warm her cold hands, the heat seeping through the gloves she wore. "We've no choice. That last attack by the Sparras took half of our territory and cost us three more lives. We're running out of food, Philippa, and we have very little fuel to keep this bloody cold out. If we stay, we will slowly starve then freeze to death."

"Do you think they'll come back?"

"The soldiers? Maybe, but I know they had other plans first."

"That government place they mentioned seems a good option."

"Yes, the regional centre is our best option, but they weren't certain it would be up and running."

"It'll be a tough journey in this type of weather. Should we wait?"

"No. If we stay and wait for a break in the weather, and there isn't one, we'll have wasted precious time. We'll just get weaker and colder by the day."

"Eighty miles. Still going for doing it in less than two weeks?"

Judy took a sip of her tea, barely able to taste anything from the over-steeped tea leaves. "I reckon we can do at least six miles a day, leaving two days in reserve."

"We can't take any longer than that. We'll have run out of food and energy by then. Anyway, Sean and Melissa are going to struggle."

"We'll help them get there."

"And George?" She indicated towards the back of the coach with her head.

Judy didn't respond immediately. She'd talked it through with Gavin, who had effectively become her number two, and they had both agreed, after consulting Philippa, that George would not make the journey. In fact, she believed that he was unlikely to live beyond another week. He couldn't keep food and water down and was extremely dehydrated from continuing bouts of diarrhoea. "My decision hasn't changed." She leant forward and whispered, "We have no option but to leave him here. Make him as comfortable as possible. We could ease his suffering, but we don't have anything to give him."

"It's callous, you know. And I don't entirely agree with you."

"The options? Stay here until he dies anyway, and put the rest of the group at risk? The Sparras want our territory, and we're not in a position to deny it to them. It's only a matter of time. Either way, we're stuffed."

"Yeah, yeah, I know. Just doesn't seem fair."

"Fair? What's bloody fair about any of this?" Judy retorted.

"I'm sorry, I know you're right."

"Is that you Judy?" came a voice from further down the coach.

Judy stood up and handed her now empty cup to Philippa. "Thank you, nice treat."

Philippa laughed. "Dishwater, my specialty."

Judy made her way down the aisle, stepping over the sleeping forms of the other patients, until she came to an occupied space in between two of the coach seats, a few rows from the back of the bus. On the left, a figure, shrouded in two unzipped sleeping bags and a red chequered picnic blanket wrapped round his shoulders, rested up on his elbows. Although his complexion was generally pale, two pink spots, almost like blusher, showed on his cheeks. He smiled. "Paying the sick a visit, Judy?"

She crouched down next to him. "Just making sure you aren't disrupting the other patients, Ollie."

"My reputation that bad?"

"Worse." She scanned his face. "Feeling better?"

He lifted his elbow, struggling to support his body on just one, but quickly put it back down and lay flat on his bed. "My wing is a lot better."

Judy plumped up a few of the cushions that had been lying by the side of his bed and pushed them behind his head, allowing him to sit up in a more comfortable position. "Any pain?"

"Some, but less every day. Philippa reckons I should get up tomorrow and start to exercise it."

"That would be progress."

"Need to be ready for the big move."

"We have a few days yet."

Ollie, a young looking thirty-year-old, was quite fit before the bullet struck his upper arm, missing the bone but tearing a long, jagged gouge along his upper biceps muscle. He would have some movement once it had fully healed, but it would never be fully functional again without treatment from a specialist.

There are no experts, no specialist hospitals, and no doctors available, she thought, frowning.

"You OK?"

"Yes, of course I am. And don't you worry. It's your legs that will be needed when we go on our great journey."

"Wasn't that a film? *The Incredible Journey*. Some animals going on an adventure?"

"Not one I've seen." She laughed. Judy noticed another body stirring, deeper inside, right at the back of the coach. "I need to go and see George."

Arriving at the rear of the coach, although her sense of smell had adjusted to the background odour, it didn't prepare her for the stench that assailed her nostrils as she leant over George's form encased in a number of multi-coloured blankets. His ulcerated arms and face, unbandaged, were free of the restrictive covers. Philippa had initially applied bandages to the slowly rotting flesh, but peeling them off when they required changing was agony as the fibres adhered to the wounds. Now she just kept them clean as best she could. Judy wasn't sure if George was asleep, or even unconscious. One thing she did know: she would be committing him to a death sentence if the group left, leaving him behind. He would die anyway, Philippa was adamant about that, but it didn't help Judy feel any better.

CHAPTER 5

PARALYSIS | GROUND-ZERO +30 DAYS
TOWER TRIBE, CROYDON

The group spent an uncomfortable night in the warehouse. Part of the roof at the back was missing so the floor was covered in a thin layer of slush. The steel sheet frame, albeit blackened, had protected much of the contents within from the firestorm as it burnt itself out next to the common to the west, acting as a firebreak, and a much larger warehouse to the east acting as a barrier in that direction. The backend, though, had caved in, hit by flying debris. A section of metal racking supported soft and hardwood planks and lengths of timber, with different sized cross sections, so Ken and Owen dragged some of the flatter planks off the slats and laid them on the floor. Helped by Mathew and Justin, they soon had an area of about sixteen square metres where they could get their feet, and their gear, off the concrete floor. Although protected from the sleet in the immediate area, the wind outside often blew sheets of wet mush from the direction of the collapsed back end of their newfound shelter, towards their position. Simon, helped by Ellie, soon had a fire going inside a now partially rusting wheelbarrow. The smell of any remaining burning paint soon disappeared as the fire increased in volume and intensity, stripping it off. They took it in turns to gather around its heat at the one end of the home-made platform. After some heavy muscle shifting the wooden planks to make a gap in the centre, the wheelbarrow was carefully wheeled into the gap in the middle of the group, allowing more to benefit from its life-giving heat. The dry space available was still not sufficient to accommodate every one of the survivors from the tower, and a second platform was completed along with another wheelbarrow brazier, wood being plentiful in the warehouse. Robbie had organised two small groups, one led by Sally and one by Aleck, to heat up water and prepare some food using the precious few supplies they had left. After their only meal of the day, Bill ordered that they were to get as much as sleep as they were able.

But now it was morning and, while the rest of the group packed up their things and had a last drink before they moved out, Robbie,

Owen, Simon, and Bill settled on one of the racking locations where most of the lengths of wood had been removed. It was big enough that all four could sit on the remaining timber with their legs dangling over the edge, just a short drop to the ground.

"What next, Bill?" asked Owen. "Those dogs are going to be a real problem when we get out of here."

"We certainly can't stay here," added Simon.

"We won't have to." Bill pointed towards the front left-hand side of the small warehouse, his torch lighting up one of two counterbalance forklift trucks, a small utility vehicle used for lifting up palletised loads to load onto and offload from flatbed lorries. "Look at those. They're powered by gas, and there's a stock of bottles over there, along with a second truck." The beam of Bill's torch moved over a stack of gas bottles locked away in a cage. Next to the cage was a second red counterbalance, its paint badly chipped.

"How will they be of help?" asked a puzzled Robbie.

"Just thinking out loud. There's two trucks, and I've seen two cages that are used for stocktakes."

"Cages?" asked an equally puzzled Simon.

"Warehouse guys stand in the cages and are lifted up so they can count or check the stock at the higher levels safely. They can probably reach to a height of the two levels above where we're sitting. I'll show you how to drive one later. My idea is that we put someone in the cage, fill it with some of those small patio bricks, normally used for making mosaic patterns, and lift it up to, say, a metre. With a driver for each truck, providing we can find a way of protecting them... Can I leave that with you and Simon, Owen?"

"Sure, we'll sort something out."

"With one truck at the back of the column and one at the front, whoever is in the cage can warn us of the dogs approaching and also fling the bricks at them. The dogs won't like the noise of the trucks either.

"Do we get to do some jousting as well, Bill?" laughed Owen.

Bill dropped down from the racking and slapped Owen on the knee. "Whatever floats your boat, mate."

"Here, boys," called Sally, bringing over a hot drink. "I'm afraid it's just water with the juice from a dozen old dried lemons we've been hanging on to."

"I'd kill for a coffee, but thanks, Sally," responded Owen. They all thanked her.

"Right, lads, once you've finish your drinks, we'll get going."

The other three dropped down to join Bill and, while Simon and Owen went to look at how they could protect the drivers in the open cabs, Bill took Robbie to see if they could start up the trucks. After a few tries and Bill cleaning and tightening the connections, the warehouse echoed with the sound of the gas-powered motor revving.

"The sound reminds me of a tuk-tuk I went in on my last holiday to India."

"Probably safer than those contraptions, Robbie," laughed Bill, raising his voice above the noise.

It took over an hour to get ready. With assistance from Ken, Justin and Aleck, and using chicken wire strapped to the frame that supported the overhead cover that was there to protect the driver should an object fall from one of the high racking shelves onto the top of the truck, a barrier that would keep the dogs at bay was created. It looks like something out of *It's a Knockout*, thought Bill when he saw the finished articles.

"Right, get ready. You know what to do. Start 'em up."

Aleck and Justin, who were the designated drivers, turned the keys in the ignitions and the two gas-powered trucks roared into life. Mathew and Robbie were each in the cages, a pile of cobblestones, roof tiles and small mosaic bricks stacked around them. Once Bill was satisfied that the motors were ticking over nicely, he gave Owen and Simon the nod and the main door was pulled inwards. Aleck pressed down on the accelerator and the first of the trucks jerked forward, shaking the thick black mast with the two large forks attached, which in turn supported the steel cage, Mathew gripping the top of the cage, that came up to his armpits, to steady himself. "Whoa," he called down.

"Sorry," yelled Aleck. "I'll get the hang of it."

Bill had given the two drivers some quick lessons, but there hadn't been enough time for them to become fully competent. Aleck accelerated slowly and drove out through the open doorway, the large wheels coping well with the layer of slush on the road, but he would need to be careful as Bill had warned him that the trucks were very unstable if you turned too fast and were liable to topple over. Aleck spun the wheel left, at the same time pulling on the lever in front of him that started the chains on the mast, which in turn started to lift the cage up.

There were a dozen dogs in a semi-circle around the entrance;

having heard the noise, knowing something was about to happen, the potential of food and another meal coming to them. But they got more than they bargained for. With the cage now raised to the height of the top of the cab, putting Mathew at over three metres in the air, and Aleck tooting the horn for all he was worth, the dogs scattered, the towering giant causing them to flee. Mathew flung half a dozen roof tiles that smashed when they hit the road, sending smaller chunks ricocheting towards the dogs. With the noise of the truck, the horn blaring, the cage towering above them, and the threat of being hit by flying debris, the pack kept its distance.

Justin then took his turn and accelerated, driving out of the warehouse, but this time turning right. He also pulled on the lever that raised the cage above the cab. He had to be more careful as he was towing a small four-wheeled trailer, not much bigger than the base of the forklift truck, with additional gas tanks to power the vehicles and which could also be used for cooking. The trailer also sported other items that could prove to be useful, particularly some of the two-by-four lengths of wood that could be used for making a shelter or burning should they need fuel for a fire. For any dogs still hanging around the right of the warehouse entrance, it was the last straw, as a second snarling giant screamed towards them, cobblestones being hurled in their direction by Robbie.

With Aleck driving a figure of eight at the back and Justin moving forward slowly, Bill and Owen ushered everyone out, and the group followed the red painted rear of the truck ahead of them. Within five minutes, there was a long column making progress along the A236 Croydon Road, the open ground of Mitcham Common to their right, and soon they would have the Mitcham Golf Course on their left. The pack of dogs followed, getting closer and closer to their prey, but with Aleck occasionally turning back, tooting the horn followed by a barrage of tiles and cobblestones from Mathew, they quickly dispersed until eventually they learnt to keep a reasonable distance and just keep pace with the refugees in front of them. Maurice, the wounds in his leg strapped up as best Ellie, a trained nurse, could manage under the circumstances, bounced on top of the booty that had been tied down to the trailer. Although the warehouse had held no food, there were items that Bill felt sure they could come back for at some time in the future. In the meantime, they had taken the most important items that could be used in the near future, but his main goal was to get his people, his tribe, to safety.

CHAPTER 6

PARALYSIS | GROUND-ZERO +30 DAYS
TOWER TRIBE, CROYDON

It took them nearly four hours to get to the other end of Mitcham Common, the sleet almost as much of an enemy as the dogs. The pack had kept their distance, and when the group stopped just before the Three Kings Pond, their objective to cut down the blackened upper trunks of a couple of remaining trees, the dogs had still harried them but maintained a safe distance, clearly willing to bide their time, and perhaps wait until someone who was too sick or crippled to walk any further would drop out, providing them with a meal.

Cutting down the trees had not been easy, but Robbie, the ex-triathlete, shinned up the trees until the trunks were thin enough for the chosen lumberjack, roped to the tree, to attack them with a handsaw. Once a notch about a third of the way into the trunk had been cut, a forklift truck pulled on a rope that was lashed to the upper trunk. Its wheels occasionally slipped in the snow, but its counterweight, which enabled the truck to lift nearly five tons in weight, helped the solid rubber tyres to grip. The treetops splintered and crashed to the ground, and the rest of the able-bodied soon hacked and sawed them into smaller logs to be loaded in the trucks' cages, the occupants perched on the top when complete. One counterbalance did get stuck, but was soon towed out by the other. Once the last of the logs were stowed, the refugees continued their journey north-west.

They made their way through what was once the leafy housing area of Mitcham, travelling in a north-westerly direction, the area more desolate the further west they went. Passing close to Cricket Green School, there had been a stand-off. A group had occupied the remains of the building, establishing a base for survivors that had grouped together into a small community. Bill negotiated passage down Church Road, convincing the half a dozen men that blocked their way that his group was no threat. Apart from scavenging for food and supplies, wood was becoming a sought-after commodity, its heat-giving properties essential for warmth and cooking in the bitter climate that had descended on the UK. Further north, particularly in Scotland, temperatures were regularly dropping to minus twenty. In the south, although the weather was warmer, the colder nights were still close to minus ten, and would get worse. The group relented, allowing Bill and his people free passage along Church Road, providing they didn't stop. It wasn't due to a moment of sympathy that they had relented, but more because Bill's group represented a threat and were fifty-plus strong, possessing a number of weapons, whereas the group at the school had only two shotguns, along with only eleven cartridges between them.

Three kilometres and two hours of trudging through snow, the cold air freezing the sleet into crystals of snow falling steadily from above, found them next to the remains of the upper buildings of the South Wimbledon underground station. It was a no-go. The mainly four-storey glass-fronted building had been smashed to smithereens, engulfing the parade of shops that used to thrive on the money spent by travellers that flocked to the station to travel to work or on other planned journeys. There had also been a bus station outside but the red buses were nowhere to be seen. Most had been requisitioned by the government at the last minute to move soldiers and government officials to their wartime locations, and for the transportation of supplies to wherever they deemed it appropriate if the country was to survive an attack. The country, the United Kingdom, though was ill-prepared. Although a few of the Regional Government Centres, not yet closed, or rapidly reinstated, were functioning, the remainder simply no longer existed. With the Cold War supposedly over, the majority of the regional government buildings and bunkers had been left to decline, or closed, or some even sold to private industry. The parade of shops that used to consist of a barber's, fish and chip shop, newsagent's, florist's, and other small enterprises considered ideal to elicit money from the travellers had been crushed beneath tons of rubble.

Once he realised there would be no access to the station, Bill wasted no time and led his group east along London Road, changing the propane gas tanks on the forklift trucks during the journey. Passing through devastated areas of the borough, the further north they went towards the centre of the City of London, the worse the destruction. They arrived at Colliers Wood tube station, but it too had suffered from the blast wave as a consequence of the explosions to the north. Again, Bill wasted no time. Joined by Justin, Robbie, and Owen, the four men poked and prodded the rubble, using thin three-metre poles brought with them from the building where they had spent the previous night.

They poked and prodded, clearing snow aside with shovels also brought with them, looking for any opening that could lead them to the depths below. After three hours of back-breaking work, Bill called a halt. They needed to find shelter and security for the night. The dogs had followed them, and their dark coats glinted wet in contrast to the white background of the snow as they stalked their prey, slowly forming a semi-circle, keeping an eye on what could be their next meal.

The rest of the group had stood watch, huddled together, shivering, eating what cold food they had available to them. Simon and Ken had completed a reconnaissance of the immediate area, a number of dogs tracking them as they moved warily along the high street. The two men brought back good news, finding somewhere they could hold up for the night. It had once been a library, the Donald Hope. The old seventies-style windows on the top two storeys had been blasted to smithereens, and the two floors and roof had collapsed in at the far end. But near the edge of the road, adjacent to the wreckage of the upper levels of the Colliers Wood tube station, the ground floor level was accessible and, more importantly, dry. Bill moved the entire collective to the library, parking the two forklift trucks across the entrance to provide security. The people trailed in through the entrance area, where readers had once logged out their choices of books and CDs and paid any fines for delaying their return. All they could access of the main library now was just a mass of black and soggy ash, the remains of the library's books burnt to a cinder during the firestorm that swept through the borough. Opposite the library was all that was left of a petrol station: a large crater, now covered in a thick layer of snow-covered dust, where the fuel tanks deep below had erupted, blasting all about them.

Under Bill's instruction, Owen started a fire just at the entrance to the shattered building, using the wood they had brought with them to get a good blaze going, followed by the logs that been cut down en route. The fire served three purposes: to provide warmth and a means of drying out their sodden clothing; the heat necessary to cook food and melt snow for water; and as a security barrier, keeping the dogs at bay.

There was an additional threat. Their presence hadn't gone unnoticed and, along with the watching eyes of the dogs, human eyes had been monitoring their activity and progress. Bill ensured security was tight before encouraging those not on watch to settle down and get what sleep they could. There was very little food to eat and what there was had been shared out. Discussing the situation with Robbie, Owen, Trevor, and Simon, they reckoned there were no more than two days of food left, and that wasn't exactly feeding everyone on full rations. For the first time, Bill experienced doubt and concern. He needed answers and he needed them quickly.

CHAPTER 7

PARALYSIS | GROUND-ZERO +30 DAYS
THE CONVICTS, CROYDON

Salt ducked to the left, just avoiding a blow as Keelan's fist powered past his head, causing the man to lose his balance and crash forward onto the ground, rolling painfully onto his shoulder. Keelan just managed to get back up into a crouch, avoiding Salt's boot as it swung close to his head. Now it was Salt's turn to lose his balance, the momentum behind the kick, and the failure to connect his boot with Keelan's face, putting him into a spin, ending up facing away from his target. Keelan wasted no time, and his muscular thighs launched his large frame upwards, his broad shoulders crashing into Salt's back, his burly arms gripping the taller man in a bear hug. Salt shook himself from side to side, desperate to escape his fellow convict's grasp.

Milo, his beady, rat-like eyes flicking from one to the other, fearful of the outcome of the battle between the two giants, finally got up from where he was squatting in the corner of the derelict house. Although terrified, he stood in front of the two struggling men, Salt unable to break Keelan's vice-like clasp, but Keelan in turn unable to take advantage and bring the taller man down to the floor. He held his fingerless-glove-covered, paw-like hands out in front of him, the light from the wood fire flickering in his pleading eyes, wide with trepidation as he stuttered a barely audible request, "S-Salt...K-Keelan...p-please stop. You need each other...we all need each other. P-please...stop fighting."

The two men responded, Salt halting his attempt to shake Keelan free, his antagonist retaining his grip but peering around Salt's shoulder to look at the pathetic figure in front of them.

"You need each other...I need you...if you...we are to survive."

Although a diminutive person, both Keelan and Salt knew that the individual in front of them, Milo, was a murderer, and in the wrong circumstances could be a cold-blooded killer. They didn't fear him but, to hear his protest, his pleading, it touched something in both of them, and Keelan's grip slowly relaxed, his arms dropping to his sides.

Salt shrugged his shoulders then wiped a smear of blood from his swollen lip. "Fuck, Milo, what's with you?"

"You were both trying to kill each other."

"Nah, we were just exercising," responded Salt.

"We gotta train," added Keelan.

Milo stopped shaking and walked over to the fire, suddenly feeling the cold biting into his body, the lack of food over the last couple of days starting to take their toll. He was joined by the two combatants who, although warm after their fight, crouched down opposite him. The fight had started with Keelan's frustration boiling over. The lack of comforts, alcohol, food, and water had pushed him over the edge, and he had blamed Salt for their current predicament. What had started as an argument quickly escalated into a row, with Keelan throwing a punch at Salt. Salt, the glancing blow splitting his lip, swiftly retaliated, leaping at his antagonist, the disagreement turning into an exchange of blows.

Salt scratched his head. No longer closely shaven, an inch-thick layer of mousey-coloured hair now covered his head. Keelan's was the same. The hair and scalp of both the men was now dirty and ingrained with dust and grit. Milo's hair had always been short but not a crew cut. It had also grown and was now lank and untidy. All three had facial growth. Milo, in his late forties, had a beard flecked with grey. Keelan's was dark and wiry, whereas Salt, who was a late starter with respect to shaving, had a few wispy facial hairs that looked almost juvenile-like.

Keelan turned to Salt. "You OK?"

"Apart from a thick lip, yeah. You?"

"A punch from you." Keelan laughed. "Didn't feel a thing."

"You've got a fucking grip though. Thought my ribs would burst."

"Glad you two are talking." Milo smiled.

"We was just joshing, Milo buddy," Salt reassured him.

Milo, rubbing his hands in front of the fire, relieved to be back by its warmth, nodded, but he wasn't sure how it would have ended if he hadn't intervened.

"But you gotta see my point, Douglas. We've come to bloody Croydon, and it's in shit state. We've run out of food, down to our last bottle of water, and are living like pigs," complained Keelan.

"I know, but I didn't expect it to be like this," replied Salt. "I thought we'd be living like kings by now. Holed up in some hotel living off the processed food that has to be out there."

"It's what we do next that matters," suggested Milo.

Keelan looked at Salt. "And what do we do next? This is your part of the world."

"The plan's the same. We find a group, one that's established, and integrate ourselves. You know the rest."

"How do we find the right group?" asked Milo, pulling a blanket around his shoulders. "We've seen groups scavenging, but they look pretty hostile."

Salt leant forwards. "Look, we need food and water. There has to be some somewhere. We find that. Then we track some of these groups, see where they go, and decide who and when we approach and simply ask to join."

"And if they say no?" asked Keelan.

"If they seem too powerful, we move on. If not, then we take out the ringleaders and take control."

Keelan nodded his agreement. He didn't doubt for one minute that they could take control of the right group. They had a shotgun and, more importantly, the state of mind and right level of aggression to take control. "In the meantime?"

Salt looked at Milo. "Milo buddy, this has to be your field."

"Mine?" His paw-like hands came up in front of him in defence. "You two are the leaders. I don't know what to do."

"Your sniffer does though. If you were on your own, it wouldn't take long for you to suss out where the right places are. Just put your devious mind to work and picture yourself all alone here. What would you do to survive?"

Keelan chucked a chair leg, already partly burnt from the fire that had engulfed this part of the city, onto the fire. A shower of sparks ascended.

Milo's rodent-like eyes gleamed, and behind them synaptic connections passed signals between each other as he processed the request. Deceit and thieving had been his life since the age of eleven; the first time he came in front of a magistrate was for 'taking a conveyance', the modern term for stealing a car.

"It's not the obvious places that should be of interest," he ventured finally. "Places like supermarkets, shops, pubs, homes, and hotels will have been targeted and stripped clean. We need to focus on the least likely places people will go to and scavenge."

"And they are?"

"I'm thinking. Give me a minute, Doug."

Salt rifled through his bag, pulling out his last bar of chocolate, a treat he had been saving. The paper had been burnt off, but the congealed mess beneath had been protected by the silver foil. He peeled off the foil and broke the chocolate into three chunks. Not of equal size but close, he gave Keelan and Milo a piece each, keeping the slightly larger chunk for himself.

Milo held up his piece of chocolate before taking a bite. "Thanks, Doug. Real treat, this."

"Where you been hiding this?" grumbled Keelan.

Milo jumped in before Salt could respond. "Factories."

"What factories?"

"These sort of factories," responded Milo, studying his last bit of chocolate before placing it in his mouth. "They're bound to have something edible."

"What, bloody cocoa beans?" spluttered Keelan.

"There's a Nestlé factory in Croydon," added Salt.

"Not cocoa beans, but they'll have other stuff. Sugar, powdered milk, water, and...I don't know...something we can eat. Anyway, there must be other factories we can try."

"Yeah, but powdered milk?!"

"Tins of beans and the like will be gone, Stan. Anything refrigerated, fresh or not in a tin will be rank by now."

"He has a point. I know there is a Nestlé's. Most of the factories will be around the same area."

"Maybe that's the way ahead," Keelan tentatively agreed. "Not just food, well hardly food, but stuff we can survive on. And we could find some decent shelter. Could you take us there?"

Salt nodded, his outlook brightening. "Sure. It's about an hour or so from here. I suggest we do circuit rather than going straight there though. We can scavenge on the way and keep a lookout for something more permanent."

"Things are looking up. My turn to produce the goods. Been saving this for a rainy day." Keelan pulled out a whisky bottle, still a quarter full. "I think our master plan calls for a celebration." He pulled out the cork and took a swig before handing it to Salt. Salt tipped the bottle, closing his eyes as he took his tipple, swilling the fiery liquid around his mouth, savouring its burn as he passed the bottle to Milo.

Salt finally let the warming liquid slip down his throat, feeling optimistic for the first time in days. "God, that was good."

The bottle back with Keelan, he took a second swig. "One more each. Then let's keep the last bit for when we get to our first factory."

Salt took another slug, followed by Milo. Then Keelan secured the bottle in his rucksack. He patted the bag. "We need to find some more of this though. Any distilleries in Croydon, Doug?"

"No, but there might be a brewery."

"I could live with that."

"Others may have had the same idea," cautioned Milo. "Best we focus on the low-key sites first, eh?"

"Yeah, sure, Milo. We get the picture." Keelan stood up and walked over to the doorway that led out of the room they were ensconced in. They were on the ground floor of a house on Stafford Road. Although the roof had disappeared and most of the walls had collapsed, this one room still had a ceiling, and with the window blocked and a blanket draped across the doorway, the trio had managed to retain some warmth during their overnight stay. Keelan pulled aside the curtain. The battered walls of the other room had held back the blasts of cold air that were now starting to gust through the city, but with the house open to the sky, a thin layer of snow had formed on the floor of the house. White flakes decorated Keelan's head and shoulders. He brushed the snow off the top of his head, drips from melting flakes running down his cheeks and neck. Although cold, it was quite refreshing, and he knew immediately that they needed to find containers for source of water as their own supplies were running dangerously low. He ran his tongue along his lips, savouring the life-giving liquid before suddenly spitting it out, wiping his mouth with the back of his hand and pulling his head back into the room.

"It's bloody snowing out there?" exclaimed Keelan.

"That's good news. Our water shortage has been solved."

"'Fraid not, Milo, it tastes foul. I can still feel it burning my mouth."

"Acidic rain, snow," suggested Salt.

"I gathered that, Doug. I've just spat the stuff out."

"That's the effects of the nuclear fallout. All the muck that's been chucked up into the atmosphere coming back down."

"We're stuffed then."

"We could boil it," suggested Milo.

"Kill the bugs, Milo mate, but that's all. We need to condense it."

"Condense what?" asked Keelan.

"Boil it, but capture the steam."

"That make it safe?"

"I think."

"You think," snapped Keelan.

"I don't bloody know. But what other choice do we have? If we don't find water elsewhere then we're dead."

"That's comforting."

"That's the situation we're in," added Milo.

Keelan glanced down at Milo. "You a smart arse as well, Milo?"

Milo dipped his head, choosing silence. Salt grabbed Keelan's arm and pulled the man down gently into a crouch. "Hey, chill, buddy. We're just trying to talk things through. We're kind of new to this."

Keelan calmed down, pulled his sleeve up, and checked his watch. "Just after eleven. I reckon we stay put till tomorrow."

"Is the snow heavy?" asked Milo.

"Not really, just seems steady. Go take a look."

Salt got up from his crouched position, shaking his stiffened legs. "We need to find some containers. Catch as much melted snow as possible."

Milo got up to join him. "Pots and pans should do it."

"Plastic bags or the like, so we can capture the steam," added Salt.

"Can you distil whisky as well?" laughed Keelan, getting up himself to join in the search for the items they needed.

Salt led the way, buttoning his jacket top button up and pulling his beanie hat on. "Let's get it done."

CHAPTER 8

PARALYSIS | GROUND-ZERO +30 DAYS
BRAVO TROOP, LONDON

Rolly checked the tripwire which was attached to a bang-alert device, ensuring it was the right height so that it would catch the foot of anyone approaching the entrance of their hide. He had two: one guarding the approach from the south-east, the other covering the north-west. It was a simple device: a spring-loaded plunger attached to a thin, almost invisible tripwire that, when triggered, struck a cap, creating a loud bang. This would have two effects: firstly, warning Rolly that intruders were close by, and secondly, frightening the individual, or individuals, that had triggered the alarm. Although Rolly, left on his own to guard the Land Rover, trailer and the troop's supplies, would be alert most of the time, he still needed some sleep. The use of Claymore mines had been discussed but, even under the current conditions, the men pulled back from the potential slaughter of innocents. Having said that, Rolly was armed and would defend their hide using lethal force if necessary.

It had been agreed right from the start that three would descend into the depths of the London tube in an attempt to access the Pindar Bunker. Not knowing what they might have to face, they agreed that the minimum of three should go on the expedition, leaving one behind to keep a low profile and protect their equipment and supplies. Rolly had been chosen for that task. He had one last look around, satisfied that the steady fall of snow was covering his footprints and those of his three comrades who had trekked towards the Oval tube station. He returned to the dark interior of the cavern, brushing past the hessian barrier, and sat in a director's chair facing the entrance, settling into its canvas back. With the gas stove on the bonnet of the Land Rover, he heated up some water for an Earl Grey tea, his favourite. It bothered him a little that the box of 200 was less than half full. Once his tea was made, the tea bag saved for a second cup, he settled back in his chair again, a sleeping bag pulled up around his legs and knees, C8 carbine on his lap, and prepared for a long wait.

Three days was the agreed time to find the bunker and explore the area. If his fellow troopers were not back by dawn of the fourth day, he was to pack up and make his way to Chilmark. If still alive, his comrades would make their way back on foot, or by whatever means they could find. Rolly sipped at the hot liquid and steeled himself for a lonely three days and nights.

Glen crawled on his stomach. The narrow channel, found after they had roped down to it, that would lead them to the depths of the tube station was inches away from his shoulders and back, jagged sections of collapsed concrete tugging at his NBC suit. He wondered how Greg was coping. Greg's pleasure in pumping weights meant he was the stockiest of the troop and would no doubt find the tunnel more than a tight squeeze. Thank God he doesn't suffer from claustrophobia, thought Glen, as he inched his way forward on his elbows. His MP5 was held out in front of him, and behind him, attached to his ankle by a short piece of rope, he dragged along his rucksack and PLCE, his Personal Load Carrying Equipment. A cold layer of sweat was forming on his back, causing him to shiver. Although still chilly inside the confines of the collapsed entrance, it was significantly warmer than the wind-driven snow outside. He eventually arrived at the end of the channel, a draught coming from the black tunnel ahead of him. He was able to get up into a crouch and turned his helmet torch on which lit up a tiled but dust-covered floor. He pulled his rucksack and kit towards him, but left them tied to his ankle. He listened. Nothing could be heard ahead of him, but Glen could hear the shuffling body of Greg some ten metres behind him. He moved forward awkwardly, in a duck walk, his equipment dragging behind his foot, the MP5 cradled in his left arm as he used his right to feel his way ahead. The torchlight lit up huge chunks of masonry, supporting parts of the roof that had collapsed inwards from above.

At the end of the low passage, Glen came to what appeared to be a dead end. He examined the area more closely, and he could see that what initially appeared to be a huge piece of reinforced concrete blocking his movement forward was actually hiding a gap behind it that would take them to the steps leading down into the ticket area, where the ticket offices, ticket machines and barriers would be found. Or so he hoped. He shuffled around the side of the huge structure, pieces of rubble digging into his knees as he crouched down low to peer around the back. He shone his torch into the cavity; a handrail and steps were visible. He switched the torch off, conserving the batteries, and waited for Greg to join him.

"God, this place is oppressive. What you got?"

"Some steps."

"Spot on."

"It's whether or not we can get your fat body through this gap."

"Hey, boss, that's not very politically correct, is it."

"I thought that was Plato talking then."

"Wanker."

A light from behind the two men shone in their eyes. "You two arguing again?"

"Get that bloody torch out of my eyes, Plato."

"Sorry, boss."

"We have a way in, but it's tight. I'll go first, and then you try, Greg. OK?"

"I'll pass your kit through after you."

"I'll ditch this as well," Glen pulled his helmet off, pulling a second torch from his pocket. "I'll go head first, but there's not a lot of space to manoeuvre, so push me from your side."

"Gotcha."

Greg moved back while Glen disconnected the rope from his ankle releasing his pack and gear and stretched out, positioning his body on the floor, lying on his side. "I'm going for it." He eased himself forward, using his right elbow as a lever, reaching out with his left hand to pull on the concrete, his gloved hands protecting him from its rough surface. Halfway into the gap, his body now arched around the mass partially blocking their way, both arms extended forward, Glen wriggled his body in waves, snake-like, kicking with his feet, moving forward a centimetre at a time. He felt a pair of boots connect with his. With his back up against the ruins of the tube station, Greg pushed against Glen's boots, allowing his fellow soldier to push back, generating some forward movement. After a ten-minute struggle, Glen was able to use his now free hands and arms to pull himself completely into the space the other side.

A quick examination identified the stairs, partially blocked by fallen debris but accessible, and he was at least able to stand up. Greg pushed Glen's kit through and got himself in position to take his turn to squeeze through the narrow gap. Even with Plato pushing from behind and Glen pulling from the front, it was a non-starter as Greg's muscular body got caught time and time again.

Greg sat down, catching his breath after the last effort. "It's no good. There's only one way to fucking do this," and he started to strip off his combats. His NBC suit first, followed by his MTP combats and shirt, leaving a T-shirt, a pair of long johns and gloves. His boots were put back on and he was ready.

"Greg," whispered Plato, "you don't need to do this. We're already acquainted."

"Wanker. Right, let's try again. Coming through," Greg called to Glen.

The detritus on the floor ground into his body as he grunted and wriggled his frame frantically in order to make progress. The concrete blocking his route tore a thin strip of skin from his stomach as he arched his body around it, pushed and pulled at both ends. Suddenly, like a cork popping out of a champagne bottle, after a powerful push from Plato, and Glen pulling on Greg's arms until they were close to coming out of their sockets, he was through.

"Birthday suit, Greg? Get dressed please."

"Boss, anyone tell you you're a wanker?"

"You, frequently. Now, get dressed."

Plato pushed Greg's uniform through the gap, followed by his and Greg's kit and then took his turn. A similar build to Rolly, but five inches shorter, he was through in less than five minutes.

"That's how you do it, mate."

"You could get through a crack in a door."

"Better than being a little on the plump side."

"Wanker."

"When you two have stopped bickering, we'll make a move," ordered Glen.

Greg dressed quickly, and they all slipped on their PLCE and pulled on their rucksacks. With his helmet back on and three torches, two from the others flickering around the black space lighting up the way, Glen led them down the steps. There was only one flight. Glen took each step carefully. Rubble from the initial collapse was strewn across the steps and down to the floor below. Greg followed behind him, with Plato as Tail-end Charlie.

Glen stepped onto the white tiled floor, although it was now grimy with dust. A musty smell assailed his nostrils – a mixture of electricity arc burns, damp, and engine oil, a smell familiar to all who have ever used the London Underground. He placed his feet carefully. Parts of the roof had caved in, leaving small traps on the floor to catch him out if he wasn't careful. His helmet torch illuminated the way ahead. Ticket offices and ticket machines were on the right, and an information kiosk on the left. Ahead, the individual barriers that controlled access to the trains below were partially covered in fragments of the structure that had caved in from above, leaving only two gates accessible on the far right. Glen moved towards them, the crunch of broken glass from the kiosks and from the skylight that had once existed some way above now smashed to smithereens. His torch cast a light over some of the circular green and white tiled mosaics: white cricketers in various poses on a background of green, reflecting the closeness of the station to the actual Oval, the famous cricket ground. As he moved slowly forwards, motes of dust danced and sparkled in front of him wherever the beam of his torch touched them. He passed between two waist-high turnstiles, stepping over the barriers, a ticket no longer required.

Turning left, the torches of Greg and Plato flickering around behind and past him signalling that the two of them were not too far behind, Glen continued warily, deeper into the Underground complex. The corridor was congested with more fallen masonry, but there was just enough space to squeeze past. The two sets of escalators were completely obstructed. The wall from the right-hand side had been pushed in by the forces from above, choking the exit point at the bottom, completely blocking any further access to the depths of the station. Glen led them to the left and, within ten or twelve strides, took them to the top of a set of spiral steps that descended deeper into the station's abyss. A buckled RSJ lay across the top of the spiral staircase, but Glen was able to step over it, and after checking the other two were with him, started down the eighty-odd steps that would take him even further towards the platforms below. The set of steps seemed to go on forever, but eventually the three men reached the bottom and moved down the corridor that would take them to the tunnels. It was an eerie feeling, the blackness of the corridors only penetrated by the light of their torches, and the silence broken only by the footfall of their boots and the clink of weapons. The familiar shape of the entrance to the platform, a curved roof spanned the platform on the other side. Prior to passing through the entrance, Glen had checked the sign on the wall which indicated they were about to enter the southbound platform. Once on the platform, he turned left. He stopped to get his bearings, using a second torch to help light up the platform walls. Opposite was a red roundel with the words 'Oval' in white on a plaque with a blue background. Next to it was an advert from an investment bank, promising the earth. A bank that no longer exists, thought Glen.

"We need to keep left," he informed the others.

"Like you, I've been down in places like this at night before. But somehow it feels a lot different this time," Greg shared.

"Feels like I'm being watched," added Plato. He shone his torch onto the railway lines, and two rats scampered past them, their beady black eyes watching their observers as they ran.

"You were. Trust those buggers to survive," moaned Greg.

"We'll be eating them in a couple of months."

"Until then, Plato, I'll stick with compo rats."

"Come on, you two, let's make a move. I want to keep going until we at least hit Waterloo."

At the end of the platform, they crossed the yellow line that ran along the platform's edge and jumped down next to the tracks, entering the coal-black tunnel ahead of them, their torchlight swallowed up by its blackness.

"Mind the gap," Greg joked as he had jumped down.

They strode along the left-hand side of the railway line, the air becoming stuffier the deeper they progressed into the bowels of the tunnel. All the extractor fans had ceased to work a long time ago, and there was no longer the rush of trains pushing and pulling the air through the tunnels. The men spoke occasionally, pointing out maintenance doors, pipework, signals and electrical control boxes, their voices echoing in the void ahead and behind them. The deeper into the tunnel they went, the more oppressive the air became. Even the beams of their torches seemed to be consumed by the darkness, just a dense wall, which appeared impenetrable.

The trio got into a steady rhythm. The tunnel curved very, very slightly to the right as the three soldiers continued their march towards Kennington, their next checkpoint. Glen shone his secondary torch around the upper curved surface of the tube. Rows and rows of cables lined the roof, drooping between each point of attachment. Lower down, he shone the beam on a yellow sign, a picture of a black steam train set in a black triangle with the warning: 'Danger, beware of trains'.

He stopped, looked back at Greg and laughed. "Keep a lookout."

"Almost be a relief to see one in this dingy hole."

"You might see one of the passengers though," suggested Plato.

"What?"

"It's haunted down here. Didn't you know that?"

"Don't be ridiculous."

"He's right, Greg," supported Glen.

"See. A passenger was killed boarding a train, trapped between two carriages, and dragged around the loop."

"Wankers." But Greg could feel a prickling sensation down the back of his neck. "Bloody fairy stories."

Plato stopped. "Hang on a sec." He widened the beam of his torch and focused it on a section of the roof up ahead. A large crack could be seen, a steady drip of water seeping out of it.

The other two stopped.

"That has to be fresh," suggested Glen.

"Looks like it," supported Plato.

"Survived World War Two, but a city pounded by nukes is perhaps a bit too much," threw in Greg.

Glen carried on walking. "Let's see what's further on."

After 500 metres of marching, they finally exited the main tunnel and were able to climb up onto the platform at Kennington.

Glen unslung his MP5 and placed it on a wooden bench attached to the wall, the recognisable red roundel with the word Kennington across it above. "Let's take five."

The other two also took off their weapons, removed their helmets, rucksacks and weapons kit, and grabbed a bite to eat, Glen choosing a tin of cold hamburger and beans, Greg and Plato opting for instant porridge followed by a swig of water.

Glen shone his torch around the platform area, the yellow line with 'Mind the gap' in white visible in the glow. Beyond, the lower arch where the train tunnel continued could be seen at the far end. He then switched off his secondary torch, conserving the batteries as much as possible.

After a short break, water bottles were secured, their helmets, rucksacks, and kit dragged back on, and, with weapons in hand, their journey continued. At the end of the platform, they dropped back down onto the lines and entered the second tunnel, no different from the one they had just left, apart from a couple of doors, locked, on the left-hand side. Glen kept a eye on the roof, but there were no further signs of cracking. After 300 metres, the track split and the soldiers took the left-hand fork, now heading north.

Interconnecting with the Bakerloo and Jubilee Lines, Waterloo, one of the larger tube stations, was their next stop. This would also be their longest stint, the tunnel stretching nearly a kilometre to the next station. The Northern Line was a deep-level tube. The soldiers were well and truly isolated between stations at a depth of over forty metres. Some of the stations on the Northern Line were more than fifty metres below ground. They walked in silence, just the hollow clatter of their boots on the concrete disturbing the peace, or the occasional scampering sound of rats and mice. On one occasion, startling them all, a bat flew just above their heads, causing Greg to flinch and curse as the air from the creature's wings blew across his face.

They eventually arrived at their destination, and Glen called them together. "This place will be a rabbit warren. I want to check it out, probe as far up as the surface if possible."

"Makes sense," agreed Greg. "Might as well suss out what's going on up there." He indicated above them.

"Let's do it then." Glen switched his second torch back on, and they clambered onto the platform and headed for the exit.

Waterloo tube station, located deep underground near the south bank of the River Thames, was situated in the London Borough of Lambeth, and London had been the number one target for the nukes sent over by Russia, so none of them held out much hope that they would be able to exit to the outside world. However, they felt it was worth the effort to try.

Greg shone his torch on a sign above and to their left. "Way out," he informed the others with a wave of his torch. "Should take us all the way up to Waterloo's main line station." As he scanned for other doorways, should they be needed, which would lead them away from the platform and steer them to the upper levels, his torch beam picked out items of clothing scattered on the ground, discarded food packaging, empty drink cans, and empty water bottles. They exited the platform and headed down one of the corridors that would eventually take them to the surface. The closer they got to the first of the escalators, a strong smell assailed their nostrils, growing more pungent as they approached the source of the stench. The volume of personal detritus also increased: abandoned blankets, sleeping bags, empty boxes, cigarette packets, empty food cans, the occasional pram or pushchair, plastic bags containing personal belongings, and other paraphernalia you might associate with people living rough.

"Keep your eyes peeled," warned Glen. "We might have company."

The three soldiers weaved through the narrow passageways,

ignoring the 'Keep left' signs, until they reached one of the twenty-three escalators that serviced the Northern Line, along with Bakerloo, Jubilee and the Waterloo & City Lines linked to it. They ascended the first set of escalators, stationary naturally. The smell of death, a rank and pungent smell mixed with a tinge of sweetness, amplified the higher they got. Glen had taken the left escalator, with Greg and Plato on the right. A steady hum could be heard as they ascended, and all three were confused as to the source of the sound. It was a long climb, and their calf and thigh muscles were tight by the time they reached the summit. The open area at the top was awash with line upon line of miniature hovels, no more than a couple of centimetres apart. Broken cardboard boxes were laid down as a barrier against the cold tiled floor, a dozen different-sized sponge mattresses, a few camp beds, sleeping bags, blankets, thick coats, plastic sheeting, refuse – all trappings indicative of homeless people. The difference this time was that there were bodies scattered amongst the allotted living areas. At least twenty were visible as the soldiers played their torch beams across the small concourse. A multitude of flies rose up in a swarm from the bodies they were feasting on, the first time they had been disturbed in weeks. Although the soldier's sense of smell was adjusting to the foul stench of rotting flesh, it was still overpowering.

The three men pulled on the surgical masks, brought specifically for coming across an event such as this, over their mouths and noses and moved nearer. On closer examination, it looked as if the individuals, men, women, and children, had died of starvation, but probably the lack of water would have been the deciding factor. Many had scalps that were discoloured, almost bare but for a few clumps of hair. Patches of dry, stale vomit, dark specks of dried blood visible, covered some of the bodies or decorated the surrounding tiled floors. Some of the corpses writhed, not through the power of muscle or still functioning nerve cells but from the thousands of maggots that riddled the bodies.

On closer examination, Plato could see that their faces and any exposed arms were covered in what had once been weeping sores, blisters that had reddened, swollen and then burst, necrosis of the exposed tissue. In other words, the cells had died. A swarm of flies propelled themselves into orbit from the bodies under examination and settled on others further away, continuing their banquet. "Cutaneous radiation syndrome."

"In English, Plato?"

"They've been exposed to an extremely high dose of ionised radiation, Greg. They've had severe damage done to their cells and DNA, and were more than likely suffering from gastrointestinal effects, hence the blood-splattered vomit plastered everywhere. I reckon they were caught out in the open, were exposed to extremely high doses of radiation, and have effectively made their way down here to die."

"They didn't die well then."

"Nope. There would be no one to treat the burns. And as for the radiation, the only way these people could have survived was with blood transfusions and antibiotics and probably even bone marrow transfusions."

"That wasn't going to happen."

Plato swept half a dozen cockroaches aside with his boot. A rat that had been gnawing on the hand of a young girl scarpered. "No. My concern is around typhus and cholera. The sanitary conditions down here, along with the bloody flies, rats, and cockroaches, don't bode well."

"This is a biological minefield," exclaimed Greg. "God knows what's floating around."

Glen's helmet torch beam moved up and down, indicating he was nodding his agreement. "Let's take the next flight up for a quick look-see. Then I suggest we get the hell out of here."

Without further discussion, Glen moved off down the corridor that was lined with more temporary homes and corpses, some with their clothing singed and faces and arms badly burnt. He reached a second set of escalators, but went no further. The pieces of rubble dashed around the bottom of the steps, larger chunks wedged between the handrails further up, and the mass of smashed reinforced concrete blocking the exit above answered their silent questions as to the reasons why the survivors had not exited the hellhole they'd found themselves in. Blackened walls were indicative of a firestorm having probed the upper levels of the station. As the nuclear strikes slammed into the City of London, catching its inhabitants completely by surprise, many, against the advice of the government, had chosen to run to safety in the depths of the London Underground tube stations. It may have been acceptable to have used the Underground network as a bomb shelter in World War Two, but the tunnel entrances were completely inadequate to survive the multi-megaton bombs that struck the city. The majority of the tunnels may have survived the holocaust, but the entrances to these places were now buried under tens of thousands of tons of masonry, rubble and other wreckage. The population were subsequently prevented from getting in, and, unfortunately, those already in situ had been unable to get out.

"I've seen enough. Let's go," ordered Glen.

"Those capable would have tried to find other exits, so it is possible that all the upper levels of London stations are blocked."

"Hopefully, we'll have a different way out, or in, should I say..." Glen didn't clarify his statement any further but headed back to the previous escalator, descending back down the stationary metal steps and returning to the platforms below. The three men clattered down the steps, not rushing, but maintaining a pace that was possible with the minimal light at their disposal. The hum of flies faded the further away the soldiers got. At the bottom, weaving through the various corridors, they followed the signs showing the various routes to the different tube lines, north or southbound, and stations. Glen knew exactly where he was headed and guided his men to the westbound platform on the Northern Line, choosing a spot at the far end just before the tunnel that would take them further west, then north under the River Thames, and to the Embankment, the next tube station, and then on to their final destination, Charing Cross or, as some knew it, Trafalgar Square.

"Right, lads, I suggest we pitch down here for the night. We've no idea what's up ahead. Could be worse than what we've seen up there. So, some hot food, a few hours' kip, then in the early hours, we'll head west, then north."

"I'll get some water on for a brew first," Greg informed them.

"I'll sort out the food." Plato started to shrug his kit off, placing his weapon close by. "Something hot will go down well in this depressing place."

"Taste your cooking already."

"A dash of Worcester sauce to kill the taste, boss?" laughed Plato.

"No Peri-Peri sauce?"

"Greg's got that. We need the stronger stuff to disguise the taste of his culinary skills, or lack of them."

"Wanker."

"We'll still take it in turns to stag on. No idea who we could meet up with in this hellhole," instructed Glen.

"I'll take the first one," volunteered Plato.

"Can I borrow your iPod?" asked Greg.

"Why? You suddenly into opera?"
"Might help send me to sleep."
"Just get that tea made."

Glen shone his torch towards the tunnel mouth. Two large floodgates blocked the beam. One of the giant steel gates was secured across half of the tunnel entrance, but the second one only half closed, allowing passage for the men to continue their journey later, after something to eat and a few hours' sleep. Spinning his torch around and concentrating the beam, he was able to see that both of the steel gates had been closed across the tunnel entrance at the other end. He wondered if the local authorities had started to close them off in a vain attempt at restricting access a matter of hours before the strikes occurred.

Rolly woke up from a thirty-minute snooze and pushed the sleeping bag down over his boots. Standing up, stepping out of it and throwing it over the back of the chair, shivered and pulled the zip of his jacket up to his chin, checked his weapon and pushed aside the hessian blind. Taking a couple of steps forward, he stopped and listened. Checking his watch, 18.40, he wondered where his three comrades were at that moment in time, how far had they got down the tunnels, and what they might have come across. He moved further towards the entrance. The pile of rectangular blocks, once the entrance to the church, were now piled up in a disarranged structure, partially covering the entrance to the cavern he and the vehicle were using as a hide. His boots crunched on a layer of snow as he moved to the furthest limit of the chamber, a steady tumble of snowflakes blocking his view beyond more than fifty metres. Moving further out, his boots sank into a layer that was close to half a metre high, the sides of the collapsed church supporting drifts of up to two metres either side, all adding to the camouflage of his position.

Rolly lifted his head, twisting his neck left and right slowly, trying to pick up any sounds that might be carried on the wind, warning him of any potential danger. He started when he saw a dark shape suddenly appear about thirty metres away, something low, an animal perhaps. Getting closer, a mongrel appeared, its ribs clearly visible through its fleshless skin. It sniffed the air, and watched Rolly warily for a few moments before moving closer. The dog now within ten metres. Rolly stooped down slowly, picking up a small chunk of brick. He stood up again, pulled his right arm back and, once the dog was within five metres, threw it with all the force he could muster. The object collided with the dog's hindquarters, causing it to jump and yelp. Rolly bent down to acquire more ammunition but, by the time he stood up again, the animal was nowhere to be seen. He waited ten minutes to ensure the dog didn't immediately reappear before returning to the warmer confines of the cavern to continue his vigil and wait patiently for his friends to return.

CHAPTER 9

PARALYSIS | GROUND-ZERO +31 DAYS
THE FARMERS, EXMOOR

Thunk...thunk... Andrew swung the axe with ease, *thunk...thunk*, the blade biting deep into the trunk of the tall, thin, straight pine. He stopped, setting the axe head on the ground, resting his hands on the handle of the shaft. He admired his work, hearing the occasional creak of the tree, the V-shaped notch eating into the integrity of its trunk, the weight of the branches above bearing down on the weakened spot. A few more swings should do it, he thought. He watched Patrick, his thirteen-year-old son, as the boy scampered around the forest, picking up small broken branches and twigs that could be used for kindle back at the farm. They would need to be dried out, the ground damp from the thin layer of melting snow. Andrew remembered what Tom had said the previous night, years of experience in second-guessing the weather in order to plan the cultivation and husbandry of his farm: cooler temperatures were on their way, but before that, snow. With the temperature dropping lower each day, he was sure it wouldn't be long before the snow stuck. Then there would be a steady build-up of white drifts covering the forest floor.

"Patrick. Patrick!"

"What, Dad?"

"Keep to the other side of the tree. It will topple soon."

"OK, Dad. Can I watch?"

"Yes, but keep well back. Who knows where it'll end up?"

Andrew hefted the long-handled axe in his hands and moved to the other side of the tree, opposite the V-indentation, ready to attack it from the other side, weaken it completely until it gave up the fight to stay vertical. *Thunk...thunk...thunk.* He stopped in mid-swing, a cracking sound suddenly emanating from the damaged area of the trunk. The cracking got louder, and the notch splintered, strips of wood breaking away from the stem of the tree, the tenuous links of the trunk snapping, removing its resistance to gravity. *Crack...crack... crack...crack.* There was an eerie screeching sound from just above the bole of the tree as the battle was finally lost, the swaying branches above whipping upwards as the trunk suddenly slewed over, the top of the once proud pine crashing into adjacent trees as the speed of its fall accelerated, stripping branches from itself and others. It struck the ground with a thud, the vibrations felt underfoot, causing Patrick to yelp and jump. Andrew smiled. The trunk, completely severed now, bounced upwards, flicked up by the upper length of the tree as it smashed into the ground, before crashing back down, resting a few feet this side of the pale yellow, splintered tree stump.

"Hey, Dad, that was spectacular!"

Andrew smiled. Patrick was happy. In fact, both children, Patrick and Tom's seven-year-old daughter Mary, were happy, a sense of freedom and the feeling of being cloaked in a security blanket, their experience at the farm slowly being banished to the back of their minds. Andrew knew that it was an illusion. They were far from safe. He looked up at the thickening flurry of snow. A different blanket will cover us if we don't get to work soon, he thought with a smile.

"Time for work, son. You cut the small branches at the top, and I'll start sawing through the trunk."

Patrick ran to the far end of the ten-metre tree. "Here?"

Andrew made his way along the trunk, stepping over the larger branches that jutted out. "That's it. Just saw them off. Leave the small ones where they drop, but when you get to the bigger branches, drag them to our collection point. OK?"

"Sure, Dad." Patrick attacked the first small branch with gusto. Andrew smiled again, knowing it would be short-lived. He now needed to get on with the task at hand, sawing the tree into two-metre lengths that could be loaded on the Land Rover and driven back to the farm. Fuel was critical to their survival, and the two families needed as much wood as possible before the winter set in with what Tom had said would be with a vengeance.

Tom cursed as he dropped the spanner, his hands numb with cold. Even under cover of the barn, the temperature inside was no more than ten degrees, and outside it was nearer zero. He wasn't sure what use could be made of the tractor in respect to farming until after winter, but at least if they could get it going it would power the sawmill, making it easier to cut up the wood that Andrew was harvesting from the forest. He reckoned there was about three weeks' worth of fuel at the farm, but they would need significantly more if they were to survive the full term of a bitter winter. He picked up the box spanner and again tackled the spark plugs. The shiny, green, almost new John Deere tractor, parked alongside the one he was working on, was next to useless. Something had been fried as a consequence of the Electromagenetic Pulse, EMP, from the nuclear explosions, and he couldn't coax any life from it at all. But the older, and smaller, Massey Ferguson had turned over a couple of times, and Tom was confident that, if he persisted, he could bring it back to life.

Maddie, a bandanna tied around her head, keeping her hair under control, stirred the stew, which was made from tins of braised beef, cubes of potato and carrots, and a sprinkling of salt. They still had half a dozen tins of braised beef in gravy, but that was the last of the vegetables. The potatoes and carrots had been found in the farmhouse pantry, but by the time the rotting parts had been sliced off, there wasn't much left. Just enough to add some additional bulk to their lunch. It had been agreed that the hot meal would be in the middle of the day. With Tom and Andrew working out in the cold, they felt that having a main meal halfway through the working day would help to keep some semblance of warmth in their chilled bodies and provide them with much needed energy.

"Ten minutes and this will be more than ready. The two men should be in soon."

"Never mind…those two, I'm hungry…myself," responded Lucy, kneading a large piece of bread dough. "The smell of baking is driving me insane." There were already two cloth-covered bowls of dough on the large kitchen table, an opportunity for them to rise before being placed in one of the Aga ovens. A loaf was nearly ready as it baked in one of the ovens. It would be a welcome addition to the stew that was also nearly done. They had enough flour to bake bread for a month, but beyond that, unless they came across some additional supplies, bread would be off the menu. Lucy rubbed her hands together, removing as much of the flour as possible before adjusting the elastic band that held her hair in a ponytail, keeping it out of her face.

The two women were like chalk and cheese. Maddie had shortish brown hair whereas Lucy's was shoulder-length and blonde. Lucy was five six and slim. However, her friend was five three and, although not fat, quite plump, giving her a round, soft face with a button-like nose as opposed to Lucy's sharper features.

"Time to get my masterpiece out," said Lucy, rubbing the excess flour of her hands.

"Can I have some?" piped up Mary, who had been concentrating on drawing a picture.

"Only if you help Aunty Maddie and Mummy with the washing up afterwards."

"Oh—"

"You can't have it both ways, darling."

"Patrick is out in the cold helping his daddy," Maddie rebuked, but mildly.

There was so much work to be done, the children would have to contribute much more than they had previously been used to. The new world was not one for games and playtime.

"I don't want to go out in the cold."

"Stay in and help us then, eh?"

"OK then, Mummy."

Just as Lucy took the now baked bread from the oven, turning it out onto a tray, the outer door of the utility room opened and a sudden cold draught could be felt in the kitchen.

"I hope they shut that door quickly," Maddie appealed.

The draught ceased, and the inner door banged open as Andrew, Tom and Patrick, devoid of their thick layers of outer clothing, but still a light dusting of snow on the two men's faces and beards, entered the kitchen.

"It's so warm in here," said Andrew, excitedly rubbing his hands together at the thought of food. He pulled a wooden kitchen chair out and plonked himself down opposite Lucy.

"The Aga helps."

"And the smell of your baking, Lucy."

"We only have enough coal for a couple of months," she reminded Andrew.

Lucy moved the now three bowls of bread dough and cleared the table where she had floured it in order to knead the dough. Tom joined them, sitting next to Andrew, while Patrick went over to Mary, cadging a sheet of paper and some crayons to join her in creating a work of art.

Tom sniffed, wrinkling his nose. "I don't know what smells better, the stew or the bread."

"The stew has been created by the chef," called Maddie.

"But the cook bakes the best bread," countered Lucy with a laugh.

"Let's call it a draw," suggested Tom.

"I'm with you on that," agreed Andrew. "So it's a draw then."

With the four adults mucking in, the rest of the table was quickly cleared, then laid with cutlery and plates, and Maddie served everyone a portion of stew while Lucy sliced into the still warm loaf of bread.

The two families were soon babbling away as if they had lived in the farm all of their lives and the situation was a natural as it could ever be.

"This is good, Mum," Patrick praised Maddie.

"Glad you're enjoying it, son, but please stop slurping," Andrew rebuked him.

"Sorry, Dad."

Andrew reached over and ruffled his son's unruly hair. "You need a haircut. We have scissors?"

"We do," responded Lucy, "but it's not just Patrick. You two men look like something from Robinson Crusoe."

"With those beards, they look like more the wild men of Borneo," joined in Maddie.

Chewing on a piece of steak, before biting a chunk out of the thick slice of bread held in his other hand, Tom replied, "God...this is good. Well done...girls. Shaving's out. We've no blades left, and God knows when we'll see the like again."

"Yes, but beards can still be trimmed," chastised Lucy.

"Yeah, yeah."

"Plans for this afternoon?" asked Maddie.

"I'll continue with the wood. We need as much as possible. Looking pretty grim out there."

"And I'll get that bloody tractor going if it kills me," groaned Tom.

"Daddy swore, Mummy," Mary shrilled.

"I know he did. He's a bad man."

"Sorry."

"Think you'll do it?" asked Andrew.

"I reckon. The carburettor's had a good cleaning, and once the plugs have dried out, it should start."

"The other one?"

"Like all the modern vehicles, it seems to have been well and truly fried."

"Having the sawmill going will be a boon. We can cut all the logs we need to see us through the winter."

"We still need to get more food," Lucy reminded them. "We can scrape by for a couple of months, but after that..."

"Andy and I have discussed it. Once we can get enough fuel for the log burners, we intend setting traps in the forests."

"Rabbits, Dad?"

"Yes, Patrick."

"We can't eat rabbits!"

"I meant hares, Mary."

"What's a hare?"

"Just a wild animal."

"Will I like it?"

"Tastes just like chicken."

"I like chicken nuggets."

"Good. So, we'll set some traps," Tom continued. "Then we'll scout the wider area. Maybe go as far as Minehead."

"Should you be going into the towns? Remember what happened last time."

"We'll be fine, Luce. Andrew and I will be careful. We'll be armed and we'll be extra cautious." Tom slid his plate, wiped clean with his last slice of bread, away from him. "That was great. Just what the doctor ordered."

"Yes, thanks, girls," added Andrew, who pushed back his chair and stood up. "Me and Patrick have work to do. Ready, son?"

"Another five, Dad?"

"Just five. Then I want to see you outside."

"Do you have a load to lug to the farm yet?" asked Tom.

"Not yet. Give us a couple of hours."

The two men kissed their respective wives, donned their thick winter clothing, and left the farm to continue the tasks they had allotted themselves. Maddie and Lucy would clear up. Then Lucy would bake the remaining loaves whilst Mary took charge of the washing up.

CHAPTER 10

PARALYSIS | GROUND-ZERO +31 DAYS
RGC, CHILMARK

The small gathering finished topping their cups up from the urn of tea prepared by Alison earlier. The meeting was being held in the canteen rather than the control centre, which was situated deep below in the bunker where operations had been previously been conducted by the region's principal officer, Douglas Elliot. The government-appointed leader, Elliot, had been found dead after the security of the bunker had been reinstated by Alan and a few of his soldiers, ably assisted by a special forces team that had arrived in the nick of time. While Alan's armed force, assigned to the Regional Government Centre prior to the nuclear strikes as part of the UK's tattered civil defence strategy, had been defending one of the supply warehouses from a large band of intruders, a minority group from the centre's own survivors, had instigated an uprising. Wanting the benefits the regional organisation could provide, like food, medical care and protection, but not prepared to contribute by providing the labour necessary for the community to survive, the mob had ransacked the food supplies held at the feeding station and the bunker complex, killing many that got in their way.

Alan preferred to hold the meeting in the softer surroundings of the canteen, rather than in the room that would be associated with the deceased principal officer. Murdered is a more appropriate term, thought Alan. Douglas Elliot had been murdered, along with Rupert Lowe, the chief scientist, Mathew Craig, the finance officer, Edward Cox, assistant to Elliot, and many others, including the senior police officer, Superintendent Collins, and the senior military officer, Colonel Bannister.

After the bunker had been reoccupied and secured, the majority of Alan's small army had completed a search for any remaining intruders that had attacked the warehouse, checking whether a threat still existed. Once the dead bodies had been collected and despite an intensive search of the immediate area surrounding the warehouse, there had been no sign of Russell, the leader of the group that had led the attack on Alan and his men. The man had chosen to run with what was left of his clan rather than hang around and suffer the consequences of his actions. The final total had been seventeen intruders killed, with seven wounded, now in hospital being cared for with whatever meagre resources the medical staff had at their disposal. What would be done with those men had yet to be decided, but it was not on Alan's list of priorities for the present. As for the occupants of the region's camp, apart from the occasional passing patrol keeping an eye on them, they had been left to their own devices. Alan neither had the time nor the resources to complete an investigation into the circumstances of the uprising or the murder of the government officials, that he was sure would come to nothing. But he would never allow security to lapse again.

"Right, gentlemen, let's make a start."

All eyes focused on Alan. There were eight people present. Dylan Wright, head of the Department of Employment, one of the half-moon lenses of his glasses cracked as a consequence of a tussle with one of the ransackers when the bunker was overrun. He was one of the lucky ones to be alive. Kate Worth, head of the Ministry of Agriculture, Fisheries and Food (MAFF), along with Cliff, the food officer, had also survived. Joe Curtis from transport had been called into the meeting as well. Although the titles were now obsolete, the civilians clung to them. Perhaps it gave them a link back to when the world was sane, or relatively so. From the uniformed side, Alan had brought in his CSM, Scott Saunders, Sergeant Ashton, now head of the civilian police force, and Eddie, the ex-REME soldier who had been responsible for saving the lives of Alison and two of her assistants when the bunker was assaulted. Once the message had got out that the bunker was now secure, a number of previous occupants had drifted back, but many of them had been found dead, or were still missing. Those occupants responsible for energy, social security, British Telecom, Department of Trade and Industry, again old titles, and other departments had been excluded, Alan wanting to focus on what he deemed to be the immediate priorities.

"Thank you for joining me." Alan scratched his dark, four-day growth of beard, making a mental note to shave as soon as possible before the itching drove him mad. "I feel it is important that we initiate some of the plans I have in mind as soon as possible." He pulled a sheet of paper from his combat jacket pocket. "Three things I want to initiate immediately—"

"Shouldn't we be confirming who is in charge?" Dylan interrupted, not making eye contact, focusing on cleaning the uncracked lens of his half-moon spectacles. "With both Mr Elliot and his number two dead, we should agree who the civilian member of the government department is the most senior and therefore next in line to become the principal officer."

"I understand the point you're making, Dylan, but the first priority is to get the region back in control. We can worry about structure at a later date."

This time Dylan looked Alan in the eye. "You mean, we accept military control of a civilian organisation until the military deem it appropriate to hand back that control?"

"Dylan, I have no intention of getting into that debate at the present time. There are far more pressing issues that need to be dealt with. Who is in charge is not at the top of that list."

"But—"

Kate Worth interrupted Dylan before he could continue. "Why don't we listen to what the major has to say before we jump to any conclusions, yes? Unless, of course, he's proposing to throw us all in jail." She looked at Alan, her head tilted sideways, her grey hair, normally clean and well-presented, lying lank over one side of her face. She looked ten years older than her fifty-two years.

"Thank you, Kate. No jail cells are planned." Alan smiled.

Heads were nodding, and Dylan remained silent.

Hearing no further interruptions, Alan continued. He lifted himself up so he was sitting on the restaurant counter, his booted feet dangling. The group he was talking to had pulled chairs and tables around him in a semi-circle. "There are three priorities as I see it. First, we get the feeding station up and running as soon as possible—"

"You can't be serious!" Dylan spread his arms out in front of him, his frustration obvious. "We have to hunt the killers down. Find those that broke into the bunker and murdered the head of our government and bring them to justice." He looked at the others in the room for support but, seeing none, looked back at Alan.

"There were hundreds involved in the ransacking of the bunker and the food stores at the feeding centre, and to—"

"There had to be ringleaders, surely?"

This time Sergeant Major Saunders butted in. "If you allowed the major to finish, we might actually get to hear what he's proposing."

Alan held his hand up. "We don't know who the ringleaders or killers are, and neither do we have the resources to find out. In fact, I doubt we'll ever know the truth about what happened."

"We let them get away scot-free?"

"Dylan, if you don't allow me to finish what I want to say to the group, I will have to ask you to leave."

At this, even Kate and Cliff raised their eyebrows.

"But—"

"Please, Dylan," Alan pleaded.

Dylan lowered his head, wanting to continue to fight his corner but equally not wanting to be evicted from the room and miss out on what was being planned, so he capitulated with a nod of his head.

Alan attempted again to brief the gathering in the canteen. "The quicker we can get the feeding station up and running, the earlier we can regroup the labour force, and then the sooner we can get back to some sense of normality. It's unfortunate what has happened, and had it not been for the outside interference, the Intruders, it's likely that all would be well now. That's not to say there wasn't some dissent, that is understandable, but we were making progress."

He looked around the room, noting the nodding heads – all except for Dylan.

"Cliff, how quickly can we get the feeding station up and running?"

"Er, I'm not sure. Maybe twenty-four hours?"

"What do you need?"

"Well, some food for a start. Fuel for the ovens, labour to carry out the preparation and cooking..."

"With as few people as possible, could you provide hot soup for an evening meal?"

"Tonight?"

"Tonight."

"I suppose."

"And some bread?"

"That's pushing, but I'll try."

"Sarn't Major, how quickly could we get the necessary supplies from the warehouse?"

"Four hours tops, sir."

"What about security?" added Cliff, nervous at the thought of being back out amongst the bulk of the community, some of them who may well have been party to the killing of his boss.

"Sergeant Ashton?" asked Alan.

The sergeant, wearing a dirty yellow fluorescent police jacket, three makeshift chevrons in black tape applied to his right and left sleeve, his badge of authority, puffed out his chest. In his late forties, he wasn't a big man, but exuded confidence, and Alan had seen him on duty many times in the past and was impressed by the way he handled the police constables and the public they watched over. Ashton stroked his grey moustache with a finger and thumb, a serious look on his bulldog-like face. "I have seven police constables, but have kept them within the bunker so far. Happy to go back out, but would appreciate some back-up from you military types."

"That's not a problem," responded Sergeant Major Saunders. "I'll assign two sections, four men in each, to back you up. Any sign of the CPS?"

"Five of the civilian police support have reported in, rather sheepishly, I might add. I plan on using them as well."

"Good," concurred Alan. "Are your police officers armed?"

"Three, including myself." Ashton tapped the canvas pistol holster strapped around his waist.

"Scott, can you see what we've recovered from our attackers?"

"Sure, sir, I'll pick them up when I go across to the warehouse." Scott turned to face Sergeant Ashton. "A couple of pistols and a few shotguns do you?"

"That would be great, sir. Feel safer already." The sergeant smiled.

"Scott, call me Scott," the CSM whispered out of the side of his mouth.

"So, Cliff," Alan continued the briefing, "you will have food and security. Dylan, can you drum up a small labour force to get some fuel and help prepare the meal?"

"They're not going to want to—"

"Just ask for volunteers," snapped Alan, losing his patience. "I guarantee you'll have some come forward, to find out what's going on if for no other reason."

"I'll help," volunteered Kate.

"Thank you, Kate. I'm sure Dylan would welcome that. You also need to start planning a workforce to get back to clearing some of the houses and farms in the area. The snow will put a stop to any farming plans for the moment, but we need to get people into some form of housing before the cold weather bites any deeper."

CHAPTER 11

PARALYSIS | GROUND-ZERO +31 DAYS
MOTORWAY TRIBE, NORTH-WEST OF CHELTENHAM

They had started off well, sneaking out at one in the morning, hoping that the other groups inhabiting the motorway, north and south of their location, would be asleep, or at least less alert and wanting to stay wrapped up in their protective clothing, preferring to stay warm than to expose themselves to the bitter cold. Gavin led the way, a reflective vest wrapped around his rucksack, increasing his visibility slightly so the next one in the column could follow in his footsteps. Judy had chosen Gavin, who considered himself to be her number two although nothing had officially been announced, to lead because of his particular skills. An experienced trekker, he could map read, which she couldn't, unless on the open road, and demonstrated a good grasp of the land they would have to negotiate. That was key to their success. The group had to avoid the towns and cities, and even villages could be a threat. She would heed the warnings Glen had given her: avoid major roads, keep away from likely target areas because of potential contamination, and, in particular, avoid built-up areas. Not only would many of the buildings be unsafe, but the area could be inhabited by dogs that would now be hungry and possibly wild. But, even more dangerous than that, they could be inhabited by people: people who would also be starving and would stop at nothing to feed their bellies and those of their families. That's the reason she had chosen to take her group south, heading for the Regional Government Centre that had been marked on her map by Glen. At least there, providing it was still in existence and was being run effectively, she could secure protection for the people that were following her and, as a bonus, relieve herself of the responsibility of looking after twenty-odd people. From the original number, one of the group had died later from a gunshot wound as a result of the fracas with the special forces soldiers, three had been killed outright. Two had died from their illnesses, losing the will to live. Three more had been killed as a consequence of defending their territory from the other groups wanting them out, and a few had left, wanting to strike out on their own.

She rearranged the rucksack, weighed down with a sleeping bag, food, water, extra clothes and other items that would be needed on the trip, higher up on her shoulders as she watched Gurvinder and Fiona trudge by. They were also laden with supplies, but both managed a smile as they walked past her. When scavenging amongst the wrecked and abandoned cars along the 1,000 car-plus stretch of the motorway, the focus had very much been on finding provisions of food and water. But, over the last couple of days, they had revisited those very same vehicles looking for tents, additional sleeping bags, waterproof clothing, boots, rucksacks to carry loads in, and just about anything that would aid their survival on the long march that lay ahead of them.

Judy started to walk back down the line, passing Andrea with her daughters, Jade, nine, and Stephanie, eleven, barely visible wrapped in bubble jackets designed for a six-foot man. She turned and started to walk alongside them, keeping pace with the mother and her girls. "You all OK?"

"We're doing well, aren't we, Jade?" Andrea responded.

"It'll be easy-going for a while, but a bit harder when we go off-road."

"We'll be fine, Judy, don't you worry about us."

Judy turned back again, wanting to see those at the rear of the column. After clambering down the bank of the M5 motorway, about 100 metres north of the A4019, she had led her group south along the edge of the M5 until they came across the A road that would take them east. Passing more walkers, she gave them encouragement, finally reaching the last in the line, Zack, following up at the rear.

"Not lost anybody yet, Zack?"

"I should hope not. We'll be in a right mess if people start dropping out so soon."

Their boots crunched on the snow as they walked along the edge of the tarmac road, the two-centimetres of snow not a problem. There was a steady snowfall, and some of the drifts alongside the road were close to a metre in height, but at the moment weren't impeding their journey. There was a light wind, and Judy prayed that it remained light, making their journey a little easier. A metre in front, she could see Mathew's rolling gait as he plodded along ahead of them. Looking past him, she could see the line snaking away from her until they disappeared into the darkness ahead.

"We need to push hard while people are fresh," advised Zack.

"I agree," Judy replied. "Not only while they're fresh, but to get as much distance as possible between us and the motorway."

"You think they'll notice us gone immediately?"

"Not straightaway, but within a few hours of daylight the lack of movement around our camp will be noticed, I'm sure."

Zack laughed quietly, clouds of frozen breath fogging the air in front of him. "If both groups move into our camp at about the same time, that'll create a big enough distraction to keep them both occupied and off our backs."

"True, but they'll know that we've left. I'm sure they'll give some thought to the fact that it's likely we'll be carrying food. With us out in the open, they may well choose to send someone after us."

"If anyone does, it'll be the Londoners."

"That's why you're at the back, Zack, and have that army weapon."

He tapped the assault rifle, slung over his shoulder, next to his rucksack. "I can point it in the right direction and shoot, but that's about all."

"We have over 100 rounds of ammunition, so let fly with a few and hope for a hit." Judy smiled beneath her scarf.

The line ahead had bunched up, Judy assumed at the point where they would be leaving the road. To continue on their present course, the group would come up against Uckington and then, if they passed through there, they would soon be on the outskirts of Cheltenham.

Zack and Judy approached Marc, who was one of the group assigned the task of directing others whenever they came across a change in direction.

"You go ahead again, Marc."

"Sure, Judy. Going well, isn't it?"

"So far, Marc."

They had turned onto a very narrow lane, one that would take them north towards Elmstone Hardwicke, and Judy picked up the pace to pass the group and get back to her assigned position in the line, which was near the front. She was buoyant, even excited. That was the same for many of the group, keen to get away from the putrid smell of their camp, the incessant firefights with other groups, and the constant fear of being overrun and any subsequent consequences. Death could be one of them, but many preferred death to starvation or something much worse.

The group snaked across to the right-hand side of the lane, the snowdrift on the left was over a metre high in places. Although many wanted to stop, Judy had cajoled, encouraged and even bullied them to keep going and was pleased with the progress made. She estimated that they had walked some six or seven kilometres, achieving that in just over two and a half hours. Now they were all stopped, either side of the lane, tucked into a stretch of hedgerow that was not banked with snow. Although initially kept warm by the efforts of walking from their old camp, that warmth would soon go as their bodies cooled. Judy thought that wasn't a bad thing, knowing that most would want to get up and move, to generate some heat and drive out the bitter cold that would soon creep bone-deep. Ollie and Daniel, wounded when the soldiers had arrived at their camp, were coping well, although this was only the first night. The group had stopped just south of a quarry and would have to turn east, skirting the southern boundary of the opencast pit to the north. Judy chatted with as many as she could, optimistic that they would complete this trek in one piece and find safety.

She joined Gavin and they studied the map under torchlight.

"I want to try and reach Hyde Lane, here," Gavin proposed.

"Why there?"

"Looking at the map, it suggests there are some buildings around there. We can hold up for a few hours, give people a chance to get a bite to eat and some rest."

"How far?"

"I'd say about three to four kilometres."

"Some won't be capable of doing that in one go."

"I know, but we can have a fast group and a slow group. The first group that arrives can get everything set up and ready."

"That sounds like a good idea, Gavin. We leave that stopover at about twelve, do half a day, stay somewhere overnight, then full days from then on."

"Shall we get them moving?"

"Yes, I'll take the slow group," volunteered Judy.

"Is that for your benefit?"

"Cheek!"

Although there were plenty of groans, eventually, tirelessly chivvied along by Judy, the column reformed, turned east and followed a path that tracked the outer edge of the quarry. Gavin pushed on at a relatively fast pace, taking the stronger ones with him, while the slower section formed their own cluster. Zack still remained at the rear, covering their backs, ready to protect the party with the assault rifle slung on his shoulder.

Margaret, one of the older members of the group was struggling, seeming to stoop under the weight of her load, and Judy went to provide what assistance she could.

"Here, Margaret, let me take your rucksack."

"You have your own, Judy. You can't carry mine as well."

"Mine's quite light. Let me carry yours for a short distance. Give you a bit of a break."

Margaret, sixty-seven next year, loosened the straps, and Judy eased it off her shoulders, slinging it onto her own. Margaret immediately wriggled her shoulders, seeming to stand taller, her pace quickening.

"That feel better?"

"Much. My feet are cold though."

"Walking a bit faster will help keep you warm. Anyway, a couple of hours and we'll all be able to rest, get warm around a fire, and have something to eat. How does that sound?"

"Lovely." Margaret sounded chirpier, and stepped out a little faster.

"I need to check on the others, OK?"

"You go on, Judy."

"Zack's behind you, so you won't get left behind."

Judy walked the line, encouraging those she passed, Jacqueline, Natalie and Wesley in particular, reaching Marc at the front of the slow group, a small torch beam lighting the narrow path ahead. Daylight wasn't far off, another hour or so. Judy approached the junction of the track and railway line up ahead. There was no sign of the faster group who had moved ahead at a solid pace as agreed. At the junction, she directed the others to turn right. William, after Marc, was the first past her.

"Nice pace, William. The going will be a bit easier now we're on the lane."

"Thank God, that last stretch was a bit rough."

He continued down the lane that ran alongside the railway line, closely followed by Jacqueline, Natalie, and Wesley, then Margaret, who had caught up. "I can take my pack back now, Judy," she said. "I'll find it easier now there's some solid ground under my feet."

"You sure?"

"Yes, and thank you."

Judy was relieved; two packs were a burden even for her.

Robert, a sprightly sixty-six-year-old was next, closely followed by Andrea and her two girls. Their father, away at the time of the strikes, had been killed whilst trying to rejoin his family. Both girls were pushing a pram each, laden down with supplies, the large wheels barely coping with the snow. But someone else would take a turn later. Daniel, another one of the group injured during the fracas with the soldiers, having been shot in the shoulder, followed. He was holding up well, and twenty-nine-year old Alysha had volunteered to stay with the slower group and provide Daniel with both moral and physical support. Judy suspected there was an ulterior motive for Alysha staying behind; she had noticed the two spending more and more time together back at the old camp.

Fiona, Ellen, Gurvinder, and Steve brought up the rear, with Zack, last, watching their backs. All seemed to be coping, so Judy walked with Steve for a while.

The snow crunched beneath their feet, the ground fairly solid. But they still had to walk with care, and all had been encouraged to pick up any sticks that were about and long enough to act as a walking stick and/or a probe. Judy constantly swung forward the two-metre staff she had found, poking it into the snow ahead, probing for any unseen obstructions beneath the snow, obstacles that could trip them up and cause injury. Not only had the nuclear strikes kicked up huge plumes of dust, millions of tons in fact, along with tons of contaminated debris, but the hurricane-force blast had strewn wreckage across the landscape of the UK. From fragments of destroyed houses, factories, garden sheds, human bodies to wrecked cars, large chunks of masonry, and even skidoos and motorboats. The lane they were now on had once been tree-lined, obscuring the view of the countryside, but now the trees were shredded and, in places, completely flattened, leaving the landscape open to view had it been daylight. Not that there was a lot to see, the curtain of snow restricting visibility.

"Making progress," said Steve.

"Better than I expected."

"I'm worried though, Judy."

"About the journey, the distance?"

"That to a degree, yes. I'm more worried about what's at the end of it. What we will find."

"The soldiers were pretty sure there was a government centre there."

"But had they actually seen it, been there?"

"Well no, but we have to take the chance."

"What are your plans if it doesn't exist, or existed but is now destroyed?"

She sidestepped an object, the handles of a twisted bicycle frame jutting up above the snow. "The truth, Steve? I don't have a plan. If we find nothing there then the group has to debate our next move."

"Would we not have been better staying where we were? We had some reasonable shelter."

"You know the answer to that, Steve. Look at it." She indicated the snow falling and the layer steadily building up on the ground. "We would have had to start looking for fuel to keep warm, exposing us to the other groups who are no doubt doing the same. Running out of food would quickly follow. What then? Attack the other groups?"

"I know, I know, Judy. This just seems a bit desperate."

"We're in desperate times, Steve."

After walking a further two kilometres, they caught up with the rest of the slow group, which had flocked together by a stile that led to another narrow track where William was directing the group.

"Over the stile, then keep going. I'll catch you up. That's it, Robert, you've got the right idea." William helped him over. "Keep your torch low in front of you and those behind can follow, OK?"

Robert acknowledged the instruction and started to walk along the track. Andrea was next with her two children, then Fiona, Ellen, Gurvinder, and Zack followed, Zack having overtaken Alysha and Daniel to help out.

"You carry on, William. I'll take over here," called Zack.

"Great, thanks."

William climbed over the stile and increased his pace to get back to the head of the column with Marc, proud that he had been given this important task. A project manager in his past life, he was glad of the responsibility, the opportunity to get people organised.

"How you doing, Daniel?"

"Just a bit tired, Judy. Is it far?"

"Somewhere along Hyde Lane. Gavin will find us somewhere to stop for a while."

"It would be nice to be warm for a few minutes. This cold is biting into my shoulder."

"The group ahead will be stopping just as soon as they find somewhere suitable."

"We can get a fire going then?"

"Of course, I'm bloody cold as well." She laughed. "You still OK helping, Alysha?"

"You bet. I'll keep him going."

Alysha and Daniel smiled at each other as if their secret was still that – a secret.

Judy watched as the last of them past her. Then she clambered over the stile herself, Steve and Zack not far behind.

A quick stopover and a warm by a fire, as promised, amongst some ruins on Hyde Lane, then at twelve they pushed on again for a few more hours. A gap soon formed between the two groups and it was two and a half kilometres before the slow group caught up with the now stationary first group. They had crept past some derelict buildings, the glow of a fire indicated that someone was using it for shelter. They got by unseen, Cameron, from the lead group, having waited behind to warn them and guide them past. They crossed the Evesham road, making their way along Southam Lane, the remnants of the Cheltenham Racecourse to their south.

Eventually, on the extreme outskirts of Southam itself, Gavin had discovered a large enough ruin where they could hole up for the night. Although windowless and roofless, the second storey having collapsed inwards, there were enough walls and a section of the ceiling still standing in one of the large downstairs rooms to provide all-round security and some protection from the wind and snow. Gavin and his faster group had already got a roaring fire going. Despite its brightness, potentially giving away their presence to others, it was necessary. Both groups had three things in common: all were tired, all were hungry, and, to a man and a woman, they were bitterly cold. The minute they had stopped walking, many started to shiver, some uncontrollably. Their outer clothing was damp from the persistent snow and, with very little inner warmth to combat the extreme cold, some of the older and more infirm members of the group started to go downhill rapidly. The two senior members of the party, Robert, quickly followed by Margaret, both bowed to the bitter cold, their thin frames unable to generate enough heat to contest the biting cold. A large saucepan of water had just come to the boil, and ten small packets of hot chocolate, those you normally found in a hotel or B&B, were added to it, and a mug each was quickly thrust in front of Margaret and Robert as Gavin banked up the fire.

Although weary and cold herself, Judy got to work: organising a fire watch, keeping the precious flames burning in order to keep them alive, others to gather fresh fuel, some to get sleep immediately so they would be able to take their turn later in the many tasks that needed to be completed throughout the night. Steve, Gavin, and William, together with Alysha, were a great help in getting to grips with what needed to be done, though Gavin was starting to lose patience with those that were happy to let everyone else do the work. Judy quickly calmed tempers, cajoled the lazier ones in the group to do their bit, and within forty minutes a sense of calm had descended on the group. After tucking her two girls up in the single sleeping bag, a tight fit but warm, leaving them with a mug of hot chocolate between them, Andrea volunteered to collect more wood for the fire. Margaret and Robert had not been allocated any tasks, Judy sure that if they didn't rest for the night and stay close to the fire, they may well succumb to hypothermia.

Fiona and Gurvinder had the first fire watch, keeping the fire burning for the next hour, to be relieved by Ellen and Zack. Judy checked on the three who, up until they had left the motorway, had been in their medical centre in the coach: Jacqueline, Natalie, and Wesley were all suffering from the after-effects of exposure to radiation. Wesley also had suppurating sores from the third-degree burns he had suffered. Philippa was keeping an eye on them. Daniel was fine. Alysha had made sure he was comfortable before she went to work collecting fuel for the fire. Judy felt sure Alysha was trying to compensate for Daniel's inability to help. Marc and Ollie were already fast asleep, at least until it was their turn to stoke the fire. Gavin and Judy, along with William and Steve, the other unofficial leaders of the group, sat together sharing a couple of mugs of hot chocolate, the effects almost immediate, the fire warming them from the outside, the hot drink from within. It wasn't long before steam was coming off their boots as the heat of the flames started to dry them and their clothing out.

Gavin drew a cross on the map spread out across his lap. "We've managed about nine kilometres so far."

"Not bad," added Judy.

"Still a way to go, though."

"The two separate groups seemed to work." Steve complimented Gavin on his earlier suggestion.

"We've a long haul ahead of us, Steve. I'm sure the slower group is going to experience difficulties the further we get."

"I agree with Gavin," supported William. "It's going to get worse, not better."

"I suppose we're all at our freshest," reminded Judy. "Even if the fittest, like ourselves, are coping well now, I'm pretty sure the journey is going to tax us all as the days go on. So, I say we keep the pace steady and see how each day plays out."

"It's a worry, Judy," cautioned Gavin, whispering. "Yes we are pretty fit compared to the others, and there's at least another five or six in the group that we can depend on, but we're not exactly overfed and on top form ourselves. Should we have to start carrying people, or their baggage for that matter, then we could go downhill rapidly."

"A toughie like you go down?" laughed Judy. "We would be in trouble." She became serious and leant into the group to ensure that only they heard what she was about to say. "We have no idea what's going on out there, but there's a good chance that the human race has been decimated. We will need each other, all of us."

"Don't be daft," chided Steve. "We know there are people about. We've been fighting them for the last few weeks."

"I know, Steve," she hissed more forcefully, "but look at them, look at us. We're fighting over a few scrapped cars, and we've been scavenging for food from car boots. We've lost a number of our group through sickness and injuries already, and, yes, we'll probably lose more. So, we need to keep those that are left alive, for as long as possible at least. We'll need them. If we keep shrinking as a group then we'll be prey to every despot and vigilante group out there." She paused before repeating, "Like it or not, we need each other."

There was silence for a few moments; then the nods slowly came. Gavin's was last, but it was there. "Do you have a rota, Gavin?"

"Yes, I have you down for second watch, then William, then Steve. I'll take the first."

"I'll check everyone, then get my head down if you don't mind."

They said their goodnights and she left the crackling of the fire, the wood smoke drifting across the sleeping forms and mixing with the steady snowfall. Most people had a waterproof layer covering their bodies, keeping them dry, ones without staying as close to the fire as possible, using its heat to keep them dry, even at the risk of getting showered by sparks or having their clothing singed.

Judy came across Andrea and Alysha, laden down with wood,

who had entered through the gaping hole at the back of what was once the rear door of the large country house.

"We've got loads." Alysha exuded pleasure at being able to contribute. "Some will have to be broken up or cut, but it'll keep us warm."

"You're doing a grand job, girls. Your two OK, Andrea?"

"I tucked them up well. They'll be fine, Judy. They were asleep before I left them."

"Well, I'm going to get my head down. Goodnight."

They both said goodnight and thanked her for everything she was doing for them. Then Judy found a spot, reserved for her amongst the bodies that encircled the fire, laid a plastic sheet on the snow-covered ground, and pulled her sleeping bag from her pack. Slipped off her boots and waterproof jacket, placing them under her pack to keep dry, and shuffled into the down sleeping bag, pulling a ground-sheet on top to keep everything dry. Using her rucksack as a pillow, she was asleep in seconds, to the crackle of flames as someone threw more wood on the fire.

William leant in towards the other two men who had remained behind when Judy had left. "We do have too many invalids in the group."

"It worries me too," agreed Steve. "They could bring us down, and no one will survive."

Gavin scratched his beard and looked at the two men who also had two or three weeks' growth. They had found fresh razor blades, and there were bars of soap available. It was just too much effort to scrape away the bristles in cold water, the same water used day after day, drinking water in short supply. The beards also provided insulation, keeping their faces partially protected from the bitter cold. We must all stink to high heaven, he thought. Body washes had been the norm in the early days, but even that had increasingly become a luxury.

"Judy's our leader."

"Hey, I'm not saying we oust her. We've survived this far because of her," reacted Steve. "I just think she can be a bit soft at times. If there's too many sick or lame in the group, we can't bloody well carry them all."

"Keep your voice down," hissed William.

"I don't disagree with you both, so let's just keep an eye on things and see how it goes. For now, you'd best get some sleep. Judy will be waking you up in a few hours to keep watch." They said their goodnights, William and Steve finding their own spots in the circle, while Gavin placed another piece of wood on the fire that had been dropped alongside it earlier by Alysha. She's hard-working, and nice, he thought as he stared into the flickering flames, mesmerised by them, wondering what would become of them, all of them.

CHAPTER 12

PARALYSIS | GROUND-ZERO +31 DAYS
THE CONVICTS, CROYDON

Milo led the way. His legs looked spindly compared to the rest of his body, the thick layer of upper clothing, topped with a thin blanket wrapped around his back and shoulders, then finally a waterproof jacket, bulking him out. Keelan looked even more of a giant than he usually did, his large frame covered by three T-shirts, a bright blue jumper and a black fleece. This was topped by a bright blue bubble jacket, torn down the left arm but still serviceable. Apart from the colour, he would have fitted in well with the well-known tyre advert. A bobble hat, scarf and black ski mittens topped the outfit off. Salt, not as large as Keelan, still a big man but taller and slimmer, was also dressed warmly. A black waterproof jacket covered his layer of clothes, with at least two T-shirts, a sweatshirt, along with a couple of scarves wrapped around his chest and waist, another around his neck, and a pair of large brown leather gloves over the top of a thinner pair ensured warm hands. The three men also wore hiking trousers and thermals beneath. Their rucksacks held a pair of dark blue waterproof over trousers, along with more clothing, a blanket and some personal items. But there was no food.

Milo took them along South End, passing Heathfield Road on the right. Although Salt knew the location of the small food factory, it was agreed that Milo was the best scout they had, instinctively sniffing out trouble. They had seen a number of stray dogs wandering around but keeping their distance so far. Once past Heathfield, the long line of shops continued. What used to be a florist, hairdresser's, local store, newsagent's and cafés were no more. All had their windows shattered, and most had roofs missing. Snowdrifts had formed along the shopfronts on the left-hand side of the road. In some, with the larger windows, the snow had built up inside, the storm of the previous night forcing the snow crystals through any opening that could be found. Not one of the shop spaces had been left untouched by scavengers, and all three men were starting to panic as their stomachs knotted with hunger.

At the junction of South End and Ledbury Way, Salt indicated to Milo that they should head right, along South End. As they continued to traipse through the snow, the hungrier they became, the icier the biting cold. Their journey eventually brought them to the factory. Milo shivered as he looked up at the red-brick four-storey building, looking very much like an old Victorian mill, although flat-roofed. Just before a path which led down the side of the T-shaped building, there was a café. Just like the factory, it was bereft of windows, and the roof looked like it had been peeled back like a sardine tin. Milo was about to lead them past the end of the café and to go right down the side of the red-bricked building when his ferret-like nose twitched, his hands up in front of his face as he sniffed, his head turning like a radar.

"What is it?" hissed Salt who tapped him on the shoulder. "That's the factory on our left."

Milo inhaled gently through his nose, not wanting the bitter cold to freeze the sensors of his already numb nostrils. "Fire? Cooking, maybe?"

Keelan joined in the huddle. "I can't smell nothing."

"There. Yes, just a hint. You old bugger, Milo," Salt praised him.

Keelan sniffed and sniffed. "Nah, you two are imagining it."

Milo sniffed again. "Roast meat, I'm sure of it."

Keelan's stomach gurgled, literally, and loud enough for the other two to hear. Equally, their bellies cramped at the thought of food.

"Where then?" demanded Keelan, his mouth watering at the thought of it, as he still couldn't smell anything.

Milo pointed at the café. "There."

"You're taking the piss," Keelan berated. "It might have been a café or restaurant once, but not anymore."

Milo edged closer to the shop front, the half-metre layer of snow beneath his feet crunching as it was compressed, but it was less noisy than if he had been walking over the shattered glass on the pavement beneath. The window frames were buckled slightly and the snow had forced its way in to cover the tables and chairs. A small counter or bar at the other end of the room protruded above the snowline.

Milo indicated with his arm that they were to follow him, and he led them past the café, turning right down the pathway with the factory building towering above on the left. Keelan and Salt looked at each other, shrugged their shoulders and followed, the thought of roast beef or something like it playing on their minds. Salt pointed towards the tall building indicating that they should explore that area next, their original objective. Milo held up his hand, and the two men following stopped, moving forward when Milo beckoned them to join him around the back of the café. There was a doorway and a window, both without glass. Those had been destroyed by the hurricane-like shock wave that had peeled back the roof, remnants of it draped over the back of the café. The snow-covered ground was littered with debris, traps ready to twist an ankle or break a leg. Keelan cursed as he caught his trousers on a jagged piece of metal, tearing a piece out of his trouser leg. Milo placed his right forefinger against his balaclava-covered mouth, indicating they needed to be quiet. Keelan nodded, realising that the presence of the plastic sheeting over the window and doorway, probably meant that the building was occupied.

Milo stepped aside as they stood close to the covered doorway, his task over. He would leave the muscle work to his two colleagues. Did he consider them friends? No, it was more of a symbiotic relationship, an interdependency that suited all three for the present. There was no debate. Keelan powered his way through, ripping the plastic from the screws that had been used to tack the edge of the plastic to the door frame. He crashed into what had been a galley kitchen, the modern stainless steel kitchen work surfaces apparatus appearing to be in one piece. A man, who was in the process of manually rotating a spit on which there were what appeared to be two small rabbits sizzling away over a fire that had been lit in one of the stainless steel sinks, turned quickly to face him. At below average height, caught completely by surprise at the intrusion, he was no match for the hammer-like fist that crashed into his face. Pieces of scarf were snagged by the man's teeth as the remnants of two shattered incisors collapsed back into his mouth, agape with shock, his nose also broken. Staggering back, the thirty-seven-year old father, once the manager of a shoe shop, partially blacking out from the brutality of the strike, fell back onto the other occupants in the room. A woman screamed and a shout from a young boy of "Dad, Dad," could be heard beneath the pile of bodies. Salt stormed past Keelan and grabbed the semi-conscious man, hauling him off the two he was sprawled on, dragging the groaning man towards the entrance, consciousness returning, dumping him just inside the doorway. Salt raised a leg before thrusting it down on top of the man's head, a crack as his skull struck the industrial-tiled kitchen floor. The crack changed to a thud as he pounded away with his boot, the skull's frontal bone above the eye socket giving way with a crunch. The woman, suddenly realising what was going on and what was happening to her husband, screamed, a blood-curdling scream that brought goosebumps to Milo's spine as he watched the events unfold. However, he put that aside to scamper to where the food on the spit, now stationary, was catching fire. He continued the rotation of the metal spike that skewered the two carcasses as he looked on.

The woman's screams were brought to an abrupt halt as the back of Keelan's hand smashed into her face, splitting her lip, two of her teeth puncturing the delicate flesh of her upper lip.

Her eleven-year-old son crawled to her side, gripping her abundant clothing and pulling himself in close to her blood-splattered face, tears cascading down his cheeks as he wept on her shoulder.

Keelan and Salt congregated next to Milo, Salt the first one to ask, "What have we got, Milo buddy?"

"Aah, rats, Doug, rats."

"You gotta be kidding," cursed Keelan.

"It's just meat, Stan."

"Meat? Those disgusting things? I'm not an animal, Doug mate."

"It's all we've got."

"Shit."

"Try it." Milo had cut a thin sliver of the cooked meat from one of the rat carcasses, now cooked completely through, chewing on a piece himself. "It tastes pretty good."

Keelan snatched it from Milo's knife, stuffed it in his mouth, and swallowed without more than a couple of chews. Salt took the piece he was offered, chewing it slowly before the hunger took over and he quickly swallowed it, gesticulating for more.

Keelan took another piece, overcoming his disgust as he was also driven by the hunger pangs that cramped his stomach. "Let's see what else they've got." The big man hovered above the woman and child, what little light there was from the fire flickering across their faces. He pulled the boy by his arm, yanking him away from his mother, who, although she tried, was still too stunned to successfully intervene and help her child. The boy was practically thrown down the other end of the room, crashing down next to his father who had about two minutes left to live, his life slipping away, the blood and brain matter oozing from the crack in his skull.

Keelan rummaged around the woman, tugging out plastic carrier bags containing what were probably their worldly possessions.

Once satisfied he'd acquired everything that was in the vicinity of the woman, he ripped the bags apart, dispersing their contents about him. He pulled off his gloves and fumbled in his pocket for his torch, the light through the opaque polythene-covered window not providing enough light at ground level. Once the torch was switched on, he knew he had about five minutes of dull light before it died again. He rifled through the family's things, assuming they were a family, finding four sealed bottles of water. He threw one each to Milo and Salt.

Milo brought him half a dozen strips of roast rat which he now ate with relish, the juices initiated by the first few bites overriding any distaste he felt. He unscrewed the top of one of the water bottles and took some swigs of water before finishing the rest of the meat, wiping his mouth with the back of his hand, smearing some of the woman's blood across his face. His belly partially satiated by the food and water, Keelan rummaged through the rest of the items laid out in front of him. The torch flickered, so he speeded up his search before the batteries finally died: a tin of peas, two tins of sardines in olive oil, three tins of soup, one of bolognese, a pack of dried spaghetti, a tin of tomatoes, and a tin of bean sprouts. "Hey, we've struck gold here, lads."

"You want some more meat?" asked Milo.

"Nah, I'll settle for some of these," Keelan responded, holding up a tin of sardines. "Hey," he called again, "check this out, they've got...hang on. One of gin and one of whisky."

The other two men squealed with delight, and Salt pounded Milo on his back, almost knocking him down. "You've done it again, Milo mate. Sniffed us out some real food, drink...and...how's the woman, Stan?"

"Give me a minute. No, make it three." Keelan unscrewed the gin bottle, pulling a face as he took a deep swig, followed by a second before he reapplied the top and rolled it across the floor towards the other two.

"Shall we chuck him out?" asked Milo, pointing to the dead man.

"He dead then?"

"Yes, Stan."

"Better not. If the dogs get a sniff, they'll be round us like flies. Secure the plastic sheeting over the door again. Now, leave me in peace, I'm busy."

Both Salt and Milo took turns sipping at the alcohol, picking the last pieces of rat off the spindly bones, choosing to crunch some of them rather than waste them. Both knew that they had struck gold, but the currency wouldn't last. Milo then went to re-secure the doorway.

"Come here, you," Keelan said unsympathetically to the woman as he turned the rapidly dimming torch off. He'd seen some batteries amongst the haul so would change them later. "You don't half smell," he uttered as he leant in closer. "But, then, I'm no rose-smelling perfume, am I?"

The woman had curled up into a ball, using the thick layers of clothing as protection, but then she didn't know who she was dealing with. One punch that deadened her leg, eliciting a yelp of pain, quickly shattered any hopes she had of resisting. From then on, she allowed Keelan to grope her at will, pulling her two sets of trousers and knickers off, peeling away at her upper clothing, heaving the last layers up and over her head. Grabbing her ankles, dragging her away from the wall so she was lying flat on the tiled floor, he then raped her. A protest from the boy was stifled by a boot in the face from Salt who then took his turn with the woman, followed by Keelan again. Milo declined, slightly sickened by events, but not daring to make his views known. Each had her three times before settling down, sharing the proceeds, eating at least fifty per cent of the food and drinking the full bottle of gin.

Using the wood collected by the family, they kept the fire in the sink going, giving them some light and taking the chill off the room. Keelan had his shotgun handy, and they chatted about what they would do next, the following day, while sharing the bottle of whisky.

The boy had been cajoled and kicked, and now he was lying next to his mother who, traumatised, just stared into space, knowing, and dreading, that the two animals would be back. She squeezed her son's hand, whispered that she loved him, and pulled the knife from its hiding place. Only a short vegetable knife, but sharp enough for the purpose she had in mind. Marion squeezed her eyes shut, clenched her teeth tightly as she sawed through the flesh of her wrist, tears of sadness, fear and pain wetting her eyes and face. She bit back a scream as she cut too deep, stopping, knowing she had done enough. Gripping her son's hand with her healthy one, she lay there, allowing time to take its toll. There was no doubt that the two big men had far from finished with her, but with full bellies, a gin and whisky-induced sleep ensured that she would die peacefully. At the moment she felt herself going, one last minute of panic, and guilt, welled up inside her at the thought of her son having to survive without her. But she knew she could not have faced having her body ravaged the way it had been again. She had seen what they had done to her husband and knew they would literally rape her to death. Her one hope was that they would leave an eleven-year-old boy to live.

CHAPTER 13

PARALYSIS | GROUND-ZERO +31 DAYS
BRAVO TROOP, LONDON

After catching six hours' sleep, followed by a small, cold breakfast, consisting of bacon grill and a tin of mixed fruit, followed by a warm drink, the three soldiers headed west for a short while before turning north, where they would pass beneath the River Thames. Not wanting to hang around once they had eaten, the three soldiers, the memories of what they had seen on the upper levels still fresh, packed up their gear and headed out. At one point, Glen, who had been counting the number of paces, recording them on a small blue and white knitting row counter to keep count, slid onto a short piece of a snapped off knitting needle, pointed upwards at the ceiling, advising them that the River Thames was now directly above their heads. It took them forty minutes to complete the journey from Waterloo to the Embankment, and all were relieved to leave the claustrophobic confines of the tunnel. The journey beneath the river had been quite short, but with the weight of thousands of tons of water pressing down on the relatively narrow, curved tunnel, the three men were not sorry to be across on the other side. It was an uneventful journey, and they had been particularly pleased to find no cracks in the circular concrete roof above them. They did encounter half a dozen dead bodies, people who had wandered aimlessly in their search to escape, and who had succumbed to thirst, hunger and physical ailments caused by the nuclear offensive and the aftermath. Although their sense of smell had acclimatised somewhat to the background aroma of rotting flesh, the aroma of cadavers grew stronger the closer they got. Following a search of the immediate area of the Embankment, checking the platforms and higher levels covering the Northern, Bakerloo, Central, and District Lines and finding nothing other than more corpses, they dropped back down onto the railway line and entered the last tunnel. This would be their last stretch, taking them closer to their goal, and to Charing Cross, their penultimate destination. After trudging for less than a kilometre, but through yet another oppressive tunnel, they got their first inkling that there could be problems ahead.

Glen, who was on point, switched on the torch attached to his MP5, as a dark shadow, initially picked out of the gloom by his head torch, loomed up ahead. "Something up ahead," he hissed, his voice muffled behind the surgical mask.

Greg, number two in the file, moved up alongside Glen. "What have you got?"

"Not sure. Looks like the tunnel is blocked."

Plato moved closer to the two men, listening in on the conversation, ensuring he knew what the potential problem was so he was in a position to react if needed.

Glen played the light beam across the obstruction in front of them. "Whatever it is, it fills up the mouth of the tunnel almost completely."

As they got closer, the outline of the front of a London Underground train became visible, one of the 1995 rolling stock from the Northern Line, the two large windows either side and an oblong one in the centre reflecting the light of their torch beams. Although covered in a film of dust, the colours of the train cab could be distinguished: grey on the top half and red on the bottom half. A single door, leading to the driver's cab, and the rest of the eight-carriage train, was situated in the centre.

"It's nothing but a bloody tube train," announced Greg.

"Should be able to pass through it," suggested Plato behind them. "They're designed to be linked together."

They grouped together around the front of the train. Several rats scampered beneath the bogey wheels. The central door was about a metre above them.

"The door's been secured with a chain," observed Greg. "We need your toolkit, Plato."

"Coming up." Plato lowered his weapon to the ground and slipped off his rucksack. They had agreed to bring a specific set of tools that they felt sure would be necessary when exploring the tunnels of the Underground. And elsewhere in the city for that matter, should they be in a position to get out of the tunnel complex. He removed a pair of bolt cutters and handed them to Greg who got straight to work. He was also carrying a crowbar, hammer, pliers, and a few other smaller tools that could be of use should they need them.

Greg hefted the bolt cutters towards the handles of the cab door and aligned the jaws with the padlock hasp that was used to secure the two chain links together. With Glen lighting up the area of work, and also keeping an eye on the door, Greg applied pressure to the two handles, grunting as he exerted physical force, the two sharpened jaws making light work of the padlock. The jaws suddenly snapped together, and the chain was free of the padlock's clutches and fell apart with a clatter, echoing in the confines of the tunnel.

Greg lowered the bolt cutters and handed them back to Plato. "That'll have woken the dead."

"Not the dead we saw back there. Let's get this door open," instructed Glen.

While Plato returned the bolt cutters to his bag, Greg clambered up onto the buffer at the front of the train, shouldering the door which, after a few shoves, gave way, then he made his way into the cab of the carriage, opening into the confines of the carriage. An overpowering smell hit him immediately, and he gagged, the putrid odour of decomposing bodies penetrating his mask within seconds. "Shit, not again." He dropped to the floor of the tunnel.

No explanation was needed, as the foul smell soon reached the other two as well.

"I'll go first, then Greg, just in case we need the firepower, followed by you, Plato," Glen ordered them. Although the other two carried a silenced MP5 each, Greg still sported his light machine gun. The MP5s would be good in close-quarter fighting and the silenced weapons would give them the edge, but Greg's 100-round LMG would ensure the trio had some heavy firepower should they need it.

Glen clambered up, the torch on his helmet and MP5 lighting the way. He played the beam across the seats, the 1995 carriage layout with a row of blue seats either side, facing inward, along with tip-up seats and spaces for wheelchairs. A third of the way along, next to a double door either side, was an area where passengers could access or exit the train, or stand when it was crowded during peak times. There were also doors two-thirds of the way along and a single door each side at the end.

The three men made their way warily along the first carriage, dodging the vertical grab rails, checking the seats and floor, overhead poster adverts of no further use staring down at them. The first carriage was empty, surprisingly no dead bodies, but the doorway they passed through, separating it from the next, had been forced open at some point to allow free access between the two. The second carriage had the decomposing bodies of two soldiers and one civilian. The soldiers were lying in the centre, across the width of the carriage, while the suited civilian was slumped up against a window facing the rear, a Glock 17 9mm pistol visible in a shoulder holster beneath the half opened suit jacket of the cadaver. All three had been dead for at least a couple of weeks.

"Close Protection?" asked Greg as he looked over Glen's shoulder.

"Looks like it. The squaddies aren't badged, but look like regulars."

"Still got their weapons." Plato shone a torch over the two bodies. Two assault rifles lay close by.

"But why are they here?" questioned Greg.

"Sentries? Keeping the poor buggers back there out."

"Could be, Plato mate. But the CP guy, now that raises a few questions. The state they're in though..."

"Make sure your masks are secure and don't touch the bodies, or anything for that matter, unless you have to," Glen reminded them.

"I'm with you on that," agreed Plato.

"They've hueyed over their kit," observed Greg.

"No signs of radiation sickness. Has to be typhus or cholera then, or something along those lines."

"There's only one way to find out." Glen continued down the centre aisle of the carriage, Greg behind him and Plato following. The next carriage was set out as an accommodation block, the odour even fouler. Sleeping bags had been laid across the width, in between the seats on each side, some with bodies tucked inside. There were seven corpses in total, four in military uniform, one a police officer and two more civilians in suits. Four were in sleeping bags, two slumped in seats, and one appeared to have collapsed by one of the centre doors. All were armed, including the policeman.

"Guard room. Accommodation block for the security guys," suggested Greg.

"Let's keep moving." Glen pointed forwards down the rest of the train. "Then we can find out what the hell's been going on here."

They stepped over the bodies, picking up any weapons they could see, their hands protected by gloves, and depositing them where they would see them on their return journey, intending to collect them and as much ammunition as they could carry to take back with them.

The fourth carriage was empty, empty of people and bodies, but not objects. Boxes of food and fifteen-litre-size containers of water were stacked down the one side along with knives, pots, and pans associated with food preparation and cooking. Some of the carriage seats had been ripped out, making room for camping tables and chairs, and in the space near two of the off-centre exits, two cookers powered by Calor gas bottles were resting on metal legs. Checking that the seals hadn't been broken on the containers of water, they took the opportunity to top up their own water supplies.

Carriage five, with at least fifty per cent of the seats removed, was chock-a-block with radio and communications equipment. A temporary telephone exchange board had been set up, two dining chairs in front of it. Communication wires could be seen trailing out of the back of it and then up the side wall of the carriage compartment and out of a hole that had been cut in one of the carriage windows, probably leading to further connections that were perhaps linked to the outside world. No bodies were visible. The carriage was stacked with a variety of different types and calibre of radio transmitters and receivers. All were high-powered and, providing there was an aerial link to the outside world, would be able to communicate nationwide or even internationally. Satcoms capability was an unknown factor. No one knew if the satellites in their geosynchronous orbit above the earth had survived. It was well known, in the circles of the privileged few, that both the East and the West had the means to attack each other's coms and photographic satellites orbiting above the Earth's atmosphere.

"What's this lot doing here? Why isn't it in Pindar or another bunker?" questioned Greg.

"Alternate HQ?" suggested Plato, picking up a logbook from in front of one of the telephone exchanges. "Listen to this: contact made with Essex 21A. *Requesting assistance.* Responded – assistance unavailable. Authority to act in any way you see fit to regain control. Authority. PM. Prime Minister?" he said to no one in particular. He flicked a couple of the upper sheets back and shone his torch down the entries. "This is telling. Two weeks ago: Romeo Three. Contact with rescue team above lost. Coms test positive. Rescue team not responding."

"Check some of the earlier ones," Glen said.

Plato flicked through some more of the pages attached to the clipboard. "Here you go. Three weeks ago: Romeo Three. *Second attempt to lift debris from Westminster Tube unsuccessful. Lifting gear irreparably damaged. Orders?"* Plato flicked forward a page. "COBRA to Romeo Three. Release authorised. Discontinue rescue efforts. *Romeo Three. Whose authority?* COBRA. Authority PM. *Romeo Three. Negative. Will continue efforts.*"

"Well, that covers some of our unanswered questions. Looks like they've been blocked in and the external rescue attempt has failed, leaving the poor buggers down here," summarised Greg.

"Could be," thought Glen out loud as he played his MP5 torch around the coms complex. "Keep the log, Plato. We can read it at our leisure later. It may give us an indication of any other survivors out there. Let's probe deeper in."

Glen took the lead, followed by Greg, then Plato. Carriage number six, was set up as some form of office: map boards had been leant against the carriage sides, lists of call signs, officials, administration hierarchy for the country, food stats, and radiation readings, showing that critical levels of radiation had penetrated the centre of London moments after the nuclear detonations. In the penultimate carriage, number seven, they came across what seemed to be a medical centre, ten camp beds, all occupied. The corpses ranged from soldiers in uniform to overweight civilians, probably civil servants or representatives from the government.

"Scout for medical supplies. If there's anything we can use, we'll take it along with us," instructed Glen.

"Shame about the food back there," commented Greg.

"We can load up with as much as possible on our way out of here."

"If need be, we can come back later, with help from Chilmark, and clear the lot out," suggested Plato.

"Makes sense, so long as no one else finds it first. We'll grab as much of the useful stuff as we can on the way out."

"Some tins of stew back there, now in my bag, so we can have a slap-up meal tonight." Greg seemed oblivious to the death that surrounded him.

"Got some morphine, Neomycin, Teicoplanin, Furazolidone and loads of other stuff, boss." Plato stuffed the ampoules and tablets into his pockets, passing handfuls to Glen and Greg as they passed, on their way to the next coach.

"It's like bloody Christmas for you, Plato."

Plato held up one bottle of tablets. "You'll no doubt be needing this one at some point, Greg."

"What is it?"

"Roxithromycin – great treatment for syphilis."

"Wanker."

Plato added some sterile bandages and other medical items to his already bulging rucksack. They moved on. Torches flickered around the last carriage with at least two-thirds of its seats removed, replaced by armchairs probably dragged down from one of the Westminster Cabinet rooms somewhere above. Wires had been laid along the outer edge of the compartment and fed into the back of two telephones on a mahogany desk, a plush office chair behind it. That chair was vacant, but four of the six armchairs were occupied – but not by the living.

Although the bodies were in the process of decomposing and their faces blotched and gaunt, individual features could still be identified. Plato shone his torch over the faces. "Pretty sure that's the Home Secretary, or at least was." The beam of his torch lit up another macabre face, the mouth wide open, dribbles of fluid, now dried, streaked down his face and suit jacket, a crystal whisky glass still gripped in his right hand, a bottle half full of Glenfiddich in the other. On his lap, an open, empty, brown pill bottle, several pills scattered on his trousers and the floor about him. "Transport Secretary." Plato moved to the next two and scrutinised them. "Don't know him, or her."

"Down here," called Glen from the middle of the carriage. Next to an armchair, a CP officer, pistol still in his holster, head hung back, mouth wide open in the agonies of death. Behind the man, a large curtain was suspended across the middle of the carriage, hiding what was beyond it from Glen. He was joined by the other two as he peered round the screen, using his MP5 torch to light up the vicinity. "I doubt we'll need any help in identifying this one."

Greg peered over Glen's shoulder. Plato pushed aside the left-hand edge of the curtain and shone his torch on a body, lying on its back on a military camp bed, blanket draped across it shroud-like.

Beyond, Plato could see the door to the second driver's cab. This was the last carriage in the train. He moved forward, the other two remaining in situ. He lifted the top end of the blanket, pulling it back and exposing the cloudy eyes, greenish-coloured skin, and the man's tongue protruding from a gaping mouth. "The swelling around his neck and facial tissues make it difficult to identify, but I'd say it's him alright. It's the PM." He pulled the blanket further down, revealing the swollen stomach. The bacteria, located in the intestines, had done their work, feeding off the dead tissue, the resulting gases causing the Prime Minister's belly to swell.

He dropped the blanket back down and returned to the screen. "What now, boss?"

"How long?"

"Hard to tell, but six to nine days, maybe."

"They're all fucked," pronounced Greg. "So we might as well head back and wake Rolly up."

"I'd rather we checked out Pindar first. You two OK with that?"

"Sure, boss, whatever turns you on."

"Plato?"

"We're here, so might as well finish what we came for."

They left what as appeared to have been the new office of the Prime Minister and Cabinet Office Briefing Room A (COBRA), the emergency Cabinet. But not looking as slick as the COBRA briefing room in Whitehall, with its large conference table and high tech screens providing up to date military and political information to help feed their decision making process.

A quick lever with Plato's crowbar and the central door leading onto the platform was opened. There was a line of small two-man tents along the back wall of the platform, the only size that fitted comfortably there. Some military and civilians had crawled into these confined spaces to live out the last few hours of their lives.

Greg and Plato followed Glen along the platform, checking the tents as they passed them. A long, thick, black cable ran along the ground in front of the portable shelters. As they walked along the platform, Plato completed a quick check with his radiation survey meter; the readings were within acceptable limits. They exited halfway along by two chairs and a desk, a phone on top of it, probably manned by security at some point in order to control access. Glen headed down the corridor, Greg and Plato close on his heels. They arrived at a concourse at the foot of two long, stationary, ascending escalators. The area was occupied by more tents, piles of food and other supplies. Here the black cable had been attached to one of two small generators, resting on short lengths of RSJs, used no doubt to power floodlights around the edge of the open space and the equipment and communications systems back on the train. But, now, they were silent. Glen, as if from memory, led them up the escalators, weaving his way through the corridors until he arrived at his final destination. When Greg and Plato caught each other's eye during a flash of light illuminating their faces, both shrugged their shoulders. They knew they were headed for Pindar, but had no idea how they were going to achieve that.

Shining his torch along the wall, Glen found what he was looking for: set into the wall was a steel door, about a metre and a half high, a sign on it showing QWHI, a large brass-coloured keyhole top and bottom on the right.

"Magical mystery tour, boss?"

"I thought you liked a bit of mystery, Greg."

"Yeah, but it's locked," pointed out Plato.

Glen produced a large brass-coloured key from his pocket.

"Alice has a key," joked Greg.

"Where the hell did you get that?" asked Plato.

"The regiment has four of these, and I'm one of the keepers. Even so, if we searched that lot back there, I'm sure we'd find another one." Glen proceeded to unlock the door, the locks taut, requiring pressure to turn the cylinder inside. But, after only a few moments, he was successful and pulled on the recessed handle, the door opening outwards towards them.

Greg's torch showing a steel-runged ladder attached to the wall, descending into the depths below. "It looks narrow," he pointed out. Although the shaft was reasonably wide, it was not very deep. The gap between the ladder to the front wall, or entrance, would accommodate a person, but not with a bulky rucksack.

"Always the obvious," tormented Plato.

"Wanker."

"It is. We need to dump our rucksacks."

"Leave them here, boss," Greg suggested.

"No. There's room either side, so keep your personal kit and weapons with you, but we can suspend our rucksacks from the rungs of the ladder, using a carabiner. Once we've pushed past them, we'll have a clear run all the way down." Glen removed his rucksack, dropping it on the floor close to the entrance. He entered the shaft head first, gripping the ladder then placing a foot on the metal rung, ensuring his boots had purchase.

Greg passed the rucksacks, one after the other, and Glen suspended them, two on the left, one above the other, the second positioned about three metres lower down the shaft. The third one, he hooked onto the right side of the ladder. His helmet clinked against the shaft wall as he climbed back out.

"You like mystery tours, Greg, so you can lead the way. I'll need to lock up after us."

"Thanks, boss."

"You're welcome."

Greg climbed in, manoeuvring his LMG, with its larger magazine, into a position where it wouldn't inhibit his descent. He was then followed by Plato with Glen bringing up the rear. Turning back around, placing a boot on a small platform either side of the ladder, put there for this very purpose, he pulled the door to with a loud clang and relocked it from the inside. He turned back round, squeezing past the suspended rucksacks and followed his two colleagues downwards. After descending for about twenty metres, he entered a horizontal shaft going left and right, and his boots soon touched the concrete floor. Greg's and Plato's helmet torches flickered around the two-metre high cable tunnel. They were all able to stand upright relatively comfortably. A plaque on the wall showed QWHI/2845, the designation for the tunnel.

"This answers why Rolly is babysitting the kit."

"It does, Greg. He'd be cracking his head every couple of seconds."

They all laughed, but quietly.

"How far does this go?" asked Plato.

"About 500 metres. I'll lead."

"It's a BT cable tunnel," surmised Greg, the darkness hiding Plato's raised eyebrows.

Glen squeezed past the two soldiers, the tunnel just over a metre wide, taking the left option and moving along at a fairly brisk pace. The silence was shattered only by the clump of their boots, their presence stirring up fine dust particles from the floor, reflected in their torch beams. After marching for just under 450 metres, the tunnel went off to the left, at a right angle, but a short ten-metre stretch, straight ahead, narrowing to less than a metre wide, continued on to a seemingly dead end. Glen led them straight on, a set of steel rungs set into the concrete wall facing them at the end. A plaque on the wall behind the ladder showed QWHI/2845A.

"Up we go then, lads." Glen started the climb up the narrow shaft, Plato next, followed by Greg, struggling to keep the LMG from scraping against the sides.

It was a short climb. Glen was at the top no sooner than Greg's legs had disappeared from view as he left the BT deep level cable tunnel. The steel door above was unlocked, with the same brass key, and opened and Glen exited, helping Plato and Greg out in turn.

"We're nearly there." Glen relocked the door, and headed off again, not waiting to answer the questions he knew would come if he dallied. Ten metres further on, and another steel door, unlocked this time, was pulled open and a second climb was required, this one much longer. After ascending thirty metres up the shaft, Glen opened a further door. This one had locks, but had been left unsecured.

He stepped through, his helmet and MP5 torches lighting up a corridor that appeared empty. "Plato, right."

Plato didn't question the order but turned right as soon as he stepped out of the shaft and lit up the corridor, his weapon at the ready should they come under threat.

"Problem?" asked Greg as he too stepped out of the exit from the shaft.

"Door wasn't locked. Just be alert. Come on, let's go."

Glen went left down the corridor, both men in tow, leading to a standard door that would take them into Court 6 of the Treasury Building. "We've just come through the protected route from the Cabinet War Room," Glen informed them. "Through there," he pointed.

Greg went first, pushing the door open and stepping into a large chamber, moving his head from side to side, sweeping the area with the torch attached to his helmet.

Bang...bang.

The small calibre bullets from a 9mm pistol thudded into Greg's body, one striking his left shoulder spinning his body round, the second burning a furrow along the back of his head. Momentum continued to turn his body until he crashed into the door, pushing it open even further, and he keeled over onto the floor in a heap. Close behind Greg, and hearing the first shot, Glen was able to focus in on the flash of the second shot, and fired a quick three-round burst in the direction he envisaged the shooter was situated, rewarded by the sound of someone crying out. A double tap followed, his torch lighting up a dark shadow next to what appeared to be a desk, a shriek indicating another round had found its target.

Glen completed a quick scan of the area before charging across the three-metre gap to secure the target. Kicking the pistol, lying close to the shooter's hand, away, he crouched down and did another 180-scan, checking for other threats. "Clear."

"Clear," responded Plato, who, crouched down next to Greg, had also checked the area for other threats. "Cover me. I need to see to Greg."

Rolly swilled his soup mug with water, then drank it, not wanting to waste the precious liquid. He scratched the heavy stubble on his narrow, sharp features, vowing to attempt a cold-water shave sometime in the next twenty-four hours. He was starting to feel a little impatient. Not with his team but just generally. Used to the physical activity of operations, or fitness training as a substitute, he was finding the waiting around a chore. Standing and shoving the hessian curtain aside, his C8 carbine in his right hand if needed, he stepped the other side of it, stopping and listening. Nothing but silence – of the man-made kind at least – but there was still a steady breeze driving the snow up against the outer walls of the hide.

He moved further out to where he could examine the area 180 degrees, the falling snow still ensuring visibility was reduced to less than fifty metres. Checking the tripwires again, making sure they would do the job of warning him of intruders, he made his way to the front of the church, ensuring he stepped over the thin thread attached to the spike at one end and the bang-alert device at the other. It was heavy going through the thick blanket of snow, but he felt happier now that he had some visibility of the road. Seeing no activity and hearing nothing but the whine of the wind, he made his way back to the hide, making a mental not that the tripwire wouldn't be of use for much longer if the snow continued to fall at the current rate.

CHAPTER 14

PARALYSIS | GROUND-ZERO +31 DAYS
BRAVO TROOP, LONDON

Plato leant over Greg who was trying to sit up. "Here, let me help you up, mate."

"Shite, I can't believe I've been hit. Caught like a bloody rookie."

"Don't worry, your guardian angel's here."

Plato manoeuvred Greg so he was sitting up, leaning him against the reinforced concrete and steel bunker wall. He unbuckled Greg's PLCE and peeled it off as best he could without exacerbating the injury.

"You don't smell like one."

Plato shone the torch in Greg's eyes before using it to help him examine the area of the wound.

"You trying to blind me?"

"Is he alright?" called Glen.

"He's complaining, as usual. Always a good sign."

"Come and look at this guy when you're done."

"Gotcha." Plato shone the torch over Greg's upper body, seeing a dark wet patch around the front of his shoulder, just below the collarbone. "I need to lay you back down again and get your kit off."

"If you were an angel, I'd welcome it, but—"

"Stop with the wisecracks for once." Plato peeled off his own helmet and gloves, but keeping them in close proximity, then placed his hand behind Greg's head to support him as he lowered the wounded man to the floor. Greg cried out, and Plato could feel the matted hair at the back of his head, wet and sticky. He rolled him on his side, straddling his friend, supporting his body with his knees. He shone the torch beam so it lit up the back of Greg's head. He could make out the blood oozing from the furrow across the back of Greg's skull, just below where his helmet sat. He probed it with his fingers to gauge its depth.

A grunt from Greg ensued. "Argh. Angel fingers?"

"Shut it, it's not deep." Unclipping Greg's helmet, Plato gently removed it from the soldier's head and placed it to one side. He reached round the back to one of his pouches where he kept his medical kit. The major items were back in his rucksack, suspended in one of the shafts, but he had enough to make do. Still supporting Greg's head with his left hand, he pulled out a sealed pack containing a large dressing, he tore it open with his teeth, extracting the dressing and applying it to the wound before allowing Greg's upper body to lie flat against the floor.

"Let's take a look at this now." Plato started to unzip the NBC suit jacket, pulling it aside. "I need to sit you up for a few seconds because I have to get this stuff off so I can get to the wound. Can you manage that?"

"Of course I bloody well can. I'm not some sort of bloody wuss, you know." Greg grunted as he sat up, helped by Plato, who kept a hand to the back of Greg's head, keeping the dressing in place. Now he was able to undo the combat jacket and push both layers of clothing off Greg's left shoulder. Plato lowered his friend down again, placing the helmet under the man's head for support. Reaching back into the medical pouch again for the pair of good quality scissors, he cut into the shirt and T-shirt, exposing the shoulder wound.

Glen completed a cursory check of the man slumped against the wall before helping him into a more comfortable position. What the torch revealed was not promising: Glen had scored at least two hits. The stranger, in his early forties and wearing a crumpled, stained, but good quality suit, stared at him through glassy eyes, a line of blood oozing from his mouth, congealing on four-day-old stubble. The pallor of his skin was indicative of something more than just the impact of being shot. The man looked feverish, a film of sweat beaded his brow, and Glen could smell stale vomit even through the mask over his nose and mouth.

The man spluttered, spitting flecks of blood as he tried to speak. "Sorry..." *Cough, cough.* "I didn't mean...to shoot. Panicked."

"Who are you?"

"Just..." *Cough.* "...a civil servant."

"What happened here? Where is everybody?"

The man's eyes flickered. He was close to losing consciousness, or worse. He opened them suddenly, and wide. "Am...I dying?"

"I don't know, but my friend will check you out once he's free."

"Did I kill him?"

"No, he's just wounded."

"That's good...it wasn't intentional. I...just fired wildly in panic."

"My friend will live."

"OK...I don't really want to live though."

"Why not? What's your name?"

"Gordon...Geoff Gordon...there's nothing left. Country's finished."

Glen supported him as a coughing fit racked the man's body. He knew instinctively that Geoff didn't have long left in this world.

"Pindar?"

Geoff smiled. "Survived the bombs."

"But not the diseases?"

Geoff's head moved slightly in agreement. "Radiation...really bad...as well...to start with. Clear now..." *Cough...cough...cough.* "Levels...dropped."

"Just hang in there. We'll get you sorted in no time."

"It was the diseases...that destroyed everything."

"Diseases?"

Cough...cough...cough.

"I'll get my friend over in a minute to take a look at you."

"You a politician?" Geoff suddenly seemed very cognisant.

Glen was bemused. "No, as you can see, I'm a soldier."

"Then tell the truth."

"It's not looking good."

"Thank you."

"What's it like outside of this bunker?"

"Outer buildings above destroyed...nuke strikes...were far more devastating than expected...EMP...damaged even...some of our protected..." *Cough.* "...radio sets."

"What disease was it?"

"Typhus...to cholera, no one was really sure. Whipped through the entire Cabinet. Everybody dead. It was agreed the sick...would leave...go to the tunnels. The healthy...would remain in Pindar. The PM, he's dead."

"We've seen him. Anyone in the Admiralty Citadel, Q-Whitehall, Pindar?"

There was no response, glassy eyes stared at him, a last spluttered response: "All gone, all gone..." Geoff's chest rose, lungs crackling as he sucked in one last lungful of air, his last breath slowly exhaled in a long sigh.

Glen shone the torch in the man's face; an empty stare returned. He checked the man's pulse, but he had seen enough death in his time to know the man was no longer in this world.

Plato put the morphine syrette down on the ground after giving Greg a shot. He then placed pieces of Celox Gauze on the entry and exit points where the bullet had passed through. The small hole in Greg's shoulder, not much bigger than a five-pence piece, was weeping blood, as was the exit wound which was twice the size. The gauze, containing a substance made from crushed shellfish, would become sticky on contact with Greg's blood, acting as a blood-stemming agent, assisting the vital fluids to clot, and helping to staunch the flow of blood. On top, Plato placed two thick wads of absorbent material, then started to bind them both, passing the roll of bandage beneath Greg's back, securing the dressings against both wounds. Greg, although pale and partially out of it thanks to the morphine shot, should be OK, thought Plato.

He was joined by Glen who crouched down next to him. "How's he doing?"

"He'll live to drive us nuts for a while longer yet."

"Will we be able to get him back?"

"Sure, give him an hour, a hot drink, and we can get him on his feet."

"Wound bad?"

"No, bullet gone clean through the muscle. No bones hit, but I will need to get rid of the crap from his clothing out of the wound as soon as we rejoin Rolly. How's the other fellow?"

"Gone to meet his Maker."

"Any intel?"

"A bit. Seems that Pindar's survived the bombs, but a high dose of radiation killed a bunch of them, and typhus has been rife, finishing off a few more. The whole of the Cabinet, by all accounts. COBRA is no more."

"Well, we've seen the PM's body. What now then, boss?"

"Get Greg sorted, then let's get the hell out of here."

They redressed Greg as best they could, using then the soldier's helmet and kit as a cushion to make his head and neck more comfortable. Plato had examined the wound at the back of Greg's head – it looked worse than it was – but Greg would no doubt have a splitting headache for a few days.

Glen boiled some water in a mess tin over a Hexi burner and was able to make two large mugs of tea to be shared between the three of them. Greg, although still drowsy from the effects of the morphine, was able to drink some, not too much though, but the little he had warmed him from the inside, helping to reverse some of the shock.

"Have I ever told you that you make a great nurse?" Greg slurred through his surgical mask. Plato had insisted they kept their mouths and noses covered until they were able to return to fresh air, just lowering them to take a drink.

"I preferred you when you were out," responded Plato.

"If we didn't need to move out soon, I'd let you give him another jab and leave us all in peace."

"That's not very caring, boss."

"We need to move out within the hour, buddy. You OK with that?"

"Sure, boss. Can you guys help me up?"

Although Greg winced occasionally, the two soldiers succeeded in moving their comrade to a sitting position, his back up against the hard wall of the bunker.

"That's better. Anything I need to know?" Greg was sounding more lucid.

"Apart from the world's all fucked?" answered Glen. "It seems that we don't have a government, or anyone in charge for that matter."

"That's not good…boss. If there's no one in charge…then every despot in the country is going to be seeking power."

"My God, for once the man talks sense," laughed Plato.

"Wanker."

"Yep, he's better," chuckled Glen.

Plato looked at his watch. "How long do you reckon it'll take to get back to the hide?"

Glen tapped Greg's leg. "What do you think?"

Greg thought for a moment. "My legs are fine. Might need some help up and down the ladders, but if it's a straight run back…could do it in a day. A long day, though."

Glen looked at Plato. "What's on your mind?"

"I'm thinking, if we stop here tonight, give Greg some…"

"Don't you worry about me."

"Let me finish. Give Greg some breathing space and some kip, he'll be on much better form tomorrow. It's 19.15 now. You could do a recce of the area on your own. You'll be faster, and quieter, and could gather some more intel maybe?"

Glen scratched his beard, then took his helmet off, scratching an itch that had been irritating him for the last ten minutes. "Good call. It wouldn't hurt to nose around a bit more. It's not as if we'll be coming back here."

Plato checked Greg with a shielded torch. The soldier's eyes were closed, possibly asleep, the effects of the morphine. Once it wore off, he could give him another shot now it had been decided they were staying in situ for the night. "Shame we haven't got our rucks with us."

"We've enough food, water and ammo. So long as we're back before Rolly starts to panic."

"He'll be climbing the walls already, cooped up in there."

"I'll scoot then, Plato, while you watch over the invalid."

"Where are you headed?"

"Back down the way we came in here. Then I'll follow my nose." With that, Glen got up, leaving his helmet as he would be able to negotiate the tunnels and shafts much faster without it. He checked his kit, gave Plato a flicked salute, and headed through the doorway they had originally come in through. He retraced the route they had negotiated earlier, descending the thirty-metre shaft, down the short corridor, then descending another ten metres until he was back in the BT deep level cable tunnel. Going down was a lot more difficult than climbing, having to find the ladder's rungs by touch as he descended. Ahead of him was the long tunnel that they had used to get here from Charing Cross, but this time, rather than going straight on, he would turn right.

The torch on his MP5 lighting the way ahead, his footfall echoing around him, Glen confessed to himself that he found the experience quite eerie. A T-junction came up on his left and he took it, picturing the map in his head: 150 metres until the end of this particular cable tunnel and there would be a final junction, the old War Office on the left and the MOD on the right, accessible by a lift shaft that would take him the thirty metres to the surface. He was there in no time at all, Plato being correct in his supposition that Glen could move much faster on his own. Taking the right-hand link, the main corridor continuing on to the south, his torch lit up the lift doors up ahead. They were closed and, shining a torch through the small glass slit, he ascertained that the lift cage was on his level. But there appeared to be no power as pushing the button at the side failed to work. Perhaps it needs a key, he thought.

Sliding his knife from its scabbard, Glen forced it in between the two doors, creating a crack between the lift doors. Easing open the gap, pushing his gloved fingers, then his hand and arm and finally his shoulder into the space, he managed to push the doors apart with his arms and buttocks. The lift cage was in front of him, and he wasted no time in entering and punching open the hatch above. Slinging his weapon across his chest, he jumped up towards the square hatchway in the roof, grabbing the edge and pulling himself up with his arms, his muscles burning and trembling as he lifted his body up until his head, then his shoulders, were through, and he was able to use his elbows to gain greater purchase, pulling his body through, dragging his legs onto the top of the lift.

Unslinging his MP5, he used the torch to examine the lift shaft, the head of it about thirty metres above. He spied a series of rungs running up the right-hand side of the shaft and started the long climb. The shaft smelt musty and of machinery and oil. His boots and gloved hands gripped the ladder well, and he was soon at the top, just resting once, halfway up. Once at the top, he went through the same process, forcing the doors open, much more difficult this time, but once done the action proved pointless: the armoured upper section of the lift shaft had protected the integrity of the lift, but the outer shell of the building surrounding was black with soot, and the smell of burnt fittings blew in through the door on a cold breeze. There was about a metre of space around the entrance. The rest was enclosed in the collapsed and scorched remains of the MOD building. The Russian missiles, followed by a firestorm, had done their job.

He pushed the doors closed and descended, knowing his next and final target would be, according the words of a dying man, in one piece.

Plato snoozed, his back against the steel wall, his head lolling to the side, taking the opportunity to catch up on some kip. He would need his strength if he was to help support his not so light fellow soldier when they moved out. Glen had been gone a few hours and on his return he might well want to head straight back, to get out of this potentially biologically toxic area, connect up with Rolly, and head west for Chilmark. Then again, he might want some kip himself before they left.

Plato started to dream, feeling a cold chill against his face, coming awake instantly as a voice uttered, "Don't bloody move."

He felt the cold touch of gunmetal against his cheekbone at the same time as his MP5, lying across his knees, was whipped from his grasp. Greg's weapon was also removed from reach as the soldier, roused by the voice, stirred. Plato mentally cursed himself for his stupidity, and hoped the intruders were friendly, although he didn't hold out too much hope.

He looked up, a torch blinding him. The voice above demanded, "Who the hell are you? You from an RGC, Territorial Army, or what?"

"We're just a couple of squaddies. We're on your side." Plato went to get up.

"Don't move!"

"Who are you then?" asked Plato in return.

"We're part of the security force."

"Security force for who?"

"That's enough questions for now. You're to come with us."

"Hey, we've found him," informed a voice across the other side of the room.

"And?"

"Dead."

"Did you soldiers kill him?"

"He fired on us first, we—"

"You did us a favour. Now, get up, but no tricks or I'll shoot. Oi," he called over to Greg, "you too."

"He's wounded. Morphine."

"Where?"

"Shoulder and back of his head."

"He'll be alright. Get him up."

Greg sensed two more people close by as he tried to scramble up from the floor, still disorientated by the drugs flowing through his body.

Rolly found them completely buried in snow, but it was fairly soft, so he was satisfied that the wires could still be tripped. He did change the caps though as they would more than likely be damp and could fail to go off if triggered. Once back under cover of the hide's overhang, Rolly studied what landscape he could see, at least as far as he could see through the steadily falling snow. Everything was now white. He estimated there to be at least a metre of snow, and that was steadily thickening. He suspected they would have a pretty difficult journey back to the RGC, and it wouldn't be easy getting away from the collapsed church's grounds. He wondered how Glen and the lads were doing, what they had discovered. Had they made it to Pindar, or at least found some form of administration still in operation? He would know soon: thirty-six hours and they would return. He slung his weapon on his shoulder and went back inside, laying his C8-Carbine on the bonnet of the vehicle. He pushed the director's chair out of the way, making enough room so he could complete fifty jump squats, 100 press ups, fifty squat thrusts, and a few other exercises to prevent his body from stiffening up from so little activity, just hanging around waiting and watching over their kit.

He would be pleased when they could finally move out. But, more importantly, having the troop back together.

CHAPTER 15

PARALYSIS | GROUND-ZERO +31 DAYS
TOWER TRIBE, CROYDON

It had been a cold uncomfortable night for Bill's group, having to use the open space in the lower levels of the library, those that were habitable. The buildings close by were inaccessible, and those that weren't were occupied by other survivors. The strength of those survivors was an unknown. Although the group had an automatic weapon, five shotguns and four pistols, ammunition was limited and, at the moment, could not be replenished. Once settled, Bill was determined to visit the TA centre he and his team leaders had discussed back at the tower. He felt going further north, or even east or west, was a pointless exercise, beyond a radius of seven or eight kilometres, the destruction to the land and buildings seeming to get progressively worse. After building a fire, they had kept it stoked throughout the night, to not only to keep warm but act as a deterrent for the dogs that had continued to follow them to the tube station.

The fire had naturally attracted the attention of other survivors and scavengers in the area, some even approaching Bill, asking, pleading, to join his group. Although down to just over fifty, having lost too many back at the tower, he was not in a position to give sanctuary to others at present. The state of the survivors they had seen was pitiful. Bill's group were on a limited diet, their faces pinched and grimy, and their clothes had seen better days, were dirty, becoming increasingly tatty. But the refugees that came appealing for sanctuary were something very different: emaciated, faces blotchy, hair loss obvious, showing the effects of radiation burns, obviously untreated, the ulcerations too sore to cover and protect them from the cold. They literally looked like bundles of rags on spindly legs, carrying or dragging bags containing their worldly goods. Others were using differing methods of transport to cart their worldly goods around with them, from the unsurprising shopping trolley and wheeled shopping carriers to bicycles and pushchairs.

During the night, there had been a particularly loud commotion, the sound of squealing and snarling dogs bringing the entire group awake and alert. Although Bill's group had seen the dogs as a threat, being hunted now by a pack of up to thirty dogs, others saw it as manna from heaven. A group that was particularly resourceful had lured the dogs, using a couple of freshly gutted rats as bait, the scent of fresh blood too tempting to be ignored, into a trap. Three nets cast over the scrapping dogs as they fought for fresh meat triggered the commotion. The snarling, baying dogs, trapped and frantic to escape, soon became entangled in the mesh of the nets and were subsequently clubbed to death by the dozen or so survivors that were waiting in the wings. The humans didn't escape scot-free. Those dogs that were not trapped were not giving up their new found food easily, and a few of the survivors felt the slobbering keenness of the dogs' fangs. But, in the end, it was a one-sided battle, the humans, who had become almost as savage as their prey, winning the day. The three carcasses were quickly dragged away, gutted, skinned and barbecued over an open fire within twenty minutes of being killed.

The leaders of the human pack, the fittest, the strongest, the most astute, bartered with the lower members for items of clothing, other forms of food – a tin of peas being particularly valuable – and for sex. The falling snow failed to block the smell of roasting flesh that drifted towards Bill and his people, and he and the other leaders planned to take a lead from what they had just witnessed. Ideas were put forward, and a number of the group were tasked with the hunt.

Bill split his group into four teams for the day, as soon as it was light enough to start. Most couldn't sleep anyway. Although plastic sheeting, again requisitioned from the warehouse, had been laid across the ground to keep them dry and an extra fire lit to throw out more heat, the night had been far from comfortable. To a man, they longed to be back in the relevant comfort of the tower block. But that was no longer possible. The threepenny bit-shaped block of office space was nothing more than a burnt-out shell. Owen led the first team, tasked with baiting and setting a trap for the dogs which, until now, had hunted them. The tables were about to be turned, and the hunters were about to become the hunted.

CHAPTER 16

PARALYSIS | GROUND-ZERO +32 DAYS
MOTORWAY TRIBE, NORTH-EAST OF CHELTENHAM

Judy was sitting by the fire, the flames kept going throughout the night by a small team taking it in turns to feed it, a boon for everyone, making the night bearable. She'd slept soundly for the first hour, but after taking her turn on watch, then going back to her bed, the next two hours had been fitful, the cold easing its way inside her sleeping bag, chipping away at what little warmth her body retained. When she did finally drift off again, her dreams denied her of rest...her nightmare of previous events returned to haunt her.

"Hi, George, how are you feeling?"

As sick as he was, he was still able to find a smile for her. "Not... too good...lovely lady. Everyone ready?"

"Yes, you know we have to go, don't you?"

A dribble of saliva ran down the side of his mouth, turning pink as it picked up some of the blood from the cracked sores which opened up every time he moved his facial muscles. Judy had asked Philippa whether or not the sores were painful. Judy was taken aback at the response: Philippa's description of how agonising the myriad of open sores George had about his upper body would be.

"Have you got a litter for me?"

A tear ran down one of Judy's cheeks. "We can't take you, George. We're just not strong enough to support your weight, particularly across country and in this weather."

He smiled. "I know that...Judy love...but I thought...I would ask."

"I'm sorry..." Tears were now flowing freely down her face.

George reached out with a skinny, shaky arm, his bony fingers touching her hand. "Hey, lovely...someone else will turn up."

Before he could withdraw his hand, Judy struck. The cushion, held behind her back, was brought swiftly to the front of her body where, gripped by both hands, it was thrust down onto George's face. She leant forwards, her weight adding to the force of her arms as she pressed down hard, smothering his face, preventing him from breathing in or out. His arms and legs started to flap, and his spindly fingers gripped her arms in an attempt to force them up. But to no avail. Now openly sobbing, Judy pushed down harder, leaning directly over him, using her chest to add to the force. Once he had stopped struggling, she held the cushion in place for at least another three minutes before being satisfied that he was dead. She stood up, leaving the cushion covering his face, wiped the tears away with the back of her hand, and walked away, not looking back, feeling treacherous and sick.

When she awoke with a start, a thin film of cold sweat across her brow, Gavin was there with a mug of weak but hot tea. He had even managed to find a sprinkle of powdered milk, luxuries that Judy was sure wouldn't be around for much longer.

"You OK? I was just about to wake you up."

"Thank you, Gavin," she said as she took the mug from him. "Just a bit of dream." But she knew, and no one else knew, that it was far from being a dream. She was sure it would haunt her for a long time to come, if not for the rest of her life. He left her, and she checked her watch, the snow-filled clouds changing from dark shadows to a lighter grey as dawn slowly broke. Even the snow had eased, not stopped, but with the wind having dropped the light fall was fluttering around her rather than being driven into any exposed skin.

Eight fifteen: she wanted to be on the move by nine. She knew that time was their enemy: the longer they were out in the open, exposed to the weather, with food and water running out, the greater the demand on their individual physical resources. She stood just as Gavin and Steve were rousing those that were still asleep or staying in situ in order to keep warm. A wave from Gavin caught her eye, and she stepped over Alysha who was in the process of dragging her legs from her sleeping bag, saying good morning as she did. Fortunately, they had all acquired sleeping bags, of differing quality though. The contents of many of the cars in their old camp had such camping items for their use as occupants fled the cities. She made her way around the outside of the circle of people until she reached Gavin who was crouched over a sleeping form inside a bright red bag. Although a plastic sheet had been laid beneath it, during the night it had slipped off, and Judy could see the dark layer of damp along the lower section of the quilted bag. A wisp of grey hair, a few flakes of snow undisturbed, were showing from beneath the beanie hat and hood that Margaret had worn the previous night, new items she had hoarded for the day they left camp.

"Is she…?"

Gavin nodded. "Sometime during the night. I did check on her before I got my head down. She was cold but breathing." He pointed at the ground sheet. "She's obviously turned over and dislodged it. Ground's sodden underneath."

A tear ran down Judy's cheek, and it felt like someone or something had gripped her heart in a vice. Day one and she'd lost someone already. "It's my fault."

Gavin placed an arm around her shoulder and comforted her. "Hey, don't be stupid. It's not your fault. It's the idiots that caused all this in the first place that are to blame. You're just trying to keep us all safe."

She stood up, drew herself up to her full height and called out to everyone. "Please stop what you're doing and gather round. All of you, please."

One by one, they responded, gathering around Judy and Gavin in a huddle.

"I have some sad news." More tears escaped, two salty lines making a passage through the grime on her face. "Margaret left us during the night. She became so cold that her body could no longer fight it. It's partly my fault. Knowing she was vulnerable, I should have made more of an effort to ensure she and the others amongst us were OK."

A chorus of, "Don't be silly, you couldn't have known, if you're to blame, we're all to blame," swamped her, and her shoulders shook as she sobbed her heart out. Gavin steered her away, nodding at Steve and William, indicating towards Margaret's still form. They knew what had to be done.

While Gavin comforted Judy, enjoying the feeling of her sobbing shoulders beneath his strong arms, the feeling of a woman's body close, something he had not experienced for a long time, Steve and William picked up the frail body of Margaret, the red sleeping bag her shroud, and carried her around the back of the broken walls of the house. They laid her alongside the back wall, flakes of snow already settling on her form. William zipped the bag right to the top, covering her face. There was nothing else they could do: they didn't have the means or the time to dig a grave. She would be left, her body would eventually freeze, and the snow would drift over her, hiding her from view.

Judy asked where Margaret's body was and went to her while the rest of the group shared a dozen tins of plum tomatoes, heated on the fire. Judy stood over the woman's body and said a few words. "I'm sorry, Margaret, I let you down. It won't happen again. I'll take better care of the others. You can rest now. No more worries about the future for you. Maybe you're one of the lucky ones, but, for the rest of us, we must go on. Take care, sweet lady, and rest in peace."

She returned to the fire, and William thrust a mug of tomato soup and a spoon into her hand. "Get this down you, Judy. The fire's dying, so we need to move soon before the chill sets in."

"Thank you." She wolfed the food down, not realising how hungry she was. She noticed her sleeping bag had been rolled up and placed in her rucksack, the wet ground sheet furled and attached by the straps on the outside. She finished her meal and the camp got ready to move on.

"Ready?" asked Gavin, handing her the rucksack.

"Yes, you lead again?"

"Of course."

She shrugged off her despondency, chivvying everyone along, placing William at the rear of the party with Steve in the middle. They assembled outside the remains of the house, and Gavin started to walk along Southam Lane. It had been agreed the previous day that Gavin would lead them south beyond the village of Southam, avoiding the built-up area and topping up their water supplies from Hyde Brook. If the water from the brook appeared too risky then they would have to make do with what they had, or melt snow, until they reached a small reservoir further south.

The first dog, a large French poodle, her usually white coat now matted and dirty, ventured forward first, sniffing around the mound of snow, the faint red outline of the sleeping bag showing through. She was soon joined by an alsatian, the two of them joint leaders of the pack. Neither had been able to dominate the other. Poodles, the standard standing between fifteen and twenty-six inches or more at the withers for a male, were successfully used as hunting dogs during the Middle Ages. This poodle, a female, standing at twenty-two inches and weighing in at eighteen kilograms, had been used by her master for retrieving game during shoots, and a tentative truce had formed between the two dogs.

The poodle scraped away at the layer of snow, the action becoming more frantic as the scent of the corpse filled the dog's nostrils. The alsatian, losing patience, lunged at the sleeping bag, gripping it between his jaws, tugging the bagged body away from the wall. The poodle flew at the other dog, sinking her fangs into the soft flesh of his flanks, snarling, twisting, manipulating her jaws to acquire a better grip and bite down hard. The dog yelped in pain, escaped, and turned back to face his attacker, lips curled back over his teeth, head low, hackles up, snarling. There was a stand-off for a few seconds, the rest of the pack, nine dogs of varying breeds, stood in a semi-circle watching, their ribs indicative of their desperate hunger, but not daring to intervene, as tempting as the body was that was waiting for them.

The poodle simply turned away and ripped at the sleeping bag, tearing the nylon covering, the synthetic cream filling of the bag sticking to her snout as she buried her muzzle deep, pulling, ripping, tearing at the bag and the woman's slacks, eventually exposing a bony leg. A tug of war ensued, the alsatian dog at the other end, its incisors shredding the zip, its blood lust up as it tasted flesh from the woman's cheek. The rest of the pack gathered closer, nipping in, snapping at the woman's body as more and more of it was exposed. Hunger driving the dogs mad, the pack took greater and greater risks, the poodle and alsatian responding aggressively.

Eventually, with an arm to herself, muzzle spotted with human blood, the poodle took her reward away to feast on it in peace, savaging any other animal that came near and threatened her prize. The two alphas feasted while the rest of the pack went into a frenzy, rending chunks of flesh from the corpse, the first decent meal they'd had for seven days. Till this bounty came along, they had fed on rats, voles, and any other small animal that had mistakenly come across the pack.

Judy walked up and down the line as often as she could, providing help, advice and encouragement. Heads were down, not through despair, but to avoid the stinging snow as best they could, their eyes reddened and skin stinging. It was eleven twenty in the morning, and they had been on the go for over two hours, stopping at the brook for water. As a consequence of the dry weather prior to the onset of snow, the brook was a mere trickle of water, the contents rank. The risk of drinking it, even after boiling, was too great. The group had been allowed a five-minute rest at the brook, but Gavin and Judy agreed that the next stop shouldn't be until around one o'clock if they were to make any decent progress. They had continued east, trudging across a field, snow and mud sticking to their boots, following the line of the brook, until they arrived at more solid ground, the B4632. After going south for a kilometre, Gavin steered them east along Gravel Pit Lane, passing a large farm complex on their right. Although tempted to scavenge, it was agreed that making progress was more important. Gravel Pit Lane led to Upper Mill Lane, the route taking them away from the eastern outskirts of Prestbury, a suburb of Cheltenham, and beyond that was the countryside. Here, Gavin eventually called a halt at the junction with Cotswold Way.

The group huddled amongst the foliage-free trees, using the stripped trunks to rest against as they eat some of their meagre rations. They had walked roughly four kilometres so far, a hard section, but Gavin and Judy reassured them that, although they still had a long stretch ahead, they would continue across a hardened surface. The snowfall was light but steady, making the going slightly easier. But it was getting to the stage where diverting from any road or decent track, heading across tracks in fields, would prove more difficult, especially where snowdrifts had built up. On a positive note, the snow meant the temperature was slightly warmer during the day, hovering around minus one degree centigrade. Roused from their resting places, groans uttered about aching limbs and the cold, Gavin and Judy coaxed everyone up, promising they would be warm again soon, once they got back into the rhythm of walking. They headed south.

Apart from a few long, shallow bends, the Cotswold Way was relatively straight They headed south with a major change of direction taking them east once they reached Arle Grove. A further three kilometres, and Gavin signalled the group to halt. He and Judy consulted the map.

She looked back quickly, visibility down to less than 100 metres, the line of individuals stretched out well beyond that. "Just as well we've stopped. People are starting to flag."

"Give them a chance to catch up, eh?"

"We're not all as fit as you, Gavin." She smiled. Generally, his sense of humour was good, but Judy felt sure that he could snap if the wrong buttons were pushed. Back at the motorway camp, he had been one of her biggest challengers. But once she listened to his argument or proposal, he generally accepted her final decision with good grace.

He pointed ahead. "The A40 is about 300 metres down there. You can just see an outline of a car up ahead, one of many abandoned cars across the UK."

"We crossing it?"

"No, I'm proposing we use it."

"Is that a good thing, Gavin?"

"Look, the snow on this road is about half a metre thick now and we can cope with it, but over there," he pointed to the fields beyond, "it will now be impassable. And look," he held out a gloved hand, "the snow is thickening. It has to be the main road if we are to get to the reservoir. We can't use the snow for water. We've tasted it."

"Won't the reservoir be contaminated as well, then?"

"Hopefully, the volume of water in it will dilute the stuff in the snow. As for the water already there, I don't know, but I'm sure that water itself can't be affected by radiation, only what gets in it."

"You mean the fallout?"

"I'm hoping that will have settled on the bottom," continued Gavin.

"You're hoping?" asked Judy.

"Come on, girl, none us know what's what anymore."

"Sorry, you're right."

"We said porridge for tonight. That'll require a gallon of water."

Gurvinder and Fiona, closely followed by Andrea and her two girls, crashed down on the bank just behind Gavin and Judy. Jacqueline, Natalie, Wesley, Daniel, and Alysha slumped down on the opposite bank.

Steve jogged up to join them, interrupting their conversation. "Marc's taken a tumble."

"Is he OK?" Judy was concerned.

"Bad gash on his upper arm, tripped over some junk at the side of the road, but Philippa is patching him up."

"Thank God we have a nurse." Gavin heaved a sigh of relief.

Zack, Ellen, and Cameron joined the group, soon followed by Robert and Ollie.

The last one to appear was William. "Everyone accounted for. I'll warn everybody to take extra care. There's so much shit been blown across the country. Did you notice the bath in the hedgerow back there?"

"Now, there's a luxury long gone," responded Judy.

Together, Steve, Gavin, William and Judy debated their next move, the rest of the group happy to leave the decisions to the four, particularly trusting that Judy would make sure the final decision was the right one.

"Gavin is suggesting we use the A40, which is up ahead, to get to the reservoir and top up with water," Judy informed the other two.

"Dodgy, but is there an alternative? This lot'll never make it across country."

"I'm not sure I'd make it either," responded Judy.

"Or any of us," added Gavin. "If the rate of snowfall continues like this, we'll just get bogged down."

"The road it is then," agreed Steve.

"Could everyone gather round please?" called Judy.

"Come on, folks, up you get," added Gavin.

Judy glanced at him sharply, wondering why he felt the need to reinforce her request with an instruction.

With a few groans, the group levered themselves up off the snow-covered bank and shuffled around the four already standing.

Judy gave them all a smile, and thanked them for pushing hard and getting this far so quickly. Philippa and Marc joined them. "How's the arm, Marc?"

"Smarts a bit, but Philippa's done a good job in patching me up."

Judy looked across at the freshly bandaged arm, the man's shirt and jacket sleeves tucked up out of the way. She noticed blood oozing through a red patch of the otherwise white gauze, drips of blood running down his wrist from where the gash had been attended to. Droplets fell onto the white snow, staining it a dark brown.

"I've cleaned it out as best I can, Judy, but it does need stitches," Philippa said defensively, noticing Judy eyeing the blood-soaked bandage.

"Will it stop eventually?"

"I don't know. I have a stapler. I could try and pin it together that way."

"If you don't mind."

"It'll hurt."

"Are you happy for Philippa to do that, Marc?"

"Sure, Judy, I've experienced worse," responded Marc, a veteran of the forces and having survived after being shot on a tour in Northern Ireland in the late seventies.

"How long, Philippa?"

"Give me ten minutes."

The group opted to remain standing while they waited for Philippa to complete the first aid on Marc's arm, their bodies cooling, stamping their feet, flapping their arms about their bodies to stimulate circulation. Although tired and weary, to a man, mentally, they urged Philippa to finish the task speedily so they could continue walking. Marc cried out twice as Steve, Philippa not having the strength to squeeze the staples through the man's skin, punched four staples into the wound, pinning the two folds of flesh together. A fresh dressing, and the group were ready to move on. The line of march was pretty much the same, except Judy swapped Steve and William with Zack and Cameron. Zack and Cameron took their places at the rear of the column, and she kept Philippa and Marc at the front where she could keep an eye on him.

It was now four thirty-five. They had made good progress, completing eleven kilometres. It was time to find a place to stop over for the night. Although not a dual carriageway, the A40 was a half decent road. A single lane of abandoned, snow-covered wrecks lined the westbound carriageway, no doubt queuing previously to get onto the M5. Although the snow hadn't been disturbed, no doubt at some point prior to the snow starting, the cars, lorries and buses had been ransacked. Judy and her group were experienced enough to know that in those circumstances, they were unlikely to find anything of value. Just a two-kilometre walk to the Dowdeswell Reservoir to go, and the group could hold up for the night. They were generally positive now they could sense the end of the day's marching was in sight.

The pack had trotted at a steady pace, probably moving at twice the speed of the human pack ahead of them in order to catch up. Her hunger sated by the human remains picked over back at the derelict house, the poodle, named Bianca by her owners, had set off, her nose sniffing at the scent left behind. It was too fresh for the steadily falling snow to obliterate completely and the trail quickly led her on the right trail, the Alsatian, Rambo, close on her heels, and the remainder of the pack following a few metres further back. She sniffed around by the brook where the human pack had stopped. Confused for a few moments, it didn't take her long to pick up the spoor leading east. Within three hours, the dogs had reached a point near to the junction with the A40. Bianca sniffed the blood around by the now exposed and rusting wing of a car, licking the drops dispersed in the snow. She didn't need much guidance now, the drips of blood acting as a large arrow pointing in the direction the human pack were moving. Heads down, noses close to the ground, the rest of the pack ran backwards and forwards, lapping at any blood spots they could find, heads moving from side to side, sniffing the air, paws padding through the snow, following the route taken by the humans. It wasn't just the blood now, but the closer they got to the people ahead of them, the stronger the odour. The pack's blood lust was rising. Not all had managed to get their fill from the scrawny woman provided for them. And since then, others had joined, content, for the moment to remain on the periphery.

Cameron tapped Zack on the shoulder, handing him the shotgun. "I'll catch you up. Going to try and get some fuel out of one of these cars."

"You sure? They've probably already been done. Sure you'll be OK?"

"Yeah, yeah. If I can get some fuel, it'll help light the wood. Bound to be damp."

"If you're sure."

"Do you see anyone around?" Cameron shrugged, arms out at chest height.

Zack laughed. "Nah, see you later."

Cameron dropped the rucksack and bags he was carrying, most of it his personal items plus the obligatory extra rations of food and water, and brushed the snow from the rear of the car, a Skoda Fabia. After a bit of an effort, he managed to prize off the fuel flap with a screwdriver. He untwisted the cap and a quick sniff test indicated there could be fuel in the tank. Rummaging through his bag, he extracted a long length of plastic tube and a thick plastic water bottle, the type used by walkers.

Bianca, a continental clip for her coat, an inch and a half off the skin. Shaven face to improve visibility, with some hair, like bobbles, left on the ankles and top of the head for additional warmth in water, watched, her muddy white coat blending in with the muddy snow that had been crushed by the passing of Judy's group. The Alsatian, held back, still smarting from the sharp fangs of the other pack leader. The rest of the group lay down in the snow, waiting.

Cameron was oblivious to their presence as he focused his attention on guiding the tube through the filler and deeper into the tank. He wiped snow from his eyes, the flakes thickening, a smile across his face as the feedback from the plastic tube confirmed it had reached the bottom. He lifted it slightly, not wanting to draw up any contaminants that may have settled on the bottom, and twisted the container base into the snow so it had a solid surface to sit on.

Bianca padded silently closer, wary, but hunger driving her onward.

Cameron, satisfied all was ready, knelt in the snow and placed the end of the tube in his mouth, sucking hard through his mouth, inhaling quick breaths of air through his nose as he sucked harder and harder, sensing the fuel ascending the tube.

Bianca, now no more that three metres away, wandered sideways, positioning herself directly behind the human.

Cameron coughed and spluttered as the unleaded petrol flooded into his mouth and he thrust the tube into the container as the fuel splashed everywhere.

Bianca struck. She leapt at Cameron's body, her front paws knocking him onto his side, her fangs bared and mouth drooling as she savaged his face. He hit out, her teeth tearing a strip of Cameron's lower lip away as she rolled over in the snow. Before he could recover and scramble up from the ground, Rambo collided with him, the fragrance of blood sending him into a frenzy as he tore at the man's face. Although Cameron managed to get a grip of the Alsatian's neck with his hands, it was a fight he couldn't win. Bianca was back, and now the rest of the pack entered the fray, nipping at his arms and legs, teeth biting through his clothing, dragging him away from the car until he was in the centre of the frenzied pack. Fangs ripped at his flesh as well as each other, and there were barks and yelps of excitement and pain. Bianca's grip on his throat, released briefly only to allow her to tighten it, securing the soft flesh in her clamp-like jaws, prevented Cameron from crying out. With bulging eyes, arms entrapped by snapping incisors, he quickly drifted into unconsciousness as the pack slowly tore the cloths from his body, ripping off chunks of flesh, gulping them down before the others could snatch them.

Gavin clapped Zack on his shoulder. "Where's Cameron?"

"He's back there." Zack pointed behind him. "Said he wanted to get some petrol."

"You left him on his own?"

"He said he'd be OK," responded Zack, perturbed by Gavin's reaction.

"We shouldn't leave anyone on their own. Judy," Gavin shouted, "I'm going to get Cameron."

"Where is he?" she asked, running over.

"Back there."

"What's that?" Her ears pricked up.

All three strained to identify the distant and muffled noises they could hear, the heavy snow acting as a soundproof blanket.

"What's he doing?" asked Judy.

"Syphoning fuel," responded Gavin.

"Why didn't you stay with him, Zack?"

"I offered, Judy, but he insisted he'd be OK."

A sudden change in wind direction brought the sounds of the furore.

"Christ, what the hell is that? Zack, with me. Judy, get some help." Gavin grabbed Zack's arm and ran towards the sounds and the last place Cameron had been seen. Judy started to call out names, seeking additional support for whatever trouble Cameron was in.

Zack nearly slipped and fell, fumbling with the shotgun, more use to handling the assault weapon that was currently with William.

"For God's sake, don't drop that," called Gavin, his own shotgun held at the ready.

The noise of the ruckus became louder the closer they got.

"It's bloody dogs," yelled Gavin. "Come on, run."

Both picked up speed, icy clouds of breath framing their faces as their lungs laboured in the cold. The swirls of snow suddenly cleared, and the sound of the snapping, snarling pack was audible. They could also see now the commotion in front of them: multi-coloured fur scrabbling on the ground amongst the blood-splattered snow as they tore at their victim, oblivious to the onlookers.

Gavin fired a single barrel into the air, not wanting to fire at the dogs for fear of hitting Cameron. He needn't have worried: Cameron had perished minutes before, his throat ripped out by Bianca. The pack, startled, scattered as a second blast from Gavin's shotgun ensured he had the dogs' attention. Just one dog was left, and Gavin looked on in astonishment as the poodle, its coat mud and blood-splattered, used to the sound of shotguns when out hunting, snarled, teeth bared, lips drawn back over its fangs, hackles up, causing Gavin's skin to prickle. The dog looked at the commotion behind Gavin and Zack as the others arrived and then raced off to join the rest of her pack who had scattered at the sound of the gunshots.

Judy shot past and dropped to her knees alongside Cameron, his bloodied clothes torn to shreds, his face unrecognisable, a hand missing. Her head drooped.

"No good?" asked Gavin, joined by William and Ollie.

She got up from the pink-tinted snow. "He's dead. We shouldn't have left him on his own."

"I'm sorry," muttered Zack. "He insisted."

"Lesson learnt," she said. "Now, let's get him covered, and get everyone to safety before the dogs come back."

"We need to leave him," Gavin instructed.

"We can't just leave him like that," responded an astonished Judy.

"He's dead, Judy, and the dogs will want food."

"That's callous, Gavin!"

"Judy, the dogs are obviously starving. If they don't get something to eat, they'll start hunting us."

"But feeding him to a pack of dogs!"

"Cameron's beyond worrying about that, Judy. If we take away their meal then we'll be on the menu instead."

"That's hideous."

"I tend to agree with Gavin," said William. Zack and Ollie were also nodding in agreement.

"We need to go, Judy. Everyone'll be wondering what's happening and getting cold waiting for us," suggested Gavin.

Judy took one last look at Cameron's mauled body and headed back to the group, anger etched on her face; not angry with Gavin, although she disliked the apparent ease with which he was prepared to abandon Cameron's body to a pack of dogs, but just angry. Angry with the politicians who failed to prevent this catastrophe; angry with herself for losing two people in less than twenty-four hours; angry with the icy weather; and angry with her seeming inability to keep everyone safe and secure. I must try harder, she chastised herself. No sacrifice was too much to get her group through this, and the weather and hunting packs would not stop her.

CHAPTER 17

PARALYSIS | GROUND-ZERO +32 DAYS
THE CONVICTS, CROYDON

It was later than planned when they left the café. Keelan's mood was foul after discovering the dead woman. He felt cheated. The boy had shuffled himself so he was behind his mother's body, oblivious to the blood, the dark patches visible on the tiled floor in what little light passed through the opaque plastic sheeting over the window. Keelan was also pissed off because he'd had to move during the night. A steady drip of water from a fragile section of the roof above him had woken him up, forcing him to shift position.

They left the boy where he was, his eyes reflecting his traumatised state. Milo, probably the only one that sympathised with the young boy, had discreetly passed him a tin of tomatoes, not realising that they had taken the only tin opener available. They had checked for dogs before leaving, but the snow, although only a light fall for the moment, was being whipped around by an ever-surging wind, making it difficult to see more than a few metres ahead.

Milo took the lead again, having earned a reputation for being observant and aware of his surroundings, picking out likely places to find food and other titbits, a true scavenger. They crossed the path between the tall building, the factory, they had examined from the outside the previous day and the café they had just left, which took them to the rear of what they believed to be a food factory of sorts. They didn't have high hopes that they would find anything. All the windows had been shattered, and pieces of flat roofing jutting out of the snow were indicative that some, if not all, of the roof was missing. The main door was a double door, solid and securely in place. But the windows along the back wall were all smashed, and access was easily gained to the inside of the factory. All three were relieved as they dropped into the room, grateful to escape the powerful wind and snow that was rapidly turning into a blizzard. The snow-covered floor reflected some light, what little there was from the darkened skies, which radiated through the window showing the space to be a toilet, male urinals along one of the walls.

Salt took the lead this time, Keelan behind him with the shotgun ready. They felt safer with the weapon, but all three were conscious that the seven cartridges were like gold dust and should be husbanded if they were to survive in this dog-eat-dog world they now found themselves in. Salt pulled the toilet door inwards and checked the corridor outside. To the left was a passageway that led to the double doors they weren't able to access. Using a torch, now with fresh batteries taken from the family they had just left for dead, Salt turned right, passing a men's locker room, his footwear sloshing through a ten-centimetre layer of slush. There was also a ladies' toilet and locker room. All were searched for useful items, but to no avail, apart from a cook's knife left in one of the lockers. There were overalls in some, but of no use to the three men.

At the end of the passage, Salt could either go dead ahead, where a door opened into a large office, or go right, a dog-leg corridor taking them to a cleansing area, and eventually around the back of the office. A dozen office desks were covered in the usual paraphernalia, with grey filing cabinets along the back wall, but everything was sodden, a steady trickle of water seeping through the false ceiling and running down the walls and false ceiling onto the surfaces beneath. A cursory search turned up a sealed bottle of water in one of the desk drawers, two pairs of scissors, and a long envelope opener, all of which were pocketed by Salt. Milo found a Mars bar, still in date, but there was mould on the wrapper that had burst open from being submerged in water. Nonetheless, he broke it into three pieces to share with Salt and Keelan.

"You're a star, Milo." Salt smiled as he chewed on the sugary chocolate that tasted out of this world after being deprived of it for so long.

"We can't survive by doing this every day though, Doug," grumbled Keelan. "We'll spend the rest of our bloody lives poking around shitholes like this just to keep our bellies full."

"That's why we need to stick to the plan: find a small group who know what they're doing and latch onto them."

"Then take control," added Milo.

"Exactly," agreed Salt.

"Yeah, and look at the family we just left," moaned Keelan.

"They were just like us, Stan, living on the edge. We need a switched-on group or family who've got it sussed," Salt coaxed.

"Well, there's sod all else in here. Let's move on. Place stinks of damp and mould." Keelan headed for the door, Salt and Milo close behind him. He took a left turn along a narrow corridor, a couple of hand washbasins either side along with slim wardrobes on each side, both with long white coats suspended on coat hangers. At the end, Keelan could only go left and had to jump over a deeper pool of water, set in the ground halfway along the next corridor.

"For disinfecting your boots," Milo advised him.

They had to go left again, down another corridor, before turning left once more. They had effectively walked around the external wall of the office they had just left. Following this last stretch of corridor, now walking parallel with the toilets and locker rooms that were on the other side of the wall, the area suddenly opened up. The three men split up, Keelan aiming for a set of metal double doors straight ahead, while Salt and Milo moved around what looked like a number of production lines, a packing machine, and stainless steel tables. The two men sloshed through the ankle deep water, moving deeper into the production area. Salt's torch beam picked out the reflection from the thick, opaque plastic strip doors, tough, thick strips of plastic suspended from the door frame, allowing access but creating a barrier between rooms.

"Jesus fucking Christ." There followed the sound of retching from Keelan.

"What is it?" yelled Salt.

"Fucking large fridge full of rotting God knows what."

"We're going through here," Salt responded, pushing his way through the plastic strips, Milo catching them and passing through himself.

There were a number of machines, signs showing them to be associated with the preparation of vegetables, rotary peelers, slicers. A sign on the fridge door opposite said 'Cold Storage Room' which, based on Keelan's experience, they avoided. Milo did find a food storage room, but for vegetables this time. It stank as they too were just a rotting mulch.

They heard Keelan crash through the plastic, fighting with it in anger, but losing it, the strips designed to withstand a battering from forklift trucks passing in and out. "This is a dead end, lads."

"I'll just check this last room, eh?" suggested Milo moving to the far end, his torch lighting up a sign that said 'Wheat Flour Storage Room'. "Hey, this looks as if it's a sealed room."

"It won't be as soon as you open that door," advised Salt, looking over Milo's shoulder.

"What've you got?"

"Could be flour in there, Doug."

"What good's bloody flour to us, Milo?" exclaimed Keelan.

"It...it's food, Stan."

"What? You gonna bake some bread?"

"No, but we can mix it with water and make pancakes or flat-bread, or whatever it's called."

"He has a point, Stan."

"We can trade with it as well," suggested Milo, excitedly.

"He has a point there too, Stan."

"You in Milo's fan club or something? Let's get on with it, then."

Milo placed his hand on Keelan's hand that had gripped the handle. "Once the water pours in, we need to be quick and salvage what we can."

Keelan nodded and thrust open the door. The three men moved into the windowless room shining their torches around the floor, walls and surfaces. Slush and water spilled in around their feet, but squeals of delight from Milo on seeing sacks of flour on a raised wooden bench echoed around the room.

"I take my hat off to you, Milo." Keelan smiled as he lifted his beanie a fraction of an inch off his head.

"What do you suggest we do now, Milo?" asked Salt.

"We need some containers to carry some of the flour for our own consumption. We can cook some of it tonight. Then we shut this door back up and come back when we have someone to trade with."

"How do we protect it? Stop some other fuckers from taking it?"

"We make this our base for now, Stan. Keep coming back until we've found somewhere better. People will be starving out there, and this stuff is worth more than gold."

"He has a point there, Stan mate."

"We start searching for suckers to trade with, then."

They all agreed.

They searched the rest of the factory, the three floors above just sales offices for the food-processing factory that had produced pies, pizzas, bread, and pastry-associated products. However, the first floor turned out to be quite a good haul. A coffee machine gave them stale but drinkable coffee granules, sugar and powdered milk. They also found some packets of crisps, a couple of chocolate bars, and pots and pans they could use to cook with. The manager's office gave up three bottles of Champagne and six bottles of Cava, no doubt rewards for successful sales reps or visiting customers that they managed to entice into signing a contract for business.

Salt, Keelan, and Milo felt like kings. Although all the outer offices' shattered windows exposed the rooms to the elements, one internal section was free of water. It was still cold, but at least it was relatively dry. The second floor was bleak, shattered windows allowing the snow to blow through, and the upper floor was completely uninhabitable with the majority of the roof lost.

They spent the rest of the day making their new digs more comfortable, using the white coats, at least the ones that were dry enough, as additional blankets for when they slept. After some coaxing from Milo, Salt and Keelan carried four of the large twenty-plus kilogram sacks of flour up to the first floor where there was a better chance of it staying dry. With cooking oil and olive oil rooted out by Milo earlier, used as a fuel to cook the flour and water mixture with, plus salt, they had a veritable feast. It was pretty tasteless, but that was countered by a tin of tomatoes and, accompanied by two bottles of Cava, they felt like kings once again.

"This is more like it," declared Keelan, settling into position to close his eyes and catnap for a while. This was the warmest, most comfortable and sated they had been for sometime.

CHAPTER 18

PARALYSIS | GROUND-ZERO +32 DAYS
BRAVO TROOP, LONDON

Glen had spent another hour or so exploring the local area. The corridor leading to the old War Office was clear, as were the ladder rungs that took him thirty metres up to a hatch that should have given him access into the buildings above. But it wouldn't budge, and he suspected it was the weight of a collapsed building above pressing down on it. He'd sat on the floor once he'd descended back down to the bottom, eaten a chocolate bar that had been found amongst the supplies in one of the tube train carriages, and washed it down with a few gulps of water. He loosened both his NBC suit and combat jacket to allow some heat to escape and cool down his overheated body. The exertion of opening the lift doors and climbing two sets of thirty-metre ladders had brought on a sweat.

After a ten-minute breather, Glen clambered up from the floor, adjusted his clothing, and headed back along the corridor. However, instead of going left, which would take him back to the MOD lift, he carried straight on down a long concrete-lined corridor until he came to a dog-leg. This took him left, left again, then right. One hundred metres further on, the corridor took a sharp left and, after another fifty or so metres, he arrived at his chosen destination. In front of him, his torch lit up a huge, heavy, red steel blast door, over two metres in height. He was sure it must weigh several tons but the door was open. Two large rotating handles controlling two thick levers, evidently to secure the door, were visible. Glen had been in the bunker before, but had previously entered from the opposite end. He shone his torch around the entrance. A second, equally thick red steel door was visible, GTD6 stencilled on it, just below head height. Both doors, when shut, protected the bunker from blasts, and, as they were gas-tight, would keep out any contaminated air, internal filters sucking in air after filtering out the contaminants. The second door was also open, exposing a blue-grey concertinaed lift door beyond it. Glen moved through the first entrance, took two long strides and was at the second door. This also had two large rotating handles, three spikes of steel, evenly spaced and sticking out at a thirty-degree angle, top and bottom. Had the two doors been closed, and secured from inside, there was no way Glen would have been able to gain access. He studied the lift, shining his torch beam through a small glass observation window, a few centimetres wide, at the top left-hand side of the lift door. He peered through it, angling his torch so he could see inside the lift compartment. He couldn't see much but was confident that it was empty.

With his back against the right-hand wall of the small chamber, protected by the two steel blast doors, and clutching his MP5 in his right hand, he heaved on the handle, pulling the lift door back and open, the clatter of the metal door as it collapsed in on itself echoing loudly in the confined space. Once it was half open, he stopped and entered the lift cage. A quick scan with his torch showed the lift control box, indicating three floors. He assumed he was at the top and that there were two other floors below. He thought for a moment, aware that if he took the lift down to a lower level he would be committed, going down to a level that may be occupied. Providing the lift has power, he thought. A risk: not knowing what he was likely to find. He made the decision and pulled the lift door closed, a steady hum coming from below of what he surmised was the ventilation system. He stabbed the button that would take the lift down to level 2, the next floor down. The lift jerked, jolting him. Then it descended ten metres, the humming sound getting louder as it speeded up, the cage, on reaching its destination, coming to a halt with a shudder.

Glen swivelled round. The exit door was on the opposite side. A yellow light shone through the small window, this time on the right of the exit door. Signs of life, thought Glen, gripping his MP5 in anticipation of any trouble. Maybe there is a government in existence, he hoped silently. Grabbing the handle with his left hand, he tugged the lift door open, pulling it back as far as it would go, the concertina panels clashing as they closed up, allowing Glen a full view of what was on the other side. He quickly took in the layout of the space exposed: a small room with a single desk, a cabinet with a kettle and cups next to it along with a jar of instant coffee, two steel filing cabinets and a small bank of CCTV monitors. Two were showing grey pictures, one the darkened area where Glen had accessed the lift on the upper floor, and the other two revealed images of other corridors, both unoccupied.

A sleepy-eyed, suited figure, slumped in a wheeled office chair, his feet up on a steel desk, an MP5 next to them, scrambled to get up, surprised by the visitor, expecting it to be his comrades returning, his foot catching the sling of the weapon, consequently pitching it bouncing onto the carpeted floor. "Who the hell are you?" exclaimed the man, expecting the return of his colleagues. Recovering rapidly from the shock of the unexpected intruder, he went for his pistol holstered in a belt clip at his waist.

Glen was faster. He exited the lift at a sprint, the butt of his silenced MP5 striking the close protection officer on the side of his head, the metal of the weapon connecting with the man's left temple, rendering him unconscious. The man collapsed, his head striking one of two steel filing cabinets before slumping to the floor, his pistol still in its holster. Glen crouched down, gun at the ready, eyes fixed on the door that led away from the small room, waiting in case someone responded to the noise created by the short-lived fight. Also, he could see a small CCTV camera in the corner of the room, at ceiling height, zoned in on the exit from the lift. He was concerned that it was being monitored elsewhere on the site. After twenty seconds, satisfied that no one was going to respond, he checked the CP officer, seized the man's pistol, removed the magazine, and ejected the round still in the chamber. He did the same to the unsilenced MP5 and placed both of them out of sight behind the steel cabinets. Then he searched the man's pockets, an identity badge showing that he belonged to SC&O19, the Metropolitan Police's specialist firearms unit. Partially hoisting him up by his shoulders, then placing his hands beneath the casualty's armpits, Glen dragged him to the lift, laying the man on his front, black plasticuffs securing his feet and hands. He slid the lift door shut before carrying out a cursory inspection of the room. Nothing of interest caught his eye. His eyes scanned the CCTV screens again, but there was still no sign of movement.

Glen opened the exit door to a corridor carefully, fluorescent ceiling lights enabling him to see down the corridor, a hooded CCTV camera pointing down directly at him. He padded along the carpeted floor, finding a door on either side towards the end of the corridor. Steadying his breathing, MP5 at the ready, he twisted the handle and eased the first door on the left open. Three desks, unmanned, along with a bank of steel filing cabinets, and six CCTV monitors, one showing the lift lobby and the corridor he had just walked down. The others were blank. One desk had some form of intercom system and a large microphone on a bendable stalk. Closing the door quietly, Glen checked the room opposite. This one had a single bed, a duvet with cover thrown back, and a couple of crushed pillows. The pillowcases had a thin black striped pattern on white, similar to the duvet cover. A wall light was on, shining above the headboard, and above it a rail with half a dozen wire coat hangers, two with white shirts and a tie slung over each one. Next to the bed was a small wooden bedside table, a three-drawer chest along the far wall, and a simple padded tubular steel chair next to it. *Is Pindar fully operational?* thought Glen.

He shut the door to that room and opened the connecting door that led to the next corridor, the make-up very different from the section he had just left. Again, the corridor was well lit, this time with half a dozen long fluorescent lights on each side, a framed painting suspended beneath two of them. Where this section of the corridor differed was that it was half the width again, and an array of cable trays ran along the centre of the ceiling supporting a mixture of wires and cables. On each side were two equidistant, vertical, galvanised ventilation shafts, about half a metre in diameter, running up into the ceiling. Glen felt a light draught from the forced air system, cooling him slightly, but the air was still warm and stuffy. To the left of the cable trays, two pipes, a third of a metre in diameter each, ran along the length of the ceiling. An attempt had been made to soften the industrial effect by the placement of four large ceramic plant pots, pale green, matching the walls, the yucca plants close to two metres in height. At waist height were two yellow, fluorescent, glow in the dark strips with signs attached indicating a fire exit back the way Glen had just come and an emergency exit ahead of him.

He checked four more rooms along the corridor: two further single rooms and two that were four-bedded. All appeared to have been occupied at some point, with evidence of the beds having been slept in and various items of clothing strewn across chairs and drawers. A third corridor produced more accommodation and a first-aid room, but the fourth corridor had a large broadcasting studio on the left and what was labelled the MOD briefing room opposite. In the studio, there was large curved news desk with three red conference chairs placed behind it, in front of a yellowish-green background with powerful-looking theatre lights suspended from the ceiling. Two rows of chairs sat facing the console, with two modern television cameras zoned in on the news desk. A few papers had been left on the chairs, but apart from that the studio was deserted. The MOD briefing room was much larger. There was a long conference table down the centre of the room banked by high-backed, red conference chairs. Maps of the world and of the UK adorned the far wall along with two large LED TVs, both with an inbound TV feed and video player. Maps and large aerial photos of the UK were displayed on the walls down the sides of the room. A conference phone/speaker system was in the centre of the table which was clear of paperwork, although several plastic cups, some with the remnants of dried coffee, had been left together with three empty spring water bottles alongside them.

Glen left the room, shutting the door quietly behind him. On passing through the door at the end of the last section of corridor, he came up against a tube shaped entry capsule. Through the tinted bulletproof glass, used to gain access to and from level 2, Glen could see a door, no doubt blast doors around a dog-leg on the other side. Signs informed the occupants that salmon-coloured papers, classified secret and above, were not allowed to be removed from the bunker. The access system on the right, needing the requisite ID pass to enter the capsule, prohibited Glen from going any further, but steps on his left did allow him to access the lower levels. A metre-high vent was set into the wall at the top of the steps and he could feel a steady stream of air circulating around the stuffy corridor. There was a white sign on a green background, an arrow pointing downwards: 'To Bomb Shelter Area'.

Time to explore further down, thought Glen.

"Get him up," ordered one of the suits, pointing at Greg who had slumped back down.

"Christ, he's just been shot," Plato protested.

"Get rid of your kit, helmet, ammo, knives. His too, then get him up," demanded the suit. "Get him up, or I'll finish the job here and now."

Plato stood up, took off his PLCE and removed his and Greg's killing knives.

"Move it."

Plato held back from taking any action, and cursed under his breath as he crouched down next to his injured comrade. Then he examined Greg's dressings and checked the soldier's pulse. "You OK, buddy?"

"Yeah, I'm OK." Then Greg whispered, "We need to take these

fuckers out. Just give me the nod. First opportunity."

The suit kicked Plato hard in the back. "No talking. Get him up."

Greg pushed back against the wall as Plato helped him into a standing position, pulling Greg's good arm over his shoulder.

The suit called over to one of his colleagues, "Adam, frisk these two, will ya?"

Adam came over, handing his MP5 to a colleague standing behind him, and while he was covered by the other two, checked the two SAS soldiers for weapons. He removed two more hidden knives, and checked for other weapons, finding a Walther PPK on each of them. "Walking armouries, these two."

"Done?"

"Yeah, they've nothing else."

"We're army. We're on your side, for God's sake," remonstrated Plato.

"We'll let the boss decide that."

"Who is your boss?"

"The Prime Minister, of course."

"But he's dead," exclaimed Plato.

"We saw him back in one of the tube stations," Greg confirmed with a croak.

"That's why we have a new one. How many are you?"

"Just us two," responded Plato.

"Not a full section?"

"We were just on a recce. Got lost amongst all these corridors." Plato faked a nervous laugh.

"Yeah, right."

"Can we at least keep our weapons?"

"Not a chance. Now, enough talking, let's get moving. Adam, you watch our backs, Frank, you take lead. Jesse, in front of these two, and I'll be right behind them. Let's go."

They got into position, Plato supporting Greg as they negotiated the exit. Retracing the route they had come via earlier, descending the shafts was a particularly difficult and slow process with no help being offered by the suits. Once down a short stretch of corridor, they were back in the BT deep-level cable tunnel. The two soldiers crabbed their way down the corridor, not enough room for them to be completely side by side.

Plato's thoughts were of how the hell they were going to get out of this, and where Glen was. Had he also been captured?

★

Glen made his way down the steps, curving around to the left, another CCTV camera potentially monitoring his progress. Now walking in the opposite direction, down a second flight of steps, he soon arrived at level 1, a sign on the door to the corridor confirming this. A second flight could be seen going down to the ground level, another sign on the wall pointing downwards to the bomb shelter. There was a deeper hum, or more of a drone, which he felt sure was a generator. He peered through the long, thin window on the right side of the door that led to the corridor. Initially, he saw nothing and was about to push the door open when a uniformed individual, red tabs showing him to be a staff officer, exited a room on the right and crossed the corridor to a room opposite. Glen took a deep breath, hesitating, wishing Plato and Greg were here with him. If he walked through this door then he was committed; there would be no going back if he was seen. But, he was resigned to accepting the consequences. It would be madness opening fire, particularly on a senior officer, at the Pindar headquarters, with a possible legal government in control.

"Sod it," he hissed to himself and pushed the door open. Although his MP5 was kept at the ready, the barrel was pointing down in a non-threatening manner.

He went down the full length of the corridor first, noting that the officer had come out of a room that was labelled the emergency briefing room, crossing over to the crisis control centre. Placing his ear to the door of the briefing room, Glen could hear sounds of movement and talking. He eased another door open at the end. A second corridor was revealed, and more doors led off either side to other rooms. One held an IT complex, the servers and hard drives humming away in their air-conditioned room, even drowning out the sound of the generator running somewhere beneath his feet. Behind another door, Glen came across catering facilities, where there was some activity preparing food, but the occupants just acknowledged Glen as he popped his head through and then got back to their tasks in hand. Other rooms were toilets, and a bunkroom that was far more salubrious than the rest he had seen so far and even had a double bed. Beyond that, more accommodation, storerooms, telephone exchange, medical centre and what looked like a breathing apparatus control room, extended duration breathing apparatus secured in large red cabinets attached to the wall. Some of the cabinets were empty, no doubt used by those that explored the city above to check the radiation and contamination levels. Apart from the officer and those preparing food, he was amazed that he came across no one else. It felt like a ghost town. At the far end of the long level 1 corridor, Glen found another set of descending steps, the thrumming noise of the generator coming from below, the air warm and slightly tainted. He clattered down the steps, conscious of time, still needing to make the decision about contacting the occupants of Pindar or returning to his men and linking up with Rolly again. The stairs swung back on themselves, and he arrived at ground level, the lowest point in the complex, other than perhaps the bomb shelter, the noise now much louder. He pushed through a door at the bottom of the stairs that led him into a corridor. The loud but slightly muffled sound of a diesel generator along with its associated pumping equipment, powering the electrics for the Pindar Bunker, emanated from behind a reinforced door on his right. Even through his surgical mask, he couldn't mistake the smell of oil and the stench of diesel exhaust. He would take a quick look along the rest of the corridor before returning to level 1.

The group arrived at the first of the red blast doors, Plato and Greg sandwiched between the four suits.

"Is this Pindar?" asked Plato.

"It could be. It's need to know, so don't worry yourself," answered the head suit with a smirk.

They passed through the first doorway, then through the second entrance, also protected by a steel blast door. Both doors were open, as they had left them. Greg had his right arm around Plato's shoulder, the left arm hanging limp, pain starting to eat away as the morphine wore off. Greg had no choice but to dig deep. The four men had been relentless in getting the two soldiers back their HQ and would not tolerate any delay as a consequence of his injuries.

"Hey, the lift's not up here," blurted out Frank, who was standing next to the lift door on the other side of the second red blast door. He turned towards the head suit. "We left it up here. No reason why it should be down below."

"Hit the button. You and Jesse watch the lift, Adam and me'll watch these two. Drop down to the ground, you two." Adam pushed on Plato's shoulder, signalling for him to get down. Plato helped lower Greg to the concrete floor, and Greg slouched up against one of the walls. Then Plato crouched down next to him, his eyes flickering over his captors.

"Don't get any ideas," warned the head-suit, indicating with his pistol what the consequences would be if they tried anything.

All eyes turned towards the lift as they heard the clunk of lifting gear as it took up the weight of the cage and started to hoist it up from the floor below.

Back at level 1, Glen made his way along the corridor, passing through the interconnecting doors moving to towards the two doors he had seen earlier, the one labelled as the briefing room and the other as the crisis control centre. Just as he was approaching the entrance to the control centre, the door handle moved, and Glen quickly dashed back and through the interconnecting door again, and peered through the glass panel, glad he'd shifted speedily as he watched at least a dozen individuals cross the corridor, leaving the control centre and entering the briefing room. He picked out what looked like a rear admiral, gold embroidery on the cuffs indicating his rank, and a brigadier and a colonel, both in combats, both armed with pistols. They were followed by half a dozen men in suit trousers, smart shirts and ties. A couple had their sleeves rolled up – not surprising, the bunker was warm, particularly so for Glen with his NBC kit over the top of his combats. Two women, both wearing dark skirts and white blouses, along three other men in full suits, followed. One of the suits entered with the group, and two remained outside. Glen was sure they had the look of close protection officers, cops in suits. I can't mistake them, thought Glen with a smile, remembering the many times he and his men had fulfilled a similar function. Well, in for a penny, in for a pound, he thought. If it went tits up, he'd be in the shit, but at least Plato and Greg would be free.

Making sure his weapon was pointing downwards, he pulled the door of the corridor towards him and stepped through the doorway, his hands held out in front of him in a non-threatening gesture. The two men reacted quickly, screaming at him to put his hands on his head and drop to the floor.

Well over the top, thought Glen.

Pistols aimed at him, the two men continued to scream orders as Glen slowly placed his hands on his head and dropped to his knees. The third CP officer that had gone into the briefing room with the rest of the crowd came out to discover what the commotion was. A fourth ran out of the crisis centre. The two nearest CP officers, their knees bent, assuming a firing position, pistols held out in front of them, moved closer to him, one step at a time, screaming constantly not to move, to interlace his fingers, to stay still…

"On your face!" screamed the nearest officer. "Hands stretched out in front of you. Then don't move a muscle."

Once Glen had complied, the closest ran to him. He pulled the silenced MP5 off Glen's shoulder, removed his pistol, rifled through his pockets, finding the Walther PPK, his second one, the first given to Judy back on the M5, and secured it. The man then took Glen's knife from its scabbard and searched his pockets a second time for any additional weapons, finding nothing.

"Right, get up."

Glen drew his body in, getting onto his hands and knees and then, with no help from his captor, stood up. He was frisked again.

"They want him inside," called an army officer who had just popped his head through the doorway of the briefing room. "Get his weapons' harness off first."

Glen unbuckled his PLCE and dropped it to the floor, one of the suits kicking it aside.

"You, this way," called the CP officer who had searched him. He was manhandled towards the door and unceremoniously pushed through, two other suited guns pulling him from the other side, pushing him down onto a chair that had been placed by the wall opposite the table for that purpose.

Glen looked at the faces staring back at him, a collection of officials sitting on plush dark red chairs around a long, oval-shaped, ash-coloured conference table, boiled sweets and bottles of spring water, along with clean glasses, set in the middle. He looked at the faces, the men clean-shaven, the women well dressed and hair well cared for. Their clothing was clean, freshly pressed. He felt dirty. His NBC suit, grimy from passing through the Underground tunnels and entrances, crawling through the small spaces to get into the bunker complex beneath Whitehall, was also torn in places. His kit hadn't been cleaned for two or three weeks now, and he hadn't shaved for at least two weeks. Although he did his best to keep his body clean, that hadn't been possible these last few days, and he was conscious of his own smell in this lightly scented room.

At one end of the room was a podium with a microphone on a silver-coloured stalk. Behind it, a tall, fairly slim civilian stood, hands resting on it. His dark blue suit looked immaculate, along with his light blue shirt and dark yellow tie. His hair, thinning a little on top, was well groomed and his jawline was firm, the opposite to some of the other probable civil servants sitting around the table. The brigadier and colonel eyed Glen fiercely. Glen was a little surprised at this. They were fellow soldiers after all. Or were they? The colonel's pips on his tab at the front of his MTP combat jacket were upside down. No professional soldier would make that mistake, surely.

"You're probably wondering who we are just as we are concerned about your identity," echoed the man's voice as the microphone magnified his announcement. "Well, I am Alex Mitchell, the Prime Minister, and these ladies and gentlemen are my Cabinet and chief advisors." His arm waved in the direction of the group sitting around the conference table. "So, that brings me to the question: Who are you?"

Glen didn't answer straightaway, a myriad of thoughts running through his mind as to what tack to take. The room was stifling, and the numerous layers of clothing that were essential outside in the bitter cold were superfluous in the confines of the bunker complex. Sweat was running down his face and neck. "Could I ask the brigadier a question?"

"It should be us asking you the questions but, as you're military, I'll allow you to confer with your senior officer first."

Glen looked perturbed at the statement the Prime Minister had made and turned to look at the brigadier. "What was your parent unit, sir?"

The officer's brow wrinkled, confused by the question. "I'm not sure what you mean by that question…and your rank is?"

"My rank is sergeant." Glen maintained eye contact with the man in uniform. "Although you are now a brigadier, you would have belonged to a parent unit, infantry battalion, tank regiment or the like. So, who?"

"Don't be impertinent, Sergeant," snapped the brigadier. "Remember who you're talking to."

"That's what I'm trying to establish: who am I talking to?"

The Prime Minister interrupted. "That's fine, Brigadier. The sergeant is quite right in trying to establish credentials before he answers our questions. Brigadier Howard was appointed by me, Sergeant…"

"Lewis, sir."

"You're sweating, Sergeant."

"It's a tad warmer in here than it is outside, sir."

"Please pass the man a glass of water, Patricia, would you?"

"Yes, Prime Minister." The woman, the person closest to Glen, got up and poured Glen a glass of water from one of the bottles of mineral water on the table. She crossed the conference room, just a couple of steps, and handed the glass to Glen who thanked her. The smell of hairspray and perfume was strong, her blouse looked fresh and crisp, and Glen couldn't mistake the wrinkling up of her nose as she leant in close. However, she did give him a small smile as she handed him the glass of water. He thanked her again and took a few sips.

"Better?"

"Yes, sir, thank you."

"Brigadier Howard was appointed by me. He has no military background, but I consider him the best man for the job."

Surprised by the explanation, Glen responded, "But where are the chiefs of staff? The Chief of the Defence Staff, First Sea Lord, Chief of the Air Staff?"

"A good question, Sergeant, which I'll answer. But, then, we need some answers from you, OK?"

Glen nodded.

"A lot has happened in the last month, as I'm sure you are well aware. The UK, as a functioning civilisation, has been all but annihilated. We had some initial contact with a few of the Regional Government Centres, but even that contact has now been lost. Apart from the devastation, the lack of food and medical supplies has had an overwhelming effect on the population's well-being. Disease has become our newest enemy. Once the first three weeks had passed and it was deemed to be relatively safe to leave the protection of this bunker, the PM naturally sent out groups to explore our surroundings. Unfortunately, the spread of disease out there struck us here. The Prime Minister, the Cabinet members that were here, the senior military advisers were all struck down by typhus. The entire COBRA group moved to an Underground station in an attempt to isolate the spread of the disease until it could be contained and treated, but that was unsuccessful."

"I saw the bodies."

"Are you on your own, Sergeant?"

"Yes."

"So, your turn to answer the questions we have for you."

"Before that, could I ask just one last question?"

"Just the one. Then I must insist that we acquire some information from you."

"Who are you and who are these people?" Glen swept his arm around the group sitting around the oblong table.

"We are the survivors. We are all that's left of the UK Government. We are all senior civil servants, so have a deep understanding of the functions of government. As a collective, we are in the best position to return the country to some form of organised administration."

"So none of you are military or elected Members of Parliament?"

"We are the Government, Sergeant, that is all you need to know," snapped the Prime Minister. "Now, tell us about yourself."

The sound of the lifting gear could be heard as it wound the lift to their level, the top of cage visible as it slid past the observation window of the metal lift door. It came to a halt, and Frank clasped the handle of the lift door.

Greg slumped forward, groaning.

"Get him up," shouted the head suit.

"He's bloody wounded and we've just dragged him here. What do you expect?" retorted Plato.

Frank hauled the door back, the clattering loud as the folds of the door collapsed. Shocked, he stepped back as he saw the struggling suited figure bound with plasticuffs, wriggling on the floor, frantically struggling to remove his bonds.

"Shit, it's Derek."

"Get him out of there," yelled the head suit.

Taking advantage, as all four of the CP officers were distracted, Greg and Plato leapt into action. Greg, who had deliberately slumped forwards on a signal from Plato, unzipping his NBC suit as he did so, grabbed the ankles of the head suit standing next to him, pulling hard on both, screaming as pain ripped through his wounded shoulder. But he was successful: the CP officer, his arms flailing as he fell backwards, both feet pulled off the floor, slammed into his fellow officer, Adam, behind him. He dropped his pistol as he frantically tried to break his fall.

Greg leapt up, ignoring the waves of pain and nausea threatening to overwhelm him, pulling a push knife, a short stabbing blade with a T-shaped handle at ninety degrees to the blade, from a slot in the lining of his combat jacket. He stepped over the head suit, positioned himself behind Adam, applying the stabbing knife to the man's throat, and picked up the pistol dropped during the fracas.

In the meantime, Plato, having extracted his push knife, flew at Jesse, stabbing the man in the neck, a fatal wound, the CP officer dropping his weapon as he clamped his hand over his severed jugular, the blood pumping through his fingers. Plato shoved Jesse aside, picked up the dropped weapon, and pistol-whipped Frank who was bending over, helping to free his CP colleague lying on the lift floor. The man slumped unconscious over the still struggling officer, and Plato turned to cover their captors and check on Greg.

But he needn't have worried; everything was under control.

Greg pulled his face mask down and uttered a word that brought a smile to Plato's lips: "Wankers."

Jesse, who had dropped to his knees, slid sideways onto the concrete floor as his life-giving blood flowed from his body.

"Do something for him, you bastards," yelled the head suit. "He's dying."

"It's fatal, and if you wankers had been a bit more considerate it would never have come to this," growled Greg.

Plato checked the dying man and nodded in agreement with Greg's assessment of the officer's survivability.

"Very interesting, Sergeant Lewis. I didn't realise that the Russian Spetsnaz were such a huge threat to our country. It's pleasing to know that we had soldiers from your unit, from the SAS, watching our backs. But that's all over. Now, it's all about looking forward, and you can help us with that."

Glen had been questioned for about fifteen minutes, and he had focused most of his responses on the operational role he had been involved in, not discussing anything post the apocalypse, other than his time spent in the first bunker and making his way to London to ascertain what governmental organisations existed. He didn't mention the Chilmark RGC, or the one they had come across on the way to Hereford. He did give them a description of what else he had seen: the devastation, people requiring urgent medical treatment, food, water, and protection. He also pointed out the element of lawlessness that was out there, outside the confines of their secured bunker.

"I trust though that your loyalties are still to the Government, and you will accept the authority that has been invested in this new institution?"

"I don't see as I have much of an option."

"In some respects, that's correct, Sergeant Lewis. The country is still under military law, and you are a soldier that comes under both that and the laws that govern your service in the armed forces. Brigadier Howard is in command of our military now."

Glen raised his eyebrows, something that didn't go unnoticed by the authoritarian Prime Minister.

"We don't have a large force. A dozen soldiers are currently patrolling areas of the City, passing the word to those they can find that government help is on its way. Then we have our close protection team under the command of Chief Inspector Jameson, who comes under my direct control, naturally. When Captain Chambers, who reports to the brigadier and his chief of staff Colonel Stewart, returns, along with his small force, I will place you under his command. An extra senior non-commissioned officer will add some rigour to the command structure."

"I'm sorry...Prime Minister, but how can you hope to provide security for the country with a force that's...what...ten, twenty, thirty strong?"

"We will gather resources as we expand our search and area of influence." Then, leaning forward, thumping the podium for emphasis, he continued, "We can gain control, reinstate government authority, and rebuild our country until it is the great country we know it can be. Are you with us then, Sergeant?"

"Of course, sir, I'm a soldier. It's my responsibility to support our civilian government. It's what's drummed into us throughout our training." Glen's thoughts however, were very different. His mind was racing. What civvy could be appointed to the rank of brigadier with no military training? Who were the rest of the Cabinet that were sitting around the table, their silence ominous? How was he going to get away from this Mickey Mouse Government and its despot leader?

"Capital, Sergeant, capital. If you go with one of my protection officers, they will take you somewhere where you can bunk down, perhaps get a shower and some clean clothes, yes?"

"I like the sound of that, sir. I'm sure I don't smell too good."

"Of course, of course. Once you've got yourself cleaned up, Brigadier Howard will brief you on our set-up and what his expectations are of your duties going forward. Yes, Brigadier Howard?"

"Yes, sir. If your officers can inform me when he's ready and of his location, I'll collect him and can acquaint him with our organisation in the MOD briefing room."

"Excellent. Chief Inspector, if you would be so kind as to escort the sergeant to his accommodation?"

"Yes, sir," replied the head of the close protection team.

Glen placed his now empty glass on the carpet and stood up. "What about my weapons, sir?"

"You're safe here, Sergeant. We're well protected by the chief inspector and his men. Once we've established your operational role, we can certainly provide you with what's needed to fulfil your duties. That's all. I have a meeting to continue. Thank you."

Glen was hustled out of the room, taken down the corridor to the right and through a couple of the interconnecting doors before being bundled into a washroom area.

"Dump your gear here and get a shower. What you're wearing is rank."

Glen bit his tongue and nodded.

"By the time you've finished, there'll be some fresh clothes brought for you. There'll be an officer outside, armed, so don't do anything stupid. There are no windows, and this door is the only way in and out."

With that, the man left Glen to his own devices. And Glen was more than happy to wash the grime off his body. He was looking forward to putting on a set of clean combats. In the meantime, his brain sieved through the options that were available to him in order to get back to his men.

CHAPTER 19

PARALYSIS | GROUND-ZERO +32 DAYS
BRAVO TROOP, LONDON

Plato and Greg shoved their three escorts over by the entrance to the lift, ordering the men to their knees, hands on heads with interlaced fingers, and to be quiet. The fourth CP officer was still lying on the floor of the lift cage, the fifth dead, lying in a pool of congealing blood.

"What shall we do with these four?" Plato spoke out loud.

"Finish them off," snarled Greg.

"Tempting. You any plasticuffs?" asked Plato, holding two pairs he had extracted from his belt kit.

"Yeah, here." Greg pulled a couple of sets from his kit and handed them to Plato.

One at a time, Plato forced the hands of the CP officers behind their backs, wrapping each of the interconnecting plastic strips, similar to cable ties, around their wrists, pulling them tight, a zipping sound as the cuffs were pulled through the locking device. He then ordered them to lie on the concrete floor, where he secured their ankles with strips of paracord. Although able to shuffle along the ground, or push themselves up against a wall, they were generally secure. However, if left to their own devices, Plato was confident they would be able to release each other fairly quickly. He whispered to Greg, "You need to stay with them, mate. If they're left on their own, they'll be free in no time. Then they could come at us from behind."

"Don't like the idea of you not having backup, but you're right: someone needs to watch over them. Anyway," he winced as he lifted his left arm slightly, "this complicates things."

"Agreed then."

"Yes, but you've got two hours. If you and Glen aren't back by then, I'll pistol-whip all four of them and come looking for you."

"Sounds good. I'll just drag this one out of the lift and go a-hunting." He pulled the officer out of the lift, and positioned all four so they were lying lengthways, singly, along the corridor. None of them could make physical contact without having to shuffle their bodies, but that in turn would alert Greg.

Greg slid down the wall opposite, groaning as he did. He sat with his legs out in front of him, watching over them with a pistol held across his lap.

Plato took his silenced MP5 which had been commandeered by one of their guards, and checked it was loaded and ready. He only had the one magazine, the PLCEs taken off them earlier, but was supplementing his firepower by taking two of the Glock pistols, carried by the CP officers, and some spare magazines. Tucking one in his waistband and one in his holster and with his MP5 slung around his neck, he was ready. He checked Greg's wound. It had burst open, seeping blood – unsurprising, considering the last few minutes – but the blood loss was minimal. "No morphine," he whispered to Greg. "Need you focused."

"Kindness and light, as always."

Plato smiled. "Back before you know it, buddy."

With that, he moved into the lift cage, pulled the door shut, and stabbed the button for 2. The rattling of the lift seemed disproportionately loud as it moved down the shaft. As it shuddered to a halt, Plato checked through the vision window. Seeing nothing, he pulled the door back, wincing as the metal door clattered back on itself. He did a quick visual sweep, noting the desk, cabinet and CCTV cameras, but seeing no guards. Looking through the window in the door to the corridor, he saw that it was clear, and noted the humming sound of the ventilation system. He went through the interconnecting door and explored that section of corridor. Like Glen earlier, he checked the rooms, astonished at the sense of order compared to what they had left outside, cold, diseased, and hungry refugees. He could feel sweat running down his back and unzipped his NBC jacket along with his combat jacket. It gave some relief, but he was still overheating, the air stifling after being in the relatively cooler tunnels. The office-like rooms were empty, as were the bunkrooms, until he came to the last one. As he pushed open the door of a four-man room, a civilian, dressed in suit trousers, white shirt and tie, sitting at the end of one of the beds, dived for his pistol lying on the bedside cabinet.

Phut...phut.

A double-tap from his MP5. A red bloom formed on the right of the man's shirt and a perfectly round dark hole appeared just above his temple as a second shot knocked the man sideways, rolling off the bed onto the floor the other side. Plato rushed into the room, clearing the rest of the space, shutting the door behind him before checking the person he had just shot. Satisfied the man was no longer a threat, Plato surveyed the room, taking in its sparse but functional features, certainly an improvement on the facilities available outside of the bunker.

Pocketing a third pistol and another couple of magazines, Plato exited the room, checking the area outside carefully. The steady hum of the ventilation system was all he could hear. Through the next door, he encountered a different style of corridor: wider, well lit, less plain with more of an industrial feel to it. He looked up at the line-up of cable trays and cables that ran along the ceiling and observed the vertical ventilation shafts standing either side. Plato smiled when he saw the potted plants, such a contrast to the burnt and wilted vegetation above them. He checked some more rooms along the corridor, on the alert, conscious that he had already come across one occupant. He found plenty of evidence, scattered clothing, empty water and coffee mugs, empty biscuit wrappers, that the rooms had been occupied.

Along a third corridor, he found more accommodation and a first-aid room, and in the fourth corridor, a broadcasting studio with a sign indicating its purpose, an MOD briefing room opposite. He suspected that Glen may well have come along this very same corridor. He listened at the doors, hoping to hear sounds that might indicate Glen's location, but he didn't enter any of them, not wanting to risk another encounter and warning the occupants of his presence. But he had no luck in finding Glen.

Looking through the glass window of the next connecting door, he spied another suited individual. The man was leaning against the wall of the corridor, a pistol in his right hand, seemingly guarding the door opposite. Plato considered his next action: should he just announce himself and ask about Glen straight up? Maybe Glen had made contact. Find Glen and whoever was in charge and this mess could be cleared up and Greg could receive medical treatment. But then he had reflected on the fact that Greg was wounded, had been left guarding four men, who had hardly been friendly, and he had no idea where his team leader was. He knew what he had to do. Shoving open the door, silenced MP5 held straight ahead, he fired two shots in quick succession. The CP officer, startled, didn't even have time to raise his gun hand before the first slug struck, hitting him sideways on in the chest, the second smashing into his skull knocking him down, his body thumping onto the carpeted floor. Plato ran quickly towards the body, kicking the dropped pistol aside, and got into position to investigate what was the being guarded, the sign on the door indicating it was a washroom. He twisted the handle, easing the door open slightly before taking a half step back, raising his right leg and kicking the door back on its hinges. Plato heard a grunt from behind the door and rushed through the doorway. The room was lit. Initially, the room appeared to be empty but when he swung round behind the door, gun at the ready, he found a rather startled Glen rubbing his forehead where the door had slammed into his head.

"Fuck, boss, what are you doing sneaking about behind there?"

A smile slowly spread across Plato's face, his scarf and face mask having been pocketed earlier when he noted that the bunker was well ventilated.

"What are you doing here? I thought you were with Greg."

"You're welcome, boss. Next time you need a rescue, don't call me." They both laughed. "What the fuck's going on, boss?"

"I'll explain later. Just the one guard outside."

"Yeah, but he won't be troubling us."

"We have to get out of here. They'll be coming for me soon."

"Is that clean kit you're wearing?"

"Yes, smells good too."

"Any spare?"

"We'll worry about your laundry another time. Let's move."

Glen exited the washroom and bent down, picking up the pistol dropped by the now dead guard and taking some additional magazines from the man's belt pouches. "His mates will be coming soon. We should move."

"What's the score here then, boss? No friendlies?"

"I'll explain on the way. Clear back there?"

"Yes, took out one Tango in a bunkroom. All being well, he won't have been discovered yet."

"One of these?" Glen pointed to the dead man on the floor.

"Yes."

"Back through the door you came through. I'll cover our six."

Plato led the way. After passing through the rest of the interconnecting doors, he turned left up the steps, then back on himself, taking them both up the second flight. At the top, next to the level

2 entry point, he turned right and followed the route he had taken earlier. They picked up speed, preferring a quick exit to silence. Their boots thumped on the carpet as they ran down the corridor, bumping through the interconnecting doors. Their luck suddenly ran out as a uniformed figure, the Walter Mitty brigadier Glen had met earlier, exited the MOD conference room, followed by a civilian with the colonel in tow. Plato crashed into them, knocking the brigadier aside. However, Plato was deflected into the wall, causing him to stumble. The brigadier fumbled with his pistol holster. The colonel, slightly faster, had his pistol out and aimed past the civilian at Plato, squeezing the trigger frantically until he realised with horror that the weapon wouldn't fire. No one had been prepared to trust a civilian colonel with a loaded weapon. Having never fired a gun in his life, the colonel hadn't cocked the pistol, there was no round in the chamber. Glen, meanwhile, fired two rounds, the sound deafening in the confines of the corridor. One hit the civilian, who, in a panic, had run in front of the army officer, in the shoulder. The second bullet tore by and passed through the colonel's throat, destroying his Adam's apple and throwing him back into the room.

Clutching his shoulder, the civilian collapsed, screaming. The brigadier, recognising he had the same problem as his junior, fumbled as he pulled the working parts to the rear, eventually letting them slide forward, forcing a round into the chamber.

Bit too late, thought Plato, having recovered his stance, and firing two shots from his silenced weapon, not that the silence mattered, the pistol shots were sure to have alerted someone. Both hit the uniformed man in the chest, a look of shock and horror on his face. He may not have lived the life of a soldier, or earned the right to die as a soldier, but he was killed regardless.

"Shit," uttered Plato. "That'll have woken everyone up. We need to scarper now."

"Go, go, go," shouted Glen.

Plato didn't need any urging as he crashed through the remaining doors, the last one bringing them both back to the small level 2 lift lobby. The lift door was closed, and Glen grabbed the door handle, sliding the door open while Plato kept watch.

Zing. Crack. Thud. Crack. There was a cacophony of bangs as bullets splintered the doorway and chipped the concrete walls around Plato.

Phut, phut, phut, phut...phut, phut.

Glen heard Plato's MP5 responding before he sprinted from the doorway, a line of bullet holes from an HK peppering the door as Plato pushed it to.

"Aargh, I'm hit," Plato cried out, dragging his left leg, suddenly losing the feeling in his left thigh muscle.

Glen grabbed Plato by his NBC suit jacket, hauling him unceremoniously into the lift, quickly following him then pulling the lift door closed just as two bullets, their force depleted by the interconnecting door, clanged up against the concertinaed metal door. Glen punched the button, and the lift jerked slightly before climbing up to the upper level. The time taken for the observation slit to pass the level of the floor seemed endless. More bullets punched into the door below them, but they were safe, temporarily.

Once they reached the upper floor, Greg, who had heard the lift starting to ascend, and the subsequent gunshots, was peering through the vision slit, looking to see if it was friend or foe about to drop in on him. A grin split his face as he recognised that his boss was returning to the fold. Once the lift had stopped, using his good arm, he helped heave the door open.

Glen pushed past him. "Let's get Plato out, and get the bloody door shut. Tangoes are right on our tail."

"Pleased to see you too, boss."

"I'll give you a hug later." Glen hooked Plato's arm over his shoulders, helping him out of the lift. Plato was limping, the bullet having taken a slice out of his upper thigh. Greg pushed the lift door until it was nearly shut. But it would only delay their pursuers for a couple of seconds.

"I'll help Plato. You watch our backs. Grab some torches. With the door half open, it shouldn't work."

Greg took two of the torches that had belonged to the cursing CP officers and handed one each to Glen and Plato. He already had one for himself. Just as he started to move forward, ready to run down the exit corridor, Plato making the best speed he could, they heard the lift suddenly move.

"Wankers can control the bloody lift with the door open," bellowed Greg. "If only I had my LMG."

The three soldiers shuffled along the BT cable tunnel, depending more and more on their torches as the light from the lift got further away. With his torch beam flickering ahead of them, Glen could pick out the tunnel they needed to follow if they were to get back to the Underground station where they originally entered. At the end of the first stretch, they shuffled right. Glen and Plato had made it round the corner, another section of the tunnel stretching out ahead, just as Greg yelled, "They're on us!"

They moved as fast as they could, but with two of them injured and Plato needing support, progress was slow. Greg covered their backs as they headed for the dog-leg that would lead them to the MOD area and the old War Room. As they turn left at the start of the dog-leg, Glen dropped Plato. His trouser leg was soaked in blood, and they would need to see to the wound pretty soon if Plato was not to lose any more blood. Greg also made his way around the corner, dropping to the floor, groaning as he wrenched his wounded shoulder yet again. He turned back to face the way they had just come, lining up the MP5 towards the blackness where he'd heard the noise of their pursuers. Glen dropped down prone alongside him.

As they waited and listened, there was the sudden glimmer of torches as their pursuers came round the distant corner, making progress directly towards their position. When the lights were less than fifty metres away, Glen jumped up and out into the centre of corridor, firing three double taps from the MP5, in quick succession, the clunking sound of the weapon's working parts resounding off the walls, the discharge of the bullets resonating in the confined space. Glen heard the satisfying sound of their pursuers crying out as the bullets struck, taking two of the CP officers down before the remainder threw themselves to the floor and started to return fire. As the rounds zipped past, like angry bees, Glen ducked back round the corner, sucking in fumes from the firing, slugs smacking into the back wall opposite the firers. He unclipped the magazine, depressed the round at the top, and shone his torch to reveal only three rounds left, plus one in the chamber.

"Time to go, they'll be up and running again soon," he informed Greg, who was helping Plato up supporting Plato with his good shoulder as he did so. "I'll fire these last four. Then, I'll be with you."

"Roger," Greg responded.

Greg and Plato made headway through the latter end of the dog-leg that led to them past the short corridor to the MOD lift, turning left rather than continuing straight on to the dead end and blocked access to the old War Office. Around the next corner, the main cable tunnel came into view and Greg called back to Glen, keeping him informed as Glen watched for their pursuers, "Going right."

"Roger," replied Glen.

Greg could see the T-junction up ahead. His friend was heavy on his good shoulder, stabbing pains lancing through the wound at the back of his neck as Plato's arm pressed down on the lesion. Going left would take them to Court 6 and the Treasury Building, where Greg had been shot, and Greg and Plato had been bounced by the police protection officers; to the right would lead them to the way they had come in at the start of the mission. Now, it would lead them back out. At the T-junction, Greg manoeuvred Plato to the right, out of sight of the tunnel they had just left. He then turned back, dropping down into the prone position, his pistol at the ready, but moaning as he put pressure on his wounded left shoulder. They were joined by Glen who knelt down next to the two soldiers and turned to Plato. "You OK, Plato mate?"

"Felt better, boss."

"You need to get back in the fight. Keep them back, Plato. Cover Greg while he puts a dressing on your leg, OK?"

"I'm buggered then," he responded with a wan smile, his face pale in the torchlight. "Where are you off to?"

"Got stuff to do."

"Doing what?" asked Greg.

Glen crouched down next to Greg and tapped him on his good shoulder. "Plato will cover you while you fix him up."

"Where are you off to. boss?"

"Need to get our stuff. We must have some decent firepower if we're to get out of this place in one piece."

"Two of us are already in pieces." Plato chuckled.

"Here," Glen handed Plato his spare pistol mags, "I'm off." He then sped down the left-hand turn at the T-junction towards where Greg had been shot and they had shot a civilian in return.

Greg and Plato changed positions, Plato aimed his pistol straight ahead into the darkened corridor where the pursuers lay somewhere. Greg had a pistol close at hand, ready to protect their position. Plato could see beams of light flickering at the end of the tunnel. The protection officers were obviously taking it slowly, conscious that they were already two men down, one dead and one with leg and arm wounds.

"They're getting close," Plato informed Greg.

"Keep me posted," responded Greg as he started to cut away at Plato's NBC trousers, then his combats followed by the long johns.

He exposed the wound, having to pull away the material that had stuck to the wound, blood oozing freely from it. "It's taken a strip of flesh from your leg, gouged a slice of muscle. No entry or exit wounds as such. Not looking nice, but you'll be back on your feet within a couple of weeks."

"Hurts like fuck."

"Stop whinging, ya tart." Greg applied a dressing to the wound, pressing it tight, Plato's thigh going into spasm as the pain bit. A first-aid dressing was then applied, Greg wrapping a bandage around the leg, binding it tight, protecting the wound, securing the dressing so that Plato was still able to move.

Plato saw a shadow blocking the end of the tunnel. His head and shoulders just poking around the corner, he fired two shots at the shadow. A cry confirmed that he had hit his target, and the shadowy figure scrambled back seeking cover. A volley of shots quickly followed and Plato pulled his head and shoulders back around the corner just in time.

Crack...crack. Crack...crack.

The salvo continued and bullets smacked into the wall behind Greg and Plato, both men pulling their heads in close to their chests as splinters of concrete flew off and bullets ricocheted around the constricted space. Plato reached out with his arm and let off two quick shots which were followed by a fusillade of rounds in response. A sharp sliver of concrete sliced across Plato's nose and face. He felt the warmth of his blood, and silently prayed that it felt worse than it actually was. He saw Greg's shadow fall on him and felt the soldier's presence as Greg took his turn to let off a volley of gunfire towards the enemy. The response was immediate: another burst of fire causing them both to duck back. The firing then became an onslaught, a sustained attack, forcing Greg and Plato to keep their heads back.

"They're pushing forward," advised Greg. "We need to exfil soon."

Round after round thumped into the wall, giving the two men no opportunity to return fire.

"I think you're right. We have to keep them back." Plato risked an arm and fired a wild shot as bullets zipped past, one plucking at his sleeve. "Shit, that was close."

"Where the fuck's Glen?" cursed Greg.

The firing continued. Both men knew why: the enemy wanted to keep the soldiers' heads down while they crept forward, getting close enough to rush the last few metres. A silent signal was passed between them and the two soldiers shuffled on their stomachs, snake-like, Plato struggling with his wounded leg and Greg feeling sharp stabbing pains as his shoulder was pulled in all directions, further down the cable tunnel towards their exit, preparing to open up on the first person that came into view. But the first person they saw, preceded by a dipped torch beam, was Glen, dropping the pile of helmets, PLCEs, weapons and other kit he was burdened down with on the floor. The LMG was slung round his neck, and he pulled it free as he dropped to the ground and signalled Greg to distract the enemy.

Greg edged forward as quickly as he was able, back to the T-junction, exposing as little of the pistol as possible, bullets zipping past. He fired a burst of shots in the direction of the attackers. That was all Glen required. Twisting the LMG round the corner, firing low, he fired a full ten-round burst of 5.56mm rounds down the tunnel, then followed it up with five-round bursts, the noise thunderous in the confined space, the flashes lighting up Glen's manic features, bulging eyes and gritted teeth. The consequence was more than crippling for the enemy: it was brutal. With over forty rounds slamming into the men who had been crawling along the tunnel, some attempting to maintain a continuous fire to cover the four men behind them who were in position to dash forward and complete the assault, it was carnage. Two were hit by half a dozen rounds within seconds, and two more were struck down as they panicked and ran down the corridor to escape the barrage of death that was picking them off one by one, the rest hugged the ground and prayed they would survive.

"Grab your kit!" ordered Glen as he got up from the floor, leaving the LMG in situ, then pulling the pin on a smoke grenade, counting down and flinging it towards their attackers, the billowing, choking smoke filling the confines of the tunnel.

Greg and Plato, helping each other, quickly crossed to the other side of the tunnel, pulled on their PLCEs and helmets, grabbed their weapons, and ran back across again.

Glen picked up the LMG, put the sling around his neck, and fired another burst into the smoke, and then joined them. "Let's get the hell out of here."

CHAPTER 20

PARALYSIS | GROUND-ZERO +36 DAYS
MOTORWAY TRIBE, NORTH OF NETHERAVON

Heads were bowed, members of the group just placing one foot in front of the other, following the path cleared by those in front. Up to a metre of snow lay on the ground in places and some of the drifts either side were so high they even towered above Gavin's two metres. Everyone was cold, many were chilled to the bone, their clothing damp, the constant drip, drip of melting snow running down faces, finding its way through gaps, through stitching, absorbed by the many layers of clothing. Their last stopover, an abandoned farmhouse east of Devizes, had given them an opportunity to dry some of their clothing, but with temperatures dropping to minus nine centigrade during the night, even with a fire that almost smoked them out, clothing couldn't be left off for long, and many allowed their clothing to steam dry on their bodies rather than face stripping off in the biting cold.

The group had even discussed remaining at the farmhouse for another day, using it as an opportunity to rest, dry more of their apparel, and recover some of their lost strength. The debate had been heated. Gavin, the loudest proponent for moving on, was eventually supported by Judy. The argument for moving was threefold: food was running short – people were eating more than planned, driven to it as a consequence of the continuous, biting cold; and the pack of dogs had been joined by other ravenous dogs, now numbering over thirty, and constantly shadowed the group as they made their way south. The group's saving grace was the weather: the thick layer of snow made it difficult for the dogs to get ahead and encircle their victims. Instead, they had to follow in the footsteps of the human pack, the snow trodden down as the motorway tribe continued their trek towards what they hoped would be a safe haven. Since Dowdeswell Reservoir, they had trudged nearly sixty kilometres over five days.

Although the temperature warmed during the day, a relatively comfortable three degrees centigrade at times, during the night it plummeted to a low of minus nine. One night it had even dropped to minus twelve. Three more of them had died of hypothermia, including Daniel. His shoulder wound taking a turn for the worst, an infection raging through his body conflicting with the bitterly low temperatures, he had eventually succumbed. And Wesley and Natalie, their bodies racked with dying cells as a consequence of radiation sickness, the abdominal pain worsening, the diarrhoea and sickness quickly causing their bodies to dehydrate. Their deaths were agonising to watch.

After another heated debate, the bodies were left as food for the dogs that were hunting them. Although the dogs were constantly hungry, the harsh temperatures ensuring other animal life remained hidden in burrows or nests, the flesh from the human bodies kept the pack's hunger pangs at a manageable level, allowing them to suppress thoughts of a suicidal attack on the live human food supply that was always in front of them. Although the weather helped keep the hunters at bay, it was a double-edged sword, and the third reason why they couldn't afford to slow making their headway south. Even though they were able to push their way through the snow, providing they kept to minor roads or hard-packed lanes, and bypassed any major snowdrifts, the going was deteriorating by the day, and there was a real fear that they would become bogged down without food, adequate shelter or, eventually, warmth. Fuel, such as branches and trees, was becoming harder and harder to get to and difficult to burn in the current conditions. They could burn whatever was in the accommodation they were holed up in but its quantity was limited.

Alysha, distraught at the loss of Daniel, had switched her attention to supporting Andrea, assisting her with her two children, the two girls, who were struggling to maintain the constant pace demanded by the adults. The prams, carrying supplies, had been dumped a long time ago, far too difficult for even an adult to push through the snow. Fiona, Gurvinder, Ellen, and Zack were holding up pretty well but Robert was suffering. Gurvinder and Zack volunteered to carry some of his load, but that just added to their burden, slowing them down.

Gavin was leading followed by Fiona, Gurvinder, Ellen, Zack, Jacqueline, Ollie, Marc, Alysha, Robert, and Philippa, with William and Steve the last two in the column, constantly looking over their shoulders on the lookout for the dogs. Judy moved up and down the line, coaxing the group to keep on the move, promising them that they were only a couple of days away from warmth and safety. She shouted over the noise of the blizzard that was slowly building up, as she approached Gavin. "We need to find shelter, give people a rest."

Gavin stopped as she came alongside. Probably one of the strongest of the group, she was shocked at how haggard he looked. Over the top of a scarf and chopped-off arm of a woollen jumper that were wrapped around his neck and mouth, a pair of sunken eyes stared out.

Gavin would normally argue endlessly to keep the group moving, adamant that the end target, Chilmark, should be reached as soon as possible before they found themselves incapable of taking another step. The majority of the group were now struggling with the bitter cold, the snowstorm driving into them, finding gaps in their protective layers, or blasting through the material of their non-windproofed garments. The minimal rations they were all on, the oppressive cold and hardship of the hike through the snow was proving too much for many of the group.

"I agree." He nodded, wiping the layer of frosted snow that had built up on his sodden scarf. "If we keep moving..." he paused while catching his breath, "...I will keep my eyes open for somewhere. But we can't stop here. If we don't keep moving on this road, we'll literally freeze to death."

"Robert's in a bad way and I need to check on Marc. I'll go back and help and cajole the others, keep them moving," Judy shouted back, the wind shrieking past her, sucking the breath from her lungs, snatching her words away.

Gavin couldn't hear fully what she said, but he got the gist of it and nodded before turning away and, with his head and shoulders bent, continuing to plough his way through a metre of snow, breaking the route for the rest of the group, particularly for the weaker and younger members.

Judy headed back down the line, the blizzard now blasting her from behind, pushing her along faster than she was comfortable with. She came across Alysha first, who confirmed she was OK but pleased that a stopover was planned. Andrea and the kids were behind her. Gurvinder, Ellen, Fiona, and Zack were next, seemingly holding together as a sub-group, probably because they were all of a similar age: Fiona and Ellen were in their mid-twenties, Zack in his late twenties, and Gurvinder, Judy knew, twenty-eight. She noticed that Ellen was carrying Robert's rucksack, but she couldn't see Robert and suspected he was further back. She spoke to all four, giving as much encouragement as she could, asking after Robert who had slowed down and was being helped by others. This was difficult under the circumstances, conversation ripped away in the blustery weather.

Further back, Judy came across Jacqueline, Ollie, and Philippa, another collection of individuals who seemed to have united into a group. Philippa was helping Robert. Jacqueline and Philippa were in their late thirties, Fiona, Judy felt sure, was a little older, maybe early to mid-forties. William, Steve and Marc were the last three in the column, Steve supporting the struggling Marc as best he could, William keeping a watch over the route behind them.

Judy leant in close to William, cupping her hand close to her mouth, up against his hooded ear. "Any sign of the dogs?"

"Nothing..." The wind took his breath away for a moment. "I've stopped occasionally, giving them a chance to catch up, but nothing. They'll be out there though." He indicated back the way they had just come. "Our scent is being blown by this lot directly to them," he yelled.

Judy nodded. "OK. We're going to take a break, so keep walking until you catch up with Gavin."

She could see the smile form behind his balaclava, and he patted her shoulder. Even the young were finding the trek hard going.

She left William and walked alongside Steve and Marc. "We're going...to take...a break," she mouthed.

Marc didn't respond, and she could see he was on his last legs. His boots were sodden as was a good proportion of his clothing. His waterproof jacket protected him from some blasts of wind, but the steady sheet of snow had worked its way closer and closer in next to his skin. His waterproof leggings, taken from Margaret after she had died in her sleep, were preventing some of the rain from getting through, but also containing the wetness of his long johns and jeans beneath them. He was dragging his feet and, as soon as Judy added the support of her shoulder, he slumped against her. She and Steve were supporting almost his full weight, enabling the man to throw one leg painfully forward at a time. His wounded arm, patched up by Philippa, gashed when he fell over and onto some junk blown down onto the roadside during the nuclear onslaught, although weeping badly and in danger of being infected, was free from pain. The layer of icy cold water that encapsulated the wound was helping to almost minimise the pain. However, it was a double-edged sword:

although the lack of pain enabled Marc to keep on the move, it was diminishing his body's ability to heal.

Twenty minutes later, both Steve and Judy were exhausted, practically carrying Marc, and their own rucksacks weighing them down. After another few hundred metres, they met up with Gavin, who was indicating for them to go left, where a path had been beaten through the snow by previous members of the group.

"Here, let me." Gavin shouldered his rifle and took over from Judy, who was clearly flagging, as was Steve, to help support Marc along the final stretch.

Judy trudged behind Gavin as he steered them along the snow-covered pathway. Occasionally, she could see thin, curved slabs of stone jutting up just above the snow. As they got closer to a small building up ahead, it suddenly dawned on Judy where they were: it was a graveyard. Perhaps we may never leave here, and it will be an appropriate last resting place for us all, she thought.

They heaved Marc through the door of what turned out to be a small chapel, William and Zack helping to support him until they could sit him down on the pews. Robert, who was suffering badly from exhaustion and the first stages of hypothermia, was there as well. Philippa came across and took over. There was a hacking sound from near the front of the small sanctuary as Ellen and Gurvinder used small axes to cut away at the solid wooden pews, cutting off enough wood to make a small fire. Then, while Gurvinder continued with the cutting, Ellen collected the small splinters scattered close by, and, using one of their dwindling supply of matches, coaxed a small fire into life, adding larger and larger pieces of kindling until it had caught and was beginning to burn fiercely. The smoke billowed up into the vaulted ceiling, finding its way through gaps in the dislodged tiles. The few windows in the building, although cracked in places, were relatively intact as was the door that Judy, the last one in, had shut behind her.

Everyone gathered close to the warmth, Judy encouraging Andrea's two children, Jade, nine, and Stephanie, eleven, to the front. The first four rows of pews, eight bench seats in total, had been manhandled into two semi-circular rows around the glowing fire. The other eight sets of pews would provide additional fuel, maintaining a steady burn. Although the entire building had been chilled, similar to the outside temperature, the enclosed space soon absorbed the warmth radiated by the fire in between a small altar and the pews. The weaker members of the group were slowly positioned near the front with the stronger ones occupying the second row. A couple of pans were removed from rucksacks, filled with snow from outside, and placed on the fire, the hissing of melting snow as it made contact with the fire a welcome sound.

Although it was cold on the periphery of the single skinned building, in the immediate vicinity of the fire, most were soon feeling the benefits of the crackling flames. The occasional downdraught from the holes in the roof engulfed them in smoke, but it was a small price to pay to be able to dry their sodden clothing and warm their chilled bodies.

Judy, assisted by Philippa, turned her attention to Marc who, although slowly warming up, appeared to be deteriorating. The wound in his arm had opened up again and was red and inflamed.

"We'll soon have you sorted, Marc," Judy encouraged him. "Have you something you can put on it, Philippa?"

"I have some Savlon, that's all. But it's better than nothing."

With Marc's outer jacket and jumper removed, Philippa was able to pull the dressing off completely. The gash was puckered, and the flesh around it rippled from being to a damp surface for so long. "Just rest your hand on my shoulder, Marc. Then I can get to the wound."

"I'll get his bed ready," said Judy.

Philippa wiped the wound with a strip of bandage, cleaning it as best she could. The staples had held two-thirds of the folds together, but the remainder had pulled free, the flesh blue at the edges and weeping blood and pus. Once it was as clean as she could get it, Philippa squeezed a small amount of the white cream from the tube, conscious that she only had one other tube in her supplies and this one was already half empty. She smeared it around the gash, Marc wincing as her fingers probed the wound, ensuring the antiseptic balm covered the exposed flesh as much as possible.

"That's looking better already." Although she smiled, she was deeply concerned by the state of Marc's wound along with his mental and physical condition. Marc managed the best smile he could under the circumstances, but his body was cold and his arm throbbed persistently. She bound the wound with a fresh dressing, but sparingly: they too were in short supply. She had even considered keeping the old used dressings, boiling them in water for reuse, but couldn't bring herself to do it. Things aren't that bad, yet, she thought. She could feel his arm trembling as the wetness started to evaporate from his body, drawing the heat away, causing him to shiver.

"Here." Judy handed Philippa a dry shirt, and together they pulled it onto Marc's shivering frame.

"Right, Marc, I've put your sleeping bag close to the fire along with your wet clothes. When we get to your bag, slip your trousers off and get straight in. Then all your clothes should be dry for the morning. OK?"

"Thank you, Judy, thank you both," he croaked.

The figure of Gavin hovered over her. "We need to talk, Judy."

"I'll just see to Marc."

"Philippa can do that," he snapped.

"Fine," she retorted. "But why so aggressive?"

"Sorry, sorry, Judy. Just so damn tired."

"We all are, Gavin, but we must remain strong. Do you mind, Philippa?"

"Sure, sure."

Judy followed Gavin over to a corner of the chapel where they were joined by William and Steve. Far enough away that they wouldn't be overheard, but close enough that they could still feel some benefit from the warmth of the fire. The fire had been moved, pushed a few feet across the floor using the back of a pew, as the melting snow had been dripping through the hole in the roof and was threatening to dampen down the fire.

Gavin crouched down next to a pew, Judy, William, and Steve following suit, and placed his map on the wooden seat. He pulled a candle from his jacket pocket, his waterproof jacket drying somewhere near the fire, and lit it with a burning splinter of wood he'd brought with him from the fire. Tipping the candle slightly so melted wax could drip onto the pew, he then pressed the unlit end into the melted wax, the flame flickering, providing some shadowed light over the map.

He tapped the map. "I'm pretty sure this is the chapel here."

"Can't be that many graveyards around," suggested William. "The map shows a chapel next to it."

Judy and Steve nodded in agreement.

"If we make our way south, we can walk about three kilometres, I reckon, where we'll reach the A303, then we can turn west." Gavin continued, "Or, about a kilometre away, we could turn right along this minor road, past Larkhill, then left down the, what is it?" He peered at the map in the poor candlelight. "The B3086."

"Why not take the quickest route?" asked Judy.

Gavin pointed to a blob on the map which he had circled with a pencil. "Bulford camp, army. And here," he slid his finger south, "an airfield. South of Amesbury. If they've been hit..."

"A strike that close – wouldn't this chapel have been taken out?"

"You could be right, Steve," agreed William. "Both would have been a target. Perhaps they missed, the missile landing further east."

"Good point," granted Gavin. "If that's the case then they may well have been at the extreme of the blast area, leaving Durrington, which is close by, and this chapel relatively safe."

"We could check out Durrington on our way," suggested Judy. "If it looks bad, we can switch direction."

"I like it, Judy. Makes sense to me," replied Gavin. "We all agreed? Judy?"

"Yes, that's what we'll do."

The others nodded their acceptance of the plan for tomorrow.

"How's Marc?" asked Gavin as he folded the map and got up from his crouch. Steve and William had drifted away, seeking a warm by the fire and a hot drink that should be ready by now.

Judy hesitated for a moment before she answered. "We're worried about his arm, but with some decent sleep and a bit of warmth, he should pull through. Why do you ask?"

"Just trying to help, make sure we're capable of the next stage of the journey. We've still twenty or so kilometres to go. We need to do that in two days."

"Two days?"

"Judy, we're running out of food, being hunted by dogs, and I'd say that fifty per cent of the group are on their last legs. I doubt all of us will make it."

"We're going to get everyone to our final destination, Gavin, and no one is going to stop me or us," barked Judy, raising her voice, heads lifted as some members of the group looked over to where the two of them were huddled.

"Hey, hey," Gavin gripped Judy's shoulder, "I'm with you, but someone has to play devil's advocate."

Her shoulders slumped. "I know. I'm sorry. We've come so far and have lost so many people already."

"They're the weaker ones, Judy. They wouldn't have made it anyway."

"You can be so cold at times, Gavin."

"Just being realistic." He bent down, extracted the candle

from the pew and blew out the flame, darkness descending around them both.

"I know, but I'm not giving up just yet."

"Fair enough."

"Let's get some sleep, eh, we all need it."

They parted company, Judy checking on Marc who, after a hot drink and a cup of soup, was fast asleep in his sleeping bag. As she sorted out her own bedding, Philippa came over and handed her a mug of hot black coffee.

"This is luxurious."

"Make the most of it. That's the last of my supplies."

"I have a few tea bags we can share."

"There's some soup been left in the pan over by the fire for you."

"I feel too tired to eat."

"You'll feel better for it, Judy, then you can sleep. I'm going to get my head down now. Goodnight."

"Goodnight, and thanks for helping Marc. How's Robert?"

"OK, but tired. I don't think he can take much more of this. Or any of us for that matter."

"I know, but we need to stick together, yeah?"

"Definitely. Goodnight."

Judy went to the fire and poured the last of the mushroom soup into the tin cup that had been left for her. Then, with her mug of coffee in one hand and cup of soup in the other, she completed a tour of the chapel, checking on everyone, finishing her soup and drink, before she too crashed out in her sleeping bag, not even bothering to undress. Her clothes weren't completely dry, but OK to sleep in. She fell asleep with the troubles of the world swirling round her thoughts but, like counting sheep, after she closed her eyes she was dead to the world in minutes. Tomorrow was another day.

CHAPTER 21

PARALYSIS | GROUND-ZERO +37 DAYS
MOTORWAY TRIBE, NORTH OF NETHERAVON

Considering the outside temperature during the night, dropping to a numbing minus nine degrees, the chapel had been quite warm. Not cosy, but warm enough to fend off the biting cold. Members of the group had taken it in turns to feed the fire with the ever-dwindling supply of broken pews. They also had a task of preventing the water from dousing the fire, the melting water dripping from the many small fissures in the roof, which slowly thawed on the roof above them.

Together with mushroom soup for breakfast, the last of their catering tins, a tin of crackers, was opened and shared out. The only way to eat the stale biscuits was by dipping them in the soup to soften them. This was followed by a hot drink of very weak, black tea. Although it filled stomachs and buoyed everyone up, the downside was that they had only one day's rations left. Tonight, they could eat, but after that, unless people had some other food squirrelled away, hidden from the group, they would be scavenging or walking the rest of the way on empty stomachs.

Judy gave the order for them to pack up and get ready to go, and Gavin, Steve and William helped and chivvied along the slower members of the group. Judy spoke to them all as a group, five minutes before departure time. They were informed of their route and encouraged to keep up the day's pace. She reiterated that they were practically out of food but, on a positive note, they were only two days away from their final destination.

When asked about what their next steps would be should government help not be forthcoming, while Judy was contemplating her answer, Gavin jumped in. "From then on," he said, "it would be a matter of pure survival, and our struggle would truly begin."

Judy countered the negativity by reassuring the assembled group that she would do whatever was in her power to keep the group safe and alive. Their spirits lifted, and packs were collected and slung onto backs. The door was pulled open, and a gust of wind-driven snow blew in, reminding them of what they had left outside.

"Back, back, get inside, the bloody dogs are out there," shouted William, slamming the door shut.

"How many?" Gavin called to William.

"I didn't get much of a look, but I'd say at least a dozen."

Gavin went to the door, cracked it open slightly and scanned the snow-covered ground outside. Although the skies were their usual dirty grey colour and there was a steady tumble of snowflakes obscuring his vision beyond fifty metres, he was still able to pick out the darker shapes of the dogs nestled up against the tombstones, the downwind side, lying protected from the wind in small circular clearings they had made the previous day. None moved, but they didn't take their unblinking eyes off Gavin for one second. He picked out who he thought was the leader of the pack, the large poodle. Curled up against another tombstone, about three metres from the poodle, was an alsatian, his eyes boring into Gavin's. The dog's tongue flicked out and the animal licked his lips eyeing Gavin up as if he was the next meal the dog would eat.

Gavin did a quick count, picking out at least twenty-two dogs, but he was sure that the tombstones hid others. He shut the door again and wiped the snow from his face. "Twenty-plus, I'd say. Not good."

"What should we do, do you think?"

Before Gavin could answer Judy's question, the rest of the group moved forward eager to hear Gavin's answer.

"Quick," instructed Gavin, "get the fire going again, and cut as many thin pieces of wood as you can. Thin enough so you can hold them in your hand."

"Protection?" asked Judy.

"We have this," Gavin indicated the assault rifle he was holding, "but we need to conserve ammunition. We need that fire stoked, Judy," he whispered, conscious that he was perhaps usurping her authority.

Judy turned towards the gathered group. "Gurvinder, Fiona, would you mind keeping the fire going. It looks like we'll still need it. Zack, organise the strips of wood we need."

"What for?" asked Zack

"Firebrands," responded Gavin.

Everyone went off to carry out her instructions.

"What I propose, Judy, is that we get onto the road as quickly as possible," Gavin continued. "Once there, we'll have the hedge line and drifting snow either side of us, so we'll only need to watch the front and back of the group."

"Makes sense," supported William.

"How?" asked Judy.

"Right, they have a free rein in the graveyard. They can easily encircle us or trap us up against the chapel, yes?"

A murmur of yeses came from the remainder of the group who were listening in.

"We have five guns. I'll want you, William, along with Steve to run towards the road as fast as possible, turn right and stop there. Any dogs that have got through or get on the road from the far end of the graveyard, give them a quick blast and keep them back. OK?"

"We're on it," William responded.

"Ollie," he called, "I want you go with William and Steve, but you turn left, watch the road to the south. I doubt there'll be any dogs but, just in case, take Fiona with you."

"Sure," Ollie agreed.

"The rest of you, listen in. Zack," Gavin raised his voice so Zack could here above the sound of pieces of wood being hacked into shape, "how many lengths, wooden torches do we have?"

Zack did a quick count. "Er, looks like a dozen. Don't forget, we've got a small bottle of fuel. We can soak some of them in it."

"Good idea, but we need some more. We need twice as many." Gavin addressed the main body of the group again. "I'll split you into two groups, roughly the same size. Judy, if you'll lead one."

She nodded.

"Zack, you lead the second?"

Zack came over, leaving others to continue cutting up wood. "Count me in."

Gavin raised his voice so everyone could hear. "Group one, Zack. Your group will need two torches each. Once Steve pulls the door wide open, William will fire two shots, one barrel at a time. While that provides a wake-up call for the dogs, your group, Zack, will charge out of the chapel screaming and yelling like you've never done before, forming a semi-circle with the chapel door at your back. Each throw one of the torches, still screaming like maniacs, at the dogs, and wave the torches you're still holding in front of you. Steve, William, Ollie, you leg it with them. Yes?"

They all concurred.

"Don't forget the screaming."

Although they were nervous, it still brought a laugh from the group, recognising the bizarreness of the situation they were in. Weeks ago, they were going about their daily business in relative comfort whereas here and now they were about to take on a pack of dogs.

"Judy, your group. The weaker and younger ones to the front, so you can make sure no one drops back. The same thing: scream and yell, but charge for the road. You will cover the gateway to the road. Keep both torches though. Me and Gurvinder will follow. Once Steve, William and Ollie, me and Gurvinder and you and your group are on the road, I'll call Zack's group back."

He turned to Zack. "That, Zack, is the cue for your lot to chuck the last of the firebrands. Run like mad for the road. Judy's group will be ready and, as soon as you run through them, they will throw one of their torches. Then we head down the road. Zack, if your group relieve Judy's lot of the remaining torches, you can follow up the rear with Steve and William."

"What then?" asked Judy.

"We walk as fast as we can. As for the rest of the way, we'll just have to take it from there."

They gathered their belongings again, pulling on rucksacks. Additional strips of wood, about two centimetres in diameter, shredded at the end so they would burn faster. Zack dipped the ends into what little petrol they had left. The torches were handed out, two each to those without weapons. Gavin and Judy called to them, confirming that they were ready and then instructing them to light the firebrands they held.

Woomph…woomph. The firebrands were lit and the torches flared. The small chapel rapidly filled with black smoke and the stench of burning fuel as they caught fire.

"Let's do it," shouted Gavin. "Go, Steve!"

Steve, who was already standing next to the door, ready to pull it open, grabbed the handle and yanked it inwards, twisting around so he was able to push it right back against the wall of the chapel. A gust of wind blasted its way through the opening, a flurry of snow blinding William for a moment as he stepped warily outside, the barrels of his shotgun aimed towards the gravestones and the dogs.

Bang…bang. He let go with both barrels, one after the other, the squall outside absorbing some of the sound waves, but there was still enough noise to disturb the dogs. At least half got up and, barking loudly, skittered further back into the graveyard, away from the building. The rest were either silent, attempting to ascertain what was going on, or snarling at whatever they thought had disturbed their peace.

"William, Steve, Ollie, go now," screamed Gavin, pushing them forward. "Speed is critical."

The three men sprinted out of the door, turning left, pounding through the half-metre thick snow on the track they had walked down the previous day. They had their guns at the ready, William having reloaded. William started screaming, remembering the plan, and Steve and Ollie followed suit. In the meantime, Gavin had urged the rest of the group to spring into action. Zack led his group out, billowing clouds of oily, black smoke around them, the flames flickering brightly, still being fed by the petrol-soaked wood. They immediately ran at the dogs, screaming and shrieking maniacally, more out of fear than the instructions they had been given. They formed a semi-circle, Zack flinging his firebrand at the nearest snarling dog, the wood bouncing off the tombstone it was crouched by, lips peeled back exposing its drooling fangs. It yelped and backed off, the snow sizzling as the hot flame connected. Zack screamed and screamed, his voice hoarse, his action shocking the others into throwing their firebrands at the dogs that were backing off, still fearful of the human onslaught.

"Wave your torches," hollered Zack as he swept his second one from side to side out to the front, the *woom...woom* sound distinctive as the flame fought against the draught caused by Zack's actions. Philippa, Mathew and Ellen joined in, overcoming their fear, shrieking at the dogs, daring them to take them on. Behind them, Judy's group ran towards the road, carrying their torches, followed by Gurvinder and Gavin. Gavin hung back, watching, waiting to give the order for Zack's group to run. As he checked Judy's progress, there was a cry as Marc tripped and fell, his firebrands flying through the air, landing amongst the tombstones, scattering a couple of the dogs. Andrea and her daughter Stephanie helped him up, and they ran to catch up. Gavin checked again: Judy's team were at the road, spreading out, flaming torches flickering red, yellow and orange across the white blanket of snow. The air stank of petrol fumes, irritating the dogs' nostrils, holding them back from launching an attack.

"Zack, now! Chuck your torches and run!"

Zack and his team didn't need a second warning from Gavin: torches were flung at the dogs, and they sprinted as best they could across the churned-up snow, screaming their heads off, heading for relative safety. Gavin was the last to make it through Judy's team who were acting as a screen, who, on cue, each threw a flaming torch towards where the dogs would have to exit from the graveyard to the road. On instructions from Gavin, the group manoeuvred into their agreed positions, picking up pace as they headed south, looking back over their shoulders for fear of the dogs following. Zack's group hanging back.

The last of the torches were thrown and Gavin left Steve, William and Zack to cover their backs as he quickly went to the front to lead the group to their next destination. Weapons at the ready, the three men constantly checked behind them. The large, dirty white poodle padded past the last of the burning embers just before the flames were snuffed out in the wet snow.

With the dogs keeping a distance of no more than fifty metres from the human pack, hunger driving them on, Judy's group traipsed south. Half a kilometre took them to the western outskirts of Durrington where there was visible evidence of the consequences of the nuclear strike to the south of Bulford Camp and south-west of the airport south of Amesbury. All the windows had been shattered and, in most buildings, roof tiles had been dislodged, the internal spaces now covered in a layer of snow.

After a short discussion between Gavin, Judy and William, conscious of the impatience being exhibited by the pack of dogs, it was agreed that they would continue south, staying on the road. It was another two kilometres and a further hour and a half before they arrived at the dual carriageway, the A303. Once they had negotiated the large roundabout, they ended up on the westbound carriageway. Both carriageways were strewn with snow-covered, abandoned vehicles, and after a cursory search of a few, it was obvious that anything useful such as food, water and medical supplies had been stripped from them. Many had rotten but now frozen corpses inside, possibly the remaining members of a group, such as the one Judy had led back at the motorway, that had chosen to stay rather than leave.

The group weaved around the vehicles, continuing along the westbound carriageway, at the best pace possible but the weight of the snow they had to plough through wearing them down. The dogs kept their distance, but continued to pad behind them. After a four-kilometre trek, passing Stonehenge to the north as they did, it was decided to take a ten-minute break. Everyone crammed into the back of a boxed artic trailer while the dogs lay down in a semi-circle, patiently waiting in the snow for an opportunity to grab a meal. They had been successful so far, so had no reason to doubt that one of the weaker humans would fall soon.

With the ten minutes up and the blast of a shotgun barrel towards the pack of hounds, killing one, a feast for the other dogs, the group continued its slog west. A further twelve kilometres found them exhausted. Even Gavin and some of the stronger members were starting to feel the pace. Marc, Robert and the two young children, along with their mother, had to be helped. Packs and other equipment had been shared amongst the group, making it easier for the four to make progress, but it put a strain on the healthy ones. Jacqueline was also flagging. Marc was almost close to death by the time they boarded a once luxury coach to spend the night in, Gavin firing a shot at the dogs again just before he pulled the stiff door to. Marc clearly had a high fever, his body burning up trying to fight the infections that were starting to rage through his body. It would be a cold, damp night as there was no fire this time, not even a hot meal nor a hot drink.

Judy knew that if they didn't make it to Chilmark soon then, apart from a few, the group wouldn't make it at all. She would have led them to their deaths. Four tins of Spam, the last of their food, were shared out amongst them. From now on, they would be burning the fat on their bodies, of which there wasn't much, to survive. Water was also becoming a problem, having no heat to melt the snow. They piled as much snow as they could into their nearly empty water bottles, and clutched them to their chests or stomachs in the hope that overnight it would have melted, replenishing their supplies.

CHAPTER 22

PARALYSIS | GROUND-ZERO +37 DAYS
PATROL, CHILMARK RGC

Bang!

"Hey, did you hear that?"

"Hear what?" responded Vic, the gunner, down inside the turret. "Hear bugger all down here."

"I dunno. Sounded like a gunshot. Come up here."

Vic clambered up and heaved his shoulders outside the turret hatch.

"Have a listen. Neil, turn her off," the commander instructed his driver via the intercom.

The Scimitar reconnaissance tank was suddenly silent as the trembling of the Cummins diesel engine, ticking over slowly, was switched off.

"What is it?" the driver called back to the tank commander.

"We don't know yet. Keep it quiet."

Corporal Danny Butler, the tank commander, and Vic strained their ears, pulling their scarves down, leaving their ears exposed to the bitter cold. The snowfall was light but steady, restricting their visibility down the A303, and was already starting to cover the tracks the treads of the Scimitar had left behind.

"Where'd you hear it?"

"East, I reckon, somewhere along the dual carriageway."

"How far?"

"God knows."

Vic looked at his watch. "Getting late, Danny. We should be heading back to camp. We don't wanna be out in this shit. Get lost and lose a track and we're buggered. Did it sound close?"

"It must have been if I heard it."

"If you heard it, you mean."

"Piss off. There's something out there. A gunshot stands out. Yeah, it can't be far away. Let's go take a look."

"Better to back off and stag off."

"Where's your sense of adventure?"

"In my frozen feet and chilled backside."

"Turn her over, Neil."

"Where we off to?"

"An adventure for Vic here," responded Corporal Butler.

"Don't overtax him."

"Shut it," Vic retorted.

The Cummins engine restarted and, on the order from Corporal Butler, the driver powered up and the Scimitar light tank crept forward. Although the grey light was still providing them with some visibility ahead and around them, the steady fall of snowflakes made it difficult to see more than fifty to a hundred metres. For the driver, it was even worse, and he was very dependent on the tank commander above to guide him through the slalom of abandoned cars. Although a passage had initially been kept clear for the use of military vehicles, the panic towards the end, in the last few hours before the majority of the UK population were wiped out, had prompted some drivers to cross the line, their vehicles stalling as a consequence of the Super-EMP nuclear devices detonated high above the UK mainland. These particular nuclear warheads had the sole purpose of destroying Britain's communications network and the majority of vehicle electrics and anything electrical that would hamper the country's ability to strike back at its Russian enemies. Although the Land Rovers could make their way around the snow-laden roads, especially those fitted with makeshift tyre chains, it was far from easy-going. So, with the Scimitar's ability to cross-country, its reduced weight, aluminium alloy armour and nearly half-metre wide tracks ensuring the tank exerted a ground pressure of only 5 psi, less than a human male at 8 psi, it was used for long-range reconnaissance.

"Left, left! Forward! You nearly hit a bloody car then," Neil heard through his headphones.

"I can't see shit down here," he responded.

Both the commander and gunner peered into the snow as the recce tank crawled forwards, weaving around the traffic jam ahead of them. Both empathised with the driver. He could see next to nothing down there. At least he was sitting alongside the engine, the warmest part of the Scimitar.

"Stop, stop, stop. Can you see that light, Vic?"

"Where?"

"Forty metres, one o'clock, looks like a bus."

Vic leant forwards, straining his neck and eyes, scrutinising the object Danny had identified. "Can't see nothing. Wait...yeah, saw a flicker of yellow."

Corporal Butler lifted his binoculars to his face, pulling his goggles up so he could align the rubber cups with his eyes. The snow didn't help his vision, the flakes were magnified in front of the lenses, but he did see a light that appeared to be moving behind the snow-plastered windows of the bus.

"Neil, we've seen something up ahead. Pull forward slowly. You're clear in front out to thirty. Twenty at the back then right stick if we need to get out of here."

"Roger."

"Vic, best get on the coax, just in case."

"Gotcha."

Vic dropped down into the turret, cocked the 7.62mm machine gun, and got ready.

Corporal Butler reached down into the turret and grabbed his assault rifle, bumping his arm as the tank jerked forward, Neil applying power to the engine, the wide tracks crunching down on the snow as the eight-ton tank rolled forwards.

"Thirty." The tank crawled ever closer.

"Twenty-five." The Scimitar's headlights now blazed through the snow, reflecting off those windows that had been cleared, picking out the snow-covered shape of the bus.

"Twenty. Stop, stop."

Danny scanned the area, picking out a variety of different shapes scattered in a semi-circle on one side of the bus. One shape became larger, appearing to move. The corporal lifted his goggles again and zoomed in to the area with his binos. "Dogs," he whispered to himself. Half a dozen of the dogs closest to the tank moved further back, wary of the grumbling giant that had just pulled up close to them. He clicked the comms button. "We've got a pack of dogs around the bus."

"Shall I give them a blast?" asked Vic, manning the machine gun.

"Negative, you'll scare the shit out of anyone in the bus."

"What then?"

"You come here and keep watch. I'll take a look."

"What about the dogs?" asked Vic, scrabbling alongside his tank commander.

Corporal Butler removed his bone dome, a large dense helmet with internal earphones, and climbed out of the hatch and onto the top of the turret. "Once I'm down, get Neil to rev the engine and pull forward a couple of metres."

"OK. Best you stay on the right. Keep between us and the line of cars."

"Sound. Where's your weapon?"

"Hang on." Vic leant into the turret and retrieved his SA80 assault rifle, cocked it, and positioned himself to provide cover. Corporal Butler clambered down the glacis and gave his driver the thumbs up when he reached the front end of the tank. He dropped down into the thick snow and could see that the wind had forced it to bank up against the long line of vehicles. He moved across to the right-hand side of the tank, put the sling of his SA80 around his neck, cocked the weapon, and got his bearings. The dogs had moved further away, now in a group of at least twenty, he thought. A large grey poodle-like dog was ahead of the rest, standing less than twenty metres away, facing the corporal, wary of the visitor, but still the dominant dog in the pack, Bianca was standing, albeit at a distance, facing the monster that had just arrived. She could sense that someone had exited the vehicle, but couldn't see them, the beams of the tank's lights blinding her and the other dogs. Corporal Butler edged forwards, jumping when Neil revved the engine.

"Scared the shit out of me," he whispered to himself.

PARALYSIS | GROUND-ZERO +37 DAYS
MOTORWAY TRIBE, A303, NORTH OF SALISBURY

Judy made her way along the coach, stepping over bodies that were strewn across the aisle, some tucked up in their sleeping bags, wet outer clothes draped over the backs of the luxurious leather seats. She used the torch, with its rapidly fading battery, to navigate through the arms and legs ensuring she didn't step on anyone. At the front of the coach, sitting in what was once the driver's seat, Zack kept watch, his turn to do the first hour. They were not sure what they needed to watch out for: the dogs wouldn't be able to get through the coach's passenger door and no one else in their right mind would be out in this weather as dusk settled in.

Judy was headed towards the back of the coach to find Gavin, who had positioned himself there, near the emergency exit, just in case. About halfway down the aisle, Judy was sure she saw something through the misted windows, something that was able to pierce through the steady snowfall, a light perhaps. She reached the back seat of the coach where Gavin was kneeling, wiping the condensation off the window just as a light flashed across it.

"You've seen it too?"

"Yes," he responded. "Best get everyone up, Judy. We've no idea who they are."

Judy went down the centre of the bus, waking everyone up. "Ellen, wake up. We've got visitors."

"Who?"

"We don't know."

"William, William, we've got company."

He yawned and pulled his arms out of his sleeping bag. "What?"

"Somebody's out there. Can you go and join Zack at the front of the bus."

"Sure." He dragged himself out of the sleeping bag, shivering with the cold as he grabbed for his still damp outer clothing. Steve also pulled on a jumper, one he had tucked up inside his sleeping bag, using his body warmth to help dry it out. Then he passed Judy to go and join Zack at the front. He also woke other people up as he transited the length of the coach.

As the occupants of the coach, now a melee of arms, legs and clothing, pulled themselves together, grumpy at being pulled out of the relative warmth of their bags, Judy made her way again to the back of the coach, where Gavin was rolling up his sleeping bag, the rest of his gear already stored in his rucksack, in case they needed to make a run for it.

"Listen."

Judy listened, trying to shut out the noise of the group rattling and clumping around the coach. Twin beams of light brightened as they swept towards the coach, and the revving of a powerful engine could suddenly be heard. "Is it a lorry?"

"I don't think so. Lights are low and close together. Scared the dogs off, though."

Zack joined them. "What is it? The dogs have congregated around the front of the coach. What's scared them?"

"Look." Judy pointed, staring into the bright illumination of the headlights as an ethereal figure suddenly appeared to their left, in between the other vehicles, coach and the mystery vehicle.

Inside the coach, everyone had stopped what they were doing, the group mesmerised by the brightness of the lights reflecting off the snowflakes that still fell, all staring towards it and wondering about what fate would befall them.

Now the figure was only ten metres away, Judy could see the combat fatigues, along with an assault rifle held at the ready.

"It's a soldier!" she exclaimed excitedly, just for a fraction of a second wondering if it was someone from the group they had messed with back at the motorway.

Zack lifted his gun but Judy pushed down on the barrel. "You know what happened last time."

Zack lowered the gun, and the soldier approached the rear window as Gavin wiped more of the condensation aside. A pair of goggle-covered eyes looked up, seeing the dark shadows of faces peering back down at him. The soldier made a signal with his right arm to something behind him and, preceded by the roar of an engine, a small tank came into view, the turret and barrel of the 30mm RARDEN cannon pointed menacingly in their direction. The soldier disappeared from view and then reappeared again alongside the coach, walking towards the front.

Judy, Gavin and Zack immediately made their way towards the front, brushing past the people still standing, forcing some to step back and drop down into the seats. They kept pace with the soldier and jumped when he fired two rounds from his SA80 at the dogs milling around near the front of the coach. The dogs scattered, the bullets clanging as they struck the metal bodies of vehicles close by. He was met at the passenger door as Gavin heaved it open, allowing the soldier to access the cab. Then it was quickly closed, more to keep out the blustery cold than the dogs.

Corporal Butler stood at the top of the steps, next to the driver's cab. The partially illuminated coach, lit up by the Scimitar's headlights, highlighted a mass of figures staring back at the visitor. He kept a firm grip on his SA80 in case he needed it. What Corporal Butler could see, in the badly lit confines of the body of the coach, was a group of bedraggled human beings. Their hair was dishevelled and all the men had beards of varying lengths, unkept and unwashed. There was an unpleasant smell of damp and a tinge of urine where, as a consequence of the cold, most would have have had to have urinated in a bottle, a journey outside amongst the dogs was obviously not recommended. Their clothing, a variety of mismatched colours, that in the normal world would have elicited ridicule, but in these circumstances anything that kept you warm and dry was welcomed, was soiled and in some cases torn.

A woman, tousled, shoulder-length blonde hair, eyes that shone bright from a pale but grimy face framed by a dark blue scarf approached him. "You're a soldier."

Corporal Butler looked down at his uniform. "Some of my buddies would question that," he said with a smile. "But, yes, I am." He pulled up his goggles and peeled off his green balaclava.

"Where are you from?" "Do you have food and shelter?" "Is the Government helping us?" Staccato bursts of questions.

"One at a time, one at a time, give the boy a chance," pleaded Judy. "Where are you from?"

"A few answers from you people would be a much better option. But, first, could you ask your people to lower their guns?"

Judy looked about her and could see that Zack and Steve had their guns pointed at the soldier. She waved them down. "Lower your guns, Steve, Zack. We have nothing to fear. Do we?" she said, turning back to face the soldier.

"No, not if you're no threat to me and my men."

"Are there many of you?" asked Gavin, who had moved closer, towering over the much shorter soldier.

"Enough. Now, a couple of quick questions. Then I need to let my men know that all is well before they start worrying about my safety. Where have you come from?"

Judy answered for the group. "Up north. We were living on a motorway, using cars, buses and camper vans for shelter and scavenging food from. It was just north of Cheltenham. Have you met up with some other soldiers? Four of them? Led by a man called Glen. I think they were special troops."

Corporal Butler thought for a moment before answering. "We have. Come to think of it, they actually mentioned you and your group and asked us to keep an eye out for you. He thought you might make the trip."

"Where are they now?"

"Gone off to London, I think."

"Where are you—?"

"Whoa, whoa, enough for now. Let me talk to my guys and let them know all is well. Then we can chat some more." He turned to go down the steps but stopped and turned back to face Judy. "Your name, love?"

She smiled at the thought of being called 'love' by a twenty-five-year old. "Judy."

He recognised the reason for her smile and smiled back. "I'd like to see all the weapons upfront though. Perhaps you could lay them on a seat here?" He pointed to the seat by the steps. "I want to bring the lads in, but would feel a lot easier if we didn't have guns pointed at us."

She nodded. He took the three steep steps, pulled the door inwards and open with a grunt, and peered around the corner, checking for the dogs. They were still there, but keeping their distance, a good ten metres, the poodle still at the front of the pack. He stepped down and the door was closed behind him. He kept to the side of the coach, checking over his shoulder that the dogs weren't closing in. They weren't.

As he got closer to the Scimitar, the welcome sound of the engine ticking over, Vic was sitting on the turret, his SA80 aimed in the direction of the coach and the dogs. "No problems then?"

"No, a bunch of civilians. A few weapons, but I reckon they're harmless."

"What'll we do then?"

"I'll call it in. Get the boiling vessel (BV) on, will you? They look like shit in there. A hot drink will go down a treat."

"I'm ready for one as well," Vic chuckled.

Corporal Butler climbed onto the glacis, then the turret, and dropped down into the interior of the Scimitar, grabbing the radio handset. "Hello, Two-Zero, this is Two-Zero-Echo. Over."

Vic clattered about behind him, checking the BV was full and working OK.

"*Two-Zero-Echo, Two-Zero-Alpha, go ahead. Over.*"

"CSM, OC must be off stag," suggested Vic.

"Zero-Echo. Location Alpha-three-zero-three, four klicks east of junction with Alpha-three-six-zero. Come across fifteen-plus civilians. Over." Turning to Vic, he asked, "BV OK?"

"Apart from this fucking leak still, yeah."

"*What's their status? Over.*"

"Pretty poor. They've walked from area north of Cheltenham. Oh, they reckon they know our SF buddies. Over."

"*Can you bivvy up for the night and escort them in first thing? Over.*"

"Roger that. Bloody cold though. Over."

"*Make a man of you, Danny.*"

"Yeah, a snowman, Sarn't Major."

"Call in at 0600. Move out 0615. Your ETA?"

"Looking at the state of them, sir, I'd say six to eight hours at best. Can you send some three-quarter tonners?"

"Big push on the town tomorrow, so no can do. Carry the weaker ones on top and make best speed."

"Will do, sir."

"Anything else?"

"Just that there's a pack of dogs, twenty-plus."

"Let me know when you're ten minutes out, and we'll have a welcoming party for them."

"Roger."

"Good luck, Danny. Hot meal for when you return. Out."

Corporal Butler placed the handset down. "How's the water?"

"Ready."

They were joined by Neil, the driver. "Where we kipping then? The bus?"

"It smells and is cold, but we'll have our maggots to keep us warm. I want us to stag on, two on, four off."

"Expecting trouble?" asked Vic.

"No, but I don't want to leave her unattended." He patted the turret of the Scimitar. "If you pull up alongside the coach, whoever's on stag can see her from upfront. Position yourselves in the driver's cab."

"Yeah, we'll close her up. She'll be fine. Shall I pull alongside now?"

"Yeah, why not? The brew will be ready by then."

Neil returned to the driver's position, and Corporal Butler went to the commander's hatch. Within a few minutes, after a bit of swivelling about on the tracks, the Scimitar was pulled up alongside, the barrel of the 30mm cannon just jutting past the front of the coach. Then, battening down the tank, the three soldiers entered the coach, taking with them three large flasks of hot water, a camping gas stove and five tins of broth along with three packs of army biscuits.

The reception Corporal Butler received on his second visit was very different. The occupants of the coach welcomed the three squaddies with open arms, and the gas stove was soon heating up soup while mugs of hot coffee were passed round, something they hadn't tasted for a while. With a biscuit each, and a small portion of soup to help shake off the chill, they were all feeling much better than they had for a long time, and conversation flowed freely between the soldiers and the civilians.

"Is the RGC safe?" asked one.

"We've had problems, but there's a strong security force, so have no fear," answered Danny.

"Is there plenty of food?" questioned another.

"There's food, not plentiful, and people are expected to work for it."

"Slave labour?" retorted Gavin.

"Hey, Gavin, give them a break," defended Judy.

"No, it's not slave labour. We have to rebuild Chilmark, cook food, collect water, and prepare the ground for planting crops. When it thaws, that is."

"How many people?"

"God, over 4,000 or more now, I think. I don't know about you people, but I'm shagged and we've got a bit of a trip ahead of us tomorrow. So, I suggest you all get your head down, yeah?"

CHAPTER 23

PARALYSIS | GROUND-ZERO +38 DAYS
RGC, CHILMARK

Once parked up in the area allocated for military vehicles, Alan and Scott sat in silence for a few moments. The blizzard that seemed to come out of nowhere in the last hour had taken them completely by surprise. Now it was buffeting the vehicle, shaking it violently. The major inconvenience of the steady snowfall over the last few days had been overcome with a little ingenuity from members of staff and the labour teams employed to maintain the camp infrastructure. But this sudden storm was causing havoc. What little the two men could see was not good. Although one was still operating, the bread ovens were completely exposed to the elements. The large canvas covers, supported by lengthy poles and sturdy guy ropes, had been torn from their position. Protected by wet-weather jackets and leggings, with layers of warm clothing beneath, half a dozen workers had been persuaded to keep the ovens working. A lorry had been parked across the front of the one working, protecting the operators from the worst of the icy winds. Bread was a staple diet for the entire camp, and if they failed to maintain a steady production, it would not be received well by the population they were feeding. A steady influx of refugees had raised the numbers to in excess of 5,000, many of them sick, suffering from burn injuries, radiation sickness and malnutrition.

"This is all we need, Alan." Scott indicated towards the blizzard blasting across the preparation area.

"I know. We have to have food ready for them tonight, though."

"We could always plump for cold rations for a few days."

"Look at it, Scott. It's now they need a hot meal more than anything. The temperature's dropping daily."

As they looked on, a twelve-by-nine tent flew past the Land Rover. It had originally been put in place to protect one of the food preparation areas. The kitchen team working there would now be completely exposed to the elements. Both continued to watch as several men, and woman, raced after it. Once caught, a fight ensued with the quivering canvas, getting it under control and bringing it back to its original position so work could continue on that night's evening meal. A work force of 200 had been assigned to the food preparation area, manning the serving stations, food preparation, and the ovens and boilers. Some of those 200 would have a full-time task, making repairs, hammering in tent pegs securing the guy ropes, preventing the structures in place from being torn asunder and blown to the four winds.

"*Two-Zero, this is Two-Zero-Delta. Over.*"

Scott grabbed the handset. "This is Two-Zero-Alpha. Go ahead. Over," he shouted above the clamour of the snowstorm.

"*We've picked up labour group one from Chilmark. Feeding station or camp? Over.*"

Scott looked at Alan. "What do you think?"

"They're not ready here. The camp. Use the excuse that we need a resource to make sure the accommodation is secure."

"Roger. Two-Zero-Delta. Move to main camp. Use the teams to batten down. Could be a mess down there. Over."

"*Will do. ETA for food? Over.*"

"Tell them delayed by figures six zero minutes. Out."

"Time for us to batten down and go for a walk."

"Do you want me to keep radio watch?" laughed Scott.

"I suffer, Sergeant Major, you suffer. Out."

They opened one door at a time, the wind almost ripping the door out of Scott's hand. With the vehicle secured and heads bowed, they pushed their way forward, feeling the force of the wind attempting to lift them off the ground. Although the substantial labour force assigned to the feeding station had cleared the snow from the immediate area over the last few days, the snowstorm had very quickly deposited a new layer. The two soldiers worked their way through the path of the storm, the icy snow stinging their faces, pricking at any exposed skin. They arrived at the first of the ovens. A figure in uniform was hammering away at a tent peg, probably a metal stake replacement that would fulfil the role much better than the smaller original that had already been torn out twice.

"Winning the battle, Eddie?"

Eddie stood up, leaning on the shaft of the long-handled sledgehammer, the walls of the tent flapping violently behind him, a pair of goggles covering his eyes. He pulled them up onto the top of his balaclava-covered head. "Sir, Sergeant Major. We will, at least, now we've got these decent-sized stakes."

"Where did you get those from?" asked Scott.

"I asked the lads up on the farm to scout around for something and they came up trumps."

"Do we have enough to secure most of the feeding station?" asked Alan, having to shout to be heard above the whistling of the wind.

"Just about, sir, the key areas at least."

"Good work."

"I need to crack on, sir, afore I bloody freeze to death."

"Likewise, we'll leave you to it."

They continued their walk down the line of large tents, and Eddie continued his hammering in of the steel stake to support one of the guy ropes for the marquees covering one of the bread ovens. Alan and Scott passed two more serving stations, the canvases flapping wildly, but Eddie and his men had worked their magic. Eddie, an ex-engineer who once served with the Royal Engineers, had re-enlisted after encouragement from Alan – if you could call saying "Yes" to the question "Will you join the unit?" enlisting. There was no paperwork, no terms of engagement, no rank given. Eddie, although in uniform, and part of Alan's security force, which included the police and the civilian police support officers, was responsible for the security and well-being of the feeding centre. The actual running of the operation was still under the auspices of Cliff, the food officer. Although the military were still a cohesive and disciplined force, mainly out of the soldiers' respect for Alan's and Scott's leadership, Alan had done away with saluting and was considering doing away with the rank structure at some point in the future. Although military skills were still required if they were to able to protect the new and growing community, a second set of skills were required: those of leadership of a disparate and wildly diverse range of people, and coming to terms with a new set of tasks needed to ensure the community's survival.

Alan and Scott checked the other two serveries and the food store, guarded by two CPSs, huddled just outside the tent for warmth, an open fire in a pit close by, logs of wood burning furiously, driven by the air current. Going behind the serveries, the two soldiers passed through the preparation areas, the workers swaddled in layers of clothing, preparing food for the boilers in two of them, large tins of kidney beans being opened ready, eventually to be mixed in with bully beef along with watered down tins of tomato soup, some salt and a large infusion of vegetable oil. Although not the most palatable of meals, it would, along with a chunk of bread, help fill the hungry bellies of the survivors.

A further two preparation areas were preparing tins of dough which would be baked into large loaves of bread, a staple diet for many of them so long as the flour lasted. The final one was focusing on making biscuits, chunky ones with plenty of sugar, baked hard. The plan was to give one to each of the workers, during the cold spell, to have during a midday break, to keep energy levels up and the work rate high. A large number would also be put into storage, as a reserve should there be a failure in supplies being brought from the warehouses, or a serious malfunction with the equipment.

Scott and Alan chatted with as many people as they could, and although everyone's main complaint was the cold, they all recognised how lucky they were to have a task to do, a very important task. They felt included and in some small way privileged to be part of a team responsible for feeding thousands of survivors. The dim light from the oil lamps flickered across the smiling faces, heads down concentrating on the job in hand, bobbing back up to join in the banter as a couple of the women teased Alan about Alison, the woman responsible for the feeding the people back at the bunker, his faced flushed. An elbow in the side of his grinning CSM elicited a yelp.

"What do they know?" hissed Alan.

"What we all know," laughed Scott.

While they were watching the biscuit-making process, a large urn of hot, sweet black tea was brought in, a treat they received twice a day. Apart from when they had their two meals of the day, it was a welcome interruption to the working day. Alan and Scott took a mug each themselves, and the workers took pleasure from the fact that the boss was giving up some of his time to spend it with them. Although initially wary of the military taking control of the RGC after Douglas Elliot and many of the others had been killed in a recent riot, Alan had given them no cause for concern, so far, at least.

Followed by a wave of goodbyes, thanks, and a few lewd jokes from some of the women, the two men left the tent and stepped back out into the blizzard that showed no signs of abating. They checked the washing area, the boilers where the stews, soups and other hot food would be cooked, and the two ovens, the heat in those spaces being a welcome relief from the bitter cold outside. The large tents were well ventilated, with an opening at the top for the chimneys that extended skyward. Crews were rotated every other day, allowing each person to take a turn working in the luxury of this warmth.

Back in their Land Rover, Scott drove them to their next port of call. This time it was to Chilmark, in particular, the hospital. It was a hazardous journey, and without the man-made snow chains, another device put together by Eddie, the journey would have been far worse. It took them over an hour to travel the three-kilometre journey. Scott pulled up next to the makeshift hospital, what was once a primary school. Two large twelve-man tents had been erected outside for people waiting to be seen. Hard wooden chairs had been provided, but there was no heating available, or light for that matter. Alan popped his head into one, the shaft of light from the open flap revealing a solemn group of around twenty people, the chairs grouped together, the occupants huddled together, desperate for additional warmth. There were a few staring eyes, but no one spoke. He pulled his shoulders back out and resealed the flap, the wind trying to rip it out of his hands.

"We need to do something about heating," Alan shouted above the din.

"I'll get Eddie on it."

"Mr Fixit," laughed Alan.

Passing through the main doors of the hospital, a CPS officer on duty, a second officer elsewhere off stag, acknowledged them both. Alan knew where to go: straight ahead would take them to the main hall, where in the past a school assembly would have been held every morning for the children but was now the centre of the hospital. The schoolrooms that were habitable, after having the single-storey roofs fixed, were used for those patients with the more serious injuries or illnesses, while the main hall housed those with relatively minor injuries. It was only because the school was single-storey that it had survived at all, its low height providing some protection from the blast wave.

Alan kept his scarf up over his nose, the smell of the makeshift hospital unpleasant but tolerable. He pushed through a second set of double doors, the steady drone of chatter from patients talking to each other from their respective beds. There was a mixture of beds, that had been salvaged from the houses in the local area, dried out and cleaned as best as was possible under the circumstances. The sound stopped, other than from nurses attending to their patients, the patients curious as to the reason for the visit by two soldiers. Out of the twelve staff fulfilling the function of a nurse, only two were in fact qualified, one a staff nurse, the other a midwife.

Doctor Batri, originally from the medical centre in Tisbury and the only doctor for the 5,000-plus inhabitants of the RGC area of responsibility, beckoned Alan over. "Major Redfern, to what do we own this honour?" The man looked tired, his face gaunt. He had never really carried any weight, but now his five foot nine frame looked positively fragile, a stained, whitish coat, stethoscope sticking out of the top pocket, hung loosely about his body. He looked ten years older than the fifty-seven years he was. Beneath the coat, he wore a set of surgical greens over a collarless shirt and pair of corduroy trousers, a pair of brown brogues on his feet. A green surgical cap kept what grey, wispy hair he had under control.

"You wanted to see me. Are you OK, Doctor?"

"Yes, yes, Major. Of course, I did, and, yes, I'm well."

"Alan, please."

"Alan, I'm fine. All I need is twice the number of staff, twice the number of beds, and some medical supplies." He leant forward, "I have twenty ampoules of morphine left, along with a couple of dozen Distalgesic painkillers. I could use all of those this minute, just to relieve the agony for some of the patients, but I need to keep them for those that at least have a chance to live."

"Tough times call for tough decisions, Doctor." Alan felt slightly guilty as he knew that his unit had stocks of morphine, painkillers and antibiotics. But his men risked their lives on a daily basis, above and beyond that fulfilled by anyone else. Only in the last twenty-four hours, two of his soldiers had been killed when a Land Rover overturned in the bad weather, the reason he now restricted the number and radius of his patrols. I must remember to check up on Two-Zero-Echo, he thought.

Doctor Batri reached back and pulled a clipboard from one of the children's low school desks behind him. "I have 432 patients in this hospi…school." He leant forward, closer to Alan and Scott. "It doesn't warrant being called a hospital." The drone had picked up again as the patients continued their conversations, picking up from where they had left off, so the doctor's statement wouldn't have been overheard anyway.

"I have split the building into specific wards. One for radiation sickness and radiation burns, one for those suffering from second- and third-degree burns, one for major bodily trauma from crushing injuries, fractures, serious lacerations...some still have splinters of glass, whipped up by the explosions, embedded in their hands, arms and faces. I have this space for general illnesses, serious infections such as tonsillitis, chest infections, et cetera. I have two more rooms. One the dying room – those in there have absolutely no hope of survival. If you think it smells in here then you're in for a shock with that room. But I have opened another ward, the reason I wanted to talk to you."

"Something serious?" asked Scott.

"Very. We may have a cholera and/or typhus epidemic on our hands. Most of the people waiting out in the tents there also have those symptoms."

"They are?"

"They're fairly easy to spot. Delirium, high fever, as high as 40 degrees C, severe headaches and muscle pain, and more."

"Couldn't you mistake it for someone who is just plain ill, like food poisoning, stomach upset? None of us are in tip-top condition."

"True, that is the case, Sergeant Major. But because of our poor general health, cholera or typhus will strike hard and fast. Once infected, the victims are debilitated within a matter of hours and, if not treated, dead in a matter of days."

"What can we do about it?" asked Alan.

"Prevention. The food preparation facilities have got to be spotless. Water purified as best you can. The sanitary conditions at the camp are still appalling, despite the improvements made. That has to be your priority."

"We keep getting new arrivals. We're struggling to keep on top of it. And this weather...we'll get a labour team on it straightaway. And for those afflicted with it?"

"Most will die, I'm afraid. Diarrhoea, dehydration, the cold, poor diet, and no treatment."

"We need to act pretty quickly then."

"You do indeed, Alan...Major. Everyone will be looking to you now to keep them alive."

PARALYSIS | GROUND-ZERO +38 DAYS
RGC PATROL/MOTORWAY TRIBE, A303

Corporal Butler grabbed Jacqueline to prevent her from falling off the cramped turret of the Scimitar as it ground to a halt. They had squeezed half a dozen of the weaker members of the group onto the flattish top of the tank's turret and glacis, the rest having to walk behind, but at least the tracks of the tank pressed down the snow, making it easier as they slogged forward in the rapidly worsening blizzard. Just as they were approaching a raised section of the A303 that would take them over Whyle Road and the railway line that ran west to east, one of the group traipsing behind the reconnaissance tank had called out a warning to stop. Robert on top of the turret had informed the corporal, and he ordered his driver to halt the vehicle.

"What is it?" the corporal shouted down to those standing huddled around the rear of the Scimitar.

"People," shouted Judy in response. "Look." She pointed east, towards the slip road that led to Whyle Road.

Corporal Butler peeled back his goggles and peered into the wall of blustery snow. For a moment, he could see nothing until a flash of yellow drew his attention. Behind the bright yellow jacket, other shapes slowly came into view, moving towards them.

Vic popped up next to him. "More refugees?"

"Looks like it."

"The major did say to round them up."

"Yep, he certainly did, so they can join the line."

The one in the lead had a thick, bright yellow bubble jacket, along with matching waterproof trousers, acting as a beacon for those following behind. In his right hand was a pole he was using as a walking stick with what looked like a kitchen or carving knife taped to the upper end. As they got closer, the leader spotted the tank and called back to the rest of the column who were trudging behind him.

Vic came up through the hatch alongside Corporal Butler and the Corporal cupped his gloved hands and called to them, "Where are you from?"

The person didn't respond, just kept on walking, joined by another, then three or four more, the rest of the assembly slowly picking up speed, grouping around their leader. Within a matter of minutes, twenty or so were almost on top of Corporal Butler and his vehicle. Judy and her followers had slowly moved away to make way for the approaching refugees, their determination obvious, but to what purpose was not yet known. A continuous stream of people came through the curtain of snow now, a crowd slowly formed up around the tank, and Judy and her people backed further away. The civilians on the turret looked on, fearful. Corporal Butler looked down at the rapidly increasing crowd, another horde close on their heels. What he could see of their faces showed them to be emaciated and ill.

"Where are you from?" he asked again.

With no answer and starting to feel concerned, he ducked down and reached for his weapon, instructing Vic to contact base and grab his gun.

The man dressed in yellow, even in his weakened state, found the strength the clamber onto the glacis. Neil, the driver, ducked down getting ready to close the hatch.

Vic grabbed the handset and transmitted, "Hello Two-Zero, this is—" But he got no further. The man in yellow, pushing one of Judy's people off the top of the tank, thrust the home-made spear into Vic's chest, the handset clattering to the floor. Before Corporal Butler could react, another of the intruders struck his bare head from behind with a club, knocking him forwards, unconscious, his head and shoulders slumped over the hatch rim. Then the vehicle was swarmed, Judy's people thrown to the ground, attacked violently, hacked with knives, machetes, axes, whatever the crowd had at hand. Neil, hearing Vic's scream as he dropped down inside the turret, his wound fatal, attempted to scramble out of the driver's hatch, but was bludgeoned senseless by the intruders.

Judy and the survivors looked on in horror as the people who had become their friends over a very short period of time were literally hacked to death. Gavin raised his SA80, angry, ready to hit out, go to the aid of his friends, but Judy placed her hand on the barrel of the gun, pushing it down. "There's too many. They will overwhelm us. We need to run."

The horde had expanded to some 300 people now, all playing some part in stripping their victims of food, ransacking the Scimitar tank of any food or drink they could find. Judy and her cluster slowly edged away, moving deeper into the cover of the snowstorm, wanting to be out of sight before the attention of the mob turned to them. Their last sights of the activity around the tank horrified them, and struck with fear they ran, even stampeded, panic forcing them to dig into the last of their reserves in order to get away. As well as the bodies of the soldiers being dragged from inside the tank, they saw a person, man or woman, unclear, gripping the bloodied remains of an arm, snapped off at the elbow, digging their teeth into the flesh, tearing at it in a frenzy, a strip torn away, blood plastered over their pale face. Another of the intruders, impatient for their share of the spoils, snatched the arm away, only to lose it to another as they in turn were clubbed to the ground.

PARALYSIS | GROUND-ZERO +38 DAYS
RGC, CHILMARK

Leaving the doctor and his team to get on with the almost impossible task facing them, Alan and Scott completed a tour of the other wards. The last one they visited was the dying room, and Alan almost wished he'd not bothered. The smell caused him to be physically sick, and he barely made it out of the door before he heaved his guts up again and again. With the combination of rotting, ulcerated flesh, urine and faeces, dressings that had turned rancid, and gangrenous wounds, the smell was beyond putrid. Scott helped him to the exit, and outside Alan bent over once more, hands on hips, his lungs heaving as he sucked in the bitterly cold but fresh, air. "Jesus, that was bad."

"We need to do something for them. What we've just witnessed is inhuman."

"I agree, Scott. There has to be something we can do." Alan pulled himself up again and took a deep breath, clearing his lungs of the stench.

They both got into the Land Rover, Scott starting the engine as the radio crackled, "*Hello, Two-Zero, this is...*"

Scott and Alan looked at each other, waiting for the call sign to retransmit, but they were met by silence.

Alan picked up the handset. "All call signs, this is Two-Zero. Received broken transmission. Radio check. Over."

"*Two-Zero, this is Two-Zero-Bravo. Four, four. Not us, sir. Over.*"

"Roger."

"*Two-Zero. Two-Zero-Charlie. Loud and clear. We've not transmitted. Over.*"

"Roger."

"*Two-Zero, Two-Zero-Delta. Clear. Over.*"

"Roger. Out to you. Hello, Two-Zero-Echo, acknowledge. Over."

Hisssssss.

"Two-Zero-Echo. Report your location. Over."

Hisssssss.

"They should be OK, sir."

"I'd be less worried if it wasn't for this weather."

"True. They've also picked up some refugees. You don't think..."

"We need to find out. Two-Zero-Delta. Your location? Over."

"Just finished escort duties from warehouse, at feeding station. Struggle moving between locations. Over."

"How many bodies?"

"Me plus three, sir."

"We've no contact with Two-Zero-Echo. Going to investigate. We're moving out from Chilmark now. Head north on Cow Drove. Follow and keep me posted of your progress. Over."

"Roger that. Moving out now. Problem, sir? Over."

"We don't know. Be prepared. Two-Zero out."

PARALYSIS | GROUND-ZERO +38 DAYS
RGC PATROL/MOTORWAY TRIBE, A303

Judy ran for her life, dodging abandoned cars, William, Fiona and Ollie alongside her, Gavin behind them, urging them on. Ahead were Philippa, Andrea with her two girls, and Zack. The remainder of the group, the weaker members, most being transported on top of the army vehicle, were all dead. Even so, the rest of the group, deemed fitter than those they had just lost, were hardly in any condition to maintain their current pace. The ones up front, fear driving them on, were starting to flag, only enough stamina in their weakened condition to keep going for no longer than a minute or so. Eventually, as if on a signal, they all stopped, heads down, their lungs heaving to drag in as much oxygen as possible, some collapsing in the snow, oblivious to its cold.

"Why didn't you shoot them, Gavin? You could have saved their lives, the soldiers too," demanded Fiona.

"There were hundreds of them, and only four of us are armed. They would have turned on us as well, and it would have been a slaughter," snarled Gavin, far from happy at being singled out.

"We should have tried," continued Fiona, panting.

"Look at you," he snapped. "You can hardly breathe. You wouldn't have been able to run another metre, let alone escape their clutches."

"I stopped Gavin from firing," Judy intervened. "It would have resulted in probably all of us being killed."

"They were eating human flesh," wailed Andrea, pulling her two daughters close to her.

"We're as shocked as you," agreed Zack. "It was horrific."

"We need to move again. There's no telling what they'll do next," warned Gavin, peering through the snow still being blasted about them. "There were hundreds of them, and if human flesh has become their staple diet, there wasn't enough there to satisfy them all."

"Gavin!"

"It's the truth, Judy, and the sooner we accept that, the better prepared we'll be."

"I'm getting cold," complained Philippa.

"We need to get moving then before we all freeze to death," Gavin advised.

The storm thrashed about them, sucking the heat they had generated as a consequence of their running. Some started to moan about the cold steadily seeping in, and it was agreed to move. Not at a run, many had still to recover from the first bout of sprinting, but at a fast walk, nothing less. Even at that relatively slow pace, the strain soon started to show in some of the weaker members of the group, having to force their way through half a metre of snow at least. Although not as emaciated as the horde that had just confronted them, they were undernourished, hungry, and their bodies in a generally weakened state. Even the more powerful members of the group, such as Gavin and Zack, and those with resilience, such as Judy, were feeling it. It was only fear that kept them going, along with the whip-like voice of Gavin. For all they knew, the mob could be on their tail, a few hundred metres away on the other side of the curtain of snow that acted as a shroud, protecting them, from being seen at least.

CHAPTER 24

PARALYSIS | GROUND-ZERO +38 DAYS
NORTH OF THE CHILMARK RGC

Driving the Land Rover north as hard as was possible, bearing in mind the conditions, Scott fought with the steering wheel as the odd snowdrift caught him out, threatening to grasp the wheels in its frozen clutches, causing the back end of the vehicle to slide. Using the gears effectively, he eventually turned right, heading east along the B3089. The narrower road ahead had deteriorated since they had last traversed it. Although the track marks left by the Scimitar tank were no longer visible, both Scott and Alan could still see the furrows made as it passed. Scott steered towards the tracks that had been left, but the width of the tank meant that only one set of wheels could take advantage. However, it still made the going slightly easier. Alan continued to try and make contact with Zero-Echo.

"I've a bad feeling about this," he confided in Scott. "For them to be out of contact can only mean they're in some kind of trouble."

"I'm inclined to agree. Any deviation from the norm, and they would have informed us or Zero-Charlie."

"Two-Zero-Delta. Two-Zero. How you doing? Over."

"*Road's...pretty bad...ETA Chilmark...figures one five. Over.*"

"OK. Don't push it. Better you arrive in one piece. Out to you. Hello, Two-Zero-Charlie."

"*Go ahead. Over.*"

"They're on the ball," said Scott.

"I want a unit sent north of Chilmark," he advised Two-Zero-Charlie. "Rendezvous junction A303 and Cow Drove. Over."

"*A vehicle already standing by, three up. Do you want Golf-Two? Over.*"

"Good. Negative to Golf-Two. If the Fox gets bogged down, we'll never pull it out."

"*Roger. On way, ETA figures four five.*"

"Don't push it too hard. Need you here in one piece. Your call sign is Two-Zero-Charlie-Alpha. Have a second unit Two-Zero-Charlie-Bravo on standby, ready to move to Chilmark."

"*Roger that.*"

"Out."

"We'll at least have a bit more firepower if needed," Scott said. "Do you think it's that other lot we kicked out? Come back for revenge?"

"Could be, but my gut says no. They'd have probably gone for the warehouse."

"Hang on." Scott drove the Land Rover through Teffont Magna, the road bending round to the left taking them north along Sandhills Road. There was a more direct route to the A303, via Cow Drove, but the first section was a heavily pitted lane, now nothing more than a snowdrift, treacherous and almost impassable. They had about four kilometres to go before they hit the A303, Scott estimating they could make it in around ten to fifteen minutes. The Land Rover rocked from side to side, buffeted by the westerly winds. The windscreen wipers were coping, barely, but enough for Scott to peer ahead, searching out any drifts that had built up across their path, Alan also looking out for any signs of danger.

"Zero-Delta. Sitrep? Over."

"*Figures five to Chilmark. Over.*"

"Roger. Zero-Charlie-Alpha."

"*One klick west of Bourton. Over.*"

"Understood. Out."

"Coming to the junction, Alan."

Alan took both SA80s out of the clips and cocked them, a round now up the spout, and applied the safety catches. He reclipped Scott's but kept his assault rifle on his lap, ready.

They now joined a decent section of Cow Drove, passing the snowbound track on their left. Scott slowed down: just over a kilometre to go. He steered over to the right, avoiding the odd car here and there, abandoned shortly after the nuclear holocaust, the drivers hoping to get onto the carriageway in their attempt to escape to somewhere safer. Or maybe they were just heading back home, wanting to die there, should it come to that.

Scott and Alan got onto the two-lane A-road, turning right, the dual carriageway section not much more than 500 metres ahead.

PARALYSIS | GROUND-ZERO +38 DAYS
MOTORWAY TRIBE, A303

The group had started to stretch out, stragglers at the back nearly

200 metres from those in the lead. Fiona, Philippa, Gurvinder and Ollie, his shoulder wound playing up, were finding it particularly hard, Gavin, along with a strong wind behind them, forced them on relentlessly. A couple of them had even dumped rucksacks and other bags and personal items in an effort to lighten the load, immediate fear overcoming the long-term anxiety of being stranded with nothing other than the clothes they were wearing. Judy was encouraging them as best she could, but she too was starting to wane.

"Lights! Lights!" yelled Zack at the front, the words whipped away no sooner had they left his mouth.

Judy and Gavin increased their speed, not having heard what he said but seeing his arm pointing forward along the road. Both of them caught sight of two points of light, illuminating a flickering display off the snow crystals.

"Come on," Judy yelled, "we've got help." She waved to those nearest to her to hurry.

William, Judy and Gavin ran back up the dual carriageway, cajoling, pulling, coaxing the last of the stragglers into making one last-ditch effort to move closer to the lights and, hopefully, safety. The carriageway ended and the group, now back together, made their way onto the narrower stretch of the road, reduced to just two lanes, a line of vehicles each side.

PARALYSIS | GROUND-ZERO +38 DAYS
NORTH OF THE CHILMARK RGC

The wheels of the Land Rover were gripping well, and Scott was able to pick up speed, the snow whipping past the windscreen as they drove directly into the wind, limiting visibility for both occupants. He pushed down harder on the accelerator pedal, hearing Alan's last call to the missing unit going unanswered.

"We need to keep our eyes peeled along here. They could be anywhere. Either side of the dual carriageway once we're on it."

Scott turned his head towards Alan and agreed, suggesting that he checked on the driver's side while Alan kept a lookout on the other side.

"Look out!" shouted Alan as he saw a couple of shadows suddenly appear in front of them, assuming a car was across the road. Scott looked towards the front again, not immediately recognising anything but slamming the brakes on hard. The Land Rover shook violently, the wheels locking and the back end coming round. Scott released the brakes but tapped them hard, steering into the skid and eventually coming to a halt, the vehicle side-on less than two metres from two figures, arms outstretched, fearful of being hit. Putting the vehicle into neutral, Scott heaved a sigh of relief. Alan flung his door open and leapt out, his SA80 at the ready. At first, he thought it could be the crew who had abandoned their tank and decided to make their way back on foot, although that didn't make sense. But he quickly identified them as civilians.

A woman ran up to him, breathless. "They're chasing us... soldiers...killed...our people...killed...cannibals."

"Slow down. Take it steady." Alan spoke firmly, gripping her shoulders. "Start from the beginning."

Scott joined him, and the rest of Judy's group slowly congregated around them, looking back over their shoulders, all trying to speak at once, to warn Alan and Scott of the threat that was out there.

"Quiet!" bellowed Scott. "One at a time!"

The group, still looking warily over their shoulders, back down the road, were immediately silenced, the authority in Scott's voice having the desired effect.

Judy continued, talking fast, but she had now caught her breath and was more coherent. "There's a mob behind us, 100 or so."

"Maybe 200 to 300, or more," added Gavin.

"We think they may be right behind us," continued Judy. "They killed some soldiers who were taking us to a camp."

Scott moved to the side, staring into the storm, assault rifle at the ready.

"Were the soldiers in a Scimitar?" Alan asked.

"A what?"

"A tank. Were the soldiers driving a small tank?"

"Yes, yes. The mob killed them."

"All three of them?"

"Yes, and many of our own as well."

"Jesus," uttered Scott. "Are you sure? Did you check them?"

"We couldn't."

Before Alan could ask another question, a shotgun exploded nearby, and a voice yelled, "They're here!"

The group scattered, leaving Alan, Scott, Zack and William, each with a shotgun, Gavin with an assault rifle, and Judy, a pistol held in a shaking gloved hand, to face whatever was coming their way.

"Scott, check on Zero-Delta."

"Roger."

Zack shouted a warning as a figure came towards him out of the gloom. His warning to stop was ineffective and he fired. The body writhed on the ground. Two more individuals came towards them. They were followed by more ragged souls, faces gaunt, staring at the small group in front of them. More quickly joined: soon it was ten, then twenty, the number increasing steadily as more and more caught up.

"Back," Alan ordered the others, "get in a line. You," he instructed Gavin, "far right." Alan was wary of Gavin, suspecting that the weapon may well have been taken off one of his soldiers.

They all followed Alan's orders, shuffling into a line, Alan and Gavin at each end, Zack, William and Judy in the middle, Scott next to the Land Rover just behind them. The mob were now spread out across the entire width of the road, Alan estimating that they were now at least 100 strong and being reinforced by the second.

"Five minutes out," called Scott.

"Take up a position on our far right," yelled Alan so he could be heard above the whining of the wind.

A man stepped forward from the group facing them

"They're going to rush us," warned Scott.

The line of the mob spread out as numbers increased. Alan could sense the nervousness of the civilians alongside him. "Hold," he encouraged. "If we run, they'll be on top of us in seconds."

Another thirty or so joined the mob, looking as emaciated as the rest. Alan scanned what little he could see of their partially covered faces: many had lesions of some sort on their faces, whether from radiation burns or straightforward third-degree burns, he couldn't tell. A few had black patches on their faces, one with the tip of his nose completely missing. Frostbite, Alan thought. The clothing they wore was in equally poor condition, tattered, damp-looking, dishevelled beyond belief. He noticed some of them were shivering, no doubt because they had ceased moving, stopped chasing their victims. But it was probably also from lack of food and adequate protective clothing to keep out the cold and the damp. Alan was fairly well fed and his apparel was dry and windproof, yet he too could feel the bitter cold and sharp sting as the wind flung icy particles across exposed areas of his skin.

The mob said nothing, didn't even talk to each other, just shuffled around, moving closer to each other, seeking a barrier from the blizzard that was lashing their bodies, seeking any warmth they could.

They will charge, and soon, thought Alan.

"We mean you no harm," he shouted above the cacophony, the wind coming from behind helping to project his voice towards the mob. "We are part of a government centre. We can provide you with food and shelter, but you will have to be disarmed."

What turned out to be their leader, surprisingly diminutive considering he was representing a group that had now grown to close to 300 people, took a step forward. "We've come from one of your government slave camps, and look where it's got us." He swept his arm to the right, indicating the mob he was leading. "Literally worked to the bone on a meal a day that wouldn't feed a dog. But the leaders eat like kings, like lords of the manor, while we die of disease, typhus, cholera..."

Alan couldn't check his watch without potentially causing alarm, needing to keep them talking until help arrived. "We also have labour teams, we have to. We're trying to make houses habitable for families and prepare the land for crops." He held his hand out, palm up. "But this weather is hampering our efforts."

"And food?"

"Those that work get two meals a day."

"And the others starve?"

"No, they get the same, but less calories naturally."

"Where's this food come from?"

"We have stocks, put aside by the Government for times such as these. They're not infinite, hence the need to be ready for when they run out."

"How many of you are there in your community?"

The man sounds educated, thought Alan. "We have a large number of families. We could absorb your group, but we would need some time to make preparations for accommodation."

The group were now packed together tightly, like emperor penguins in the Antarctica, using body contact as a windbreak as they became colder and colder standing around.

Alan heard the crunch of snow behind him as his four additional soldiers, from Two-Zero-Delta, moved slowly into position. Sergeant Major Scott Saunders had instructed the unit, by radio, to stop 100 metres back, debuss and approaching on foot so as not to spook the intruders lined up against their commanding officer and the few armed civvies. The four men stopped level with the back of the Land Rover, awaiting for further orders from their boss.

The leader started when he saw them, and Alan quickly raised his hand in supplication. "They're just the rest of my patrol. They're no threat to you."

"Why should we trust you?"

"I understand your reservation," replied Alan. "Just come with us. I'll radio ahead, and we can get some hot soup ready for when you arrive. Then find you some temporary accommodation and get you out of this." Alan indicated the gusting snow that was quickly chilling them all.

The leader turned to his group, and a heated discussion rapidly ensued. There appeared to be a yes and a no camp, and Alan ran through the options in his head should it go either way. Absorbing them into the camp wouldn't be easy. An additional 300 refugees would use up supplies more quickly and place a strain on the rest of the already overstretched facilities. But, equally, if they were to survive, the RGC needed more people. Out of the current 5,000 population at the centre, not all of them were well. The diet, the workload, not to mention previous illnesses, burn injuries and radiation sickness were also taking their toll.

The debate heated up further, and Alan was becoming increasingly concerned, recognising that, although they had the upper hand in respect of firepower, they were vastly outnumbered. If they decided to launch themselves at Alan and his small force, the mob would take casualties, but Alan and his men would also be quickly overwhelmed. He looked over his left shoulder, caught Scott's eye and made a fist. He knew Scott would know the significance of the gesture.

It looked like the group was separating into two opposing camps, with the original leader standing with the group on the left and a verbose pseudo-leader attached to a separate group, of equal size, on the right.

Alan glanced over his shoulder again briefly and saw Scott disappearing from view. He hissed, as loud as he dare, "When I give the word, we run...get behind the Land Rover...be ready to open fire."

"Will they attack?" asked Judy nervously.

"Just run when I shout."

The group had now definitely split into two, the leaders poking fingers at each other, their voices increasing in volume, not only to counter the sound of the steadily increasing blizzard but also to appeal to the other group to follow their lead.

"Move back slowly. Keep your weapons pointed forward."

They all looked at Alan, following his instructions and his lead, watching him step back, trying to ensure they kept pace with him as he took another. They had gone half a dozen steps, in line with the bonnet of the Land Rover, when the new leadership challenger noticed.

"They're escaping," he screamed. "Don't let them get away."

"Run!" yelled Alan, turning on his heel and sprinting, grabbing the arm of Zack dithering at his side, who then accidentally fired the shotgun he was holding. The crash of the gun, pellets firing wildly into the air over the heads of the crowd, drew the attention of those that had missed their leader's call. Individuals from both groups leapt forward, running maniacally towards the soldiers and the civilians.

On cue, Scott and Corporal Brodie pulled the pins on their grenades, drew their arms back, stepped forward a pace, Corporal Brodie moving from behind the Land Rover where he had been hiding, Scott next to the bonnet, and threw their explosive packages overarm towards the now baying mob. The effect was shattering. Scott's grenade exploded first: four victims, three men and a woman, were violently flung apart and upwards, knocking others aside as slivers of hot shrapnel sliced through their clothing and wasted flesh. Their screams were drowned out by a second explosion. Corporal Brodie's grenade landed at the front of the mob, blasting those at the front with a hail of hot gases and red-hot shrapnel.

The shrieks of the wounded competed with the howl of the wind. The mob tripped over each other, punching and kicking to escape the death those still alive felt sure was also waiting for them. Alan had moved his men forward and into a line, ordering the civilians, even those armed, back behind him and his soldiers. Now, he and his five men faced the rabble who, realising there were no more explosions and no gunfire, came forward again, stepping over the groaning, writhing and thrashing bodies of the fallen.

In the meantime, Alan had instructed the rest of his men to move forward, keeping the line intact, weapons at the ready, until they were at the front of Alan and Scott's vehicle again. Pale, confused, fearful and pitiful faces looked on as the original leader stepped forward, walking around the figures on the snow-covered ground, one reaching out, trying to clutch the man's trouser leg, begging for help.

Ignoring him, the leader continued until he was two metres away from Alan. "I am sorry my people attacked you. They were unprovoked, I know, but scared and misled."

"Your people?" asked Alan.

"Wrong terminology, perhaps." He smiled, the wrap he had had around his mouth pushed down. "I'm representing a group of survivors at their request, not a role I had chosen willingly, who want me to help them get out of this hell we've found ourselves in."

"Where are you from?"

"Basingstoke, a so called government rescue centres.

"What happened?"

The man shivered slightly and took off his pair of round, wire spectacles, one with a crack in the lens, and wiped them free of snow with a rag he pulled with his pocket. Then he placed them back on his face. "Where do I start? There was a three-way power struggle right from the beginning, I suppose. The army, the government officials, the remaining survivors."

His group slowly shuffled forwards, shoulder to shoulder, keeping what heat they generated for as long as possible. Their posture wasn't threatening, they merely wanted to listen to what was being said, to be party to decisions that could and would affect their individual lives going forward.

"The government didn't want to feed us until a four-week period was up, claiming that many were still to die, and the food was in short supply and couldn't be wasted."

"And the army?"

"My name is Emanuel, by the way."

"Alan."

"Army?"

"Yes. I'm in command of the security forces…and the Regional Centre."

"What happened to the officials?"

"Let's hear about you first, OK?"

"I understand. The army released some food, not much. It transpires that the government stocks had been destroyed by fire, and what effort had been made to stockpile food before the bombs had been left too late. The threat wasn't seen as credible." He laughed.

The survivors had now stopped shuffling and the leader was

rooted in the front row. The agonies of those wounded behind them could no longer be heard. Not only had the weather turned significantly colder in the UK, but there was no longer any room for sentimentality.

"It started off well, as well as could be expected under the circumstances. But the soldiers, the police, they were struck down by disease. Typhus. It spread rapidly through the soldiers, and that's when the bureaucrats took over, but that didn't last long."

"That's when the mob took control," suggested Scott.

Emanuel turned towards Scott. "Yes, the mob, and that's exactly what they were, took over." Emanuel's group continued to huddle together, those on the outside shuffling their way into the inner segment to try to evade the biting wind. "We feasted for a couple of days, like kings, I might add. But it dawned on the leaders that the stockpile of food and other supplies was dwindling fast, and personal survival kicked in. The chosen few, about 100, I'd say, hunkered down with what was left, shooting anybody who attempted to get a share, and took care of themselves."

"And the rest?" asked Alan, but already knowing the answer.

"The sick and dying, well, they did just that. Died. The healthier of us tended to split into groups and slowly slipped away, searching for shelter and food. But without food, shelter was pointless. If we'd stayed in one place to keep warm and dry then starvation would have killed us all. Saying that, we're not much better off now. Look at us." He had to slip his arms from those pressing on each side to indicate the group he was leading. "We've been wandering for nearly two weeks, starving, almost comatose on occasion such was our weakness through lack of food. So, what happens next then…Alan?"

"Providing your group…" Alan raised his voice so everyone could hear. "Providing you are prepared to follow the rules, our rules, you can join our population. But be assured, I, we, will not tolerate any sort of behaviour that destabilises our community. Anyone who does not comply will be evicted, and we will use armed force if necessary. Do I make myself clear?"

Alan saw lots of nodding heads, and Emanuel spoke again. "I thank you on behalf of my people, and I promise you we will integrate with the community already in place. We thank you for showing us pity."

"It's not pity," responded Alan. "If we're to survive the weeks, and months, and even years ahead of us, and they will be tough, we need people. But people who are prepared to pull their weight. Right, organise your group into—" Alan stopped as he heard another vehicle inching its way towards them.

"Two-Zero-Charlie-Alpha," called Scott.

"More soldiers?" asked Emmanuel.

"Yes, we're well able to protect ourselves and our community. That protection is now yours too."

"Thank you. What would you like us to do?"

"Have your group start to form a column. There will be two Land Rovers up ahead and one following behind. It's a few hours' walk to the town, but there will be hot food waiting for you when we arrive."

The military organised themselves into position, Two-Zero-Delta tasked with checking on Two-Zero-Echo before following up at the rear. Told that their comrades were likely to be found dead, there was suppressed anger amongst the soldiers. A couple of the soldiers were more than capable of driving the Scimitar, so would follow on behind the rearmost Land Rover. Two-Zero-Charlie-Alpha led the way, the original group rescued by Two-Zero-Echo walking behind. Then Alan and Scott, followed by the line of survivors who they had rescued.

Alan and Scott, along with the other soldiers, needed to bite deep into their resolve to allay their anger at not only the deaths of their comrades but the manner in which they died. Within an hour, the military vehicles were making progress, a steady seven kilometres an hour, a long column of fatigued souls, heads down, battered by the ever more powerful snowstorm, barely able to place one foot in front of the other, but knowing that if they stopped now, separated from the group, they would never move again. Still, every three or four kilometres, someone would drop out. A friend, husband or wife, sibling or other close relative occasionally did their best to persuade the individual not to give up, but they in turn had barely got enough strength to continue the journey themselves. One couple, in their early sixties, at the end of their tether, dragging their feet, one after the other through the snow, suddenly walked away from the column, dropping down next to a gate that led to a field. Lying side by side, arms around each other in a final embrace, they waited for the arms of Morpheus, the god of dreams, to release them from the realities of their current existence.

CHAPTER 25

PARALYSIS | GROUND-ZERO +38 DAYS
RGC, CHILMARK

Alan watched from the Land Rover, the engine ticking over to keep the inside of the cab warm, as the ragged line of survivors queued up for a bowl of hot soup, probably the first hot meal they'd had for weeks, perhaps even longer than that. Although marquees had been erected over the two main serveries, those queuing outside had to face incessant blasts of icy snow whipping at their exposed bodies, sucking away the heat faster than the emaciated forms could generate it. On the outside, Alan kept a poker face, concerned about showing weakness, his leadership established, but he knew that could change at the drop of a hat. Inside, he ached for the people in the food line, and those living on short rations as a consequence of being unable to work, not able to contribute to the security or rebuilding of a society that was gradually finding its feet, albeit after a fragile start.

Once the people had been served a bowl of hot, thick soup, heavy in fat content, ideal for feeding their deprived bodies, they staggered, all but spent, to the home-made benches and tables, two canvas barriers shielding them from the worst of the wind. It had been agreed that, once they had finished their first bowl, they could rejoin the queue and receive a second portion of the life-giving food. Eddie, in charge of the feeding centre, had organised for each of them to receive a half-loaf of bread to take with them to the camp. There was a labour force of sixty, coaxed out into the blizzard by Eddie with the promise of a can of beer each, twenty per cent of the cans still held in the stocks at Wincanton, once the task of erecting half a dozen twenty-man tents was completed. The three or four hundred survivors, no one had yet done a full count, would have to spread themselves amongst the tents, squeezing in wherever they could, forty to sixty in each canvas accommodation. Tomorrow, Dylan and his aides would sort, log and assign duties to those fit enough to work, although Alan doubted many would be fit for days to come.

There was plenty to be done. Alan had ordered that they have forty-eight hours to recover before being set any labour-intensive tasks. A blast of air filled the cab as the door of the Land Rover was opened and Dylan literally collapsed into the passenger seat. "God, it's like the Arctic out there."

"The boffins we have left seem to think this cold weather snap will be with us for a few months at least."

"They're always pessimistic. If we left it up to them, we'd still be sealed in the bunker doing nothing."

"Well done to your team getting some hot food on the go for those poor buggers out there."

"That's what I wanted to see you about, Alan. I know I agreed to this, but we've made a mistake allowing such a large number to join in one go. God, it's nice and warm in here."

"What am I supposed to do, Dylan? Leave them out there to starve and eventually die?"

"I…I don't know. But I hear they're cannibals. Christ, Alan, are we going to be safe in our beds?"

"They haven't eaten for at least two weeks. In this weather, walking the country like they've been doing, even 5,000 calories a day wouldn't have been enough. They've had nothing, zero, zilch."

Dylan's head dropped. "Yeah, I know. It's just—"

"My boys will be keeping an eye on them. Those ten extra CPSs we've trained will lighten the load on everyone as well."

"That was a good idea of yours, although I know you were reluctant in the early days."

"I was kind of still living in the old world then. But we need to move with the times."

"I'm scared, Alan."

Alan turned to look at the employment chief and could see the fear in the man's eyes. Normally very vocal during meetings or discussions, Dylan came across as confident and determined to have his say or have his ideas implemented. So this shook Alan somewhat: one of the more resilient members of his team showing a weakness. He needed everyone to be strong if they were to get through this hell, to survive.

"We've got it under control, Dylan."

"Got what under control, Alan? The food stockpiles won't last forever. How long? A couple of months, maybe three? What then? Plough fields and plant crops? Look at this shit."

Alan was shocked when he saw the tears running down the man's cheeks.

"Look, Dylan, I need you to be strong. There's thousands of people out there who are going to die if we don't see our plans through."

"Plans? What bloody plans? We're living hand to mouth and from day to day. The labour gangs can work for about three or four hours a day in this, and we can't even see what they've bloody done!"

"Hey, hey," Alan patted his shoulder, "that idea of yours to use large buildings and warehouse spaces as large inside gardens is a great concept which we can build upon. We can plant some winter crops, partially sheltered from this weather. It'll work."

"Yes, we need to give it a try at least."

Another Land Rover pulled up alongside, and Scott leapt out and ran over to Alan's vehicle.

"The sergeant major wants you." Dylan brushed the tears from his face. "I'll get cracking. And, Alan, thank you. I wanted your job, but you're the best man for it. You're our best hope."

Before Alan could respond, Dylan exited the Land Rover and Scott quickly slid into the passenger seat, along with another flurry of snow.

"Shit, boss, what's wrong with your radio?"

Alan checked. "Sorry. Turned it off for a few minutes."

"Well, get it back on."

"Why? What's up?"

"Turn it on."

Alan switched the radio back on and Scott contacted the RGC.

"Zero, this Two-Zero-Alpha. Transmit the first recording. Over."

"What recording?"

"Listen."

"*This is Zero. Sending now.*"

There was a hiss of static; then a recorded voice could be heard over the radio: "*...foxtrot-three-five...Air-Force...can you...us...need... assistance. Po...is...but..Please respond...batt...dying. Any...sign...this is...zygzxs...one...mwbnd...ndnwdn wkdnn...*"

"*That's the latest transmission. Over.*"

"Roger that. Anything from the previous transmissions? Over." Alan asked over the radio in response.

"*Pretty much the same.*"

"Have you tried to contact them?"

"*Yes, sir, but no response.*"

"Checked our transmissions?"

"*They're positive. We're transmitting OK. I suggest they're not receiving.*"

"Keep trying."

"*Roger. Out.*"

"We could do a triangulation on the radio traffic," suggested Scott.

"What then?"

"Investigate?"

"Who do we send, Scott? The population is fairly stable at present, but we know how quickly things can kick off. I don't believe we should send valuable resources out, especially in this." Alan indicated the blizzard lashing at the windows of the Land Rover.

"Track down the location? Then decide?"

"I'll go with that. I'm off to check on the camp. You've got a visitor by the way."

Scott left the cab, holding the door open for a figure swaddled in clothes, which looked to be a woman as she swapped places with Scott. Scott slammed the door shut and ran to his own vehicle.

The woman pulled back the hood of her waterproof jacket and the hood of a man-sized sweatshirt beneath it, pulled down a fleece neck warmer, and flicked her lank hair, freeing it up. "I hope I'm not intruding?" She shivered as she spoke, struggling to form the words, her face and lips blue with cold.

"That's OK. Take your time, warm up a bit first. Here," Alan pulled out a flask from between the seats, "Alison made me a flask of coffee before I left. It should still be warm."

"Thank you, it'll make me want to pee though," she chuckled.

Alan responded with a smile and poured her a cup full.

She sipped it gratefully. "Mmm, nice. Not had coffee since… God, I can't remember when the last time was."

"How can I help you?" asked Alan, not rushing her, but he still had a few things to do before he called it a day.

"My name's Judy, by the way."

"Yes, I remember. Mine's Alan."

"You've already helped us, Alan. I just wanted to thank you."

"So, you've come from a motorway up north. Camping out in cars, I believe."

"Yes, but the fights between factions were getting worse, and food was running out. Some soldiers came to our motorway camp—"

"Ah, so you're the group we were warned about."

"Warned?"

"Not in a dangerous way, just alerted to the fact that you might make the journey south."

"Glen? Is he here?" Her eyes lit up and her cheeks, now warming up as a consequence of the heat inside the vehicle, flushed. "Sorry, he helped us out."

"After a shoot-out, I believe."

Judy felt the warm blush spreading to her neck. "Yes, it was a mistake on our part. Is he here?"

"No, he and his men have gone on a mission on their own."

Her face dropped. "London. He said they were going to London. Will they come back?"

"That was his plan."

Her face brightened again. "Will you tell him I'm here?"

"Of course. How are your group settling in?"

"Fine. We're all just glad to be here. A hot meal and a tent for us to shelter in has worked wonders. It's nice to feel safe again. Thank you for keeping us away from the others. What will you do about them?"

"Why?"

"They're cannibals, of course."

"We'll keep an eye on them. We've all been driven to do things out of character since death has intruded into our lives."

She finished the coffee and handed the cup back. "Thank you."

"Some more?"

"No, but thank you. As I said earlier, I now need a pee." She smiled.

"I'll drop you off at the camp. That's where I'm going next."

"You're fine. I'm helping out at the feeding station. Someone called Ed said he'd find me a job."

"It's good you're getting involved."

She pulled the two hoods back over her head again, tucking her hair in, and opened the door. Just before she pulled her neck warmer up over her mouth, she said, "This is our home now."

CHAPTER 26

PARALYSIS | GROUND-ZERO +38 DAYS
THE FARMERS, EXMOOR

Andrew and Tom had driven along the narrow road that ran alongside the Washford River, bypassing the small village of Luxborough, and continued west for another couple of kilometres before heading south towards the crossroads of Church Street and the B3224, and then heading north-west for Wheddon Cross. They would also avoid that village. In fact, they wanted to avoid all signs of life – human life that was. What they were seeking was wildlife, or at least signs of it. The going had been tough, the steady snowfall over the last few days making the roads treacherous in places. Once, they had had to dig their way through a snowdrift that blocked over half the road. In places, the road was pretty well protected, the trees helping to shield the routes they were using from drifting snow.

Both knew that they had to complete these forays now. Leaving it any longer was out of the question. If the snowfall continued at the current rate, the entire countryside and outlying areas would be paralysed. Pulling over at frequent intervals, where there were clear lanes or tracks leading deeper into the wooded areas, both searched for prints left by a deer or other wild animal or even domestic animals gone astray. They had come across two cows, but both had been dead for sometime. Despite the fact that they still had some supplies left, that would perhaps last them for a couple of months if they were used sparingly, the two families knew that, if they were to survive, they needed to become completely self-sufficient as processed food ran out and became more scarce as time ran on. They had debated the issue at length around the kitchen table. Unless there was government intervention, and once the remaining processed foods in the UK ran out, people would be on their own. The population would be left to their own devices, left to struggle, left to survive.

Initially, Tom and Andrew had been reluctant to go out together, leaving their wives and children to fend for themselves while they were away. But, if they got into difficulties on the snow swept roads, it needed both men to dig or, using a hand winch, to get their vehicle out of it. Both Lucy and Maddie had protested vehemently about their husbands believing they couldn't fend for themselves. Maddie's outlook in particular had changed significantly. After her experience with the gang that raped her, and attempted to rape Lucy, she had acquired a strong-willed streak and was less likely to bow to the decisions of the rest of the group. Not in an antagonistic or aggressive manner, but as someone who was more prepared to stand her corner now. And to protect her son Patrick and her husband Andrew, she would kill, of that she had no doubts. Tom and Andrew had trained both the women in the use of the shotguns, and talked through the security measures they should adopt until the men's return. Even Patrick had been given some rudimentary training in the use of the weapons. When Tom had suggested that Patrick was too young to handle a gun, it was Maddie who pointed out that he wasn't so young that he couldn't be murdered by a predatory gang. It was agreed that the two men would travel together, the defence of the farm in the hands of Lucy and Maddie.

Tom and Andrew came to the end of that section of the B3224, and, rather than going south towards Bridgetown or north to Timberscombe and wanting to avoid Wheddon Cross, Andrew steered the Land Rover south-west, following Hare Lane. The high hedgerow in places had acted as a buffer against the snow squalls, helping to shield the road from the worst of the snow, but he still encountered high snowdrifts. This meant he had to manoeuvre the vehicle right to the edge of the road, and even then it was a miracle at times that they managed to get by. Their next major crossroads was when they reached the A396, which they also crossed. Going north would have led them directly to the centre of Wheddon Cross. But, for the time being, both men wanted to avoid the villages. Their bad experience back at Sherston, where, over a week ago, they had been overpowered by a gang and Maddie raped and Lucy nearly raped, and having lost their farm, burnt down by the Reynolds family, had made them more cautious of places that could be inhabited.

Andrew reduced power, changed down, and crossed over the road, powered up again, and took them along Thorne Lane. Although the snow had been heavy, the blizzards driven down from the Exmoor hills, most of the snowfall had drifted up against the hedgerow to the north, on their right, leaving the left-hand side of the lane relatively clear. Whenever they came to a difficult section,

Andrew would tap on the brakes, conscious of the Land Rover's poor roadholding ability on slippery surfaces. In fact, early on in their journey, taking a bend too quickly, he had nearly spun the vehicle off the road. After travelling along almost five kilometres of the lane, Andrew steered them almost completely back on themselves, following the B3224 for roughly the same distance.

Both men were quiet, Tom knowing that any distraction could potentially result in Andrew crashing the vehicle. They passed the leafy village of Luckwell Bridge to the south as they crossed the River Quarme, starting to climb as they headed north-east. A couple of kilometres west of Wheddon Cross, Andrew completed another U-turn, avoiding the village to the east, heading west then north-west. The Land Rover climbed steadily. They were now at a height of 200 metres, the strength of wind intensifying the higher they got, buffeting the sides of the Land Rover, Andrew gripping the steering wheel tightly, constantly adjusting the line of travel to keep them straight. A sign for Combeshead Farm on the left and open fields either side, the countryside became barer the higher up they got. They crossed the River Avill, and Tom suggested that before they curved around to the north and headed back, stopping off at other locations on their return home, it would be a good idea to head for the summit of Dunkery Hill. The hill, next to the nature reserve, could be used as an observation platform, enabling them to scan the horizon, check out the landscape. Andrew agreed and turned off the road onto a hard-packed lane, the buffeting of the winds strengthening as they steadily ascended towards the 500-metre summit. Beneath the snow, either side of the track, was typical scrubland found on high ground, on this occasion on top of Devonian sedimentary rock, with little or no trees to break up the force of the wind that was battering away at their Land Rover.

"Sure this is a good idea?" Andrew laughed but didn't take his eyes off the track ahead.

"I'm beginning to wonder myself. Shall we turn back?"

"Not possible on this track…Whoa!" Andrew voiced his surprise as the Land Rover bounced. First, the driver's side front wheel, then the rear wheel, dropped into a pothole hidden by the snow.

"We've only 600 metres to go. Might as well get to the top."

"I hope the view's worth it. Not sure we'll see anything in this lot."

"Might see some smoke. Places to avoid."

"Or contact should we need help."

"Good point."

The engine growled and the vehicle jolted as the wheels struck hidden rocks along the final stretch, the wind howling and whistling around the hardtop roof at the back. Approaching the top, both could see the summit cairn of the Dunkery Beacon dead ahead. Andrew steered round to the left and pulled up just on the other side of the ridge, slowing to a halt.

"I'll do the next stint," volunteered Tom, turning to pat Sam's head. The dog was waiting patiently in the back.

"Please, my arms are throbbing."

The windscreen wipers flicked left...right...left, clearing the snow, and the wind lessened slightly as they were just on the other side of the summit.

"Snow's eased off a bit," indicated Tom.

"Take a quick look then?"

"Might as well."

Andrew turned the key, switching the engine off, the rumble of the diesel engine replaced by the steady whistle and groan of the wind. "One door at a time though, yes?"

"You first, then."

"No, you, please."

"Come on then, Sam, we're the guinea pigs, it seems." Tom smiled. The collie's ears pricked and his pink tongue licked his lips in anticipation of freedom.

Sam didn't need a second invite as he clambered over the front seats, dropping onto the passenger seat as Tom exited, a blast of wind and flurry of snow filling the cab. As Tom stepped down, Sam darted past him, seemingly impervious to the cold, just pleased at his liberation from the vehicle. Tom pulled his scarf close around his face, adjusting his bobble hat and the old swimming mask he used to wear on the farm, then pulling the waterproof hood, which immediately filled with air, up and over, pulling the drawstring as tight as possible. He reached back inside and grabbed his shotgun, holding the door to inhibit his and its movement, preventing it from being torn from the body of the cab. He slung the gun over his shoulder, the barrels closed but no shells inside. Those were kept in his pocket. To have the gun broken, with two live cartridges in the breech, in this sort of weather, common sense told him, was not recommended. He then grabbed the binoculars from the footwell and closed the door. Sam looked up at him longingly and got the nod. He tore off, bounding over the banks of snow, some that were taller than him in places. But the dog didn't care: he was free.

Andrew came round the front, pocketing the Land Rover keys, single-barrelled shotgun in hand, and joined Tom. "You look like something out of one of those kids' movies with those goggles," he joked.

Both had to raise their voices to be heard above the howling wind.

"That hat, with the furry ear muffs, is reminiscent of an American frontiersman. Sure your name's not Davy Crockett?"

"Touché. Are you going to use those binos?"

Tom waved him to follow and walked away from the vehicle, striding through the half-metre layer of snow, the wind flicking at his clothing, threatening to wrench him off the hill. He pulled the face mask down around his neck, raised the binoculars to his eyes, and looked north-west. Being at the highest geographical point in Devon would give them, but for the snow, a good view to the north and north-west. The slope dropped away towards a national nature reserve. On the hills above it, further north, sat Stoke Wood, Parsons Wood, Allercombe Wood, and Sideway Wood. Tom scanned as far east as he could, slowly moving his line of view until he passed the northern point of the compass. He lowered the binos and shuffled his feet until he faced north-west, hearing Andrew come alongside him on his right. He put the binoculars to his eyes again and almost jumped backwards, an object filling the lenses that looked out of place on the white landscape, but somehow familiar.

"What's up?"

"I'm not sure what I've just seen. Hang on while I have another look."

Tom repositioned the binos, zooming right out so he had a wide field of view. He homed in on the object, somewhat darker than the surrounding snow. It was white, but an off-white, different from that of the crisp white snow adjacent to it.

"It can't be," Tom exclaimed. "It's the tail of an aircraft, I'm sure of it. The snow's making it difficult to pick anything out clearly."

"Here, let me have a look."

Tom pulled the strap from around his neck and handed the binos to Andrew, who immediately, through fear of losing them, placed the strap around his neck.

He scanned the area as best he could, zooming in to the shape that Tom was referring to.. "It's the tail of an aircraft alright, but it's end on, so no wonder it was difficult to pick out. I can't see any markings. It's big, maybe one of those jumbo ones. Hey, look, I can see a wisp of smoke…I think."

Tom took another turn, focusing straight in on the tail now he knew where it was. "Yes, I can see it. Next to a mound, sticking up in the snow. The mound's quite big. Maybe another part of the aircraft?"

"Possibly. If it's crashed down there then it'll no doubt be in pieces."

"You're probably right there, Andy. I can distinguish some different colour tones. I'm sure there are some other chunks of debris down there."

"What do we do?"

"Try and get there, of course."

"Why?"

"If it's an airliner, it will be stocked with food."

"The fresh stuff will have gone off though."

"But not the water, crisps, nuts, et cetera."

"True. Not forgetting the alcohol. Could quite fancy a tipple of brandy."

"We go down there then?"

"We need to be careful."

"I agree. Getting there is going to be tricky. We'll have to drop back down the other side, and find a track to take us west to the next knoll."

"That's true, but I was referring to danger of a different type – people."

"Good point. If there's a fire then that must mean a person or people."

"We've had two close shaves in as many weeks. No chances this time. Right?"

"Right."

"We shoot first."

"I'm with you. We have our families to consider."

Tom called the dog over, and they returned to the Land Rover, Sam pleased to be back inside, sheltering from the wind. Tom and Andrew plotted their route. With a map on the dashboard, picked up from a deserted garage, the two men studied their options. They agreed they would reverse their route for about 500 metres; then take a narrow track that ran west, just below the high ground, sheltered from the wind, until they struck the junction. From there, they could drive north-west and get closer to the scene of what looked like an air crash. This element of the journey was the most treacherous yet, and Tom often had to switch to low-ratio gears to negotiate some of the rougher sections. It took them two and a half hours to drive the three kilometres, and what little light there was was disappearing rapidly. It was agreed that, once they got to the junction, they would camp up, have a hot drink along with some hot food, and then climb into their sleeping bags. The plan: to approach the site during daylight hours.

Refuelling their bodies, then tucked up inside their sleeping bags in the back, Sam lying on a blanket between them sharing their warmth and giving some in return, they slept, secure in the knowledge that Sam would warn them of any intruders, wind or not.

CHAPTER 27

PARALYSIS | GROUND-ZERO +39 DAYS
RGC, CHILMARK

Down on the second level, Alan was sitting in the office at the far end of the bunker, chatting with Scott and Dylan, discussing the next stage in their plans to enhance the Regional Government Centre and the surrounding area so they were better able to support the population for which they had assumed responsibility. Alison was also sitting with them, after bringing a tray of sandwiches made with fresh bread brought from the bakery, despite the continuing blizzard, at the feeding station, along with a large pot of tea.

"Mmm, these are great, Alison," complimented Scott, his mouth full as he chomped on the food.

"Yes, you've even made the corned beef taste good," added Alan.

She beamed at the compliments, particularly from Alan. Scott looked at each in turn, seeing the connection, knowing that Alan had not spent the previous night alone. He smiled. He was pleased for them both.

"What are you grinning at?" asked Alan with a furrowed brow.

Scott took a mouthful of sandwich. "Just this…tastes really good."

Alan frowned at Scott again, suspecting there was more to it than he was letting on.

Dylan, confused by the turn of the conversation, also added his compliments. "Delicious, really delicious."

"Well, I'll leave you men to planning our future. I promised Ed I'd help out at the centre."

"He's dragging everyone in to work for him," laughed Alan.

"I've already allocated another twenty people to his group," Dylan imparted. "But he's doing an excellent job in getting things organised."

Alison left, and they continued their conversation. The three men were sitting around three Formica-topped desks that had been pulled together, various maps, lists and charts strewn across them.

Dylan picked up one of the lists and read from it. "We now have three barns cleared and waterproofed, and there's a stack more we can utilise at Dinton. Tomorrow, we'll put the JCB to work, digging for soil to transport to the barns. Its going to be bloody hard work though. They'll have to clear the snow first."

"We have no choice," added Alan. "We have to grow some form of crops. Vegetables, at least. We have a pretty good stock of seeds."

"More space will be needed though," added Scott. "With over 5,000 mouths to feed, that'll need a lot of veg."

"What about the cattle?" asked Alan.

"We now have seven," Dylan responded. "They're in pretty poor shape, though."

"What are you feeding them on?"

"There are a few tons of oats that were damp. Not fit for human consumption, although that criteria has changed somewhat, but we can use it to feed the cows."

"How we going to feed them in the future?" asked Scott.

"We've got five ex-farmers in our community, and between them they're working up an agriculture plan for going forward." Dylan held up another list. "It's this bloody snow. Stumps us every time."

"Housing?"

"Now that's where we're making some progress, Alan. Pulling a list together of all the different trades we have has been a boon. Seventeen houses watertight and relatively clean."

"How many will they house?"

"We've planned on three families in each one. To start with, anyway. Four families for the larger ones. I'd say up to 200 people, no more."

"Just a drop in the ocean," retorted Scott.

"It's a start, Scott," countered Alan.

"It's a great start," Dylan continued. "We have some more houses we can reclaim in Chilmark. I'm already planning to send a team to Tilbury and Fovant."

They heard the clatter of boots and were soon joined by one of Alan's soldiers and the doctor from the medical centre in Chilmark.

"You can go now," the doctor snapped at the soldier.

The soldier raised his eyebrows, but Alan nodded, saying, "It's OK. And thanks for bringing the doctor down."

The soldier left.

"Take a seat, Doctor." Alan indicated the chair in between Scott and Dylan. "The solider is acting on my instructions, so I would appreciate it if you treated him, and others for that matter, with respect."

The doctor scowled for a few seconds but then relented. "Sorry, just tired."

"As we all are. Here." Alan pushed a cup over to him and poured the doctor a drink. "What's troubling you? Something bad, I fear, if you've braved the weather out there."

"That is an understatement, Major." The doctor looked at each of their faces in turn.

"Spit it out, man," demanded Scott.

"Typhus, we have a major outbreak of typhus."

"In the hospital?"

"Yes, you know that, Major. But, now, at the camp as well."

"Have you been there?"

"No, but there have been a steady stream of patients making their way to the hospital."

"How did they get there?" asked Dylan.

"One of the lorries. After it dropped off a gang of labourers. Then it went back to pick up a second batch. We have a real problem."

"Typhus. How serious is it?"

"Serious? That's an understatement, Sergeant Major. This is epidemic typhus. In a generally healthy population, without treatment, you can expect the fatality rate to be somewhere in the region of ten to fifty per cent. With antibiotics, the fatality rate would be significantly less. We simply don't have enough medicines to treat them."

"And the bad news, Doctor?" asked Alan, grimacing.

"The old and seriously sick? One hundred per cent. The fit, and I use that term lightly, as undernourished as they are, along with the weakened state most are in, seventy per cent, or more."

"How has it been started, or spread?"

"Lice, Major. Hygiene is not the priority for most of the population. In this weather, with the facilities they have at their disposal, even those that recognise having a clean body is a must struggle."

Alan turned to Dylan. "Can we divert resources to improving or increasing our washing areas?"

"We can, but it will mean shelving our plans to house more people in other areas."

Alan rubbed his eyes with the palm of his hands; then scratched at the stubble on his chin. He desperately wanted to shave, determined to maintain some level of self-respect, despite the circumstances. The Regional Government Centre was still functioning as a complex, providing hot water, cooking facilities, fresh water and sleeping accommodation for the seventy-six occupants, but Alan seemed to be always in demand. The government officials, soldiers, police and other bureaucrats, would be the last to be rehoused. It would have to happen eventually, particularly when the fuel situation became critical and the machinery within the bunker broke down and became irreparable.

"What about the new arrivals?"

"They're in a pretty weak state," Scott advised.

"I'm a bit worried about their past exploits though" concern in Dylan's voice. "Cannibalism, who'd have thought it."

"Let's hope we never get that hungry," cautioned Scott.

"But can they do anything?" Asked Alan.

"A few hours a day, perhaps?" suggested Dylan.

"Then do it. Use them."

"And if they refuse?"

"Evict them."

"Not hold food back first?"

"We've seen the consequences of them being without food. I don't want a repetition."

"They could die if they're thrown out of the camp."

"We're all at risk if we don't do something. They work, starting first thing. Latrines and washing areas."

"We'll have to scrounge some more tents."

Alan looked at Scott. "Can our lads help?"

"Zero-Charlie is the best option. I'll get them on it."

"Good. Well, Doc, we'll make a start."

"That will help, but we need to do a full search of the camp, identifying those who are showing symptoms and isolate them."

"That's a big task," exclaimed Dylan. "Moving 5,000 people around in these conditions, they'll not be happy."

"We can check the labourers as they report for work and divert those that are ill. Can we have some of your nurses to help with the diagnosis, Doc?"

"I can let you have three, maybe."

"That will have to do. Dylan, can you put one of your deputies in charge?"

"Sure, MAFF should be able to do it."

"Kate? That's worse than having a matron in charge," laughed Scott.

Sergeant Thompson crashed through the door into the office. "Boss, you gotta come and listen to this."

"What?" asked Alan, standing up, automatically picking up his SA80 that had been leaning against his chair.

"You need to come now, sir, before it's too late."

Alan flung his webbing with his ammunition pouches over his shoulder and headed for the door, Scott close behind him. "Sorry, gentlemen," he said, turning to the doctor and Dylan. "I'll have to leave it with the two of you for now. I'll catch up with you later."

Sergeant Thompson, Alan and Scott ran down the corridor, up two flights of steps and along almost to the far end of the upper corridor where Bennet, one of the soldiers, was manning the radio. "I've lost it, sir. Sorry."

"Shit," responded the sergeant.

"I got a recording of it, though."

"Well, bloody play it back then," Thompson instructed, clearly frustrated that Alan hadn't heard it first-hand.

There was a hiss of static then a recorded voice came over the speaker. The voice and content were unrecognisable. "*Какова ваша позиция? на…*"

"*В ста километрах от нашей цели...Подтвердите, когда вы упали. Из*"

"What the hell is that?" exclaimed Scott.

"When I first heard the transmission, it was pretty broken up," Bennet informed them. "That was strength four four."

"And it sounds Russian. Your thoughts?" asked Alan.

"If anyone will be able to tell us then it'll be Kothari, he's into eastern languages. "

"The inbound comms are strength two two, but the outbound comms are four four."

"What does that suggest to you?"

"The inbound is stationary and some distance away," replied Bennet. "But the outbound is closer. The comms have improved over time. I reckon it's moving."

"Makes sense." Alan turned to Scott. "An aircraft?"

"Possible. Comms getting stronger suggests that, whoever they are, they're perhaps getting closer to us, the UK, that is."

"Military?"

"Can't see it being anything else. If it was civilian traffic, why would they be flying here? The UK is done for."

"Rescue mission? Come looking for help?"

"Thing is, we don't know, sir. We've assumed that Russia has been hit just as hard by nukes as we have. I'm sure our subs, and the American ones would have launched. Maybe we're wrong, perhaps the Russian's first strike was so effective, we've been unable to respond."

"I doubt it. We know we had at least three nuclear ballistic missile subs out there. That's a lot of firepower. And don't forget the Americans: their subs have far more firepower than us."

"I still don't get the Russian transmissions, if that's who it is."

"Or the other one we heard yesterday for that matter. Do we have a fix yet?"

"Only that it's to the south-west, sir," answered Bennet. "Nothing more."

"Busy times ahead, Sergeant Major, busy times ahead," mused Alan.

CHAPTER 28

PARALYSIS | GROUND-ZERO +39 DAYS
BRAVO TROOP, EN ROUTE TO CHILMARK RGC

Glen passed item after item to Rolly as he unloaded the trailer. The blizzard slammed into them, pummelling their bodies with its wrath. Rolly, the taller of the two men, literally had his feet whipped from under him, crashing to the ground, arms and legs flailing, the box of food he was holding splitting open, contents scattered amongst the surrounding snowdrifts. Many of the items they were unloading from the trailer, had been acquired from the tunnels in London.

Glen, Greg and Plato had returned to their forward operating base (FOB) and met up with Rolly. Glen and Rolly patched up the two injured soldiers, Greg and Plato, as best they could. Making them as comfortable as possible on collapsible camp beds, sleeping bags pulled over them, the two soldiers were pumped full of antibiotics, had saline drips attached, and were given a hot meal. The two wounded soldiers, weapons close by, were left to defend themselves while Glen and Rolly returned to the Underground station to collect as many weapons, boxes of ammunition, bottles of water and food as possible and took it all back, laden down with thirty kilogram packs, to their FOB. It had been tough going.

On the third trip, they encountered security forces from the despot Government. Shots were fired, and two close protection officers were killed. A truce was agreed and, after a conversation between Glen and the captain in command of the military element under control of the pseudo-government, they were allowed to continue their scavenging unmolested, providing it was for the last time. One interesting element of the conversation between Glen and the officer was that the captain inferred he didn't actually support the regime. Although Glen didn't divulge the location of the RGC they had come from was at Chilmark, he did provide Captain Chambers with a location and a set of prearranged signals to enable them to meet up if that was the course of action the captain wanted to take.

On return to the FOB, and once the Land Rover and trailer had been packed to bursting, completely overloaded, with Greg and Plato crushed in the rear seats, they headed west, back towards Chilmark and the Regional Government Centre that had tentatively become their new home. The journey had been a nightmare right from the start. The steady snowfall had turned into a blizzard. The entire UK was whipped by the heaviest and most violent storm in living memory, and the mainland was, in effect, paralysed.

Despite the weather, the four soldiers made progress, all of it in four-wheel drive, some of it even in low-ratio gear. Although this burned up fuel at a much higher rate, it did mean that additional jerrycans of fuel were used up, relieving the overloaded trailer of some of its excess weight. They consumed as much of the food as possible, further reducing the burden and providing the wounded soldiers in the back with some additional space. Greg's neck and shoulder wounds were healing well, but Plato's leg injury was constantly weeping blood and a worry to them all. Glen was torn between continuing the journey, making it harder for Plato to recover, or to stop for a few days giving Plato some respite from the constant jolting of the journey. But, choosing the latter option meant that, as a consequence of the ever worsening weather, they risked getting bogged down and stranded for an indeterminate period of time.

Once they got to the north of Winchester, the trailer gave up the ghost, the trailer pin snapping. Rolly, who was driving at the time, wondered why the going was suddenly a little easier. He quickly discovered that the Land Rover had been relieved of pulling the ton weight behind it. Now they found themselves transferring all they could manage, giving priority to the few weapons and small amount of ammunition they had. Then it was fuel, which they could also use to melt the snow for water, then food. Rucksacks and sports bags used to transport the goods from the Underground tube station were now suspended from the sides of the Land Rover. Rolly's comment that they looked like travellers was apt.

Once they had finished, and abandoned the half-empty trailer, they made slow progress, not wanting to tax the engine too much. Greg had advised them on how best to make repairs afetr the overloaded engine faltered, the vehicle grinding to a halt. A temporary fix, but enough to get them moving, and they were on their way again.

"Can this get any worse?" Rolly questioned, his arms constantly jarred by the forces transferred from the wheels up the steering column.

"God knows," responded Glen.

"He knows fuck all anyway," piped up Greg from the back, making the sign of the cross on his chest.

Greg and Rolly laughed at Greg's sarcasm, knowing the soldier was a staunch atheist.

"How's Plato doing?" asked Glen.

"He's asleep. I'll not be sorry when we get him back."

"We'll make it," answered Glen. "Even if I have to carry you both."

CHAPTER 29

PARALYSIS | GROUND-ZERO +39 DAYS
THE FARMERS, EXMOOR

Andrew pushed his sleeping bag down his body, shivering as the cold struck him, his breath forming clouds in he confined space of the rear of the Land Rover. Even with the inside of the Land Rover being frosted, Andrew caught a whiff of the dog's coat, having dried out overnight. Sam licked his hand, and Andrew ruffled the dog's head and ears before quickly pulling on a jumper. He would leave his waterproof jacket, which was hanging over the headrest of the front seat, where it was for now. Kneeling in the cramped space, his head catching against the roof causing a small cascade of snow to tumble down the partially snow-covered windscreen, he quickly rolled up his sleeping bag, making space so he could heat up some water. He would make them both a hot drink to have with two tins of smoked mackerel in spicy tomato sauce for breakfast. Once they were up and about, Sam would get his usual tin of dog food, of which Tom had a reasonable number in stock. Andrew felt the urge to pee, but tried to suppress it, not wanting to put his boots on just yet. During the night, the temperature had dropped to minus nine degrees centigrade, and there was a layer of frost on both the inside and outside of the windows, condensation from their breath adding to the thickness of the layer of crystals on the inside.

Tom, lying alongside him, groaned and sat up, rubbing his aching muscles, the dense foam sleeping mat providing some protection against the hard floor of the vehicle, but not enough. He kept the sleeping bag around his shoulders as best he could, retaining the last vestiges of heat he had generated overnight. He ruffled Sam's neck. "Good lad." Then he turned to Andrew. "I'm too old to be sleeping out overnight in the back of a Land Rover. Every bit of my body aches."

"Better than pitching a tent out in that lot." Andrew smiled. "I'll get this gas stove going. Then we can have some coffee." A cloud of hot breath swirled like a shroud in front of his face.

"Yes please. Not sure I can move without it."

"Do you want your mackerel delight now or wait for your coffee first?"

"I'll wait. God, what happened to bacon and eggs or croissants or even just a slice of peanut butter and toast?"

"Torment yourself, Tom, but not me, please." Andrew grinned. "Mackerel and sauce it is then."

Within a couple of minutes, the water was getting close to the boil, and the temperature in the back of the Land Rover steadily rose. Tom was able to shrug off the sleeping bag with some comfort but pulled on a sweatshirt to retain some warmth. Sam looked on as the two men tucked into the flat tins of fish, spooning chunks into their mouths, the aroma of spicy sauce filling the confines of the vehicle adding to the rather pungent like smell from Sam's coat. Food eaten, a second coffee started, and Tom began to pull on more outer clothing, preparing for the shock of facing the bitter cold that awaited them. Tom would need to let Sam out and then feed him. He also needed to relieve himself, the cold starting to work its magic on his bladder, particularly after two tin cups' worth of coffee.

Tom pulled on a sweatshirt over his T-shirt. "Well, we'll get to see what that plane is all about soon."

"I'm surprised there are any survivors. A large airliner crashing onto the deck like that can't bode well. They're damned heavy, and the ground's pretty solid."

"There's smoke."

"A lucky survivor, maybe."

"Or unlucky, depending on which way you look at it."

"Or perhaps some scavengers have come across it and are camping there while they strip it clean?"

"Maybe. What're you saying, Andy? That we're scavengers?"

"Our new trade, Tom."

Once they had finished their second cup of coffee, both went for a pee, Sam doing likewise before wolfing down a tin of meaty chunks, then racing around in the snow again. It had ceased snowing during the night as the freezing cold set in, but Tom could feel the first flakes stinging his face as the day started to warm and the gentle breeze picked up speed.

The engine coughed and spluttered before turning over, shattering the silence of the area about them, Tom adding to the noise as he scraped the windows clear of ice and snow. Both now back in the cab, Andrew driving again and Sam in the back once more, Tom consulted the map, ensuring he understood the likely terrain they would find beneath the snow. The tyres crunched over the snow as Andrew increased the power to the engine, the deep tread of the tyres gripping well as the Land Rover pushed through the snow that had banked up against the lower part of the front grill. Tom had wired a sheet of metal to the front of the Land Rover, across the lower part of the grille, to prevent the snow from forcing its way into the engine compartment as they moved forward, the large protruding bumper forcing a passage through the snow. The Land Rover crawled along the track, low-ratio gear having been chosen for this first stretch, Andrew finding it difficult at times to even identify where the track was. The occasional post, or cairn, stacks of stones on the side of the track, poking up through the snow, gave him a hint of its direction. The two men had estimated the plane to be three kilometres north-west of their current location. Tom had searched for the plane's tail through his binoculars, but the falling snow, although fairly light so far, still restricted their vision beyond more than a few hundred metres.

"This is going to burn up fuel," warned Andrew as he weaved along the track.

"We'll need those three jerrycans to get back, that's for sure."

They had travelled roughly three kilometres, heading for a position just to the west of the second knoll, the ridge in between the two high-points. The ground to the left of the track sloped downwards towards a depression, the River Exe running along the valley floor below them.

"Making good progress. If it wasn't for the snow, we'd get a view of the crash site."

Before Tom could respond, the left front wheel rode up onto a hidden boulder, sliding down the other side of it, the impetus pushing the front of the Land Rover to the right, jarring its occupants. But the real problem for Tom and Andrew was that the back end slid sideways into the slope, the three-quarter ton vehicle pressing down on the weakened edge of the hidden track, the surface crumbling, the spoil below giving way, the rear wheel dropping nearly a metre, forcing the bonnet and right wheel up into the air, and the vehicle grinding to a halt.

"Damn." Andrew cursed as the Land Rover then slid backwards, the rear bumper and tow bar digging into the ground, fortunately preventing the vehicle from slipping any further down the slope.

Sam whined as he placed his front paws on the back of the front seat.

"Down, lad, it's alright. Nothing to worry about."

Sam dropped back down, but remained standing.

Andrew pressed the accelerator pedal down, and the vehicle jerked forwards slightly before the right front wheel, now up in the air, spun freely and the rear wheels struggled with the loose spoil and icy snow.

"We have to get out," said Tom. "We'll not do anything staying in here." He grabbed his coat, opened the door, called Sam after him, and stepped down warily from the passenger seat. Andrew, in the driver's seat, was even more careful: the front on his side was sticking upwards, and he had to drop down to the snow-covered ground once he left the cab.

They both circled the vehicle. The Land Rover's back end was well and truly dug into the ground, two lines of darkened earth splashed across what was once virgin white snow, spray from the spinning wheels. Andrew kicked the rear wheel, buried nearly to the upper part of the tyre. "I knew it was too good to be true."

"Hey, we've done pretty well to get this far without an incident. Don't beat yourself up about it. It was bound to happen."

"Still, it's a bloody mess."

Tom held out his gloved hand, noticing that the snow had stopped. Daylight was strengthening and visibility improving although still dulled by the overcast, dust-filled grey skies. "It's stopped snowing."

"That'll make it a bit easier at least."

"Let's check out the trees then. There's a couple behind us that the winch should reach."

Both headed for the front end of the Land Rover, Andrew leaning into the back via the passenger door to grab something he needed while Tom scanned the area with the binos, the lack of falling snow, the first time for a number of days, gave them a clear field of view. "Andy. Here, quick."

"What is it?"

"Check this out." He handed the binos over, and Andrew zoomed in to where Tom was pointing. Sam also joined them, sitting close to Tom, touching his master's legs.

"What am I looking for?"

"The plane's tail."

"Got it. I can see…stars and stripes. It's American."

"I know, but what's it doing out here?"

"On a routine flight and crashed? Maybe it was hit by the blast from a nuke?"

"But civilian flights were banned a couple of days before it all happened. On both sides of the Atlantic, including Europe."

"Military flights only, I remember now."

Andrew searched for other sections of the plane. Although still two kilometres away, he could pick out at least two other parts of the aircraft's fuselage – at least, that was what he thought was hidden beneath the snow, including what could possibly be the cockpit. He could now pick out a ragged trail of debris, partially hidden by the snow, but the darker sections he was sure hid a number of man-made objects. Andrew could also see the cowlings of at least two of the powerful turbofan engines. "Let's make a move."

They turned their attention to the vehicle once more. Tom clambered up onto the bonnet, then the spare tyre, so he could access the low-sided roof rack that ran the length of the cab and rear section, while Andrew disconnected the drum on the winch and started to pull the cable towards the tree they had agreed would be the best to use. Neither fancied the alternative of hammering stakes into the ground. Tom reached for the ties that held the metal perforated ramps he intended to use to help them get out of their predicament. Once unsecured, he dropped four of them onto the ground, alongside the cab, followed by a shovel. In the meantime, Andrew had unravelled the cable, pulling it out as far as the tree, wrapping it around the trunk, back on itself, then clipping the gated hook onto the cable and pulling it tight, making sure it was secure. Returning to the Land Rover, Andrew assisted Tom with positioning the ramps, one in front of each wheel, although the front right was jutting up in the air at a difficult angle.

Once they were satisfied that they had done the best they could, Andrew restarted the engine, went round to the front of the bonnet, reconnected the drum to the motor and, using the remote, pressed the button that would wind in the cable that was extended forty metres across the snow. It worked fine, and he kept tapping the button until the cable was taut, digging into the trunk of the tree, gripping it successfully.

"Ready," Andrew informed Tom.

"OK," Tom called back. "Start winching."

The cable stretched slightly as Andrew applied power to the drum, flexing, thrumming, creating a trench in the snow as the pressure increased, the three-quarter ton weight not an easy bulk to move. Meanwhile, Tom ran from wheel to wheel, checking on the position of the ramps, kicking them against the wheels when necessary. The pitch of the whining winch deepened into a drone as the motor fought with the weight of the Land Rover, the tree bending slightly but holding. Andrew was conscious that if the trunk of the tree snapped, he could well be on the receiving end of the cable as it whipped towards him at breakneck speed. Just when Andrew was despairing that it wasn't going to work and was on the verge of stopping the winch, the rear wheels moved and the body of the vehicle jerked in retaliation, tyres connecting with the ramps, guiding them out of the holes that had gripped them until now. The winch motor speeded up, and the higher-pitched whine returned, the right front wheel of the Land Rover dropping down with a thump as it connected with the metal ramp lined up beneath it. The wheels turned more quickly as they rolled forward at a steady pace, all four of them now on the ramps. Then moving of the ramps, it was now back on the track, and safe.

With the power off, Andrew went and disconnected the cable from the tree while Tom returned the ramps to the roof rack. Then he turned the motor up to full speed, winding the now loose cable fully in. Ramps and winch secured, and after congratulating each other on the successful extraction, they continued their journey. After an hour and a half spent rescuing the Land Rover, and another two hours making slow but steady progress through a metre-thick layer of snow, they finally arrived at a junction, with more of a poor quality lane that would take them a sharp right north-east in the direction of the downed aircraft. Turning onto the snow-covered lane, Andrew drove them towards this location, halting within 500 metres of the crash site.

They both got out, Sam following on their heels, and examined their objective one more time, conscious of the potential risk they were taking, thin tendrils of black smoke could be seen drifting skywards from the other side of what they guessed to be the cockpit, the upper part clear of snow. Tom guided the binoculars a full 180 degrees one more time before both got back into the Land Rover and drove along the last stretch.

Looks like survivors, Tom thought. He checked out the other pieces of wreckage before returning his focus to the cockpit, zooming in, his eyes wide with shock as he realised what he could be looking at potentially. "Bloody hell, check this out!" He handed the binos to Andrew.

"What is it?"

"Have a look at the cockpit."

Andrew did as he was requested, the cockpit filling the lens, picking out the small windows used by the pilots for viewing landings and take-offs, reflecting some light off the royal blue paintwork surrounding them. Moving his focus further down to the back end of the section, to the right of the main cockpit, he could pick out the letters U…N…I…T…the word ending where the cockpit had been violently torn from the main body of the VC-25. Andrew mentally filled in the gaps and what it may have read in full: United States of America, further evidence supplied by the stars and stripes flag on the very large tail section.

"It's definitely American."

"Keep looking."

A line of circular windows ran along the rear of the cockpit, between the gap between the upper darker blue and the light sky blue at the bottom, also separated by a yellow band. When he got to where the aircraft door had been opened, a partially collapsed escape slide visible, the lower section lying limp on the snow below, he could see to the left of the doorway was a badge. He steadied his hands, kept the binoculars as still as possible. His eyes went wide.

"See it?" asked Tom.

"It can't be."

"That's what I thought, but look at it closely."

"I can't make it out clearly, but it looks like a seal, the sort you find on the US President's podium and documents. I can make out the eagle, but not the words. God, no, it can't be!"

"I think it is, Andy. I think that's Air Force One."

For more information about Harvey Black, his works and background information, including maps and photos, visit his website at www.harveyblackauthor.org.

Lightning Source UK Ltd.
Milton Keynes UK
UKOW02f0055040916

282124UK00004B/88/P